LINDBERGH'S SON

Also by John Vernon

LINDBERGH'S SON

JOHN VERNON

VIKING

VIKING
Viking Penguin Inc., 40 West 23rd Street,
New York, New York 10010, U.S.A.
Penguin Books Ltd, 27 Wrights Lane, London W8 5TZ
(Publishing & Editorial) and Harmondsworth, Middlesex,
England (Distribution & Warehouse)
Penguin Books Australia Ltd, Ringwood,
Victoria, Australia
Penguin Books Canada Limited, 2801 John Street,
Markham, Ontario, Canada L3R 1B4
Penguin Books (N.Z.) Ltd, 182-190 Wairau Road,
Auckland 10 New Zealand

First published in 1987 by Viking Penguin Inc.
Published simultaneously in Canada

Grateful acknowledgment is made for permission to reprint
excerpts from the following copyrighted material:
Autobiography of Values, by Charles A. Lindbergh.
Copyright © 1976, 1977, 1978 by
Harcourt Brace Jovanovich, Inc. and Anne Morrow Lindbergh.
Reprinted by permission of the publisher.
The Spirit of St. Louis, by Charles A. Lindbergh.
Copyright 1953 Charles Scribner's Sons;
copyright renewed © 1981 Anne Morrow Lindbergh.
Reprinted with the permission of Charles Scribner's Sons.

LIBRARY OF CONGRESS CATALOGING IN PUBLICATION DATA
Vernon, John, 1943–
Lindbergh's son.
I. Title.
PS3572.E76L5   1987   813'.54   87-40043
ISBN 0-670-81553-5

Printed in the United States of America by
Arcata Graphics, Fairfield, Pennsylvania
Set in Videocomp Electra
Designed by Kathryn Parise

To Ann

We had opened a new field with the perfusion of organs. A lifetime could easily be spent developing it. But suppose we solved all problems. Suppose we could install artificial hearts and transplant limbs at will. Suppose, even, that we could learn to remove one man's head and transfer it to the body of another. How much closer would we have come to solving life's basic mysteries? Even with his fragment of chicken heart, I realized, Carrel had not achieved eternal life, for it, too, kept dividing into new individuals and generations, just as man did—and the dilution of identity was similar.

Charles A. Lindbergh, *Autobiography of Values*

PART 1

1

All this began long before I died and they cut out my brain to keep it functioning. At least they found out nothing was the matter with it, no lesions or watery pulp. Now I think it's in the Smithsonian; footsteps, voices, cavernous echoes.

It was March of 1985. I was driving up Route 17 on my way to IBM in Owego to check out their new CAD software for the company. All week I'd been playing with our new terminal with the grid, trying to get the hang of it. I'm convinced that we're nearing the uncertain end of something in this century, maybe the end of physical reality itself, and the new world at the tunnel's exit (while computers blip and hum in the light) will be more like a radar screen, a place of sharp angles and white/green dots and electronic pulses and grids and keyboards.

The Windsor exit was coming up. I had a few hours to kill so I took it, because I hadn't seen the old place since closing it up last September. I could check for winter damage; we planned to stay at least two months this summer, and weekends the rest of the time. Maybe plant a garden. Pork Vining would take over at the office, I'd been grooming him for it all year. Pork and the new computer. At last I'd have a real vacation.

The Windsor exit swoops down on a ramp across the Susquehanna River and lands you at Route 79 on the edge of the village. I went left under the highway, then right on Trim Street up into the hills, past three centuries of houses clumped at the highway entrance: a solid eighteenth-century saltbox, a gingerbread Victorian, and some runty little raised ranches, tight as bird

3

cages, all in a row. Up into the hills: past the cinderblock VFW, past tar-paper houses and failed farms, up to where the bare trees, black in March, open up for three miles of pasture and fields on either side. The road still climbs here. You pass mobile homes and rusting farm machinery and one majestic colonial, then turn left at the Beagle Club on Ballyhock Road, through woods again, over a ridge, down to a valley and more yellow pasture, and the house I was raised in, for part of my life.

George shingled it when I was twelve; before that it was clapboard. I planned this summer to take off the shingles and paint the clapboards, because this was a real upstate farmhouse, and should be white, the color of milk. Everything around here used to be dairy farms; the milk truck came once a day and hauled all the milk to Crowley's in Binghamton. Now one farm still hung on further up Trim Street, but the rest were all collapsed barns and weeds. The roof of your house goes bad, the plaster falls in, pipes freeze, so you plunk a mobile home on the front lawn and move into that, because who can afford repairs? Just the ones who move away and start their own companies.

I pulled into the driveway as far as the back porch. Behind the house was the barn, and to the right of that, where the drive swung around, the chicken sheds and other outbuildings housing everything from a half century's accumulation of tires to an antique cutter and piles of old horse collars.

Then I thought I heard a noise from the house. A door banging shut, or something dropped to the floor, muffled inside the house somewhere. The shades and curtains were all pulled shut; I'd left them like that last September. Through the little screened-in back porch on its concrete slab, even the shade on the kitchen door was drawn, I could see. It was late afternoon, when the light in March gets long. I approached the porch slowly. When I unlocked the kitchen door and stepped inside, another door banged shut somewhere, or maybe a window, or a lamp pushed over—it was loud, it stopped me, I held my breath. It seemed to come from the side porch or the sitting room.

We always used the kitchen entrance in back; the front door hadn't been opened in years; it faced directly onto the lawn, which lapped right up to it without a walkway. Another door led to the side porch from the sitting room beside the kitchen, and it was from that direction I'd heard the noise. Crossing the kitchen, I said "Hello?" not too loud, not too casual—firm and quizzical, you might say—and opened the sitting room door, but found everything there undisturbed. Sheets covered the furniture and dust covered the sheets. The door to the porch, however, was unlocked; and out the window, beyond the porch, something or someone disappeared into the bare lilac bushes across the road, a figure or shadow obscured by the branches, I was certain I'd seen it. Behind those bushes were centuries of forest.

As a rule I'm not a paranoid man. I once found a needle in a loaf of bread (I reported it). I'm too wide awake for paranoia, I see things in the clear light of day, and I have a good memory; it's all I have left. I can remember my birth, as my mother's system was deficient in oxytocin, which passes through the placenta erasing memory as it goes. Also, I've been endowed with the faculty of controlling my dreams, of accelerating their course at will and turning them in any direction I wish, without waking up. I daresay paranoid people can't do this. Paranoiacs are at the mercy of their dreams and their insufficient memories, which throw shadows across their lives.

So I dismissed this mysterious figure in the bushes and commenced my inspection of the house, walking past ghostly lumps of furniture covered with sheets, and pictures turned to the walls for the winter: a habit (or superstition) I'd learned from my mother. It appeared that nothing was missing and nothing damaged. The place looked bored, martyred to the winter. I've often marveled at the patience of furniture. Nothing had stirred in the last eight months. It smelled musty, but there was little you could do about that after a long winter. Gaps in the floor between the pine boards opened directly into the cellar, which always dripped from its bulging stone walls.

Upstairs, cluster flies lay thick as fur on the sills of the window in the walk-in closet. I couldn't tell whether they were dead or alive. We never used this bedroom, as it faced the road, and the back bedroom was the only upstairs room with a heat register. I listened to my heels echo from room to room; the rugs were all rolled up in the attic. In the small room we called the study, I stared out the window across the back porch roof at the huge gray barn, the chicken sheds all askew, the lawn sloping down to pasture and hills a half mile away, with their black and red trees showing last year's brown leaves on the dull earth between them.

All the kitchen drawers held mouse droppings. We'd learned long ago to pack away the silver and leave the drawers empty. I shook them out on the floor and swept.

The downstairs bathroom occupied the entire back length of the sitting-room wing; the side porch wrapped this wing on its north and east sides. I'd always loved the generous space of this bathroom, large enough for board meetings. The floor here was pine planks too. One clawfoot tub, a sink, a commode, some wicker chairs and a wicker table, and an old black Salvation Army vanity with a three-paneled mirror.

That's where I found it.

It was sitting on the depressed section of the vanity, below the main part of the mirror. I recognized my number at once—030 30 2973—but the name was different. It wasn't my name. The funny thing was that I'd lost my wallet with almost one hundred dollars, pictures, credit cards, and my original Social Security card almost a year ago, in a boating accident on the Hudson. I never saw any of it again. The credit cards had all been canceled and new ones issued, but I was still waiting, after nine months, for the Social Security Administration to issue a new card.

Like the one I'd lost, this one was old: fuzzy-edged, creased. It looked like it came from the forties too. I dislike puzzles; they distract my concentration, harassing the edges of consciousness, until, like the weakened banks of a river, they threaten to collapse. Puzzles make me think reality has come down with an illness. I pocketed the card and promptly forgot it, like the figure in the bushes. I double-checked the locks on the doors, closed up the house, toured the barn quickly out back—ancient hay in its loft from ages ago—then drove back to Trim Street, and down to Route 17.

I learned later that one little tear in the screen or veil means that nothing is ever again what it seems. All becomes transformed. A woman lives with her husband for thirty years without once hearing him raise his voice, then discovers that he's been torturing cats on the side, or molesting children, and her world turns strange. Two weeks later I was playing one-on-one with my stepson on lunchbreak, in Newburgh, in a playground next to a boarded-up school about two blocks from my office. David worked at Kentucky Fried Chicken; he'd been there about two months, a new longevity record for him. David was Helga's only child by her first marriage; we had no children of our own. I'd never met his father, who lived in Virginia Beach and refused to see him. I could well understand this—the boy was unruly, insolent, sullen, defiant, and had been in trouble with the law—but wasn't paternal instinct supposed to screen out such faults? In my case, lacking this instinct, I conceived of a sense of duty to the boy, to compensate for his father's deficiency. Since the winter had begun to abate we'd coordinated our lunch hours at my suggestion (or insistence) in order to play basketball and take some fresh air. His Kentucky Fried Chicken was a half mile away. Now and then Pork Vining came too, but today he was off, having worked nights all week. It was a Friday, the first week of April.

David flopped around on the court, perpetually at odds with the long hair that fell across his eyes, pushing it aside, taking shots on the run, off balance, hardly bothering to aim—but the ball fell in regardless. His eye was deadly, but he dribbled with his elbows. He kicked the ball, stumbled, lunged at it, a windmill of arms and legs, then flipped it over his shoulder to the hoop and scored. I gave him plenty of room; lacking control, his knees and elbows commanded respect. At any rate, I couldn't keep up with him.

If he started to lose, he became upset and his nose bled. At my age, I had to rely on a two-handed set shot I'd been perfecting for more than thirty years, over a period during which such shots had become obsolete. He teased me about it, I let him tease—it showed some affection for his stepfather—but when I wanted to I could beat him with this set shot, and watch his nose bleed. I carried handkerchiefs.

At the age of nineteen, he was nearly an alcoholic. Helga refused to see or admit this. He left each evening and came home drunk, and spent weekends partying at houses of friends. He'd already been arrested for drunk driving, a year ago. He'd spent forty-five days in jail, attended a clinic, stopped drinking for a month, smoked pot instead, but the pot drove him back to alcohol. This year he'd signed up for six courses at Dutchess Community, then dropped out after three weeks. In October he hitchhiked to Florida with a friend and worked as a roofer and drywaller, but came back in December after his boss made a pass at him. Helga gave him money for an apartment in Newburgh, but he didn't pay the rent, he drank it; now he was living with us in Highland. He had a trail bike, an infernal, noisy machine, but regularly siphoned gas from my car. He wore one earring that resembled a ball bearing.

In the fourth grade, his mother had found almost two hundred dollars he'd managed to save up extorting payments from his classmates. This was the year Helga and I married.

I liked the boy, but watched him carefully. When I walk down the street, I can see people making up excuses for themselves. David never had an excuse. Helga was the only one who hadn't written him off, but that was because it had never occurred to her. If he needed money, she always gave it. She wasn't especially generous, she just never kept track.

Someone was watching us play. Outside the tall chain-link fence of this playground, where the circular drive curved around to the boarded-up door of the school, was a bench, and on it sat an old, fat woman, very short, and another woman, middle-aged.

I was conscious of an audience; they'd been here before watching us. In fact, they'd been coming for almost two weeks now, sitting on that bench and pointing with gestures that suggested they were talking about us. Nodding or shaking their heads. Disagreeing. I decided to forgo my set shot, but held it ready to lure David in. He didn't fall for it. I wanted to drive for the basket and show off my speed, what was left of it, but first he had to commit himself. I faked the set shot. He stepped toward me, arms aflap. His left leg shot out across my path, but I can only drive right, and had already committed myself, putting the ball to the pavement, and thought I'd dance over that sprawling leg, almost did, but caught my trailing foot on his calf, which spun him around all the way against the back of my hips. It must have looked like he'd decided to tackle me. As we both went down I heaved the ball at the basket, underhand, and by miracle it went in. I jumped up right away, brushing my pants, listening to hear what my insides would do.

Since reaching my fifties, I'd begun seriously, religiously, in exercise or leisure, at meals and especially at bedtime, to heed my insides, in particular my chest, as though some hidden god in there were mumbling and it called for interpretation. Sometimes at night it prevented me from falling asleep, the things I heard: a little buzz, a kind of muted humming as of an engine that won't turn on, followed at last by my weak brag of a heart, too brittle and insistent for my peace of mind. During exercise like this I pictured it hanging there in my chest, suspended on the tangled skein of arteries and veins it served, reverberating like a gong, striking itself, proclaiming itself, angry and old and red-faced and small. I pictured the cavity of my chest with this lumpish bloody head. It made me think of those spiders you see in the mountains above timberline who string their webs between boulders. Gripping the entire web at its center, they shake it without mercy back and forth, like a prisoner shaking his bars, if anything should come near and brush the web, should touch just a strand. I stood there with my hand on my wrist.

"Coop," said David, "you scored!"

I thought of the lump on my neck, its root trailing down toward my spine. I pictured my cloudy intestines, as I'd once seen them on the X-ray screen during a barium enema. How little experience of our insides we have! I was a priest examining the entrails, my own. But most of all I listened to this magnified heart beating in my fingers, and tried to decide if the fluttering of my chest was coordinated with it, or purely independent. Often at night I woke in sudden fear because a little swelling bubble close to the entrance of my heart had popped. Sitting up, eyes wide open, I took my own pulse, which raced with fright, but felt regular neverthe-less. And sitting there, I wondered: just how was your heart attached, anyway? A little foot, or neck, such as clams have? And what did that grip? Bone, muscle, flesh? Only this comforted me: taking my pulse. It calmed me down, I could feel it grow slow. Standing there in that basketball court, hand on my wrist, I made a perfect circle. It bore some relationship to sucking one's thumb, I realized. But no more reckless drives to the basket, not against someone whose every limb snagged.

"Mr. Cooper?"

I felt foolish. "It's down to eighty a minute," I said. The fat lady stood at my elbow. Her mannish face went down in two slabs, straight into her shoulders. No curve or oval to it, and no neck. Liver spots all over her face. Short, curly hair. Her mouth was funny, out of control, and she was all of four feet high.

"This is your sister," she said. She held by the elbow the other woman, the middle-aged one, whose eyes were out of kilter. Her brown hair fell to her shoulders. This woman's mouth was grin-ning, but mainly I couldn't stop watching her eyes, one of which was higher than the other and in appearance sprung or wobbly, like a button on a spring.

"My sister?"

"I took care of you as a child," said the fat woman. She stared at my face like she knew it intimately. Asked me to bend down with such authority that I did. "Just as I thought," she said, pulling at my collar. I realized she was examining the lump on the back of my neck, which was really a birthmark; it looks like a toad or raspberry. It was cold out, so the birthmark must have been red.

"Changes color, does it?"

"Yes," I said.

"Red in the winter? Brown in the summer?"

"How did you know?"

"Your toes overlap," she said.

I blushed. It was like she had seen me naked.

"Allergic to milk?"

I nodded.

"Tomatoes?"

At the mere thought of tomatoes I break out in a rash, and I could feel my skin going prickly even as she said the word, the bumps raising, the birthmark starting to spread. She was fingering the scar beneath my bottom lip, and I was still bent over, feeling foolish. I straightened up and asked the other one her name.

"Carol Lyndhurst," she said.

Lyndhurst? It rang a bell. In fact, it made me downright uncomfortable. But what I said was: "Then you couldn't be my sister. My name's Cooper."

"But your father?" said the fat one.

"His name was Williams. He died when I was eighteen months."

"What did he do?"

"Drunken stockbroker."

"No, you're wrong," she said. "Your father's name was Lindbergh and he was a famous aviator."

"And this is my sister, whose name is Lyndhurst?"

"They changed it to protect him."

Somebody protect *me*, I wanted to say. These people make me nervous. I wanted them to go, but I didn't want to lose touch either. David stood about ten feet away, spinning the ball off the backboard into the hoop with his right hand, retrieving it with his left, keeping the circle going. Every now and then he glared over at us impatiently. He wondered the same thing I did: What the hell did these people want? I became suspicious. I could feel myself growing angry. You've got the wrong man. Leave me alone. I held out my hands for the ball, and David threw it, skimming the top of the fat lady's head.

But walking back to the office later on, by myself, I pulled out the Social Security card I'd found in Windsor. It was my number all right, etched on my brain: 030 30 2973. And my first name, Charles. But the last name was Lyndhurst. Charles Lyndhurst.

When I died, plenty of people showed up at my funeral—the curious, the maladjusted, the beautiful, the wealthy. My death was featured in the *Poughkeepsie Journal.* There were wreaths and floral sprays worth hundreds of dollars.

It was only later, after everyone went home, that they took out my brain and put it in this jar.

Knowing what I know now, I can see that their reasons for doing this were good ones. But that day, walking back to my office, I simply shook my head and smiled and thanked God I was nobody important. I was a water engineer. And I thought, at least we have our feet on the ground, we engineers, we have to. How could I have been someone named Lyndhurst, let alone Lindbergh, when I was already Charles Cooper, a water engineer? I got water to move from one place to another: around shopping centers, through roads, into storm drains, under bridges. I got water to go into people's houses, where they could drink it and wash their dishes and flush their toilets into septic lines and sewers I also designed. The year before all this began, my firm, Hudson Valley Consultants, completed forty projects with a total paper value of $2.6 million. This bought Helga and me a winter vacation in Egypt, and gave Pork his promotion and computer. With his big hands and big face, Pork now sat or stood at this computer all day long like a dwarf regarding with wonder a cache of gold. It shone in his face. Pork had always shown boundless enthusiasm for work I'd usually done with my left hand, since what I really wanted to be was an architect. I only finished a year of architecture school. I did, however, manage to design two houses, the one we were living in, and one for a friend, which he never built. What a heresiarch of architects I would have made—a heresiarchitect! Our house had concrete floors (you don't have to level concrete) and resembled a sprawling, multiwinged garage. I believe in simplicity, in liberating objects. All the pipes were exposed, you could see water heaters, furnaces, pumps, wires; these were part of the furniture. I don't believe in hiding anything. I like to see space take revenge on those who walk through it. Lots of windows, but they were small. The living room wall had a row of ten windows. Simple materials; a corrugated metal roof. I sent in photos to *Progressive Architecture,* but they never used them.

There was not a single bored object in our house. It sat on top of a perfectly conical hill studded with apple trees, an orchard we leased to the man we'd bought it from.

I also designed a recliner bicycle with far better balance than the available commercial models, with a nylon shock-corded ziparound compartment for rain. I rode this bike to work before we moved to Highland.

"Great manicotti," said Pork that evening. He reached for the dish without being asked, but Helga nodded her permission, smiling. Pork's large hands dwarfed the serving dish. His nose, mouth, jaw, forehead, eyebrows, and ears were all huge for such things, completely out of proportion to his short stature. It was as though he grew in clumps or burls, not up but out, into knotted dead ends that swelled with the growth. His gestures came in clumps too, brisk and short and explosive. To sit, for him, was not always comfortable; he preferred to keep his chair back and sit on the edge of it, hunched over, as though ready to escape. Or maybe it was to leave himself room to punch and swing his arms as he talked. He sat with his feet planted firmly apart, like somebody standing, forearms resting on the edge of the table, massive hands open, waiting.

He nodded when he talked or ate. I'd discovered this was infectious; when you talked with Pork you felt yourself nodding.

"I'm pleased you like it," said Helga. "Coop made it."

"Coop? You cook?"

"I cook on the weekends. I used to be a chef."

"No kidding?"

"Glad you like it," I said. "You're easy to please, Pork."

"No, I'm not. I'm very, very choosy, believe it or not."

"I know," I said. "Very discriminating. David says he saw you in KFC last week."

Pork thrust his face out toward David, mouth half open. Then he grinned; he laughed, nodding, and clapped his big hands. "He gave me two extra wings."

Across the table, my stepson blushed. I felt myself watching fragments: Pork's large face, each feature independent, David's hair covering one eye, one cheek, Helga's big-boned, high-cheeked mask. Helga was tall, taller than me. After fourteen years of marriage, I still felt self-conscious in her presence. My fingers were often dirty (from my pipe) but I didn't notice it unless she was around. Stubby fingers, each one blunt and thick, with wide tips and dirty nails. My arms went heavy when Helga walked into the room. I preferred to stay seated, but Helga always seemed to be off somewhere else, always on her way. She sold real estate. Lately, her sales had taken her more often to Manhattan, several times a week, but these sales and commissions she preferred not to talk about. She kept it on general terms. The commissions all went into her own bank account and investments, and I had no idea what she was worth.

When Helga smiled, fine spidery lines appeared around her mouth and eyes; there were gaps between her front teeth. Other than this, she looked ten years younger than fifty-three, her age. She was very tall. When she sat in a chair, as at dinner, talking, she had that kind of subdued attentive look, all eyes and ears and bright smiles, she made that extra effort to be engaging, that convinced you she was eager to be going, she was planning her next move, even among company. I'd always been persuaded she loved me, despite the fact that she had something better to do.

"We get calls from the city," Pork was saying, "to subcontract work in our own backyard!"

"So Coop tells me," Helga said, smiling at Pork. She'd finished eating first, as always. Very small portions.

I was toying with my food, pushing it around with a fork. I could feel my blood sugar rising, that inner radiation or feeling of dissolving which spreads across the body lining, the interior padding (I imagined it like a suit of armor with upholstering inside), which made of me a separate room inside the room I was in. See what a happy family we have, I thought. David was busy staring at his plate.

"You like manicotti?" I asked him.

"It's okay."

"How come you're not eating it?"

"I'm not hungry," he said. "I stare at food all day."

"Then you come home and stare at it some more."

"You should see the grease," he said. He was trying to be nice, I could tell. He addressed the whole table, but called me by name. "Coop," he said, "you know what Paul told me? At night they fry dogs. It's the Vietnamese, they break in at night. Or maybe they have keys. They use the vats of leftover grease and fry dogs they chopped up, which they stole from the suburbs."

Pork laughed out loud, Helga smiled indulgently. I was feeling pretty good too, and wanted to get something started right away. I didn't want to waste any time. "Son," I said, and paused. "Call me Father."

"What?"

"You could say Father, Dad, Pop. Don't call me Coop. It doesn't show respect."

"Come on."

"I'm not going to raise someone else's son if he won't call me Father. Yes, Father, No, Father. Say it."

"Are you serious?"

"Coop," said Helga.

"Are you serious, *Father*? Say it."

"Bullshit on that."

"See what I mean?" I grinned at Pork, and poured myself more wine. We were on the Chianti Pork had brought, since I'd told him we were eating Italian. I glared at David, who was looking at his mother. *Can you stop him?* his face said. *Here we go again.* He turned toward me.

"Stop staring at me."

"Stop staring at me, *Father*," I corrected.

"*Cut* it!" He stood up. "Will you stop staring at me?" The look in his eyes was desperate.

"I want some respect from you, son."

"Fuck your respect," he said, walking out of the room. A few seconds later he slammed the front door. I heard his trail bike start up and zoom off. Helga stared at her plate for a minute, then offered Pork more manicotti. Her serenity was stubbornly oblivious, and I wanted to crack it, but didn't dare try. Not Helga. I felt myself grinning.

"Spunky kid," I said.

"Maybe you shouldn't insist," said Helga.

"Lots of balls," said Pork.

"Smart too," I said.

"Oh?" said Pork.

Helga watched me as I spoke. I was still seeing fragments and pieces of faces; she seemed to disincorporate as I talked. I could see the front of her face and her profile both. My own face felt heavy, like a horse's, and I could feel it changing. "Going to MIT next year," I lied. I don't know why I said it; David had dropped out of high school. I'd toyed with the idea of letting him work in the office this summer, maybe as a gofer, but he could try a little drafting too. Pork could teach him.

"MIT? No kidding."

"Full scholarship."

"That's wonderful," said Pork. "You never told me. Talk about hiding your light. What's he plan to major in?"

"Aeronautical engineering." I was beginning to feel proud of David.

"Wow! That beats us by a mile, huh Coop? We'll still be building sewers while he designs space stations."

"Space stations, thrusters, jet planes. He designed a modified combustion chamber for jet engines. Drew up the specs, made a few drawings. Think what he could do with that CAD, Pork."

"Fascinating!" said Pork. I could tell he was impressed.

"He's smart!" I said. "Boy is he smart. He did something to his car, he gets a hundred miles to the gallon."

"Even motorcycles don't get that," said Pork.

"Right now he's working on a fantastic industrial air-conditioning system. You need an in-ground swimming pool to make it work. Motels could use it. Apartment houses. It requires a liquid he invented with a salt solution and something else, which freezes at forty-eight degrees Fahrenheit. Salt, vinegar, I don't know what else. Garlic, I think. Little cartridges of the stuff, underwater tubes and pipes."

Pork watched me as I talked, but I could see the smile was fading from his mouth. "Garlic?" he said. Helga had gone to the kitchen to make coffee.

"Salt, vinegar, something else. You renew the cartridge once a year. It converts a swimming pool into a huge refrigeration unit. You have to cover it with a tarp to keep the sun off."

"I see," said Pork, avoiding my eyes. He was looking around the dining room, pretending to admire it.

"This grew out of a science fair project. He threw something in the high school fountain, turned the water to jelly. They looked at it closely, found the pipes had burst. You don't believe me, do you?"

Pork smiled uneasily, but had trouble keeping his eyes on my face. "Sure, Coop. What the hell."

"Everyone want coffee?" Helga asked from the kitchen.

"You don't have to be so polite," I said to Pork. "Save it for the office. Sylvia told me you were unhappy about something, some paper she forgot to order?"

"We ran out of Xerox paper."

"So that gives you the right to use abusive language to the secretaries?"

Pork watched me from across the table, eyes wide open. He looked like he wanted to do something with his hands, hide them or cut them off and throw them out the window. In the posture he'd assumed, the hands, resting on the table, were only inches from his face, which was drooping forward like a great sunflower bending its stalk.

"My mother used to say, get the *best*, Charles. Buy the best things. Don't stint on what you buy." I was holding up the Chianti he'd brought.

"Sure thing, Coop."

"Hell, you can afford it, Pork. Did I tell you Albany called? The Superfund office. They're letting contracts to look into groundwater contamination. Guess how much."

"Half a million," he mumbled.

"Three point eight million dollars. Three point eight million. Pork, can you hear me?"

He was folded up like a gnome, shrinking into the parts of his body that weren't oversized. He didn't fit together anymore. I thought of Mr. Potato Head, he looked like. Forehead, nose, ears, hands, feet. My mouth felt sticky, things went in slow motion. Pork came from Boston.

"I mean, Pork, we're good friends, I can tell you this. You're the best damn engineer I've ever met. Imagination? Brains? You can take a concept and—and *realize* it. Everything you touch, you improve. And you bring contracts in below estimate. That's important, we can't ignore that. Don't think I haven't noticed it. Also, you're a nice man, people like you. As far as drafting goes, you can draw circles around any damn engineer I know. So how come you're so cheap?"

"Coffee!" Helga sang from the door. I stood up and walked past her, trying not to run, but couldn't help brushing the tray with the coffee cups she held in her hands; one spilled and crashed to the concrete floor behind me. I was biting my thumb as hard as I could, at the base, trying to draw blood. In my study I slammed the door and kicked a chair across the room. Great friends, I said out loud. What shits. I've got shits for friends!

But what about Milton Berle? Johnny Cash? I didn't know these people from Adam, but I heard myself replying, Shits, all shits. Princess Di? Stravinsky? Christ, what friends. Screw them all. Screw the afterlife. Screw Canada! Screw large corporations! I was shaking my head, pacing the room, swinging my arms, baring my teeth.

In my study I had my own phone with a separate number, so David couldn't tie up the line. I dialed my lawyer.

"Hello James? You home?"

"Charles?"

"How much would it cost to change the firm's name?"

"Charles, it's Friday night. I have guests."

"A ballpark figure, James. I need to know now."

"Change the firm's name? I don't know. Why bother? You'd have to refile incorporation papers. Just the fee, I'd imagine. Fifty, sixty dollars."

"How does Newburgh Engineering Associates sound?"

"Sounds fine. So does Hudson Valley Consultants."

"What about Cooper and Son, Engineers?"

"Your stepson joining the company, Charles? That's wonderful."

"Cooper, Vining and Cooper?"

"Sounds like lawyers."

"Aeronautical Associates?"

"Charles, I must go. We have guests tonight. Why don't you think about it and call me on Monday. You have to consider— think about the other costs too. Refiling is nothing. There's your name in the phone book. Signs, stationery, advertising. Name recognition, do you want to lose that? So on and so forth."

"Hudson Valley Refrigeration? Hands across the Hudson? Catskill Water and Air?" But the line was dead and buzzed in my ear. I listened to my heart beating on the phone. Carefully, I replaced the receiver, then felt for the pulse on my wrist with my thumb, the one with the tooth marks.

2

Helga was gone the next morning; David still hadn't come back.
My head was full of cement, my heart of shame. A brain in a jar
can't feel guilt, but a body can, as guilt is primarily a phenomenon
of radiation, triggered by memory. It behaves like contagion. The
memory of some deed or trauma spreads through body tissue and
accumulates in certain pockets, especially the fatty deposits
around the heart and lungs. I found a tin of Borkum Riff, lit my
pipe, and sat there on the floor of my study—where I'd slept the
night—nursing my guilt, sucking at the pipe.

The room was full of dirty things. I noticed them for the first
time, it seemed. Socks and underwear, ashes, pipe cleaners. On
the backs of chairs, on the floor, and every other place. I looked
closely at some indecipherable dirty thing next to a chair leg on
the floor, all covered with dust and hairs. It smelled bad. Everywhere there were dirty things, and little things that break.

It was raining out that morning. I had some letters to mail.
Section by section, limb by limb, I heaved myself together and
searched the house for my rubbers. Coop gets ready to go out in
the rain. Along the way I made some instant coffee in the kitchen,
and carried it around while I looked for the rubbers. I put the
coffee down someplace, on a dresser or something, but then I
couldn't find it, so went back to the kitchen and made another
cup, but couldn't find the sugar. I'd just used the stuff, but now
where was it? I opened every cabinet door looking for the sugar,
and left each one open, just to spite Helga. Or David. I slammed
my hand hard against the refrigerator. I looked in the silverware

drawer and found an old pen, and decided to write a note to David, apologizing for last night, but couldn't find paper, not even a little memo pad. We usually keep one on the refrigerator door, attached by a magnet. On my hands and knees I looked under the refrigerator. Sure enough, there they were, the magnet and clip, the memo pad. I felt good because I'd found them. I fished them out with a knife from the silverware drawer, shook off the crumbs and grease and dust, and sat at the table to write to David, composing in my head the right words to use. But I couldn't find the pen.

Just then the doorbell rang. I still wore last night's clothes, wrinkled and disheveled from a night of sleeping in them, and looking down across the slope of my chest and paunch and lap I noticed for the first time the stains and dirt there, and brushed at my shirt and pants with a shudder. Then I stood up. Coop answers the door.

At first I couldn't recognize the creature standing there. She smiled and blinked, her eyes were out of joint. "Hello," she said. I looked around. The rain had stopped, and I noticed my rubbers just outside the door on the flagstones, pooled with water.

Then I realized who it was: the woman from the basketball court. Not the old one who'd felt my neck, but the other one, my so-called sister. Carol Lyndhurst. Behind her was a younger girl, maybe sixteen or seventeen, with frizzed hair, chewing gum. "May we talk?" said Carol.

"Sure," I said, regretting it at once. With a little sweep of my arm—half shrug, half sweep—I stumbled back. "Come on in."

Inside, I offered them coffee, but explained I couldn't find the sugar. Carol said she drank it black. I don't drink coffee, said the girl, with an edge of defiance. It reminded me of David.

"Coke?" I said.

"Not at ten in the morning."

This was fortunate, as we had no Coke. Carol introduced the girl as her daughter, Valerie, and we shook hands. She was chewing gum. I don't know why this annoyed me, but it did. No Coke at ten in the morning, but gum, yes. She was pretty, in a mousy sort of way, like a—what were they called?—gun moll from the thirties. I noticed a scar above her lip.

I made a big pot of coffee for Carol and me, and went off in search of my pipe and tobacco.

"You don't remember me, do you?" she asked when we were settled in the living room. She had a very husky voice for a woman.

"Yes I do. The basketball court yesterday."

"I don't mean that."

Valerie sat, or sprawled, on the couch below the windows, thumbing through one of David's motorcycle magazines, the ones with cleavage and gleaming exhausts. I sat in one of the mission oak rockers, lighting and relighting my pipe—it was stubborn that morning. Carol sat in Helga's favorite recliner, the kind that swivels and tips back, both, and she couldn't stop wriggling and moving in the thing like a schoolgirl.

This living room was long and not too wide, and opened out into other wings of the house on either end. I've already mentioned the row of windows, ten of them. Each with a shade. Across from that wall was a moss rock fireplace fifteen feet wide, the kind you see in hunting lodges. On the concrete floor was my favorite oriental, a Hamadan we'd bought in Iran before all the fuss there, whose dimensions—it was half rug, half runner—had determined the shape of this room.

Beside my chair I had a stand-up ashtray we'd salvaged from the Nelson House, an old hotel in Poughkeepsie, before it was demolished.

As I said, I have a good memory, but parts of it I block out; it makes life easier. On the other hand some things, when they stare you in the face, you can't block them out, they nail their welcome in. Right through the brain. "You don't remember me, do you?" she asked again, and as the words came out, I did; I think it was the voice that did it first, but once I'd recognized that, her face began to assemble itself, the distortions collapsed, the twisted mouth, the lines, the eyes askew and popping, all dissolved. These ghostly features had been there before, almost forty years ago, but latent, whereas now they were achieved. Her face had accomplished its destiny. She wouldn't have been so darkly beautiful then, I realized—so *ferocious* in her beauty—if the seeds of this equally ferocious ugliness hadn't been there. Her face was throwing itself together right in front of me; inside it, like something dimly seen in a thicket, was the girl I'd known, the first girl I'd loved. Her face had that echo now, just as—even though I couldn't know it at the time—it had this echo then.

I've since learned that memory is an acid; throw it at something and you alter it forever.

"Bernice," I said quietly.

"Carol," she said. "I changed it."

"Why Lyndhurst? Why that name?"

"It's not really Lyndhurst anymore, it's Englehard, but I don't like to use that. My ex-husband."

I looked over at her daughter, who glanced up at me briefly with a look of pure impudence. Take your feet off my couch, I wanted to say. "How long has it been? Thirty-five, forty years?" Bernice shrugged, looking around the living room. She reached down and felt the Hamadan, then flipped a corner over to count the knots. I asked her if she ever heard from Raymond, our cousin. Or was it second cousin? He was my uncle's cousin, she replied. I'd always thought of him as one of the cousins, but then again Bernice was a cousin, and she had cousins of her own, other family on her mother's side. Or was it her father's? I saw family trees branching like candelabra.

"Raymond's dead," she said. "Died of an aneurism."

"He used to tell me—remember, I went to school with the nuns? They taught me religion in the day, then, when I came home at night, Raymond said it was all lies. He told me not to believe a word of it."

"That sounds like good old Raymond."

"Consequently, I grew up with two sides of my brain, you could say. An entrance and an exit. I saw houses, but there was always the suspicion that they could have been painted props. For all I knew the rocks could be papier-mâché. Hollow."

"Ha ha, that sounds like you, Charlie."

"Bernice," I said.

"Carol," she replied. "Call me Carol now."

We talked like this, not saying anything, but I was hardly paying attention anyway. Names came up; flotsam on the tide. Meanwhile, beneath the names, the undertow carried me away. I saw the place on East Seventy-eighth Street, the library filled with books I read, wholesome books, *Treasure Island, Captain Blood, The Count of Monte Cristo,* Tom Swift, Dickens, old twenties textbooks on aeronautics, ballooning, biplanes, warfare. My USA puzzle map, my mother in her wheelchair, the huge mirror in sections the length of the hallway outside the maid's room. Flowers everywhere. Cranberry glass in carved niches. Orientals. Long flowing walls; they were fabrics, not walls.

Tall Cousin Raymond with his thin straight hair and easy way of joking about everything. His flat nose, buttonhole nostrils, and sagging eyes. He gestured off the terrace to the view of the city and the East River below. "Real life," he said. "Stay away." He sat me on his lap and showed me strange, erotic pictures in a book, dreamy scenes with forests of lines and folds and clothing, between which you could make out monstrous, stylized sexual organs. These pictures filled me with sadness and fear.

In her wheelchair, my mother insisted upon being cheerful. She was brave and kind, she tried not to complain, but I walked around in mortal fear of seeing her wheelchair come buzzing around the corner of a room before she'd had the chance to compose her face, which would therefore reveal the pure wretchedness of her life. Did I see this or imagine it? Beneath her good humor was fear, and beneath the fear tyranny. I realize now that others saw this, but I can't be certain I knew it at the time. It seems that everyone avoided her. I remember clearly that only Bernice wasn't intimidated by my mother. Dana, Patrick, Charlotte—the other cousins—all avoided her. Younger than Bernice and I, they had better instincts: stay away from tyrannical women in wheelchairs. I was told they were children of my mother's late sister-in-law. She'd taken them in. Their playroom lay deep in the inner recesses of the apartment, and only occasionally did they come spinning out of it like whirlwinds, down hallways, into bathrooms, in mortal danger of encountering my mother.

Once I opened one of the bathroom doors and found her lying on the floor by her wheelchair, legs jerking spasmodically like an insect's. Her skirt was down, the room smelled foul, but she didn't ask for help, she just lay there half propped on an elbow with a flat look of bitterness in her eyes. I'm not sure she recognized me. I shut the door and walked away.

I was fourteen or fifteen when I went to live with my mother, wearing tweed knickers and argyle socks which my new city cousins ridiculed. It was 1945, the war had just ended, everybody talked about it. Toy bombers hung by strings from the playroom ceiling. My mother was new there too, it appeared. For my first thirteen years she had lived in the hospital while I stayed in the country in Windsor with George and Louise. Then she had pills to make her feel better, so she could live at home and I could be with her, but by then she was almost a stranger. Uncle Chuck showed up on weekends, Bernice's father. He came around more often than he used to, I was told, because the war was over. Who else? Aunt Phyllis lived with us for a while and once strung a clothesline across the terrace—I'm pretty sure of this—but Bernice took it down. I was told my father was dead; Mother kept pictures of him on her dresser: a handsome man with rimless glasses and painted cheeks (in the photograph) and thin, modest lips. She called him a drunkard.

Mother had cauliflower hair and soft white skin, and kept oxygen tanks in her room to breathe with. Not always, just when it grew difficult. She died when I was a junior at Yale. As I had crew that weekend, I couldn't go to the funeral.

My mother and Raymond didn't get along, but for some reason

she was obliged to put up with him. I think Uncle Chuck had something to do with it, but what she told Raymond was, *If I weren't sick.* This was a threat with universal application and boundless possibilities, since no matter how well she became, she was always sick. And brave about it. I don't know now if I dreamed it or it happened, but she slapped Raymond once at the dinner table, I think. And my cousin Raymond with his red cheek laughed.

He brought home friends. Did I imagine this, or was one a bus driver? He wore a uniform. Sitting there across from Bernice, who was wondering out loud what became of a certain piano teacher we'd had, while her daughter waved pipe smoke away with her hand, I saw half-remembered faces, ghosts from the past—they crowd around still—each in small black and white, like newsreels in cavernous theaters where anything could happen in the dark. Some of these were Raymond's friends, some not. Men in homburgs, camel hair coats, silk scarves. I was fourteen years old. They came and went quietly. One night they burned a lot of papers in the fireplace. They made phone calls all day and never grew excited.

When my mother was away one time for tests, Raymond threw a party, to which some of these men came. Others showed up too, in V-neck sweaters and brown and white shoes; the women wore pleated skirts and scarves around their necks. Some blacks came; "Negroes" we said then. This second group of younger people laughed out loud and danced, and gathered in humming knots away from the men in suits and silk ties. They seemed to laugh at everything. Raymond taught me to mix drinks for this party. When guests left, I had to bring their cars around front, from the garage downstairs. One man in a three-piece suit offered me a twenty—he was drunk—but I told him, no thanks, I'm being paid. In slow motion now—it looks like a dream—I see him take a swing at me out on East Seventy-eighth Street, an erratic haymaker wide of its mark, while someone pulls him back to his car, arms around his waist, where he folds in half at the door and disappears.

Plenty were left from that party when mother came back. She showed up the next morning and found the place full of strange, limp bodies sleeping on the furniture amid glasses, ashtrays, napkins and crumbs, in the dining room, living room, den and library. I heard castanets. Then what I noticed was Raymond's wet head and the angelfish sliding down his shoulders, while the sound of the crash woke everyone up, and, from the doorway, where I'd just entered the dining room, I followed the great gush of water up the credenza to the hooked end of mother's cane caught in the gaping hole it had opened in our great forty-gallon aquarium.

For a moment everything was still, except the dripping water. Then Raymond jumped up, mumbling something about Uncle Chuck—wait till Uncle Chuck sees this—and my mother buzzed off in her wheelchair, triumphant and imperial.

"More coffee, please." The veins around Bernice's eyes were visible. "Look, Charlie, can you do me a favor? Poach me an egg. I'm starved."

"Maybe Valerie can do it."

But Valerie appeared shocked by the suggestion. She smiled sweetly and shook her head no, then lowered her eyes with disgust to her magazine.

So, still foggy with ghosts of the past, I cooked Bernice some poached eggs and toast, and even threw some bacon in the microwave, while she walked around the house on her own, opening doors, looking in closets. I heard her exclaim something indecipherable from the vicinity of our bedroom. When the food was done I called her, and she immediately walked in, as though she'd been waiting in the hallway. "Remember this, Charlie?" She held in both hands a silver goblet from my bedroom, made with a chaste inverted Gothic arch on a pedestal foot, one of the few things I still had from East Seventy-eighth Street; I'd taken it to Yale for a beer mug. It was English, eighteenth-century.

Bernice clung to it like a priest at Mass. "What's this worth, five or ten thousand?"

"I don't know."

"You just leave it out in your bedroom? This is a crazy house, Charlie."

"Be careful what you say, I designed it myself."

"I mean, at least you could *paint* those pipes." She nodded across the kitchen, still holding onto the goblet with both hands. Suddenly it dropped to the concrete floor with a pure single note, and Bernice regarded it with a crazy grin. "Oops."

"Bernice!" I retrieved the goblet, but found it to be undamaged.

"Silverware, Charlie." She sat to her breakfast. The goblet I placed in a cabinet, with care, then found her a knife, fork and spoon in the dishwasher. "Valerie! You want some bacon? I can't eat bacon," she said to me.

"No Mom."

"Charlie?" She pushed me her plate. I picked up the bacon with my fingers and ate it like jerky as we talked.

"So Bernice, Carol," I said. "What have you been doing all this time?"

"Nothing very exciting. I worked as a stewardess, airlines, I taught school. That didn't last long. I'm looking for work now, Charlie, as a matter of fact. I have lots of experience with planning classwork and getting satisfying results for the students and myself. I noted the job advertisements up in—I wasn't looking just for jobs, oh shit. Just scouting around up there. I'll tell you about it later. Anyway, I have not seen my finances match my abilities yet, so far as the exact amount of what I'm worth on the pay scale goes." She spoke between mouthfuls of poached egg, discreetly chewing. I couldn't help feeling that the parts of her face went off in about ten different directions as she ate, but that might have been me—a residue from last night.

"You were a stewardess? Did you go to college like you wanted?"

"Oh you remember good. I went to college and learned to play trumpet, but it made me tired. Charlie, you've come a long way, *I* should say, for somebody who got thrown out of his home, then later on didn't you run away? I was thinking of this the other day. It's been a long time."

"What college?"

"Oh you would ask that."

"What airline?"

"TWA, what else? The best, the first. When my face was still pretty. This house is so big."

I couldn't hold it in anymore. There's no doubt that this was Bernice, but she'd changed drastically. Years ago, when I first went to live on East Seventy-eighth Street, she'd been haughty and rich, the princess of that huge apartment. She'd even bossed my mother around. But she'd hardly spoken with me at first, she'd treated me like a poor relation. She was, what? A year older than me. Several times, when I first moved in, she made me play games with her and one of her friends. I was the piano mover who came to the door. She tipped me a dollar and dismissed me with the back of her hand, but as I was leaving she said, What's this? *Marks* on the piano. See this scratch? See that smudge? I had to take them off. They made me polish the piano. Then I was required to play them a song, to make sure it worked. Then one of them—Bernice it was, usually—told me to take off my shirt. They wanted to see the new hairs on my chest, which they plucked with tweezers, squealing with joy and horror, affecting patrician British accents they'd learned by listening to butlers. How disgusting, they said . . . "Bernice, Carol, what happened to you?" I blurted out.

"What?"

"You were richer than anyone."

"That was all charity, Mr. Jones."

"You didn't act like it was charity."

"We lived there by the grace of God, Charlie."

"You paraded around like you owned the place. I felt like, like—a country hick. I still smelled the hay in my pockets, from Windsor. I was afraid there was always cowshit on my shoes. You looked down your nose at me, Bernice. It drove me crazy, I bit my own thumb. I used to scrub myself down in the bathroom. I was thinking I carried the farm in my face."

"You did."

"I was ashamed, I've always been ashamed ever since, of the hair on my body. It was just coming in. On my back, on my toes."

"You were my teddy bear."

"You used to walk around, Bernice, with your fifteen-year-old butt—you held it like somebody holds a present, like Daddy's little girl, and she shakes it like this, just a tiny bit, to see what's inside. You know what I mean?"

"Oh Charlie."

"I never knew any girls before then."

"I thought you were a stocky stud farmboy."

"Like the hired help."

"You didn't take long to adjust, Charlie. I saw you changing every day. New York City did wonders for you. I saw you naked once."

"Where?"

"In the bathroom. I peeked through the window from the terrace, outside. Naturally, this was before we—before you and I . . ."

Bernice saw me naked! I smiled in the kitchen, and listened for Valerie turning the pages of her magazine out in the living room.

"More coffee, Charlie."

"I'll have to make another pot."

"Good. Make lots. I'm a coffee freak." She smiled up at me a weird, querulous grin, fractured and warm at the same time. She was satisfied, she'd eaten her eggs, and took the opportunity now to study me closely. "You haven't changed much, Charlie."

"You too, Bernice."

"You've gained some weight. I see you still have all your hair. Those pouches in your cheeks. Your face sags a little. Do you exercise?"

"I gave up jogging. I feel a hundred percent better since I did."

She asked me about my wife, my family, my work. I must have

been doing pretty well to afford this hill and this house. When would I finish it? Finish what? I asked. The *house*, Charlie.

Bernice, the house is finished exactly as it is. It's supposed to be like this. Oh, she said.

But I must admit I was taken aback by comments like this, as well as by her manner and appearance. We'd reversed positions; now I was well off and she was the poor relation, now I knew about things and she displayed her ignorance. But ignorance is relative. In the matter of social status, we're all at the mercy of our ignorance, and our betters get to be that way by perceiving its exact dimensions; they can read what we don't know at a glance, whereas for us it's a huge blank space, like the cave we carry around at the level of our eyes, out of which we peer.

I asked her what she meant about East Seventy-eighth Street, that it was all charity. If it was charity it never stopped coming. My mother's estate put me through college, and still laid an egg worth eight hundred dollars a month. I said this with some reluctance, since it was evident that Bernice was receiving nothing. Why? I'd been mailed a check every month since my twenty-first birthday.

That's not from her, said Bernice. That's not your mother's estate.

It comes from a law firm on Liberty Street, I said. Also, there's the house in Windsor.

But Bernice insisted that none of this had belonged to my mother. My mother didn't have a thing. Then she dropped a bombshell I immediately tried to ignore: That house is mine as much as yours, she said. That house in Windsor, Charlie.

Bernice, you were married? You have a lovely daughter. Married, divorced, separated, widowed? We walked back to the living room with fresh mugs of coffee, and I tried to pay attention to everything Bernice was saying, but all I could think of was the place in Windsor. Was this why she'd shown up now? She'd try first to claim it nicely—to the degree that she was capable of being nice—then if that didn't work, I'd hear from her lawyer.

But my heart was in Windsor, all the heart I had left. Windsor was where I'd been kicked out of the garden, so I could go and live with my mother in the city. The three or four weeks we stayed there every summer renewed me for the year; it was the first home I had, and still the only one.

Bernice was talking about her husband, but apparently in order to do so she had to go back to the first thing she remembered in her life, sitting on the toilet getting her hands and feet washed by a woman with bright red nails. This was going to be a long story, and I only half listened. I was thinking about all the agony I'd felt when I had to leave Windsor for the city. The only thing I had going for me was my age, and the books I subsequently found in the library of my prison on East Seventy-eighth Street. When I read *The Count of Monte Cristo* and *The Man in the Iron Mask,* I was able to imagine myself suffering heroically, and could anticipate looking back much later with pity and admiration for all I'd endured in the difficult time of young manhood. I even felt a little self-conscious and embarrassed at what my future self would think of me, since I assumed he'd be wise and forbearing, but maybe a little impatient too. After a year or so of living in luxury, and following the example of people like Jim Hawkins and Huckleberry Finn, I ran away, but only made it as far as Yonkers. Six months later I made it all the way back to Windsor by thumb—this was years before they started the four-lane Route 17—and was shocked to find the place all shuttered, the barn empty of cows, weeds in the pastures, George and Louise gone. That night I slept in the barn and breathed its ghostly animal smells, but when I hitched back to the city the next day I'd already become an adult; that is, whatever before had been solid inside me was now honeycombed with loss, I harbored labyrinths and passageways, and knew instinctively how to behave upon returning to East Seventy-eighth Street: with hypocrisy, disdain, and outward compliance. Inside, peering out from the inner jungle I'd raised, I watched everyone and everything. No one knew if I thought good or evil. Already, the place seemed stale and old—it promised to be always the same—whereas I was changing, I conceived of ambitions, I hated everyone and everything around me, but learned to act correctly to them all. I gradually adopted that icy politeness laced with reserve which manufactures social inferiors. I patronized my younger cousins. I learned what to say to the maids. Looking back at it now, it seems that even my mother conceived of a fear of me, mixed with respect and admiration. But none of this behavior was for her, nor was it for Raymond. I'd chosen my target, the object of my fantasies of voluptuous revenge: my cousin Bernice.

Forty years later, the same Bernice sat in front of me talking, incoherently at times, about her ex-husband and the daughter he'd seeded, who was just about the age of Bernice then, and who regarded me now with utter disdain. At least, so it seemed. Bernice was working her way around to the frat party at which she'd met her husband, but digressed whenever she remembered what she thought at the time, about anyone and anything. It was a toga party at an unnamed college, though I gathered from the context that this was upstate New York. The party had a Roman theme. They had a fat guy dressed up as Bacchus, the god of wine and sex. Everyone threw grapes at this target, but I thought at the time (said Bernice) what a mess. Flattened grapes all over the floor. This was intentional; it made dancing dangerous.

They served pre-made drinks in baby bottles with the nipples cemented on. At the time, in the early fifties, there was a lot of talk about getting rid of your inhibitions. They brought in a whole side of beef and everyone tore at it with their hands. The climax of the party was a crucifixion. They actually crucified someone, tied him up on a cross with ropes and smothered him with flowers.

"That man," said Bernice, pausing dramatically, "the man they crucified became my husband. That should tell you something about him. Actually, I remember thinking at the time he looked a little more mature than the others. I noticed that when they carried him in they were careful about it. When I noticed he was a little receding in the hairline department, I was happy to find out these weren't all juveniles at this party. All the people I corresponded with thought I needed a more mature man. I admired a lot of my professors, especially when they acted inspiring. I noticed there were ways to get busy and approach the possibility of friendship with these sorts of men, for example my girlfriend Kathy, who also required a more mature individual. . . . We studied very hard, both in and out of the classroom situation . . ." Bernice had begun to fidget in her chair once again, twisting her face alternately into masks of triumph and apprehension, screwing her topmost eye up over my head to peer into the past. She chewed her words, she paused, she became confused. I watched a shadow of pure anger pass across her face and freeze it.

"He was already graduated, but he came to all the fraternity parties. He ran a collection agency. That should give you a thought, Charlie. We got married for ten years. His sister moved in, in the context of looking for work, but what she seemed to be was fat, and she had two or three guys over at once. He was married once before and had already suffered the loss of a son. Adhesions from an appendicitis operation."

Bernice went on to talk about her husband's mother moving in and taking charge of the refrigerator: I'd go to the refrigerator and Mrs. Englehard would say, what the hell are you doing in the refrigerator, and I'd say I wanted something to eat, and she'd say you can't eat anything.

She divorced Mrs. Englehard's son when she caught him one time standing over Valerie's bed in the middle of the night, stark naked. This was when Valerie was eight.

Valerie appeared unaffected by this story, which she'd probably heard before; she remained buried in her magazine. Then the talk shifted slightly. Bernice's voice became husky, or hoarse. She began reproaching herself with Valerie's lack of a father—whom she never saw now—and started condemning herself in general terms as unworthy of Valerie, who never looked up. She couldn't even provide her daughter with a permanent home; or hadn't been able to so far, and I cringed, thinking of Windsor. Bernice was in the act of raising her voice, becoming almost hysterical, when I heard the back door open. It was still Bernice's, or Carol's, face that seemed strangest of all: head bowed in modesty, mouth bent and twisted, one eye pointing up, the other half shut. Leaning forward, legs apart, her back was arched, and she appeared to be forcing her head down against the inclination of her neck to raise it. In this posture, she was on the verge of discovering that her husband's obvious malice in failing to love either her or her daughter was shared by the world, when David walked in.

I jumped to my feet, solicitous and polite. I still hadn't seen him since last night. Had breakfast yet, son? Yes. Lunch? No. I invited everyone to stay for lunch, but Bernice and her daughter were making ready to leave; maybe David's manner told them something. Was he shy or sullen? Guilty, perhaps; after all, he'd been out all night. He hung his head, averted his face, refused to look at either me or Bernice, but I took him by the arm and introduced him to Valerie (I admit that I turned to wink at Bernice) and told him with a laugh that she liked motorcycles too. They regarded each other shyly, but I noticed they were soon talking about something as Bernice searched for the door she'd come in, head in a swivel.

Where can I find you? I asked Bernice, just to be polite. Don't worry, I'll find *you,* she grinned. She was walking out the kitchen door—Valerie and David had preceded her outside, and were admiring his bike propped against the garage (the kickstand was broken)—when I remembered to ask Bernice about the woman at the basketball court, the funny-looking old one. Who was she, Bernice? She thought you were my *sister.*

"You mean you didn't recognize her?" I assured Bernice I didn't. "Well, she's old, Charlie. I think she's a little senile now."

"What's her name?"

"She says funny things, she's a riot."

"Bernice, who is she?"

"She," said Bernice, "is the woman you think was your mother."

"What?"

"Her legs got better, Charlie. The way she told me about it, the possibility of getting busy and giving up the wheelchair was just an idea that came around to her one day. So she got up and walked again. Just like that. I always thought," she said, climbing into her car, a half-rusted Valiant, bobbing her head up and down, left and right, and cracking her smile like a nut in her teeth— Valerie was already seated next to her, and David leaned above the girl from the window, talking—"I always thought she'd out- live us all." She started the car and crept off on our private road, snaking down through the apple orchard on switchbacks, leaving me there with my hand on my pulse in a state of sudden fright.

After they left, I lay down to rest and to think about all this, but couldn't take it in—couldn't encompass it. I remembered what I'd said to Bernice, that my brain had an entrance and an exit, and felt the various names and faces we'd been resurrecting, especially my mother's, tumbling out of what looked like the mouth of a culvert, and at last thought I was rid of them all when the phone woke me up. I must have been exhausted.

It was Helga, calling from the city to explain that she'd be there until Monday. Her buyer had a Monday-at-two-thirty deadline, and she thought it best to stay over. When she hung up, I dialed Pork to apologize for last night and expound on the recent pres- sures in my life by way of explanation, such as my problems with blood sugar—which he already knew about—and my current concerns about David, as well as other family matters, financial concerns, distant relatives showing up, and so forth, some of which were of course subsequent to last night, but I didn't tell him that. It all just came to a head, Pork. I can't drink too much anymore, especially good wine. As a matter of fact, until last night, I hadn't had anything to drink for a month. It just sort of exploded in my brain.

But that Albany contract? The Superfund money? That's for real, I told him, that's something we'll talk about Monday.

Pork said he understood, boss. He sounded preoccupied. I asked him if he needed anything. In the mood I was in, full of doubts and apologies, I would have given him my house or car. We could go out to dinner tonight, or go to a movie, take our minds off the pressure. No, he had a date tonight. I wondered with a flash of pain—I couldn't account for it—who Pork was dating, and how he was in bed. I felt sure he was exceptional. I hung up happy for Pork, and vaguely uneasy about everything else.

We could patch it up. Actually, I liked Pork. He'd been with the firm for two years now, and his work was impeccable. But this was a friendship that needed repairs, I'd been so—such a bounder, as we used to say.

3

Bernice had to be wrong about my mother. My mother was dead, cremated according to her wishes. After her funeral they mailed the ashes to me at Yale, and I still had them someplace at Highland, in a cardboard box with the mailing wrapper still on. Preceding the ashes, a letter from a lawyer I'd never heard of had arrived, explaining that my mother had wanted her remains to be sprinkled on the East River in New York City, and could I do this for her? Certainly I could, though I hadn't gotten around to it yet. After thirty years.

At Yale, where everyone knew everyone else's origins, mine were in the closet. I was a loner. Subsequently, with scrupulous care, I carried her ashes from Yale to Albany to Nyack to Newburgh to Highland, the first item packed on all my moves, the first put away, deep in a closet. That they were my mother's ashes I had no doubt. Otherwise, why would they make me so uncomfortable just to handle? Therefore, Bernice, or Carol, wasn't telling the truth, though I couldn't very easily grasp why.

Shortly after her visit, however, I understood more. Bernice was a liar—that much was clear. She was after something, she wasn't to be believed, and this I learned from, of all people, her daughter. The letter I received from Valerie smelled of perfume or baby powder; enclosed were three small pen-and-ink drawings.

*   *   *

April 12, 1985

Dear Mr. Cooper,

As David's father I deeply hope you'll understand why I'm writing this to you. I've begun this letter millions of times (well . . . maybe not *millions*), not to mention having to hide it from my mother, which if she found out about it she'd have a fit. You don't know how hard it was to pretend to be reading your son's creepy magazine when I was there in your house, while all the time I was thinking that maybe you *knew* what was really going on. It's more like the type of feeling you get when you want to say something but you know you can't? It's not exactly that, but I was just *bursting!* Then it gradually occurred to me, because you have a kind face, and after some things my mother told me about you, like you wanted to be an architect, and you used to draw all the time, that maybe you could see whether the types of drawings I do show any evidence of art talent or whatever. Or maybe they don't. I really like the tree, I was looking at somebody's art . . . Rembrandt or somebody . . . and it seemed to show realness . . . or hardness. Actually, I don't know if I should call realness *hard,* I will just have to think about that one again, but anyhoo . . . Do you think I have talent? When I saw you I thought you had such a kind face, and I really wanted you to know what I was thinking. It wasn't just about my drawings and stuff, never mind that, that's not the only reason why I'm writing this letter. I don't know about this. I think I should warn you to be careful of my mother and don't trust everything she says (anyway I don't). I sat there on that couch thinking if only you could read my mind. You didn't seem very interested in me, but that's okay, nobody is. Well, that's life folks. When I was sitting there I actually tried sort of to beam my thoughts right into your brain, but I guess it didn't work. I really could have cried. This is why I simply had to write this letter.

Do you recognize the building as your office? Mom

took me there. We parked across the street all day, I don't
know what she was doing, looking for something I guess.
Writing things down. I suppose I don't exactly like how
heavy the top part seems, like it's this huge heavy object
somebody just dropped on the street. I'm not too sure.
Then again its angular shape came out pretty well. Sort
of like the Flatiron Building.

The other one is the Hudson River around Stony
Point. We sleep in the car there sometimes in the parking
lot, I mean my mother and me. I haven't been back to
school in weeks. I haven't seen my father in a million
years, but that's another story which my mother got
wrong too.

Yours sincerely,
Valerie Englehard

A kind face? I walked to the bathroom, to check it in the
mirror. I think you could see it that way. There were definitely
signs of kindness in the eyes. For one thing, they were soft. The
bags underneath were kind. Never mind the anticlimax of the
pupils themselves, which seemed to peer out of the fleshy caves
around them from a great, great distance, and were pretty much
opaque—even when staring at themselves—as though the gates
had closed on the lights at the end of the tunnels. Bernice was
right, about the pouches; my whole face had a certain puffy
quality, but the skin was more abraded than soft. An astute person
might interpret this as kindness. My brown hair hadn't even
begun to turn gray—of this I was proud—so the quality of kindness had to be in the face itself, and in those expressions most
natural to it.

With a face like that I could forgive Bernice, but for what? Her
hard-as-nails but soft-hearted daughter had warned me of something, though precisely what it was I couldn't say. It intrigued me,
though. After all, we were old friends, Bernice and me. To say the
least. But had forty years changed me as much as her? When you
are the change—not just the process but the result—of course you

don't notice it that much, because you are the change. And she'd seen me naked at the age of fifteen, she'd taken the trouble to peek through a window, when at the time I thought she disdained me. Despised me! So even before what happened later, she was *interested* in me.

Therefore, the past never stays the same. The amount of the unexpected in its mixture is quite high, even higher than the future, which is handicapped anyway by not yet existing.

Meanwhile, I had the Superfund contracts to deal with. This was a busy time at work; the contracts had been broken up by the State Budget Office into numerous subcontracts according to complicated guidelines handed down by the federal government (where the money originated) and the GAO. You needed more computers than we had to keep track of all this, but with the help of Pork and his new programs we managed to make substantial bids on four subcontracts, with respect to examining groundwater contamination, and this occupied much of the following weeks.

I didn't hear from Bernice again until the end of that month. It was a Monday and I'd taken the day off from work to drive Helga to La Guardia. That is, she drove and I came along to take the car back after dropping her off. It was my car, the Volvo.

Helga was flying to Orlando, Florida, to see her eighty-six-year-old father, who was ailing. His circulation was poor; one foot had been amputated. Now, in the hospital, he'd lost the will to walk, and she wanted to see what she could do to get him out of bed. Her brother Theon and sister Rika lived in Orlando too, though Max (her father) had only recently moved there from New York, where he'd spent the last forty or fifty years importing printed cloth from Scandinavia. This was a business he'd more or less fallen into after failed investments in the declining textile industry of Massachusetts and New Hampshire.

Max was a German immigrant. His wife had died before Helga and I married, and they seldom talked of her. I gathered that she'd had some sort of exotic but shameful occupation, such as professional roller skater, or trapeze artist.

Maybe that accounted for David: a recessive gene. Driving

down the New York State Thruway south of Newburgh on a cloudy, brooding day, Helga and I talked of David, who had quit his job at KFC and hadn't been home now for three days. The sky looked like the inside of someone's head, and I had a migraine, as I always did before driving into the city. "Did he tell you about the speakers?" she said.

Something in her voice made me think he should have. There are shades of intonation only I can detect in Helga's noncommittal tone—an imperceptable, slightly German lilt at the end of a question that betrays its caution. Helga grew up speaking German at home. "He mentioned something," I said.

"What?"

"About the speakers."

"What did he mention?"

"About buying the speakers?"

"Did he tell you about his friend's receipt?"

"Which friend is this?"

"Steve."

"That's the dark-haired one."

"Steve has the dark hair, yes." I could tell this story would cost me money. "It seems that this Steve was buying speakers in a music store. For their band. He gave the man a check for the money, for which the man gave him a receipt. Then he discovered there are none of these speakers in stock. They are out of stock. So the man gave him back the check, but Steve did not give back the receipt. He has told you about this?"

"He mentioned a receipt." Actually, we hadn't talked about it at all.

"It was David's idea to return to the store two weeks later with the receipt." Helga's English was faultless and precise, except for a shade of *v* inside the *w* in *with*. "Viff," it sounded like, a little.

"Don't tell me," I said. "He walked in with the receipt and walked out with the speakers."

"But his friend had already cashed the check. Which his mother had written."

"I know the whole story."

"Then you must know that the police are involved. And Steve's parents, who want the money to be paid."

"Honey, it's not as bad as all that. I'd say it's more or less a prank your son played on his friend."

"Oh?"

"You know, a practical joke? David means well. He told me all about these speakers, which he has every intention of paying for."

"I'm relieved to hear it. The speakers cost three hundred dollars."

"I gave him the money. I'm giving it to him."

"That's very generous of you. You have already given it?"

"Not yet."

"Because I'm afraid that if you had, he has spent it by now. Wherever he is."

"He'll show up."

"I admire your confidence." Helga's face was shading to thoughtful anger. She said nothing for a while, watching the highway. It hadn't rained on us yet, but the pavement was dark from a recent storm and the tires hissed through patches of wet.

"Steve's mother was quite upset on the phone," she finally said.

"When was this?"

"Last night. I wanted to speak to you about it."

"Why didn't you?"

But now Helga was beginning to pull out of the conversation. There was something else, something she wasn't saying. I could see the account sheet in her mind: relief on the one side that David's theft would be paid for—though she could have done it just as easily, of course—while somewhere in the opposite column was a debit pertaining to David, or me, or life in general. Times like this, she withdrew politely. She smiled to herself, treating human failures with a certain disdain. Had David mentioned the visit of Bernice? This I hadn't told Helga about; in fact, I had no intention of telling her. I thought of the silver goblet, still on a shelf in one of the kitchen cabinets. "David's showing signs of pulling himself together," I said.

Helga smiled to herself and glanced out the window to her left.

She held the Volvo at exactly fifty-seven, in the right-hand lane. In her view, fifty-seven was allowed by the fifty-five-mile-an-hour speed limit, but no more than fifty-seven.

I should mention that Helga and I had never had a fight. She walked away if I became abusive. This was why she drove when we traveled together; I couldn't very well mistreat someone in control. Besides, when my blood sugar rose I got claustrophobic, I had to move around, I couldn't be in a car. Once she had to stop and let me out. This didn't bother Helga; she found me later, wandering in a cemetery. She drove me home, sprawled in the back seat.

Helga had always been a woman of business. We understood each other instinctively. I thought of our marriage as linking solitudes. The convenience side of it partially filled our usual sense of loss. I didn't exactly love Helga, I feared her. She was taller than me. I feared loving her, so the love pretty much trailed behind like a dog with its tail between its legs.

And Helga on her part regarded me with an equanimity very close to love, for a woman of business. I'm sure it was love, or nearly so. We lived with each other always on the verge of love.

I must emphasize that Helga was what other women call extremely handsome. She carried herself well and tall, and her high cheekbones protected the rest of her face when she smiled. I think she was probably happy, and even when she cried, for example (without making a sound), just as when she smiled to herself, this was an expression not of that happiness that comes from fullness of being, but of happiness sufficient to float yourself along on the daily round from one thing to the next.

She was a person incapable of lying. This I deduced from both the beautiful German lilt in her voice and the quality of patient and intelligent explanation in her conversation. You could trust this woman with your life, or, failing that, just listen to her speak. We'd met fifteen years ago doing amateur theater in Nyack, and that was what had first struck me—her voice. Actually, we'd first met much earlier than that, but I won't go into the circumstances now. Gradually, our marriage became an accommodation, but as

far as I could see all marriages were. Accommodations. She asks
you kindly not to force the trash down into the kitchen receptacle
because this makes it more difficult to dump into the garbage
cans, and you gently retort that she shouldn't start *new* bags of
trash out there on the floor of the house you built until the
receptacle is *filled*. That sort of thing. Helga and I engaged in
such trivial conversations for the first few years, but later didn't
bother. In other words, we each adjusted to the annoying things
the other one did, most of the time.

Actually, we ceased to care that much. Accommodation in
marriage is oiled by disinterest.

She did what she wanted and kept her own hours, though with
courtesy—she usually phoned or left notes. When I saw married
couples at parties whispering intimately to each other, or on the
lawn of their homes raking up leaves together, I realized that
other people's marriages are the real mystery in life. After all, I'd
only been married once, Helga twice. And I'd waited till forty
because I was a loner, as I said. One of the positive aspects of it
was that in marrying Helga I married into something I'd stopped
having long ago, a family. I don't just mean David. Our feelings
for each other, Helga's and mine, were actually somewhat frater-
nal, in addition to being conjugal, and at times it seemed that she
would slip right through my defenses as only a brother or sister
could. We shall see what this led to. Furthermore, it gave me a
kind of passive vicarious satisfaction when Helga went to see her
cousin Woody in the city, or her father in Orlando, as though
these family visits discharged a duty for both of us. It made those
nights and days I relaxed at home alone more companionable.

Helga had been buying tenements in Manhattan and Brooklyn.
Her cousin Woody on the Upper West Side acted as her partner.
Not only was she a broker, she was now becoming a landlord,
although her cousin generally managed the property, or hired
management firms. Thus, Helga did not receive phone calls at
four A.M. complaining about leaking pipes.

So I asked her if she'd bought any slums lately. It wasn't

malicious, just a little joke to take her mind off whatever it was stuck on, the negative side of the balance sheet. But her smile disappeared, and she reached forward to turn on the radio. Someone was playing an old Captain and Tenille.

I turned it off. That was something I could do. "I don't buy slums," Helga said, forgoing the radio. She even smiled a little, once more. She went on to describe how Woody had just spent over five thousand dollars on storm windows for a building they'd bought, and almost ten for a new boiler.

"So raise the rent," I said.

"This is not possible. Rent control."

"You get tax credits, though, right?"

"Yes. Why must you be contentious?"

"Helga, this is just a conversation we're having. I'm interested in your work. You've sat down and figured out, I assume, how long it will take your improvements in this building to pay for themselves?"

"Eight years."

"How many apartments?"

"Six."

"Total rent?"

Helga turned to me, still smiling. "Coop, you exasperate a person. You are not the only one in this marriage with a business sense. Furthermore, we are allowed to pay tenants to move."

"You pay them to move?"

Helga nodded. Now her smile had broadened. I could tell that she thought she didn't want to talk about this, while secretly enjoying it. Aside from David, this was her life: buying and selling, building up equity. You bought new buildings using old ones for down payment, and as the pyramid grew so did the excitement.

Aside from David—and me, of course. But in fact I was just a small part of it. I tried not to resent this, and when she was absent I usually didn't, but sometimes it was bothersome to feel extraneous in the very presence that makes you so. I had an urge to be driving. "How come you pay them to move?"

"So we may raise the rents on those who then move in. There

are other options. The tenants may buy us out and go co-op. Or we may convert to condos."

"Or you could just collect the rent and take a loss. Sometimes it pays to take a loss." I unbuckled my seat belt.

"Sometimes."

"Helga, I'd like to drive for a while." I was sliding over in her direction, and reached for the wheel.

"Coop!"

"It's very simple, you just sort of slip under me." My hands were on the wheel, my legs already hooked over hers. We were on 287 approaching the Tappan Zee Bridge. "David taught me how. He never taught you?"

"This is dangerous, Coop!"

I pressed my right foot down on top of hers, the one on the accelerator. She gave a little squeal as the car shot forward. Up to now the traffic hadn't been too heavy, but approaching the bridge it was starting to thicken. "It's only dangerous if you stay here, Helga. We can't both drive." But her hands still gripped the steering wheel. Two children sitting cross-legged in the back of a station wagon passing us waved. It was Saturday morning. In the rearview mirror I noticed a white Oldsmobile only inches behind us. "Helga, just let me get in here."

"Do you want to kill us both?"

As I mentioned, we'd met doing amateur theater in Nyack, almost fifteen years ago. At the time she was still living with her first husband. This was before I started Hudson Valley Consultants, when I worked for the state DOT. It occurred to me at the time that nobody teaches anyone how to love in this country. I'd had several girlfriends each year, before Helga; they all left me, by mutual consent. Helga was different, she stuck it out. In return, I assisted her in raising a child whose problems no one could lay at my door.

That was Helga all over: staying power. That was how she won everything: she didn't fight, she didn't budge. There was something in her, a core you couldn't touch. I took my foot off hers. We were almost at the toll booth, and the traffic had begun to slow down. "So drive," I said. I unhooked my legs and slid back over. "You're a good driver." Just before the toll booth I clipped on the seat belt again; in New York State it's the law to wear seat belts.

She drove the rest of the way in silence. When I pulled out her bags at the drop-off at La Guardia, she even pecked me on the cheek to say good-bye; but she averted her eyes. She had two bags, one in each arm, and shook her head at a porter standing there. "I'll call you," she said, and walked off very tall. I felt myself slinking back to the car and slithering into the driver's seat, with absolutely no stomach for driving all the way home to Highland.

I decided to look up her cousin Woody, and parked at the airport to find a phone; no answer. I bought a *Times* at a newsstand, and sat in a lounge going through the housing ads. Rents, I was shocked to learn, were astronomical, even in Brooklyn. Seven, eight, nine hundred dollars a month. Buildings started at two hundred thousand, and these were all in the Bronx, stripped of plumbing no doubt.

Helga was into some very high rolling, but there was something about it she wasn't telling me. For one thing, she had to be worth a lot more than I'd ever suspected. It would be interesting, I thought, to look up last year's tax forms. We always filed jointly, but Helga took care of it, with the help of my accountant. I did the house payments, she bought the cars. I paid for insurance policies, medical bills, repairs, and stolen speakers, while Helga took care of groceries and household items. Separate bank accounts.

I found a bar and drank until noon, feeding my thirsty blood sugar. I like airport bars: no regulars. Airports are like life on earth: your ground time is short, you soon become separated from loved ones and belongings, and when it's over you rise into the sky. But most of all you feel yourself a stranger, a shared condition imposed by the circumstances. You feel at home.

I drove back to Highland at fifty miles an hour. On the road I noticed something funny; a white Oldsmobile followed me nearly all the way back, even off the thruway. It made me uneasy; I'd seen it before. But when I stopped to gas up in Highland it was gone.

At home, this dot-matrix letter from the Social Security Administration was waiting for me:

> Social Security Administration
> Dept. of Health and Human Services
> 6401 Security Blvd.
> Room 4100 Annex Building
> Baltimore, Md. 21235
>
> April 23, 1985
>
> Mr. Charles Cooper
> Box 17A, Ingraham Hill Road
> Highland, New York 12528
>
> Dear Mr. Cooper,
>
> In processing your request for a new Social Security card, we have discovered that your number was inadvertently assigned to someone else.
>
> We would appreciate it if you would make an appointment with your local Social Security office in Kingston in order to file an application for a new number.
>
> Enclosed, find a printout of your record of employment and benefits accrued, according to our files. In your application you must request that these benefits be assigned to your new number. Be sure to bring this letter with you.
>
> If I can be of any further assistance in this matter, please do not hesitate to call. We apologize for the inconvenience.
>
> Sincerely,
>
> Richard Foster
> Benefits Administrator

I found this to be all very proper and efficient—even if eight months late—with the exception of my employment record, which unfortunately showed me working as a clerk at Pearl Paint on Canal Street in Manhattan, then in a flag shop on Broadway, for an advertising agency on West Seventeenth, as a librarian for the city, and finally, for the last ten years, for the city welfare agency. But this was typical: in the age of computers, the past became hot-wired. This one was going to be fun to straighten out; or I could just forget it, and retire on Helga's wealth.

At first it was funny, but then I grew angry, and kicked a few chairs around. David was out; the house was mine alone. Basically, this was all a pain in the neck. Also, it was fishy. I *liked* my old number, it was part of my selfhood; why did they want to take it away?

I pulled out the card I'd found in Windsor and walked through the house with it on my palms, as though on a pillow. Charles Lyndhurst? 030 30 2973? Your card, sir. I was shouting out his name and number like a bellhop when the phone rang.

"Charlie?"

"Who's this?"

"This is Carol, Charlie. I'm calling from Windsor. Please come and collect your son."

"You're calling from where?"

"From Windsor. From our house. Valerie and I moved in last week, and for the last day or so your son David has been hanging around, the one that we are talking about here. Excuse me, your stepson. I am one-hundred-percent certain that he and my daughter are sleeping together, and I would appreciate it very much if you would come up here and take him home. Tonight. Before it's too late, Charlie."

"Bernice, what gives you the right—" But she'd hung up already.

4

I climbed back into the car and began the three-hour drive to Windsor, thinking dark thoughts. It was six P.M., near dusk; the world would be dark when I got there.

Could it be that everyone more or less indulged me because they thought I wouldn't be around much longer? They knew my heart was bad; they saw me taking my own pulse. What a trick I could play them by staying alive!

I felt puzzled and afraid about Bernice; all I could think of was her in that house with her daughter. And David too! The last few summers he hadn't even bothered to stay with us in Windsor. Thinking of them, I imagined myself growing angry and throwing everyone out; then I slammed my fist on the steering wheel, having become the creature I'd imagined.

At the same time, I wanted to convince Bernice and her daughter of my underlying goodness. David also. For one thing, I knew I was good because I often became depressed. If I wasn't good then I wouldn't care, and these depressions I felt would go away. Sometimes I wondered if that's how Helga lived; she acted without attaching herself to the outcome. It was Buddhist. I felt that if I tried that approach the world would just as soon pass me by, leaving me drunk or dead or unhappy in a doorway, so exhausted by it all that whatever desperate efforts to scream or shout I made would be smothered by a kind of inner muzzle.

There were times I had to assure myself I was an actual person; with my fingers and thumb I felt my face.

In my opinion, humans are the lowest animals. What other

species tortures its own kind? Someone in a mental home had both ears completely bitten off. A family wouldn't let the doctors amputate their mother's gangrenous leg; they wanted God to take her naturally. These are things I read about in the *Daily News*. In America, pain has a sentimental face; last week, the *News* ran a picture of a child's sneaker on a country road. The child had just been killed by a truck.

Often I calculated how long I had to live. At fifty-five, I could count on twenty more years, as long as I didn't swerve into oncoming traffic while driving to Windsor at dusk. But then when I got to be seventy-five, I'm sure I'd be counting on at least five more years. Five years is a long time. Suppose it wasn't five, suppose it was three? From a certain point of view that's a long time also. Hell, a *year* is a long time. A *month* could be eternity. A week, a day. You appreciate each day. Therefore, I'm convinced that as you grow older you are no closer to death, and no farther away, than you've been all your life.

Of course, you're no longer young, you've lost that. Everyone loses it unless a truck knocks your sneaker off and you stay eight years old the rest of your life. What if I'd been hit by a truck at the age of eight? Then I wouldn't be driving to Windsor to kick my cousin out of a house I'd lived in when I was eight. I wouldn't have these problems because I'd be innocent, forever.

By now the car was plunging through a tunnel of light created by its own headlights. I was somewhere west of Monticello, and slowed down, remembering deer. One summer on the way to Windsor a deer broke its neck running into the side of our car.

If I'd died at the age of eight—or two, or five, for that matter —it would have fossilized my childhood. But it felt that way regardless. East Seventy-eighth Street had intervened ages ago and effectively pressed down upon that earlier time in Windsor, turning all the first deposits of memory to fossils. I had the gift of remembering my birth, which happened at home. I could remember the first bright lights, the sheets, the hovering adults, the low crib beside the bed, from which I looked up at the room.

I remembered sucking like a greedy little pig. But after that everything faded or scrambled, and then I was in Windsor, delivered by my mother in her wheelchair—and some other adults— into the hands of George and Louise Lockwood, my guardians or foster parents, I'm still not sure which. They took care of me while mother was in the hospital, but once I moved to East Seventy-eighth Street I never saw them again. Thinking back on it, what seemed striking about George and Louise was that they didn't have any children of their own, even though they were older, say fifty or sixty. They had dogs, and cows. I lived there in isolation from other children and in proximity to animals. We had neighbors up the road about a mile—the Pattersons—but these we seldom saw. About the only time we gathered with other people was Sundays at church.

So I kept to myself; what choice did I have? Bringing me up, George and Louise insisted I be good, but good had more to do with being in the right place than doing the right thing. Cows were good when they headed straight for their stalls going into the barn, and boys were good when they didn't get in the way. It was only later, on East Seventy-eighth Street, that I learned (with pleasure) to be bad, because there I had a co-conspirator, Bernice. In Windsor I could be good just by standing in one spot. I learned how to be alone, and I've had that core in me ever since. There was a way of finding yourself in an object in front of your face—a leaf or the hinge of a door—which I discovered how to cultivate. It required staring at something until you dissolved into it. Louise called these incidents my spells, and took to seizing me by the shoulders and giving me two or three good shakes when she caught me at them. This she did with routine determination, the way you'd punch a washing machine to get it going again.

Driving to Windsor, I saw George and Louise, I saw the house and barn, the barn's inside, the long silent line of the back ends of cows. They were faces with high bony cheeks. I saw things up close, where a child can't miss them. They tattoo your memory. I saw Louise's white and milky face, a face that seemed in retrospect incapable of guile. She was pear-shaped, she did everything out loud—wondered or worried about annoying details, trivial irritations—until George shut her up with a crude, sharp insult. He was thin, a wheezing reed of humanity whose strict moral sense didn't necessarily exclude a bottle or curse (Louise's did), but always in the barn.

In the skin of George's throat his Adam's apple declared its independent existence by fluttering and bobbing, even when he didn't speak. He winked at me in the barn after delivering an especially cutting remark about Louise, who was back in the house. What exactly was it? It was something I'd always remembered but never really thought about; or maybe I simply hadn't remembered it before. Some things we don't remember so much as remember that we later remembered them, probably in a less innocent time. In my car at the age of fifty-five I remembered lying on my bed at East Seventy-eighth Street at the age of sixteen, struggling with lust, or shame, or resentment, while remembering George busy at his milking when I was eight. I remembered remembering that he squeezed between two cows, pushing one aside, swinging a strap across the other's back, and hanging the milker on the strap.

Now I remember: *Push over Louise.* That's what he said. Louise was not the cow's name. He glanced at me and winked.

In a corner of the kitchen, an old iron safe blocked the cellar door. A towel hung on a nail in the door jamb for us to wipe our hands on after a meal. We were clean that way. I was taught to be sanitary. If I wet the bed, Louise made me walk around with the wet sheets over my head. Did my mother know this, when she came to visit? *He wet the bed again.* Lying on my bed on East Seventy-eighth Street, I could still smell those sheets, I smelled them so much I buried my head in the pillow. In my jar I remember remembering remembering.

Didn't Louise make me wash the sheets too? Defect of memory. The cold, wet sheets all balled up in a washtub? This could have been later, at boarding school, I don't know.

Memory eats its way out of your brain like cows in a barn filled with hay. One winter a little girl visited, and stayed a few weeks. Together we explored the barn, entering it through a door on the lee side, where the snow wasn't deep. First it was dark, then out of darkness crept the old barn objects: harnesses, pitchforks, jugs and bottles, an old couch, wagons, sleds, a tractor, a truck. Toward the barn's center was a solid wall of hay bales. We entered a tunnel, crawled through bales of hay, climbed another tunnel, this one vertical, up a makeshift ladder of wood slats nailed across structural members of the barn. On top, we crossed a floor of bales to the back of the barn where the cows came into view below us, steaming and chewing. Working their mouths from side to side, they chewed slowly, patiently, like prisoners digging a tunnel. By spring they'd be out.

Later, in the house, we found a flashlight, this little girl and myself, and inside the closet next to George and Louise's bed (they were downstairs) shined it on our nether parts. We took off our pants and checked it all out. But Louise caught us and spanked our bottoms for being in her closet.

All at once, driving to Windsor, I realized with a shock of triumphal shame that this little girl who visited us must have been my cousin, Bernice. The layers fell from her face and I saw it shining there in the flashlight's beam. Bernice, it was her! It had to be. Even on East Seventy-eighth Street, I hadn't realized this; she probably hadn't either, as we were different creatures by then. I felt like I'd found an old key in some rubble. If that was Bernice in that closet, it almost explained what happened eight or so years later at the age of sixteen on East Seventy-eighth Street.

I thought of bringing this up with her when I got to Windsor. Then I remembered what she was doing right now: moving into my first home, trying to squeeze me out. What gave her the right? It was there I grew up!

Of course, Bernice was my cousin, but I wasn't sure on whose side. Until I moved to East Seventy-eighth Street I saw few relations. In Windsor, my mother came once a year, maybe less.

Except for a man named Johnny who drove up from New York every fall to hunt for a week, she was our only visitor. And the girl in the closet that time—Bernice, or whoever. She may have accompanied my mother on one of her visits, I can't remember. And neighbors who dropped by, but not too many. It occurs to me that they were discouraged. My mother did own the house, that was clear. George and Louise were more or less tenant farmers. Or, she bought the house from them later, after paying them so much to bring me up. This, I would point out to Bernice. The house was mine for every conceivable reason, from the legal to the sentimental. I saw calves born there, I saw chickens and deer killed and gutted. I worked hard there, I found myself in work; it gave me something to push against. Farm work of course is something to be despised. Farmers hate it. It's the same every day, every year, for endless cycles of years, and no vacations. But I longed to help with the haying or the milking, all the more so because for a time George was reluctant to allow me. Perhaps he had instructions from my mother. I'm sure he did. Didn't he complain about this? Also, I should mention, I didn't go to school. Louise taught me at home, and once a year an official from the state administered a test.

Why this was I don't care to speculate. The school was too far away, most likely. The fixity of memory you shouldn't poke at too much, though it's tempting. For example, who was Johnny? He came up every fall to hunt, but also, if I remember correctly, stayed one entire summer, and parked his black Packard in the barn. It was Johnny who made use of the iron safe in the corner of the kitchen. George never opened it, just pushed it aside to get into the cellar. But Johnny took papers out and put papers in, and a phone was installed that summer with which he often called the city. I think it was the city. Also, when a car pulled into the driveway, he generally disappeared into the barn.

He wore city clothes: worsted pants with cuffs, good shoes, white shirts.

He was probably a friend of the family, or maybe George's

brother. Then again he might have had something to do with my mother. Driving to Windsor, I tried to picture Johnny—who was dark and short, with a black pompadour—in relation to the picture of my father on my mother's dresser on East Seventy-eighth Street, described by mother as the portrait of a drunkard. He'd died shortly after my birth.

But nothing clicked. In Windsor, Johnny was simply part of the yearly cycle. It's only later that one might have cause to wonder about such things, but by then it's too late. You let in little gusts of possibility and too many anchors pull out, in your mind. A wind billows up, your tent fills with air, and all the stakes you'd carefully placed pull loose one by one until there it goes, whatever prudent shelter you'd made of the past. It feels like the top of your head flying off.

Also, it's bad for your heart, which has a tendency to gear up when your memory reveals too variable a content. But driving to Windsor, I couldn't stop probing and poking. I hadn't thought of that time in so long, and this unexpected stream of memory now was overly rich, like breathing pure oxygen. It gagged me, filled my brain, but I couldn't stop.

In the barn, Johnny let a calf suck his thumb. This calf looked up with goofy, helpless gratitude, or half gratitude, half puzzlement, while Johnny glanced over at me, laughing. Later I tried it myself.

He butchered a dead cow. Or was it a deer? To remember correctly, I followed a kind of inner pipeline back to East Seventy-eighth Street and me lying on my bed in lust remembering Windsor. By means of this device I had the impression of restoring my original memory to an accuracy it had never actually possessed. I found that I could bring it into focus. In fact, I could govern its clarity. *Help me get that cow that died.*

"What cow?"

"The one that calved." George was on his tractor.

I must have been ten or eleven years old, and all I remember thinking was: He wants me to *help* him. As it happened, this was the commencement of a summer in which I was finally allowed to work. Work filled my limbs, which at that age felt like parts of inflatable furniture, expanding and popping out to some prearranged yet indistinct shape.

We dragged the dead cow up from the pasture by means of a chain wrapped around its swollen midsection. Outside the barn, Johnny stood wearing a long gray raincoat and galoshes; he was actually juggling his knives, I think. In this version he juggles his knives like a circus clown. Then he lifts his arm, pauses, and with a kind of skewer or awl in his fist swings down in a vicious arc and punctures the cow's swollen belly, after which he lights a match and holds it to the hole, where a blue flame pops up and burns. It went out on the cow in seconds, but stays in my brain, blue and detached.

A sheet of blood unfurled when Johnny cut from her chin to the udders in one smooth motion. He'd done this before with deer, though I'd never seen it. In his raincoat, although it wasn't raining, he opened the slit and reached inside. Butchers need raincoats to keep off the smell. George helped him pull out the slippery coils of the cow's intestines, but once they started pulling the stuff came boiling and foaming out on its own and wouldn't stop. Memories of this colored, or were colored by, my worst dreams later on, dreams of blood and knives and bowels that refused to stay put. The nature of things was a precarious holding back; anything could split, entrails could erupt and cover the earth with their slippery worms, and it hardly mattered whether they did or not once you'd glimpsed the loathsome possibility. It was monstrous and wonderful to have this peek at the forbidden insides of things. What a secret. What a dirty secret! No wonder it felt so tender beneath your navel. Standing there, a space swelled open inside me, a soft labyrinth, something I knew wasn't me, though it was.

Next came the cow's four stomachs, each of which Johnny slit for my benefit to show how green pulp turns brown. He reached around for more stuff in there, up to his elbows grinning back at us, while our dogs and others from up the road gathered around the piles of offal to sniff and snap at it, wasting no time.

Later I ate meat from that cow with guilty greed, in silence. It was sweet. At the supper table, Johnny talked city talk, wise cracks about nothing. About entrails. He possessed a wise-guy wizardly quality, the man who'd just revealed the mysteries of nature, mysteries you either already knew and didn't much care about, or didn't know and didn't want to know. The line between the two was knowledge, and the thing about knowledge was you couldn't go back to not having it again.

Swooping down on the exit ramp across the Susquehanna River onto Route 79, then turning left in the direction of Trim Street, I felt exhausted, shaken by all this remembering, by the vision of entrails erupting from memory. And I didn't like the way things felt different or uncertain now, as though the facts of memory had lost their chastity.

It was only nine o'clock. On Trim Street I drove past the first group of houses, then pulled off the road just beyond the VFW in order to lie on the seat and catch a little sleep before confronting Bernice. By the time I awoke and started back up the hill, it was after eleven, but I felt a lot better; I felt young again! Or at least wide awake. I drove up Trim Street to Ballyhock Road, and down Ballyhock to my first home.

5

I stumbled on the concrete step at the back porch, as Bernice hadn't bothered to leave the outside light on. Unconsciously I'd pulled out my keys approaching the door, but once there I wasn't sure if I should use them. The screen door to the porch was unhooked, but the kitchen lights were off. Through the kitchen door I could see light in the living room; standing on the porch, I listened to the house. I raised one fist to knock, but held it cocked while inserting my key, the sound of which roused Bernice.

"Charlie, it's open!"

She walked from the living room half bent over, peering out at the kitchen door with a *Vogue* in her hand. "It's about time, Charlie." She flicked on the kitchen lights as I stepped inside.

"Bernice, what is this?"

The kitchen had the look of being lived in: dishes in the sink, crumbs on the table, avocados on the counter, as well as potatoes, a knife and cutting board, wedges of lime. Beneath a tray of half-melted ice cubes was a puddle of water. A pan on the stove held greenish liquid.

I could see well enough into the living room to know that the sheets had all been removed from the furniture. The rugs were on the floor. "Bernice."

"Call me Carol." She was grinning like a happy home-owner, beaming pride as I looked all around us. "What can I fix you?" In a cabinet she opened was gin, bourbon, Scotch, vodka.

"Bernice, this is bizarre. What gives you the right—"

"Shhhh," she whispered, pointing at the ceiling and winking. "I think they're sleeping."

"I thought you wanted me to take him home."

"I do. But they might as well just sleep right now, Charlie, it's late. I think they're exhausted." More winks.

She was wearing some sort of high-necked old velvet dress and an oversized gunmetal blazer with big collars. It was strange. She looked slim, even sexy, but wide and short, like some football players. I noticed a large scab on her chin. Bernice was a year or two older than me, but she hadn't aged well, unlike Helga for example. She walked fast but unsteadily, bumping into things, and reached for the gin in the cabinet she'd stocked. "Bourbon," I said. She opened a bottle of Ten High, poured some into a glass with ice, and was about to add water at the sink when I took it from her hand.

"You know how it is, Charlie, they're just kids. Let's allow them that. I noticed it doesn't matter if you're teenagers, pigs, dogs or maybe even snails for all I know. Even pigs feel like gods when they fuck." She was tiptoeing into the living room, talking over her shoulder, and when I followed I found myself tiptoeing also. To the right were the stairs going up. Everywhere else in the living room, tucked in among the familiar furniture, the couch, chairs, lamps, chests, tables and so forth, were things I didn't recognize, objects on tables or inside inverted bell jars, or on glass shelves in glass cases: precious stones, shells, jewels, carvings, jade, little ivory crickets, expensive knickknacks. Most of my pictures were gone from the walls and others put in their place: Degas prints, etchings of furniture on eggshell paper. The lighting here was subdued; I noticed Bernice had thrown scarves across all the lamps. The shades were drawn, the house quiet.

On the wall beneath the stairway were taped some drawings in a style I recognized. One was of the barn behind the house—my barn—and another of the Baptist church up the road. "What's this?" I asked. "They have realness. Hardness."

Bernice clapped her hands. "Charlie, that's just what *she* says!"

"I don't know if I should call realness *hard.*"

"She's good, don't you think? My daughter. Remember, Charlie, you used to draw."

I sat on the edge of a chair near the fireplace, and Bernice sank into the couch with her legs tucked under her, completely at home. We faced each other in silence, though Bernice still smiled and wouldn't stop staring at me.

"Who's your interior decorator?" I asked, but *sotto voce*, looking away.

With a sinking heart I wondered what the hell I'd gotten into, or how I could extricate these people from my house. They'd managed in a very short time to root into the place, to render it cozy; and as much as I feared and resented it, another side of me saw it as funny—or at least crazy—so I even felt myself relaxing. The bourbon helped. I looked around the living room. Hermit crabs, they say, will suffer themselves to be torn apart rather than relinquish the shells they've chosen for a home. David had brought home a pet hermit crab at the age of ten, but unfortunately I'd stepped on it one day. The memory made me writhe on the edge of my chair, then I found myself laughing. I was jiggling some coins in my pocket.

"I'm glad you find it funny," she said.

"So tell me Bernice, Carol, you have papers to show you belong here?"

"My papers are just as good as yours."

"A deed? Title? Mortgage? Codicil?"

"I had keys, Charlie. That should tell you something."

"Where the hell did you get keys? You have nerve, is what you have. I've been fixing this place up for thirty years, you think you can just come in and take it over? This is where I grew up, Bernice. What the hell is this? Where'd you get this crap?" I was feeling cozy, so it gave me a certain satisfaction to shout and stand up and handle some of those foreign objects she'd scattered through the living room. The one in my hand was a delicate

Limoges vase from the mantelpiece, the kind that holds one
flower; I was waving it around.

"Charlie, you break that and I'll cut off your manhood with a
fingernail clipper."

"Ha ha, that's a good one, Bernice."

"I should know." She was grinning, but her face had darkened.
It occurred to me that someone had once thrown acid in it. All
at once I recognized this vase and everything else, the knickknacks, the jewels. They were things from Bernice's bedroom on
East Seventy-eighth Street—not only the largest bedroom in the
apartment, but one she'd redesigned herself to accommodate her
collection of junk. Along two walls a cabinetmaker had built
ceiling-high glass cases to house her countless artifacts, her curi-
osities, parchments, birds' nests, precious stones, shells of all colors, geodes, crystals, mounted fossils, petrified wood, carnival
glass, dolls, dried flowers and every other imaginable portable,
precious, fragile or bathetic thing. The cases were there to protect
such delicate objects from her clumsy hands, which sooner or later
would have broken them all.

I looked down at Bernice with the vase in my hand and tried
to imagine what it felt like to have breasts. I remembered a long
time ago when I first entered her room on East Seventy-eighth
Street and stood there in awe, fingering the lump on the back of
my neck. Fingering this lump was a nervous habit.

"Charlie, put that down and get me another drink, will you?
Gin and tonic." She held out the empty glass in such a way that
you couldn't refuse. Carefully, I replaced the vase on the mantel,
and picked up a crystal dish instead. With Bernice's glass in one
hand and the dish in the other I walked into the kitchen.

"Tonic's in the fridge," she sang from the living room. I put
her glass in the sink and carried the crystal dish back to the living
room. At the fireplace, I placed it gently on the hearth tiles then
stepped on it hard. It cracked apart.

"Charlie!"

I went back to the kitchen and mixed Bernice a gin and tonic, very strong—half gin. "Here's your drink," I told her in the living room. I noticed my own glass empty on the mantel.

"Charlie, you bastard."

What I wanted was to smoke, but I'd left my pipe and tobacco in Highland. I walked back to the kitchen, opened the cellar door—where George had once kept his safe—and flicked on the light. I walked down the unsteady steps. Down here was another world, very damp, and small creatures and insects scurried around in the corners as I descended. All the walls were laid-up stone, but they bulged out in perfect curves from the pressure of earth and water behind them. Water trickled through stones here and there to the floor. I felt cobwebs on my face; it was cold in the cellar. On the wet dirt floor, with a ditch running through it to guide all the water to a drain in one corner, wide plank boards had been laid for walking. I looked around, at the furnace, the water tank, pump, tangles of wires, old radios, boots, a TV set, some old broken chairs. Ceiling tiles in a muddy corner soaking up dampness like sponges. "Charlie, what the hell are you doing down there?" I heard Bernice stand up overhead.

The smell of sewer gas in the cellar was faint that night, but perceptible. This was a complicated problem we still hadn't solved caused by the septic field leaching back into the cellar along some old clay tiles lined with stones from a dry well. In rainstorms it was worse, and the smell rose into the house. How would Bernice like that? I prayed for rain.

Once a backhoe had located that dry well, which had formerly been the main septic tank. Hidden just beneath the grass on the side of a slope behind the house, it burst like a blister or pimple when the bucket sank in and released a foul-smelling viscous black liquid which ran down the green lawn beneath the wire fence to the pasture below, leaving a trail of ancient grease. This was shit, piss, soap and garbage most likely from the time of my childhood with George and Louise—some of it my own—erupting like a little nightmarish volcano. It was stuff you weren't supposed to see, coils from the earth—otherwise, why bury it?

I ran back upstairs, through the kitchen, out the door, to get the flashlight in my car. On the way back through the kitchen I took a big slug of bourbon from the bottle, knowing instinctively it would be my last that evening. Bernice stood at the living room door, but I ignored her. "What's the flashlight for?" In the cellar the first thing I went for was the furnace. It wasn't enough just to pull the switch on the fuse box; I took out the fuse and yanked a few wires loose as well. "Charlie, what the hell's going on?" I took out the filter and threw it across the cellar. Ice clinked in Bernice's glass as she descended the stairs. Party in the cellar.

I went for the pump box, turned it off, removed the fuse, pulled on some wires. I turned on the faucet to drain the pressure tank; water poured out with a powerful rush, digging a hole in the dirt beneath it. "Charlie!" With a pipe wrench I kept on a cinder block beside the pressure tank, I began removing plugs to drain the various cold water pipes running through the cellar, then remembered the electric hot water heater. Without water, the element might burn itself out, maybe melt. Or would it shut off automatically? I went for the heater to turn it off, but by then Bernice had roused herself and lunged for it too, so that in reaching for the switch I found my hands on her hips instead. I had to push her aside; she stumbled and fell. One arm landed in mud from the pressure tank. "You bastard!" she shouted.

I was very calm. I felt in control. "Bernice, you don't understand. If I don't turn this off we could have a fire." I pulled the switch, took out the fuse, and threw it all the way across the cellar, where it smashed against the laid-up stone.

Something wet and abrasive landed on my neck; Bernice had thrown a handful of mud. "Turn that back on," she said. Standing up with a grunt or snort—and lowering her head like a bull—she wiped her muddy arm on her dress.

I clawed at the mud on my neck, scraping it off, and started for the main fuse box, switching on the flashlight. The only problem, I was breathing heavily, and could feel my heart in my ears and my head. The fuzz in my head felt enormous, and my head felt soft and heavy, like a cephalopod's.

Bernice got there first, with the pipe wrench in her hand. But it wasn't the pipe wrench that stopped me as much as her face: wild, muddy, contorted, with swollen lumps of anger showing in red and white patches, or maybe the flashlight made it look that way. She grinned like an ape, showing teeth, and, bending over, pipe wrench in the air, actually began scratching herself with her free hand. Her dress was torn at the shoulder.

I looked around the cellar, confused.

"Charlie, what I want you to do is please don't do anything funny, just leave on the lights, you could leave on some lights and tomorrow I'll get somebody to fix all this. You're making a lot of noise, Charlie, you might wake the kids, I might have to call the cops, I don't know. I might just go out of my head myself."

"Fine. Go right ahead, Bernice."

"Carol, my name is Carol, Carol. Don't call me Bernice anymore, it is Carol, Carol, Carol, Carol."

"Okay, Bernice."

"You bastard!" She lowered the pipe wrench. "You make me sick, you bastard. With all the people everywhere who don't even have a pot to piss in and you own two houses and you do this to me? The problem with you is, people like you, you don't even know how to suffer." She dropped the pipe wrench. I felt behind me and sat on the cellar steps. I don't know how, but she'd managed to put her finger right on it—I was not a person who suffered. This was actually an uncanny observation. Every time I began to suffer, some fleecy substance like hair or lint grew up to protect me, raised its fuzz across the walls of my body like the thickets in *Sleeping Beauty*, and I fell asleep inside.

"You could say that," I said. "About suffering."

"Oh Charlie, Charlie. How pampered can you get? I bet all your life someone picked up after you." She was walking toward me, half bent over, and the husk or burr in her voice had split open, so it sounded like a growl. "You *can't* make me move from this house, get busy right now and make up your mind about that completely once and for all, you can't. Call me by my name, Carol."

"Listen, Carol . . ."

"Oh yes listen I'll listen. You can clean this up later. I won't be hysterical, it's wasted effort, I'll listen, sure. Stand up, Charlie. I'm itching all over for one thing, my eczema, I'm just about ready to tear off my clothes. *I'm* not cleaning this up. You can fix it tomorrow, let's go upstairs. Charlie, I think I wet myself."

"What?"

She was grinning triumphantly. "See?" On the front of her dress was a big wet stain.

"God, Bernice."

"It's a problem I have."

I felt like crying, I felt nervous, like throwing things down to smash them. At the same time a kind of helpless exhaustion had taken over, weakening every muscle. But Carol was laughing. Not uncontrollably, not laughter on the verge of sobbing, not like she'd break down into little scraps of helpless person in my arms. It was confident laughter. Laughter in control. Not derisive either, more like indulgent. She was laughing at me, at my confusion, and now that she was standing in front of me she looked tall in that cellar.

"Charlie, get up." She took me by the arm and led me upstairs. I could smell the urine on her clothes.

Entering the kitchen, I heard someone scrambling up the stairs from the living room to the second floor. I noticed the vodka was out on the counter. The toilet flushed in the back wing—last flush of the night, since the water was off—and Valerie came tiptoeing through the sitting room and across the kitchen, smiling demurely. "Hi, Mr. Cooper." She waved her fist at me up and down, with one pinky finger extended. All she wore was a bright red T-shirt down to her knees, with the word JESUS written in a yellow slash across her breasts. In the living room she bounced up the steps to the second floor.

"Bernice, you have some bread around here? Just plain bread."

"You want anything on it, Charlie? Your son likes cream cheese." She opened a cupboard and pulled down some wheat bread.

"Just plain bread." I stuffed four or five pieces in my mouth, turning my back to Bernice out of modesty, so she wouldn't see what a pig I was. And it helped, the lumps of bread in my stomach; I began to feel better, and breathed out all at once, realizing I'd held my breath while eating.

"Charlie, fix me a drink."

I made Bernice another gin and tonic and we both walked back to the living room. Looking around at her collection of things, I remembered again her room on East Seventy-eighth Street. Upstairs we could hear activity now. I heard David's voice. Shouts, giggles, springs in a bed. Someone ran in a circle up there. Then the sounds became more rhythmic; a part of the bed began knocking the wall. It felt embarrassing, but it also felt, what? Cozy. "Charlie, I could use a back rub. Rub my back." Bernice was stretched out on the couch, on her belly. "It's a car crash," she said.

"What's a car crash?"

"I'm still trying to collect on what happened. My knee, which won't bend all the way. My weak kidneys. Sometimes a sore neck, I noticed I was feeling dizzy a lot, and this lower back, there, that's good, just a little lower please. Shit, I feel dizzy. Hit it please, Charlie. The way they massage."

I struck her back with the sides of my hands to the rhythm of the knocking bed upstairs while everything spun around us in a whirlpool of alcohol, or memory, or both. Here I was being kicked out of this house for the second time—it was just as incomprehensible as the first—and I was rubbing the back of the person doing it. The first time I had no choice, I had to go and live with my mother, who was better then, due to the miracle of pills. But my first painful year on East Seventy-eighth Street wasn't made any easier by the girl whose adult back I was rubbing now. The very same person! But forty years later. She taunted me then, she bossed me around, she paraded her superior carriage for all to see, but especially me. She must have been at the peak of her beauty at the age of fifteen or sixteen. This is when some girls look like foxes; even Valerie had that look a bit, shading more to rodent. Were foxes and rodents related? Bernice wore a big bush of hair flared out on top like a crown, in the style of the forties. It was so long ago, in another world, but the years seemed to go soft in my hands. They melted away. Her crazy grin now was sly and aristocratic then, or at least that's how I read it; my wealthy cousin with the milky skin, the beautiful snout, and the mane down her neck. Bernice with the sharp, sexy walk, whose power was scorn.

It drove me crazy. I think Cousin Raymond saw this too; looking back now, I could see that he enjoyed watching my torment, and he devised occasions for Bernice and me to be together—radio parties, outings to Central Park—in order to observe with amusement Bernice's disdain and the tortured ambivalence of a farm boy who couldn't stay away from her, but couldn't get close either without painful shyness and a thickening of the tongue.

I picked up some nervous habits. I remember I enjoyed fingering the lump on the back of my neck—the mole, or birthmark—though Bernice ridiculed me when she noticed. Also, I stole bread dough from the kitchen and played with it in my pocket, squeezing and rolling it between my fingers. I could make a little human figure in less than a minute, with one hand. And if Bernice did or said something cutting or sharp, which happened once or twice a day—that is, when she bothered to notice me—I snapped off its head.

After a year or two, though, I was better. I learned by imitation, and Bernice was my model. What to do, what to say, how to treat the servants. I learned that when asked or offered something you said no. To spurn an offer not only acknowledged its generosity as a fiction, it also reminded the one who made it of his or her position, thus guaranteeing future offers to spurn. In Windsor, if

Louise offered me doughnuts I took them gratefully. On East
Seventy-eighth Street, a different code prevailed; food was a luxury to be left out to rot, toys were pageantry, lavish and useless.
Now and then I wandered down to the playroom of my younger
cousins, who possessed every expensive toy imaginable, huge
stuffed animals and motorized ride-around cars, as well as skittles
sets, large dollhouses, and an elaborate train set with model vil-
lages and tunnels. My cousins all were much younger than me—
Charlotte was six—though Dana, the twelve-year-old, thought of
himself as my compatriot. He and Patrick followed me around,
imitated me, and in general offered themselves up as my protégés.
I did condescend to play with them now and then, though I knew
from the beginning that their room of expensive and conspicuous
toys was the visible embodiment of boredom.

Next to it was a schoolroom where a succession of tutors taught
my cousins. Only Bernice and I went to school outside, being
older.

Most of my free time I spent in our library, which was largely
for display too. No one else used it except my mother, who only
occasionally buzzed in on her wheelchair for a volume, then left.
I read all I could, especially the most dog-eared books, such as
boys' adventure stories and tales of chivalry and escape and battle,
even love, as well as books about planes and aviation in abun-
dance. I loved the dark paneling, the thick rugs, the parquet floor,
the smell of varnish and leather and something else—dust. In the
library I could brood for hours alone upon the books I read, and
upon my ambitions.

From books, I learned that there were two ways to win a girl's
love: by spurning her (like food) or by rescuing her. I ran through
fantasies of rescuing Bernice; she'd been kidnapped and I found
her in the basement of a tenement up the East River, untied her,
and rowed her back home. She fell through the ice skating in the
park, or broke her ankle or wrist on a horse, or was pushed or fell
off a subway platform dangerously close to the third rail, from
which I snatched her back.

Of course, Bernice had never been in a subway. We all had a chauffeur to take us places. But in my quest for knowledge, independence, love, or whatever it was—revenge, I'm sure—I'd ridden every subway line in the city and all the boroughs repeatedly, until an underground map of New York in full three-dimensional relief had taken possession of my mind and pitted and perforated it with endless, forking possibilities. I was drawn to the subway as to the bowels of that real world which Raymond had advised me to stay away from. I knew all the levels of the various lines, the elevated tracks, the tunnels underwater, ghost stations, ends of lines, closed and unused tunnels. I knew the only place the subway rose up and crossed a street at level grade, East 105th Street in Canarsie. A man in a little hut cranked down the crossing gates. I learned if I had to transfer on a ride to take the front or back car and be the first on the stairs. I discovered the Myrtle Avenue line in Brooklyn where the old cars dated back to the nineteenth century. Summers, crossing the Manhattan Bridge, I always stood outside between cars to cool off.

For a sixteen-year-old, the subway was knowledge in the form of power. I knew where to get off to play pinball, go to movies, buy a hot dog, browse a bookstore or stand just inside the door of a nightclub in the late afternoon (Fridays especially) to hear the musicians jamming or rehearsing. I dreamed the subway too: dark tunnels leading to multileveled caverns with trestles and tracks jutting out into space, or gripping precariously an overhead ledge.

Of course, my mother didn't know I'd ever been inside a subway station. I could do this because once I'd become routine in that apartment, supervision was minimal. Bernice and I had the freedom to come and go pretty much as we pleased until dark. If I didn't show up in my room after school, Mother assumed I was in the library, or out at some museum, or playing the Count of Monte Cristo with Bernice.

This was my first admission to her life, our game, the Count of Monte Cristo. We played it in the basement, on the roof, or evenings in the library, which was at turns my prison or her convent or the hold of a ship carrying us to freedom. Bernice especially enjoyed those parts in which I was tortured or starved, so I multiplied them to suit her (she hadn't read the book) and she invited a friend to play too. Our friends from school weren't allowed to visit us at home, with one exception, a young girl whose mother often came to see my mother. She paid her call and spent long hours talking with my mother in her bedroom, or playing cards in a corner of the living room, and her daughter always accompanied her.

This was the girl who, with Bernice, had tormented me when I'd first come to live on East Seventy-eighth Street. They pretended I was the piano mover, they ordered me around, plucked hairs from my chest. She was a year or two younger than me. I won't give her real name here, for reasons I'd prefer not to go into. I shall call her Karin.

Karin was a skinny intellectual girl with blue veins showing beneath each eye, and thin, whitish hair. She was bilingual, she spoke German as well as English, a fact I found tremendously impressive. Her mother possessed a thick German accent. They both looked like they'd never seen the sun, however, and Karin's skin had a kind of cheesecloth texture. Eventually, she developed a crush on me while playing our game, the Count of Monte Cristo. This wasn't the way it was supposed to happen. It was Bernice I'd designed the game for, Bernice whom I wanted to impress with my determined patient bravery in the face of imprisonment and pain. But Karin's crush could be useful, I decided, and I resolved to exploit it.

Behind Bernice's back we kissed. I touched her breasts, hardly larger than my own, and felt the frail cavity of her chest beneath the pressure of my nervous hands like something made of dead sticks.

Bernice had ballet one evening a week until eight—I think it was Tuesdays or Wednesdays—after which she came home and we met in the library and finished whatever episode of our game we'd begun that afternoon. She always arrived on the button, at eight twenty. One evening when Bernice had ballet, Karin phoned for her, and I took the call. Could she come over and play the Count of Monte Cristo? Of course she could. Bernice would be home any minute, come right away! She lived just down the block.

It was seven thirty when Karin arrived; we met in the library, where I confessed my subterfuge. Bernice wouldn't be here until nine, I said, but I'd lied to her so we could be alone. I spoke as myself and as the Count of Monte Cristo, dragging my wounded leg across the parquet floor to embrace her against the library table.

This episode flares up with embarrassing clarity now, decades later. I'd already developed sufficient hatred for the life I was leading, in which I saw myself as a victim, to have no qualms about victimizing another. We kissed and fumbled with each other's tense bodies. She trembled so much I thought she'd shatter. Just thinking of what I'd planned made me horny enough to burst, but I had to skewer my desire at the time. By eight-fifteen I'd convinced her to touch me, and her frail hand stroked my pants. But I told her it wouldn't work that way, I'd have to take it out, I even offered to pay her, not that she needed money—just to give her something to refuse—and though she averted her face, and stood as far away as she could, her hand was on it when Bernice walked in, and remained there when its owner, with a squeal, tripped, or fainted, or pretended to faint, pulling me to my knees with such surprising strength that I cried out in pain.

Bernice took it out on Karin, as I knew she would. She was banished from the game and our lives, and never appeared at the apartment again, though she did send me notes proposing rendezvous in secret places in the Park. I left these out for Bernice to find, and even met Karin outside a few times. At home, I pretended to languish; I couldn't play games, I stayed in my room. Something had changed, the game had lost its boundaries, and I mourned in prison for my banished love. What had actually changed was Bernice's attitude. The unstable compound of her superiority had undergone some sort of chemical reaction, had been neutralized, though she didn't realize it at first. She no longer taunted or ridiculed me, and several times a day, at the dinner table usually—since I avoided her the rest of the time—I caught her watching me thoughtfully, staring at me furtive and foxlike, as I'd once stared at her.

Bernice suggested new games for us to take up, or outings, or visits to pay, walks to take together, but most of these I declined. I deliberately forgot appointments with her. She bruised her wrist and I pretended not to care. Gradually, she was forced to pursue me. She initiated physical contact, as I pretended not to understand or be concerned. At last, she proposed the same awkward expedient she'd intruded upon in the library, but I refused, on the one hand because, though I'd planned that drama with Karin, it was nonetheless mortifying to think about—impossible to repeat with Bernice—and on the other because I was holding out for more. I wanted her to feel the power of my disregard as I'd once felt hers, but the more I scorned her the more she came back.

The upshot was that she gave herself to me a month or so after the episode in the library. She invited me to her room one night and surrendered according to the unconditional terms I'd dictated long ago in my mind.

After that, we began to enjoy ourselves. Now that we'd reached a kind of balance of power we could drop the masks. I learned that her earlier scorn was as much of a pose and a game as my recent, though I was careful not to admit my stratagems. I also learned that she'd only been living in the apartment a few months before I arrived, but when I asked her where she'd lived before that, or with whom, she became evasive.

In bed, we were awkward and shy and perfunctory at first, since I knew little more about the mechanics of sex than where to put it, but after a while Bernice began introducing little variations that made me suspect she had outside coaching. She acquainted me in tactful ways with the secret parts of her body, and taught me how I might help her achieve what I always achieved with ease. But who taught her this? Certainly not me, though we had only each other to learn from, or so I assumed. Cousin Raymond? I think now it must have been him: Raymond home from his club, in the wee hours of the night, after I'd parted from Bernice; but this only shows how ferocious her newly awakened appetite must have been.

He taught her well, and so taught me. She made love like a man, as though the instrument were hers and she were the one pushing it in and out. She controlled the tempo, never frantic or mounting, and came all at once without warning, came with a jerk, breaking her hips against mine while suddenly, spasmodically squeezing her legs together. It was unexpected and absolute: a sudden massive contraction, a snap, a crack in her breathing, and a kind of withdrawal at the peak; then it was over. She never made a sound.

We went on like this for several months in perfect ignorance, since we made no gestures toward birth control. Despite my suspicions that there was someone else, these were still the happiest months of my life. We played footsie under the dinner table too, and touched each other shamelessly in the hallways or behind my mother's back, and whispered dirty words in each other's ears. Dana and Patrick caught us necking and we had to pay them to keep their mouths shut. Such blackmail was not to be sneered at in that apartment since, however luxurious the place was, the younger children barely had access to money. What use could they have for it? This my mother asked when they pestered her. They had all they wanted, they possessed every toy imaginable, and if they wished for a new one all they had to do was tell her and she'd send a servant out for it right away.

Actually, they wanted money to buy cigarettes—or to pay me to buy them—so they could smoke in secret in my room. Dana was twelve and Patrick ten.

I sympathized with them partly because I was still a child too. Bernice and I were becoming adults, but by means of an extended childhood, in which we lived outside the world of consequences. It was a curious happiness we enjoyed. On the one hand I was in heaven, crazy with joy, and on the other I knew I was following a routine I could almost take for granted. The smug ego happiness of a teenager fucking, but I wasn't really smug. For one thing I suddenly loved everyone. I was cheerful and gay with silly, scornful Raymond, and dutiful and warm to my anxious mother, both of whom must have suspected such unprecedented behavior. I'm sure we thought we were fooling them all, whereas in reality every deed and word and glance exposed us, and we might as well have made love on the dining room table. Desire charges the atmosphere anyway; everyone feels the new current in the air, feels the temperature raised a few degrees. But these aren't matters adults with lives of their own readily admit to themselves, especially if it means trouble. I'm sure my mother preferred blinders, until even blinders didn't work.

Besides, she'd been acting strangely lately, my mother. She'd never been particularly strong, and her face was often a mask of anxiety. With the uneasy but shrill authority of a paranoid autocrat, she sent her food back to the kitchen repeatedly, uneaten, untouched, and spent half the day at the oxygen tanks in her room. She never went out, though this wasn't at all impossible with her wheelchair; she'd had a ramp installed a year or so ago at the building's entrance. It was hard to know who was in charge in the apartment anyway, who gave the orders for dinner, who organized the complicated day. Not my mother, who was acting more and more confused and withdrawn; not Raymond, who was drunk or out most of the time.

But when she burst into Bernice's bedroom like a freight engine that night, shining a flashlight from her squarish wheelchair on Bernice's back—she was on top—and began raving about Uncle Chuck, wait till Uncle Chuck finds out, Uncle Chuck won't stand for this, I learned who was in charge. Of course, Uncle Chuck was Bernice's father, or so I'd been told. For me and the younger children he was simply Uncle Chuck, though *Uncle* seemed more a name than a relationship, more an umbrella we'd found ourselves under. Even now—or especially now—I see him as the one who pulled the switches and gave the orders, who left instructions for the week and paid all the bills, while he lived his other life.

Uncle Chuck in his leather jacket, silk scarf, et cetera. He came on weekends, or every other weekend, or sometimes only once a month.

This time he came in the middle of the week and immediately began making arrangements to send me to boarding school. Bernice announced with defiance that she was pregnant (she hadn't even told me) but Uncle Chuck made it clear that in that case she would have an abortion. She vowed to refuse, he locked her in her room, and went about organizing our permanent separation with methodical patience. During my last days on East Seventy-eighth Street, Bernice and I found it nearly impossible to communicate; at night, servants were posted outside our bedrooms, and during the day we were forbidden to speak to each other. Only Raymond proved helpful; amused by the whole affair—he even cracked jokes about it at the dinner table—he delivered letters between us. Bernice resolved to bring the baby to term and we made plans to run away and be married, but they never succeeded. I was banished for the second time in my young life, packed off to boarding school, Westfield; and Bernice was—but I still don't know what happened to Bernice. When months later, I ran away from school and let myself into our apartment on East Seventy-eighth Street with my key, I found it like I'd found the house in Windsor years before, empty and stripped, all the furniture, rugs, even books gone. I saw my mother now and then after that, always at school, to which her money purchased me readmission no matter how many times I ran away, but after a while most of my dealings with my family were through a law firm on Liberty Street in the city. During the first year I ran away from school so often I began to think of the place as home, and in fact after that I began living there summers, with the family of the headmaster, who had no daughters.

It was only later, when I was at Yale and after my mother died, that I was told the house in Windsor was mine. It was left to me in my mother's will.

"Charlie, what's that noise? Oh I shouldn't have said it, unh Charlie *there.*" I heard a door or window slamming shut, scuffling feet, possible giggles, but I couldn't stop now. Bernice's hips broke against mine and I doubled my effort, rode my urgent heart, tried to outstrip it, and finally came all at once with a shout, pouring forty years of unused scorn and desire back into my Bernice, and gripping her shoulders while she squeezed her legs tight to milk the last drop. "Oh Charlie," she said. I realized how much I loved that husky voice.

We were bunched up on that couch, each of us well over fifty years old, having short-circuited an enormous gap, when it dawned on me that someone was watching. I remembered David—Helga's son!—and stumbled off the couch in the dark, popping loose from Bernice and groping for my pants, while bumping into tables and chairs and knocking over a few shells and figurines. "Charlie, be *careful.*" I was dripping all over everything too. But nobody was there. At the bottom of the stairs I stopped to listen. Nothing.

So I made my way back to the couch, smashing more delicate objects on the way. By now she was laughing, we were drunk, it was crazy. I squeezed in next to her, trying unsuccessfully to be quiet. We didn't wish to disturb the young lovers upstairs. Inches away from each other's faces, we placed our fingers to our lips and whispered "Shhhh," wearing goofy smiles. Then we made love again. Everyone says you never forget the first time, but how many are privileged to go back to it, albeit with creaking older bodies somewhat ravaged by time? Even pigs feel like gods. I realize now it was the example of David and Valerie, the sexual current in the air, pheromones they released, which impelled us to this folly—for folly it was, it turned out to be.

The next morning we had breakfast in the kitchen, trying to maintain our adult dignity while winking and cooing and holding hands across the table, with egg on our lips. Actually, I was instigating most of this foolishness, since Bernice seemed a bit thoughtful and withdrawn. Hungover, she said. I couldn't stop watching her. In the morning light, at that kitchen table, I realized just how beautiful she was. Her whole face grinned, not just her mouth, as it does with partial people or hypocrites, and in the force of that grin what difference did a few lines or wrinkles make? They merely rippled the surface. What I saw was the real Bernice now, my Bernice, still short and impulsive and sudden and ardent, whose body dovetailed perfectly with mine even after forty years, as though we'd actually been one person in some earlier existence. It felt like coming full circle.

We debated whether to wake the lovebirds upstairs. We could cook them a breakfast and bring it to them in bed.

But I thought better of this. I didn't want David to see me there that morning. I helped with the breakfast—scrambled eggs, hash browns, coffee—then tiptoed into a corner of the living room while Bernice carried it upstairs on a tray, singing their names as she climbed to ensure they'd be decent, or at least disengaged.

"Charlie," she shouted down, "they're gone!"

I climbed the stairs and walked into the bedroom. You might expect disheveled sheets, bedclothes on the floor, tissues all over, glasses, spilled ashtrays—but instead the sheets and blankets had been neatly folded and stacked on the bed, and the room was tidied up. On the stack of bedclothes a note was pinned: "Gone to Florida with David Mom. Valerie."

"On a trailbike?" said Bernice.

Back downstairs we continued acting silly, or I did. I'd begun to feel a bit foolish—the thought of David sneaking out didn't help—but couldn't stop myself sucking in my paunch and strutting around as though twenty years younger. I felt proud of my appearance, but knew I'd better not look in a mirror. Eating David and Valerie's breakfast, I pointed out to Bernice that I have small ears. "That's something attractive to women. Connotes understanding. Small ears, small hands."

"Wrong, Charlie, women like long ears. No matter what they say. Small-eared men sit around all the time lackadaisical."

"Small, *circular* ears," I said, "means you'll live a long time, without sapping your strength."

"I've noticed big ears means you know all about affirming life."

"Big ears take everything in. Like a big nose that has to smell everything."

"Women like that too. I know."

We talked nonsense like this for half the morning while the glow took its time wearing off. By noon, I'd begun feeling the first twinges of guilt, and Bernice had grown completely silent. And I couldn't forbear, though more calmly this time—resigned, even, to the inevitable—returning to the question of her claims on this house. After all, I said, we were just cousins; and at that, the guilt crept a little higher, since we didn't now, as cousins, have the excuse of being randy teenagers anymore.

I stood at the table, and leaning over, fumbled for an embrace. But she turned away. I tried nibbling her ear, but she jumped up, walked across the kitchen and swung around with her crazy grin flashing. "Cousins? That's just it, Charlie, you keep on saying cousins."

"Okay, lovers." I smiled and blew a kiss.

She looked out the window, saying nothing.

"Old lovers reunited," I added.

"Try brother and sister," she finally said.

"Very funny." I reached for a chair, to steady myself. She was looking right at me now. Beautiful Bernice.

"That's what we tried to tell you before, Cleo and me, which is what I found out. We're not cousins, Charlie. I'm your sister."

"Bernice." I sat down.

"Carol."

"But we just, we just—"

"And we did it before too, a long time ago. Anyway Charlie, I had too much to drink last night. I couldn't restrain you. I can't have children now either, if that makes you feel better."

"*Restrain* me?" I began to feel nauseous, without any fuzz to protect me. No cozy blood sugar to cushion the blow. At the same time I was just sitting there helpless, with the sun coming through the kitchen window on a lovely spring day. This woman was my sister? The girl I'd once loved and had just made love with? Twice! No wonder they'd insisted on aborting what I'd planted in her forty years ago.

"In terms of age, since I'm fifty-six years old," she was saying, "and you know what happens at that age of course." By now her face had shot off in a hundred different directions, I couldn't hold it together anymore. "So if I'm your *sister*, you see what I mean? So far as understanding why I'm here? I have just as much right to live here as you do, and besides I don't have a nice posh house in the Hudson Valley, as a matter of fact I don't have anything anymore, Charlie. I want to talk about that."

Just then someone rang the doorbell. I stood up gripping the edge of the table. In my chest, that little bloody devil or god—I was never sure which—was pounding his gong, sounding the alarm. With my hand on my pulse I moved in a daze very slowly and carefully (so as not to spill) toward the kitchen door. I noticed out the window a white Oldsmobile in the driveway.

"Is your name Cooper?"

I nodded. This strange-looking creature at the door had a spongy brown face and watery eyes. His short hair resembled the fur of a mouse, and came down in a peak on his brow, with two quadrants of scalp pointing up on either side. His lips were thin, loose and sensual, and he needed a shave. Small, round ears. About forty years old. I noticed he wore gloves without fingers on both hands, and a scarf around his neck even though it was warm outside. He stood before me stooped, almost hunchbacked, but tall and thin. I later learned that he was neither hunchbacked nor bent, but possessed extremely large shoulderblades, the size of plows or meathooks, from which the rest of his back seemed to hang. In the shape of his face and long square nose and small watery eyes he looked like a baboon.

"Mr. Charles Cooper?"

I nodded again, smacking my lips, taking swallows. I knew it was rude, but my hand had found my pulse again. Meanwhile, Bernice was slipping into the living room with face averted, as though she wanted no part of this. He glanced over at her briefly, nodded his head, then looked back down at me with an expression of extreme severity and triumph.

"My name is Charles Lyndhurst. I'm your son."

PART II

6

The first thing I did was to hand Charles Lyndhurst his Social Security card and marvel at the amazing coincidence which had given us different names but the same number, et cetera.

But he gave it back to me. It wasn't his card, he said, it was mine. He knew because one of the ways he'd found me was by hacking through computer files of the Social Security Administration.

How could it be mine, though? My name was Charles Cooper.

No, he said; you think it's Cooper, but it's really Lyndhurst. He was Charles Lyndhurst, Jr., he should know. I heard Bernice cough in the living room.

And as he said it, I almost believed it. Why not? I might as well be Charles Lyndhurst, Sr. It sounded distinguished enough, though I was in no mood to be so honored; in fact, I felt I'd been coated with a kind of slime. It was curious slime—these were real people, they weren't monsters. One was my sister and one was my son. It's just that we'd been too intimate in the process, so that —if what they said was true—my sister was also the mother of my son, making him my nephew as well. Unholy and unnatural.

And he *was* my son, it became pretty evident. He was the product of the alliance between Bernice and me, since Bernice, as it turned out, had managed to avoid that abortion. Uncle Chuck couldn't very well do it himself, and he was called away, he had to go on a long journey, leaving my mother and Raymond to carry out his orders, but Bernice talked them out of it, had the baby, and put it up for adoption. This was the story that came out in little chunks as the three of us suffered a conversation like a meat grinder in that living room in Windsor, and I performed the necessary calculations in my mind as best I could. Though he looked like he'd never been a child, but had leaped full blown and monstrous from my overheated brow, nevertheless I had to conclude that Charles Lyndhurst, Jr., could very well have been born in 1947. Meanwhile, Bernice appeared chagrined and refused to look at either of us, junior or senior. She studied the floor. I think the shame had reached a flood stage in her and she only really felt it now, when it finally spilled over. I was still in a daze; I felt like I'd been fed a large Valium/Demerol cocktail, or someone had been punching my head for about an hour. I kept on adding and subtracting dates and ages. I tried to follow the story but kept on forgetting things, and had an overwhelming urge to be back in Highland or Newburgh, to be smoking my pipe or designing new sewers or riding in the car with Helga.

Only Charles Lyndhurst, Jr., was in control. In his careful way he seemed exultant, as though he'd finally *caught* us. Next, I thought, we'll get a lawsuit. I once read of a man who sued his parents for circumcising him when he was born. What of suing your parents for not aborting you? For bringing you into this godforsaken life?

He was a strangely supercilious person, and spoke with fastidious care and politeness. A tax collector, perhaps, or a public executioner. *But he was my son.* As it turned out, I knew his entire employment record, since, whatever he claimed, the Social Security Administration had scrambled our files. Or perhaps he'd scrambled them himself by hacking. You worked at Pearl Paint on Canal Street? I asked. Yes, he said. Years ago. Cocking one eyebrow, I leaned forward and asked whether he wasn't now employed by the New York City Welfare Agency.

Yes I am, he said, sitting up with a smirk, and raising his own eyebrows.

I should mention that until this point he'd been sitting bent over as though at a desk with an attitude of extreme but ironic violence toward the work before him. Also, as he'd explained to us, not without a significant glance—as though we were to blame—he had hypersensitive fingertips and had grown his nails long to protect them. He wore gloves without fingers so the fingertips could breathe and the nails have room to grow, but also because his extremities were often cold. In fact, sitting in that living room he pulled out a stocking cap, as the heat was still off and this was a cold spring day in early May.

He wanted to know how I knew these things about his work, and I acquainted him with my letter from Social Security. But this only proved what he'd told me, he said: that my name was Charles Lyndhurst and I was his father.

By now I'd decided that if the two were so connected, I'd just as soon keep my real name, Cooper. I looked over at Bernice for help, but this proved to be a mistake, as, in profile, half turned away, she resembled the Bernice of old, she could have been sixteen, and I felt as though someone had peeled the skin off my heart. I could feel myself losing control of everything; if I picked up one of her figurines now I'd drop it immediately, as she'd dropped my cup back in Highland. She had managed to resurrect my love, to drag it up from some very murky depths, only to reveal at the last minute this extreme repulsion—this slime—attached to it. I couldn't look at her anymore, and turned to Charles Lyndhurst, Jr.—from the past to its living issue. It was all right in front of me, everything I'd been remembering for the past few weeks, the corpses I'd dug up. Some of them, at least.

I suddenly felt guilty about Helga, my wife.

Then I decided to treat this whole business as preposterous, and regard Charles Lyndhurst, and even Bernice—and the stories attached to them, the rags of memories, ghosts of the past—as a pack of cards. This made me feel better. Soon I'd be rid of these ridiculous people who were trying to convince me that I was someone else, and could resume my own life. I'd always prided myself—except when my blood sugar rose—with having a firm sense of identity, and a rock-hard feeling for the real. I'd dug up the earth enough times building bridges, laying pipes, and so forth, to know that corporeal reality was intransigent and largely inert. It liked to stay the same, and you couldn't change it just with words. Of course, there were practical matters involved. What did Charles Lyndhurst want? Money, most likely. And Bernice? My house. The easiest to deal with was the former, whom I could pay to leave me alone. I could write him into my will if he wanted, if that would make him happy and go away.

But then I thought: *He's my son,* and my heart geared up so quickly, so suddenly, like a lurching machine gun, that I shot up from my seat all at once. I stood there looking around at the living room, confused—I almost wondered where on earth I was. But I didn't know what to do, so I sat down. Even then Bernice didn't look at me.

Meanwhile, Charles Lyndhurst was talking about how he'd found us. Evidently Bernice had heard this story; he'd located her first, about a year ago, and had mercilessly pestered her for information about me. But she had no idea where I was; indeed, it was largely through him that she'd found me herself. For the last ten years or so he'd been searching through hospital files, through the records of adoption agencies, baptism records, even the computer files of the Internal Revenue Service and the Social Security Administration. It became an obsession, he told us, to learn who his biological parents were.

The question suddenly occurred to me: Did he know or suspect we were brother and sister? I looked over at Bernice, and for the first time since he'd arrived found her watching me, as though she'd read my mind, although of course it was that phrase *biological parents* which had done it. Her eyes were wide open, they contrived a plea, and just barely perceptibly she shook her head, while her mouth formed a little circle: *no.*

So we had something to hide from Charles Lyndhurst, Jr. That felt good, especially given this atmosphere of creeping revelations. He seemed to be taking joy in finally dragging relentlessly all this knowledge into daylight. He told us about himself too; he'd been raised by a childless immigrant couple in the Bronx, who waited until his twenty-first birthday to tell him he was adopted. There came a period of gradual shock and gradual withdrawal; he left home and turned his back on these "parents," thus breaking their hearts. But to his credit (I thought, with what should have been paternal pride) he re-established his relationship with them later, once he'd conceived of this campaign to find his real parents, a campaign so victoriously concluded today. Every year for the past ten years he'd spent his holidays with them. He bought them presents at Christmastime. When their apartment house in the Bronx was burned down, he helped them find a new place in Manhattan; in fact, they were living in his building now. Once he could draw the line, he said, and dispense with ambiguities, once he could think of them as the kindly couple who'd raised him, and of his biological parents (that phrase again) as some wholly different people as yet unknown, then he could treat them as, what? Good friends. Or more, people to whom he had an obligation, an ersatz filial duty. He saw them often, bought them groceries—they were elderly now—and intended to bury them too. Everyone needs somebody to bury them.

But what do you want from *me*? Now that you've found *me*, what next? I thought of all sorts of complications, not the least of which was Helga, to whom I'd prefer not to have to explain any of this. Besides, I was getting suspicious; I couldn't even bring myself to embrace this—person, although I suspected that that's what he wanted most of all: a tearful reunion, a glass of champagne. Where were my paternal instincts? Bernice had skinned my heart, but our son was casting it in iron once more. I was scared. I could sense his regret fighting with all that triumph and satisfaction he'd beamed at us initially. This was a day he'd been looking forward to for more than ten years, and now he found himself confronted not with loving parents but uncomfortable, guilty, reluctant strangers. Or, he'd seen that from the beginning, seen it in my eyes at the door, and in Bernice's shrinking manner, and that's why his smile was so ironic now. He was tasting the ashes of his own victory. On the other hand, this expression of distasteful, smirking irony was so firmly seated on his face I realized it was habitual, and I wondered exactly how he could have broken his adopted parents' hearts. A son like this would freeze hearts, not break them. Or maybe it was their fault; they'd abused him, in subtle or not so subtle ways. This was in all the newspapers now, on the TV relentlessly, the horrible effects of child abuse. *Someone* had to be responsible for this man.

Then I thought again: *He's my son.* And I detected something in his eyes, or thought I did—an appeal behind the supercilious irony. Maybe it was just the regret surging up, winning the battle. It occurred to me all at once that he was the one truly scared. I thought I spotted a *resemblance* too, a diabolical parody of Bernice's twisted smile and my own puffy features, and looked away in horror, I couldn't bear this anymore. I wanted to run out of that room forever. Let Bernice have the house and live in it with him, I could buy something on Cape Cod or the coast of Maine, I could afford it. Helga had always wanted that anyway. Live on the ocean summers and retire there.

"Dad," he'd just said, and I winced. He paused and swished the word around in his mouth, deciding its flavor. I couldn't get over that fuzzy hair, that elongated baboonlike face. Those were things I'd have to ignore as I grew to know my son. "Dad, you can't imagine what it means for me to say that word. Dad." He spoke biting his words, which gave them a certain fastidious precision, and it sounded as though he'd learned to fight his Bronx accent by bleaching the vowels, then squeezing them with his larynx, thus making them neutral—though this wasn't entirely successful, as the Bronx broke through in careless moments anyway. "I grew up calling another man Dad and found out the word was a sham. Now you've given it meaning again. Dad. That's what I want, you ask what I want, I don't blame you for asking, this must be quite a shock for you. I can't very well expect bear hugs and tears, not right away at least, Dad. And you too, Mom." He looked over at Bernice, whose eyes were on the floor. But most of the time he spoke exclusively to me. No doubt Bernice had already gone through this. "This is enough, this is heaven enough for me, to sit here and call you Dad, no matter how cold your initial response. I understand completely, I'm fairly certain I'd act the same way, I'm no prize, I grant you that, ha ha. But I'm all you have." And he smiled at each of us. "What I want, since you ask, is the chance to call you Dad. And Mom. Or your preference, Father and Mother. I'm new to this. Maybe we could have lunch together in the city. A father-and-son lunch. The chance to see you both at Thanksgiving or Christmas. Perhaps we could exchange gifts, as parents and children do. I suspect I was robbed of my childhood in retrospect. It's a fascinating question: What would I have been had *you*, my real parents, brought me up, instead of Mrs. and Mr. Fisch? Oh, I don't blame you. You did what you had to, I'm sure. You probably had no choice in the matter! You never gave it a second thought, you had more important things on your minds, grand schemes no doubt. Even if they didn't succeed, they never do, do they? The grandest schemes, the wildest dreams. We learn as we grow older—after all, I'm middle-aged too, I'm almost forty. We almost belong to the same generation! We learn in middle age to appreciate small things. A quiet evening at home with one's parents. The manly embrace of one's father at the train station. A letter, a card, a thoughtful word. These are the things we remember and cherish, the all-too-rare moments together, the small talk, pet names, good-night kisses. The signing of the report card. All those little things you deprived me of. Oh yes I know what you're thinking, I had these things, yes. But not from my parents. From two kindly strangers. Imposters. They meant well, their discipline was harsh, but I survived that. I survived a great deal, including the severest blow of all, the news of my adoption. But it made me wonder. Were my parents still alive? My *biological* parents? I tried to picture them, to imagine their lives. I wondered if they ever thought of me. Did they wonder where *I* was, or what *I* was doing? What kind of people put their child up for adoption? Perhaps they were desperately trying to get in touch with me now. It was all a mistake, they regretted their folly, even—or especially—twenty or thirty years later. So, while I was looking for you I imagined that you were looking for me. Perhaps we passed each other on the street. I tried to picture your faces. I constructed composite photos on the flimsiest evidence. No evidence at all, really. For example, Dad, I assumed you'd be tall, but we can't all be tall, can we? I tried to imagine what sort of work you'd be doing. A profession, I assumed. A banker, bald and distinguished. Perhaps a writer of mystery stories. A university professor, a doctor, a chain saw company executive. I never thought of a water engineer, that's original! I imagined all sorts of romantic reasons why you had to give me up for adoption too." He glanced over at Bernice with a smirk, looked back at me, dropped his smile and lowered his voice. "Why did you, really?"

Bernice and I looked at each other in subdued panic, fumbling for words. Did he know we'd just become lovers again? "We were young," she mumbled.

"Fifteen years old," I said.

"Our parents wouldn't let us get married," Bernice added.

"Yes, how marvelous, just as I imagined! You must have been two lovebirds, eh?" Turning his face so Bernice couldn't see, he winked at me. "This is exactly the way I pictured it. *Some* things we imagine, when we learn the truth, it doesn't disappoint. You'll have to fill me in on all the details, Dad. When we have lunch together. Now that I've found you"—and here he straightened up and shot me a glance full of significance, his face tightening around the eyes—"I won't give you up. You can count on that."

He went on like this—the memory of it is pain—for what seemed like all afternoon, but when I glanced at my watch it was only three. He took this as a hint, the glance at my watch, and treated it with resentful sympathy, weaving apologetic but ironic references to my busy schedule and upcoming appointments into his monologue, as though to hold me there but at the same time save face should I insist on going. I took him up on it and pleaded something in Highland that evening—cocktails, dinner—anything to get out of that house and collect my wits.

As we walked to the door, in a desperate rush now, and with a clinging voice, he told me about himself. Yes, he worked for the city welfare agency, as a manager of buildings leased by welfare. He gave me his card. I live in the city, he said, I play the piano, and I'm chairman of the local Right to Life Committee. This sounded like those capsule biographies on game shows.

There was an awkward scene at the door. Evidently, Charles Lyndhurst would stay and visit with Bernice a bit, so he saw me off. Bernice stood behind, in the doorway to the living room holding her arms, framed there squat and forlorn, deeply so—my heart went out to her, but laden with guilt. I had the feeling I'd never see her again, banished from her sight, like the Count of Monte Cristo. There was no question of embraces, with either mother or son, but I didn't know quite what to do with my arms either, so Charles Lyndhurst, Jr., and I shook hands briefly, half turned from each other—his hand was firm, long and bony—and then I was gone, trying not to run to the car, and later restraining myself so successfully from speeding down Ballyhock Road that I crept along it at fifteen miles an hour.

The first thing I thought was that these were two people someone had hired to drive me crazy, maybe Pork Vining. Or, the world had gone mad—they were changing everyone's names—but I could hold out, I had to, I had work to do.

Upon more calm reflection, driving back down Route 17, I felt sorry for Bernice stuck back there in Windsor with the man who was our son. I vowed to leave her alone in that house and propose a vacation to Europe this summer with Helga. We could skip Windsor this year. And when the time came that things settled down, I might tell my wife about my long-lost sister who had shown up unexpectedly, down on her luck, and was living now in our house in Windsor. Until she found work. But I wouldn't allow them to meet each other; that would be too much.

My sister! I could feel the gears in my life changing, though of course nothing had really changed except what I knew. Objectively, things were the same. This thought offered a crumb of comfort which I gobbled up quickly. If things were the same, things could go on being the same: my work, home, marriage, life. Maybe lunch once a year with Charles Lyndhurst. Why feel guilty about things that happened forty years ago? Though of course, I reminded myself with a twist of the knife I hadn't managed to pull out yet, some of it happened last night.

If she was my sister, was she my mother's daughter, or my father's, or both? Who were our parents? But here I found myself crawling out on limbs precariously weakened by my fifty-five-year-old body. If things were to go on being the same, questions like that could wait. When you dig up the past you find corpses, after all. Buried children. That's what the past is, the part you can't see: you can't see it because it's buried. I began to resent all this business, this disruption of my life, which I'd been somehow trapped into actively abetting. It was like scything your own legs from beneath you. I felt persecuted. These people were nice, I even loved Bernice, though what *kind* of love was another question now, but beneath the veneer they were taking my house—or she was—and disrupting my tranquility, perhaps deliberately, who knows? They were endangering my heart, and I'd better forget them. Except on carefully planned holidays.

But it wasn't easy, resuming normalcy. Over the next few weeks I was inattentive at work, and even Pork buried in his CAD noticed it. I forgot things, I missed appointments. Little annoying mistakes nipped at my heels, circled my head. Cutting my fingernails with a clipper I cut into one of my fingers, and it wouldn't stop bleeding. For this I blamed Bernice. See what happens when you mix the same blood? You should have told me! But forty years ago, she didn't know either. Or did she?

I woke up one night with my heart beating faster than I'd ever heard it beat, and sat bolt upright. I'd just remembered something in my sleep, but then lost it when I woke up.

I began receiving annoying phone calls, the kind where the

other end hangs up in silence. One day I came home to find the front door wide open and no one in the house.

Suddenly, my company was slapped with two lawsuits. One was pure annoyance, but either would absorb the $25,000 deductible on our liability insurance, and mean higher rates next year. We had helped draw up a new assessment schedule for the City of Poughkeepsie Water District, and so were being sued—along with the city—by a big hotel who claimed their assessment was too high. The other one was more potentially damaging. A teenager went off the road thirty-eight feet into a ditch which was part of a drainage system we'd designed for a newly incorporated section of Newburgh. His lawyer was an ambulance chaser who'd decided to sue the city, the construction company that had dug the ditch, the company that made the pipe for the ditch, and us, the firm that designed the whole thing. The boy would be in a wheelchair the rest of his life, so this was his one big chance to cash in, not that I wanted to deny him, but what the hell; thirty-eight feet off the road? He must have had radar to find that ditch. The question I couldn't decide was, should we get a lawyer, or let our insurance holder provide one? They had the greater incentive, but either way we'd have to pay, and through the nose. But the strange thing was, I couldn't decide. I agonized over it, and at the same time found myself simply letting go of it mentally. My mind went soft thinking about these lawsuits, and I had to ask Pork to take them both over.

I received a phone call, collect, from of all people Helga's sister in Orlando, Florida. Keep your boy away, she said. Fifteen minutes later the phone rang again. *Heartline!* I shouted in the kitchen. It was David this time, calling collect from a phone booth across from his aunt's house. At ten o'clock at night he wanted to know if I could possibly go out right now and Western Union him forty-five dollars? Normally I would have turned this over to Helga, but she was in the city for the weekend. Valerie was in the phone booth too, and shouted, *Hello David's father.* David talked semicoherently for a while—though I found myself preferring it to Charles Lyndhurst's coherence—and the story I pieced together was this: he and Valerie had found an apartment outside of Orlando, and he'd taken a job drywalling, but his pay had been lagged and they didn't have money to pay a deposit to turn on the electricity so they could start using their new VCR.

I went to Western Union the next morning, Monday, and sent him a money order for three hundred dollars. Without, however, telling Helga when she returned from the city. Helga knew where he'd gone, as it turned out, but not who this new girlfriend was, and I declined to inform her. Was it my imagination or did we communicate even less frequently now, Helga and I? Just to look at her was to immerse myself in guilt. Still, I couldn't help but make comparisons. Helga was my wife, but Bernice was my first love, and now the latter had turned out to be my sister. This felt like a form of narcissism after which any other love was doomed to fragmentation, unable to restore that terrible unity.

I forced myself to talk with my wife. I embraced her with ill-concealed desperation, which she was polite—or uninterested—enough not to acknowledge. Our embraces had always possessed a certain chaste quality regardless, associated in my mind with the Puritan costume of the play in which we'd met in Nyack, Miller's *The Crucible.* She was Goody Proctor and I was her husband. What silent reserves of resignation and strength Helga called upon in that role, while I blundered and stormed about, under the amateur actor's illusion that passion should splutter. This was a production of the Hudson Players, a group that met nights at the Unitarian church.

Actually, for reasons I won't go into now, I'd simply shown up during the first week of rehearsal and taken the role of the Reverend Parris, which our stage manager had reluctantly been covering. A week or so later when the director's son came down with a kidney infection I took his part, John Proctor. It was thrust upon me, you might say. As John Proctor I grew to know Helga, my stage wife, in ways I haven't been privileged to since. I'm convinced that the missing factor in most marriages is a strong sense of your role and your lines. I don't mean the proper roles of husbands and wives, God knows—no one agrees what those are anymore—but a sense of destiny in the daily drama you enact, a feeling that your existence is in the process of being transformed into fate. In the daily drama—as opposed to the one on stage—the cues are all off, the blocking inadequate, the show lacks necessity. You slip in and out of each other's arms, you go for days misunderstanding something the other one said. You don't in general feel there are any gods you need to please or even prod into recognizing your existence, and so your lives become all loose ends trailing. Squids passing in the night.

But on stage you have a script. You have an audience who doesn't know the ending. With this firm ground beneath us, Helga and I began spending much of our free time together, though she still lived with her husband. At the time, I was working for the DOT office in Poughkeepsie, designing bridges. I'd had a succession of live-in girlfriends, but Helga was the first to be married. She was thirty-eight, her husband owned a chain of tire stores. I knew I was grazing dangerous territory, but as it turned out I never did meet him. He came to one of our final performances, and such was the power of life on stage, that is, on display, that he sensed immediately what was happening between the principle players and left his wife the following week.

A year later, Helga and I married.

And now I must confess that I planned it all that way. I intended to steal another man's wife. I waited for her after rehearsals, I even hung around her house at night, across the street, under a tree. I pursued her from the very beginning, my own Goody Proctor, loyal and cold, but with a warmth of devotion and an inner dignity not even an ecclesiastical court could touch. I knew enough not to confuse Helga with the role she was playing, but I also knew that she brought to it an extraordinary sense of sympathy and understanding. And me, what did I bring to my role? All us misunderstood good people with a sense of principle need a consort. For the first time in my life I saw marriage not as something to be desired, but as a necessity. It was two against the world. It had simply never occurred to me before that the actual purpose of marriage was to double your solitude. This is undoubtedly why I never fulfilled my ambition to become an architect: I didn't know what houses were for.

We lived in Helga's place a few years and endured her son's problems as a child—or I did, as Helga's position with the State Board of Realtors kept her away from home much of the time. I was in transition. I'd quit the DOT and was consulting independently. Later on, I started Hudson Valley Consultants and Helga left the board to pursue her own investments in real estate. We built the house in Highland on property she received as partial payment for a restaurant she'd sold. None of it was real, of course; I realized that in moments of lucidity. The only real part is we grew older. Life became spongy, lacking a script. It became a constant effort at revision, and so nothing changed, as nothing was attached to an outcome. In this, I suspect we were perfectly normal. We reeked of normality, except for David, who was six when we married, and who extorted money from other children and hid his spoils inside a coconut.

It was pouring that Monday I sent David the money order. Helga showed up for lunch, unpacked, then left for her office. I'd been planning to go into work late myself, but with the rain coming down hard like that—all over the state, said the radio—I decided to take the day off.

And it didn't let up. Minor flooding in lowlands. By late afternoon I wasn't surprised to receive a phone call from Bernice in Windsor. Bernice! Her husky voice went straight to my heart, confusing it with shame and regret.

"Charlie, I hate to say this but I smell something bad in the house. What could it be?".

"Is it raining out up there, Bernice?"

"It's pouring."

"What you smell is septic."

"Septic, what septic?"

"It's the leach field from the septic tank. Sometimes when it rains it backs up into the basement, and the smell rises into the house."

"Jesus, it's rank. Septic?"

"It usually stops a few hours after the rain stops."

"What happens if it rains all day?"

"It smells all day. Problem with old houses."

"Charlie, my *God*, I can't stay here with a smell like that." Despite myself, I couldn't help smiling.

"Oh God, it's *awful.*"

"Light some incense, Bernice."

"You think I carry incense around?"

"We keep it in the silverware drawer. Way in the back."

"Oh Charlie." Her voice trailed off, and together we endured a silence of ten or more seconds, though it seemed like five minutes. We listened to miles of phone wire hiss.

"Bernice, Carol, can I ask you something?"

"What?"

"When we were—when we lived on East Seventy-eighth Street, did you ever know someone named Johnny?"

"Johnny who?"

"I don't know, just Johnny."

"No. I don't remember."

"What color was Uncle Chuck's hair?"

"Uncle Chuck?"

"You know, your father."

"My father?" She paused. "Oh, I get it. My father. His hair was brown. No, it was black."

"Was his last name Lyndhurst?"

"That's the name he gave me."

"A tall man, right?"

"I don't know, Charlie, he could have been tall. Maybe he was short. I can't remember that good, it's a long time ago. You want to know the answers to these questions, you should ask Cleo. She's the one that told me you were my brother."

"Cleo?"

"The woman you think was your mother, this person we are talking about here. Cleo Dannen."

"Christ, Bernice, her name was Cooper."

"No it wasn't, it isn't Charlie. It's Dannen. You can ask her yourself. She's eighty-five years old but if you catch her on the right day her mind's still sharp. I'll tell you where she lives if you come up here and fix the damn septic."

"That's all right, Bernice, that's fine," I said. My head was swimming with names, and I was angry. People took them off and put them on like hats. "Why did she change her name?"

"She didn't, Charlie. That was always her name."

"Her name was Cooper, she named me Charles Cooper, and now she's dead. Cooper, Cooper, Cooper," I shouted. "I have her ashes right here in the house. Someplace."

"You have her ashes? This is something you collect?"

"Bernice, why would she tell me her name was Cooper if it was Dannen?"

"When did she tell you this?"

"When I was a kid. I don't know, she must have. She named me Charles Cooper."

"That's something you'll have to ask her about. You could ask the ashes you said you have. I guess you've got somebody's ashes there, Charlie, but they couldn't be hers."

The only problem was I couldn't find those ashes, which had my mother's name on the box. I was sure they did. I'd looked just the other day, in my closet, in the attic, in the various spare bedrooms, but couldn't find it.

"Where does she live?" I asked.

"Come fix my septic and I'll tell you."

"*Your* septic. You think that's *your* septic?"

"You think that's your mother?"

I opened my mouth and nothing came out. Then I swallowed and tried again. "Okay, Bernice," I said. "Sorry I bothered you, Carol."

"You didn't call me, I called you."

"You might have to camp out or something until the rain stops and the smell goes away. You could sleep in the barn."

"Oh thanks."

"Is Charles Lyndhurst there?" I couldn't say *our son*.

"He went home after you did."

Then we both fell silent again. I knew what that septic smelled like—it was horrible. But I was angry too, and confused by all this, as well as by the things we weren't saying, the guilt and the shame mixed with persistent, lingering, unwilling, unreasonable affection. At least on my part. I remembered how I used to think that that smell was a plague for a guilty conscience, although at the time I didn't feel I'd done anything in particular to be guilty about. Just general things: my personality, my life.

This time the silence lasted. Gently, quietly, I pressed down on the button—for some crazy reason I thought of smothering a mouse—then lifted it up and heard the dial tone.

7

"Coop, it's the age, we *had* the age of 'knowledge.'" Pork put "knowledge" in quotes, as though it were a quaint anachronism.

"You want to call it that."

"Some people call it the age of information now." Through a haze of smoke, Pork gestured with his meaty hands, growing excited. I was making clouds and clouds of smoke, lighting and relighting my pipe, cleaning it out, filling it again, lighting, relighting. My fingers were black, and my plate, with flakes of dried fish still clinging to its edges, was covered with mounds of pipe tobacco tailings. Pipe cleaners bent in every kind of shape.

I knew Helga didn't like this—she preferred I smoke alone—but it was Pork's apartment, I couldn't very well ask to use his bedroom. Besides, constant smoking was an outlet for my blood sugar. I could sit there and bubble and percolate, but *sit* there. I didn't have to get up and smash all the windows. I think Helga must have sensed this, or she was just being polite, sitting forward at the table with her chin on the backs of her fingers, smiling attentively—as though the conversation *interested* her.

"But I'm absolutely convinced," he said, waving the pipe smoke away—his hands made superb fans—"we're entering the age of *intelligence* now. Not just information, *intelligence*. The possibilities boggle the mind. My God, what you can access. You can access *any* damn thing. Everything!"

"You can access the gods."

"Who knows?" Pork flung his hands up high, glanced at the ceiling and laughed. We did too.

"But this age of intelligence," Helga asked. "It requires us to think, does it not? Surely these machines cannot think for us?"

"You're absolutely right," I shot in. "All it is, Pork, is better ways to find out what everyone else is thinking. Anything, not to have to think yourself."

"First of all, better ways," he said. "That's quite an understatement, Coop. There it is in a nutshell, better ways. You have a little calculator the size of a watch can find the square root of one thousand eight hundred and sixty two point nine three in a fraction of a second. Better ways! As for machines thinking, depends on what you mean by think."

"I'll say."

"What's thinking but access? Making connections. Neural links . . ." He spread his fingers. "Networks, layers of networks. And networks connecting networks. With computers, everyone has computers, you can think bigger. Think *more*. More storage, more links, more, more—"

"More useless information. More wasted paper."

"The way I see it," said Helga, "the machine is only as smart as the one who presses the buttons."

"No, yes. You're absolutely right," said Pork. "But the one who presses the buttons. Suppose he has access to—"

"To everything," I said.

"To the wisdom of a mountain," said Helga. She was almost as good at Pork baiting as me, and instinctively we glanced at each other, smiling. This was out of affection for Pork. Everyone liked to see him get excited.

"I see thousands, hundreds of thousands of machines. Each with hundreds of thousands of bytes. It's like one big brain. You can't think of a brain as a little compact thing anymore. It's like brains are inside out. A city's a brain. A network, all the computers in Boston, or in upstate New York, let's say. These make a brain, or part of the bigger brain."

"So the thinking goes on without you."

"In a sense."

"You can go for a walk or something. Fall asleep while you're thinking." Actually, this was beginning to disturb me.

"You don't have to worry about forgetting something," said Pork. "Your brain's hooked up to a bigger brain. One that's more efficient. It's like a beehive, or an anthill. One individual goofs off, it doesn't matter for the general effort. And thinking—you'll have to stop thinking about thinking like it means 'concentration.' It doesn't mean concentration. You can spread out thinking. Thinking at leisure. Pick it up, put it down."

"And if somebody dies," I said, "while he's doing this thinking, no sweat, it goes on without him."

"Exactly!"

"No death, no loss, no horrible things."

"Well, there's always human life, Coop. I'm not talking about that. Maybe you place too much importance on thinking, in that respect."

"Maybe you don't place enough."

"I see what he's saying," said Helga, who I knew felt constrained to act as mediator. She could tell if I got too close to the edge. "All these little brains you talk about." She held up her finger and thumb as though to indicate their size. "Plugged into one large brain." She spread her hands. "But you still have room for the individual. We've been doing this for years already, watching television. Turn it on, turn it off."

"Machines, can they dream?" I asked. "Can they die, Pork? Can they suffer a sense of loss?"

"Of course not. I'm not talking about that."

"You don't sense the limitations of what you've been saying. Ask a machine what's the most horrible thing. You have a program on horrible things?"

"I don't need a program."

"So tell me what's the most horrible thing." Of course, I knew, but I wasn't telling. But I did feel like asking: Can machines commit incest?

"Premature death," said Pork all at once.

"Depends on how premature," I said. But I didn't like this answer. It crawled all over me. "I'd say torture," I said. "Torture's worse than premature death."

"What a morbid conversation," said Helga, though she still looked attentive, still smiled—how? Indulgently. Kindly.

"First, premature death," said Pork. "Then torture." He was quieter now, and more thoughtful, I could tell. But he spoke of these matters without hesitation.

"What about loss of loved ones?" I asked.

"That's next."

"You've got it all figured out."

"That's because I've had it all, Coop. In reverse order."

"When the hell were you ever tortured?"

"None of your business. In North Vietnam."

"Oh, I'm sorry, I didn't know." Pork was looking right in my face. He'd joined the firm little more than two years ago, as a kind of senior partner—I knew he was good—but Vietnam? He'd never mentioned that. Was it on his résumé?

This was the first time Helga and I had been to Pork's apartment together, though I'd come here alone after work a few times. Pork had made me drinks and we'd talked about life, girlfriends, childhood, computers. Not once had he mentioned Vietnam, so I guessed it was a sore spot.

Pork's apartment was a modest little place, dark, with cream-colored walls and motel furniture. A fifties brick apartment building, two stories, near downtown Newburgh, on a four-lane boulevard.

"Well look," I said. "At least you escaped premature death."

"So far," he said, nodding.

"You're both wrong," said Helga. She picked up her fork to push around some uneaten food on her plate, and still wore the faintest of smiles. "The most horrible thing is suicide," she said.

"Talk about morbid," I said. I was cleaning out my pipe again, anxious to fill it with more tobacco. We both looked at Helga, expecting more. I wished we were back on computers.

"The thought of suicide," she said, "is the most frightening thought an individual can contemplate. It may very well be that the other things you speak of, such as the loss of a loved one, may suggest this thought. But once you begin to entertain it, you find yourself alone. This is thinking for which no computer will help. The mind seats itself alone before a mirror."

Neither of us had an answer to this. Sounds like you've thought about it before now, Helga. She was right about suicide. I began to grow frightened. I felt that I had to make smoke.

"Self-annihilation," she said, "is thinking the unthinkable. One thing the mind cannot encompass—no matter how large these computer brains become—is the thought of ceasing to think. Of causing itself not to think anymore."

"Pulling its own plug," said Pork.

"We read of people with fatal diseases who do this," she said. "But perhaps the disease affects the mind. They do not have this experience of placing the mind before itself to contemplate its own disappearance. Perhaps the pain distracts them. They cannot have this pure experience. I imagine the same may be said of torture. I apologize," she nodded to Pork, "if this brings up painful memories for you, this talk of torture. I feel presumptuous in mentioning it. But I think it must be that torture is like noise, very loud noise, unbearable noise, for which covering your ears with your hands would be useless. It is the distraction which tortures; the sense of being nailed into your body. The mind becomes irrelevant in such a case. It shrinks to a reflex. All it can do is scream."

"Exactly," said Pork.

"Coop, must you?"

I was manufacturing smoke, billowing clouds of smoke, and I think I'd probably unconsciously blown it, or most of it, in Helga's direction. She turned her head, coughed into her fist—or feigned a cough—and waved at the smoke with her other hand. Where had this talk of suicide come from? Through the smoke I saw Pork staring at Helga with what appeared to be distended features. There was a long minute of silence, as Helga had apparently finished what she had to say, and neither of us knew how to respond. Staring at Helga, Pork looked expressionless, carved out of stone, but I sensed this meant awe.

"Helga," I finally told Pork's mountainous profile, "is very different . . ." I wanted to say different from me, we were so unlike. It was homage I was fumbling toward, praise of our marriage, of how opposites attract, but my tongue had grown thick.

"And Coop is very much the same," she smiled.

"Helga likes things stable," I said. "Secure."

"And Coop likes them capricious."

"That's not true, I like stability too." I sucked at the pipe, which was going out again. "I've learned to appreciate stability," I said.

"Coop may have told you," said Helga, "about some of the problems my son David has."

"Coop told me," said Pork, nodding. He was still turned to Helga, nodding his head in sympathy now.

"We've discussed the importance of a stable environment for a troubled boy growing up. His problems undoubtedly stem from the lack of a father. That is to say, his own father, his biological father, left me when the boy was a child. Coop has done all that he possibly could in admirably filling the role of a father. Whatever sense of self-respect David has been able to recover is largely due to him." She looked in my direction, and Pork finally turned to stare at me too, nodding away, with, however, a certain blank skepticism in his eyes. I could tell he was remembering the scene at our house three months ago, when David stormed out. An aberration, Pork.

"What's he doing now?" asked Pork, although he knew. I'd told him at work a few days before.

"He's just married a beautiful, talented young girl," said Helga. "An artist. They're living in Florida." And this was true. We'd received the announcement in the mail the previous week of David and Valerie's marriage in Orlando before a justice of the peace. What were they hiding, not to invite us? Even Helga's brother and sister weren't there.

Of course, Helga didn't know of my link with Valerie. But how long could I keep it from her? I was beginning to feel imprisoned by my secrets, living with them hand to mouth, day to day, trapped.

"Well, congratulations," boomed Pork, clapping his hands. The sudden explosion of those hands made us jump, and cleared a pocket of air in the smoke. This was just the excuse Pork needed to channel us all back to happier thoughts. "Champagne," he said. "Leroy's had a special." I cringed at the thought of drinking Pork's cheap upstate New York sparkling wine, but I was wrong; the special was on Moët & Chandon. Pork passed out three glasses without stems or stands—shaped like cornucopias—made of crystal; you had to hold them in your hands until the champagne was gone, then lay them flat on the table. This was how they did it in France, he said.

"In parts of Germany as well they have this custom," said Helga.

"What about North Vietnam?" I asked. Helga looked at me sharply.

Then Pork opened the bottle with one twist of his hand, and we toasted David's marriage, as he'd planned.

Later on Pork brought out some Indian pudding. For all his presumed amazement at my cooking three months before, he'd turned out to be pretty good at it himself; poached red snapper with ginger, plus a nice spiral bread with scallions, some buttered fresh peas and braised Belgian endive with pine nuts. All his own recipes.

It was cozy that evening in Pork's apartment, with the windows open, curtains blowing in, and cars whizzing by on the avenue outside. Their tires made a sound like masking tape ripped off a wall. Pork brought out some mock-ups for his Thunder Mountain Lake brochure, and who was I to spoil his fun? This was a subdivision he was planning in the Catskills, second homes, not a company project, a personal investment. He was doing it on the side, but sometimes I had the suspicion he made use of our CAD when he had to. Actually, he'd proposed that Hudson Valley Consultants take it on months ago, but I was too preoccupied with other things. We had enough business, we didn't need more. Sometimes Pork's ambition frightened me. We could open an office in Kingston, he said. An office in Manhattan!

But in my quest for stability, I found myself preferring things as they were, on our modest scale. When I retire, Pork, you can do all this, you can answer to David, chairman of the board.

He wanted Helga to handle sales for this project. The real estate firm she worked for in Newburgh was one of the largest in the Hudson Valley, and she had connections in Manhattan as well. But Helga appeared skeptical at first. We pulled up our chairs on either side of Pork at the dinner table and bent over the proposed brochure he'd spread out among plates pushed aside. "What's this lake?" she asked.

"That's Thunder Mountain Lake, what it will look like. We haven't built it yet."

"How can you have a photograph of a lake you haven't built?"

"I mean that's a lake, it looks like the same kind of thing. That's the basic idea for the lake. We want it to look just like that."

"But you have this photograph on the cover of your brochure? Who is this woman walking the dogs?"

"Friend of mine."

"Nice dogs," I said.

"Samoyeds."

"And here you have a site plan. Preselected homesites." Helga was being professional, I could tell. She read from the brochure. " 'In Thunder Mountain Lake, deer and wolves range across your view, unconcerned by your home beside a migration route protected by the New York State Department of Environmental Conservation.' *Unconcerned*," she said. "You have asked them?"

"We set aside land for open space, for the deer to migrate." Pork was arranging the salt and pepper shakers on the table as though to demonstrate; these are the deer, these are the wolves. Wolves?

"Pork, there're no wolves in the Catskills."

"We could introduce them."

"Say good-bye to your deer."

" 'A carpet of multicolored wildflowers crowds the edges of a walking path beneath majestic mountain peaks,' " Helga read. " 'At the end of the path, trout leap in your own mountain lake. A myriad of small animals around your home mingle the events of their lives with the events of yours.' "

I couldn't hold back. "My God, Pork, who wrote this crap?"

"*I* did," he roared. "I had help," he said more quietly. I took this to mean his friend with the Samoyeds. I could tell Pork was trying to control his temper. This was Pork the proud salesman. Did he want us to buy a homesite?

"Here you have fifty-seven homesites," I said. "You have roads?"

"All paved."

"Utilities?"

"Sewer, water, electricity. Also, fire hydrants and street lights."

"What's the density?"

"One point three acres a lot. Including open space."

"And you think you can build this without disturbing the squirrels?"

"I never said that, Coop. There's bound to be, you'll have some disturbance there. In the process of building."

Helga read more. " 'Careful planning and attention has been given to preserving and improving the beautiful yet delicate environment of Thunder Mountain Lake. Our goal is to demonstrate how humans can live in the mountains without crowding out the animals.' "

"You bring in the animals after you build the lake," I said. "Like a zoo. Fire hydrants for the wolves to piss on. Did you think all this up, Pork?"

"My friend."

"I mean, why? Why not just sell off the parcels instead of dressing it up with this—with this hypocrisy? How much are lots?"

"Sixty-five thousand."

"For a *lot?*"

"Includes utilities."

"Jesus, Pork, you think there's that kind of market?"

"Excuse me, Coop, this has been planned very carefully. We labeled all the bushes to keep them or move them, so the bulldozers won't touch those bushes we labeled. What's wrong with this? These are good ideals."

"You mean making money?"

"Commitment to the values of a natural environment."

"If you're committed to the values of a natural environment, just leave it alone. Don't build anything."

"So where would we be, where would anybody be, the whole world thought that way, Coop? We'd all be living in Co-Op City."

"That's what *this* is."

"May I take this, Pork?" Actually, Helga appeared interested. "I could show it to some people."

"It's not etched in stone, we can change some things. Some of the wording," he said. "Show it around, get some ideas."

"There are many people in the city who may be interested in something like this," she said. I knew this was just what Pork wanted to hear.

"Sure go ahead take it." With his big hands, he pushed the mock-up at Helga. Then he snatched it back, ran to his bedroom and returned with a leather case, to zip it up inside. I took this as our cue—or excuse—and stood up, looking around.

"Where's my jacket, Pork?"

"You didn't bring one."

"Oh." Something didn't feel right. It occurred to me Pork had invited us here solely for the purpose of selling his Thunder Mountain Lake. "Pork, you can buy a goddamn big house with the money from this," I said. "You could build your own private landing strip. How many partners?"

"Four, I have." He watched me carefully. We were both short. Helga stood at the table taller than either of us, with the leather

case under one arm. "It's still not too late," he said, "to get
Hudson Valley Consultants in on this." It sounded almost like a
threat. Would Pork go off and start his own firm?

"No thanks," I said, "we've got enough work." But I didn't say
what I wanted to say. I worked with subdevelopers all the time,
and had never met any who'd bothered to dress up landbusting
in these sorts of terms. "You get it by the planning commission?"

"It's just the county board up there. It's pending."

"What county?"

"Ulster."

"I can see where a board might like that description."

"Sure." Now he looked proud.

Helga shook Pork's hand and smiled, slightly bent over. "I'll let
you know about this," she said.

I winked at Pork—I'm not sure why. At the same time, I
resolved that Hudson Valley Consultants would never touch
Thunder Mountain Lake. It wasn't our style. Therefore, I
thought I could afford to say a kind word about it, and shaking
his hand (this was when I winked), mumbled something about
how pretty his brochure was. It would sell lots for sure.

"You think so?" Pork asked with some warmth. He was nodding too.

I liked Pork. I did.

Riding home with Helga up 9W, I decided to get out of the
car—she was driving as usual—and opened the door. "Coop!" she
shouted. The car was doing forty, maybe fifty, but I'd forgotten
it was moving. She pulled over and stopped. "What's wrong with
you?"

"I don't know," I said. My arms were shaking.

She leaned across me, closed and locked the door, and drove
us home while I sat there in confusion.

A few days later I received a call from Bernice. Actually, Bernice
phoned quite often, mostly about matters concerning the house.
Was there a toaster anywhere? Mousetraps? Who do you call for

clogged sinks? The septic problem hadn't recurred, since—as I explained—when the soil dries out once the summer gets going it acts less as a saturated sponge passing leachate along. I knew all about these things; wait until fall.

I'd had several calls from Charles Lyndhurst, Jr., as well, who felt it his duty to remind me of his existence. He wanted to set up a time for our lunch in the city, but I pleaded pressing business at the office, putting off the inevitable. In fact, we'd hit a lull at Hudson Valley Consultants. We could easily take on Thunder Mountain Lake, as Pork pointed out, but I grew stubborn on this point. I wanted a vacation, for one thing. What about Europe in September, Helga? No, she couldn't. She might even be forced to forgo a vacation this year, she was too busy, but I could go stay in Windsor without her, I should feel free. She was so thoughtful and insistent about this that in one of those black moments of paranoia—the sort of thing I rarely experienced, actually—I thought she was trying to get rid of me.

About David she appeared unconcerned. Curious about his new wife, but in no rush to meet her. They would visit soon enough. Thanksgiving, for example. That was fine with me. Thanksgiving was five months away, and as far as I was concerned five months was a lifetime.

I asked Helga if she'd seen my mother's ashes—the box from the crematorium. Had she run across it anywhere in the house? In a closet, or the attic? No, she hadn't noticed it. Why do you want them, she asked.

To sprinkle them on the East River.

And why would anyone want to sprinkle his mother's ashes on the East River, may I ask?

Her final wishes, I said.

I see. And she died how long ago?

Thirty-five years. More or less.

And this is an act for which you must—Helga paused—muster resolve?

Helga's irony was the thoughtful variety, containing all the appalling innocence of the sensible and level-headed. I dropped

the subject, but kept my eyes out for those ashes, which had to
be around someplace. Meanwhile, I still received each month in
the mail my eight hundred dollars from Faber and Lodge on
Liberty Street in the city. I passed my fifty-fifth birthday with a
minimum of fanfare. And I went to the Social Security office in
Kingston to straighten out my records and obtain a new number,
like a good citizen. In other words, normalcy had a foothold, and
might actually have re-established itself if Bernice hadn't called
to tell me that Cleo Dannen, the woman—she said—I thought
was my mother, had been struck by a car and might not survive,
as she was eighty-plus years old. She was in intensive care at Bronx
Hospital; Bernice gave me the room number. I drove down that
evening.

8

She'd been hit while walking on the sidewalk outside her nursing home in the Bronx, a place run by an order of Portuguese nuns. One was with her when I got to the room, but discreetly left. The car had actually run up on the sidewalk and knocked her down, struck a lamppost too, but managed to drive off. Two broken legs, a broken hip, a mild concussion, and various internal injuries. One of her legs was in traction, attached to a complicated mechanism of wires and pulleys. I wasn't quite sure what to call her. Mom? I expected she wouldn't recognize me anyway, and in fact when I walked in the room all she did was stare.

The problem was, I didn't recognize her either. Though she was the same woman who'd approached me on the basketball court that day in Newburgh with Bernice—overweight, very short, with a mannish face, bullish neck, curly hair, and a strange mouth more or less twisted out of control—I couldn't see any connection with the person I remembered as my mother. Her complexion was light, like my mother's, but her eyes were less expressive, more like slits in a bunker, as her face was quite flat. She'd lost weight since that day in Newburgh. I remembered my mother's eyes being full of watery anxiety, and her face as puffy and cloudy, that is, it had contours and hills, it was more of an actual landscape than this one before me, which resembled the sheared surface of a rock split in two. Then again, age erodes different faces differently. You never can tell where your own will wind up, and even if you see it later as a form of destiny—it was there all the time—still, there's no way to locate this destiny like a hidden plum or nut beforehand. With Bernice I'd seen the years melt away like a revelation; her face, the one I'd known, was still *there*. In a certain primordial way it was even now the same face, despite all the changes, including the vast change from beauty to ugliness (though I really couldn't see her as ugly anymore).

But with my mother, or Cleo Dannen, or whoever she was, the revelation I'd expected didn't come, and I wondered again if this weren't a hoax. Bernice's next step would be my eight hundred dollars a month.

I didn't know what to say. The shape of her in that bed was pathetic. I remembered her as short in Newburgh, but lying down she looked cut in half—a small round stump with arms and legs attached. Her lips were chapped—cold sores, it looked like—and liver spots covered her ravaged cheeks and forehead. I felt sorry for her and regretted I'd come; she was such a dwarflike, weakened creature, a blister of humanity, barely clinging to the little bit of life she had left, that it made me feel young. She looked at me puzzled. For a strange moment I felt like the wrong person. Bernice had called someone else's number, or I'd been switched in my bed, or my brain had been transplanted. I didn't recognize *myself.* Then a funny thing happened. She rang for the nurse, and when the nurse came, told her with a firm, careful voice, surprisingly strong, "There's a strange man in here. Get him out."

"Excuse me, Mrs. Dannen? I'm Charles Cooper, remember? Or Charles Lyndhurst, you spoke with me in Newburgh with Bernice, I mean Carol? Carol Lyndhurst?"

"Carol Lyndhurst?"

"You were—you said you took care of me when I was a child. You felt the lump on the back of my neck."

The nurse was actually a candy striper, and stood there with a foolish grin on her face. Kicking strange men out of rooms wasn't something she'd been trained in.

Cleo Dannen lay there watching me, narrowing her eyes in anger. Then it struck me that it wasn't just anger; it was anger laced with fear. She turned away, looked at the wall, squirmed in

her bed for a moment, and finally muttered with a sigh, "Oh yes."
I nodded to the nurse, and she walked out.

"What do you want?" she said.

"Are you my mother?" I didn't feel like wasting any time.

She turned to me again, and this time the fear, or anxiety,
passed unsullied across her face like a perfect shadow. She looked
around the room. This *could* be my mother; her anxious nervous
gestures were similar to those my mother had habitually made,
moping around the apartment in her wheelchair. She had a tic
too, she was jerking her head, half sitting up, I think she was
drooling, and all this did make me think of the woman I remembered as my mother. Not that my mother ever jerked her head;
it was more a quality of impending menace, which she simultaneously seemed to be threatened by and threatening. Then I saw it
wasn't a tic; she had the hiccups. "Your mother," she said—and
she added maternally, "Charles," as my mother had forty years
ago, drawing the name out and rounding it off—"Your mother
was the most beautiful woman in the world." I must say that
made me feel good; but I wasn't sure if she meant herself, speaking in the third person, or someone else. Meanwhile, I was looking
for a glass to get her some water when I spotted an old photograph
on the table beside her bed. That is, first I saw it, failing to
register, then it seemed to have leapt from my very mind or heart,
and with an involuntary shudder I thought, *my father.* Or (since
everything was now going soft and uncertain): the man who my
mother—or the woman I'd thought was my mother—had once
made me think was my father. He'd yellowed a little in the forty
years since I'd seen him on the dresser in her room, but still wore
the same rimless glasses, the same rouged cheeks, the same
slightly ravaged look of a financier down on his luck. A drunken
stockbroker.

Suddenly I was sucked back. Perhaps by a process of osmosis,
I recognized the woman before me, more from her voice than
from anything else, a firm staccato all the more firm for the
quivering eyes and face that housed it. I saw her in her wheelchair

forty years ago lurching around a corner straight at me. The motion rippled out to faces, rooms, streets, some I'd never remembered until now. One face in particular stood out, and I realized this was because I was hearing it described. "She was tall and beautiful. *Hic.* She had round, brown eyes. Her brown hair was silky and smooth, and her legs—her legs were quite long I remember, as well as her arms." As Cleo Dannen spoke, all this struck me as essentially correct, or at least as something that should have been correct. Maybe it was the word *tall.* I was probably acting out a lifelong fantasy, compensating for my stature, but I thought I could *see* this tall, beautiful woman, and those long legs, those long thin arms lifting me up. How could anyone forget such arms? "She hennaed her hair, though, didn't she?" I asked.

"Yes, she did."

My God. Her face came back to me with all the force of something vividly seen, shining in sunlight. This face was very oval, eyes yellowish or brown, round as coins, and her nose rather flat but round, and turned up a bit. Mouth wide and full. In my earliest memories, she was the space in the air, the hole. In my memories of being born, or lying in the crib, watching faces descend, grow larger, break up—as a fish might understand human faces from its bowl—hers was the face I saw now, no one else's, the one I'd forgotten most likely because I'd been so close to it, down there in that crib, tucked in between the bed and the dresser, the round, wooden pulls of whose drawers I could touch.

Cleo Dannen was hiccuping rapidly now, hand to her mouth. It was all growing clear. Cleo was the person I'd thought was my mother, who'd puttered in and out of my youth in her wheelchair—my nanny, I suppose—and this other tall, brown-haired woman was my actual mother, she must have been; as to why I'd forgotten her all these years, me with my excellent memory, who could tell? At least I'd always thought it was a good memory. Better than most.

As for the man on the dresser, the drunken stockbroker, he

wasn't my father, of this I felt certain. He was a fiction, even if he was Cleo's actual husband, or ex. In fact, his face looked phony—it always had, it suddenly struck me—unlike the absolute reality now resurrected of my true mother's face.

Then I realized it wasn't so much the details of her remembered face that felt so real as the quality of intimacy they contained, or gave off. Some faces feel like our own in reverse, as though their contours possessed the secret of faces known from the inside. We only know two faces from inside, our own and our mother's; and the latter knowledge we gradually lose, so that eventually her face throws itself together in more or less conventional (if beautiful) ways, as having a nose different from other noses, eyes all her own, distinctive lips, ears, hair, neck, and so forth. But some of that secret knowledge remains and clings to the lines of that nose and those eyes; children trace it with their fingers in daydreams the way they trace words or pictures in a book, in fact the way I traced it now, standing there, a child reclaiming the hidden contours of my mother's face. The difference was that my knowledge of her actual face—the one everyone sees—was so weak or nonexistent as to have completely vanished until Cleo Dannen had just brought it up. But why? Somewhere was a rupture. I felt divided in two by this face. Even now it was beginning to fade, though I'd seen it as though in a bolt of lightning just moments before.

In the smooth passage of my early life was a dangerous crack, which ate memories of mothers. Gradually her face disappeared along with other more shadowy half-remembered faces, and the bed, crib and dresser too. First I tried to remember what had happened, then attempted to remember remembering, but with Cleo Dannen below me hiccuping open-mouthed this was nearly impossible. I threw out lines and lines, anxious filaments of myself, but nothing snagged. I was probably assuming grotesque postures too, twisting around like a circus contortionist, trying to remember, and what did that poor woman lying there think? At last a shape contrived itself in my mind. It was disappointing, actually: a large room with plenty of light, that's all. Then it was gone. But I sensed the important thing wasn't so much the room as the fact of its loss, somehow associated with my mother's. This loss was part of memory too, as opposed to being a failure of memory. It was something substantial, the more I thought of it. Actually, it felt like a wedge forced down into my physical brain. It was painful, in fact. I could choke on this memory. And wasn't I wrapped in a blanket as well? I could very well have been lifted up bodily. Colder rooms, come to think of it, and a smelly car seat, then more strange rooms, and arms and legs not anyone's, not my mother's. Wet clothes, hunger, and other things too. Dirt in my mouth, whispered voices, an empty city street at dawn. A blow to my head! All this could have happened long before Cleo Dannen appeared and pretended to be my mother.

"What happened?" I blurted out. "Where did I come from?"

"You came from an angel."

"That's what *she* used to say," I remembered.

Cleo was watching me and hiccuping violently, which forced her to talk in spurts between hics.

"Sir, I'm sorry." A doctor or intern—he wore a white smock— touched my elbow and guided me gently toward the door, before bending down to Cleo on the bed.

"What was my mother's name?" I asked her.

"I don't know. *Hic.* She never told me."

"*Sir,*" said the doctor, sharper this time.

"And why did you say my father's name was Lindbergh?" I shouted. The doctor scowled over his shoulder at me, raising one eyebrow, while his candy striper actually began pushing me toward the door, ineffectually however. Then he turned back and prepared an injection for Cleo's arm. She was a paroxysm of hics by now, and glanced around frantically with blank, frightened eyes unable to take hold of anything. She looked at the wall, the doctor, the door. All at once someone was pulling me from behind. Cleo appeared to be absolutely terrified, and her body, despite the traction, squirmed on the bed like an infant's, and even began bucking or jumping. But her answer came clearly, with a firm, calm voice. Perhaps the injection was already taking effect, because the hiccups stopped all at once as she spoke, and she actually shrugged, she may have even laughed uneasily, looking up at the ceiling in mock impatience. "Oh *that,*" she said. "That just came to me." Her eyes rolled up and the lids snapped shut, but the words still came out, though more slowly and distended. "That was just to get your attention." Then she was asleep.

In the hallway, I turned to see who'd been dragging me so ignominiously out of that room. It was a man about my age, but taller, more brawny, dressed in bulging polyester. An ex-football player now selling insurance, or perhaps simply the local torturer at the health club. His face was tanned and sleek, better preserved than mine, though more or less creased across the middle, so that the brow and chin were dominant. His nose was just an ordinary nose; it occurred to me that he knew this and resented it. How else account for the vindictive expression on his face? He seemed to have a grudge against the world.

Standing there facing him, I felt the weight of my own face, and the uneasy suture it made with the world. I'd always associated my puffy eyes and more or less flaccid features with the woman lying on the bed in there, or with what she used to look like, but as it turned out she wasn't my mother. Then the face in front of me opened up, spoke, and presented living proof of the unpredictable destiny of faces. "Stay away from my mother," it said.

"Your mother?"

"I don't know who you are, or what you have to do with this . . ." He gestured vaguely at the whole hospital; I noticed his hands kept balling into fists. "But if you come in here again and upset her I'll kill you."

And he looked like he meant it.

9

Charles Lindbergh never finished college because he wanted to go barnstorming instead. He bailed out twice flying the mail from Chicago to St. Louis in the early 1920s. In the twenty-second hour of his transatlantic flight in the *Spirit of St. Louis* in 1927 he saw ghosts; he felt himself departing from his body, into the plane, the sky, the clouds, but a long extended strand pulled him back. He thought just a few French aviators would be waiting to meet him at Le Bourget airport in Paris, and was completely unprepared for the thousands who wanted to touch him, who tore pieces of the fabric from the fuselage of the plane, and the thousands more who couldn't get into the airport, lining the roads around it in their cars at ten o'clock at night. This man hadn't slept for three days. He awoke the next morning at the American embassy with the American ambassador's personal valet, Blanchard, at his bedside announcing that his bath had been drawn. Outside, on the street, the crowds had been forming all night, waiting for him to exhibit himself. He saw black socks on a chair beside his tub turned halfway inside out—the easier to put them on—and wondered whose they were. He thought he was in a movie.

He was a man after my own heart, though I was by no means the only one. I learned all this in the public library in Poughkeepsie. He won the Orteig Prize, received the Cross of the Légion d'Honneur; the mayor of Paris gave him a gold medal. He flew to England, where the king asked him how he peed on his flight. A battleship met him when he returned to New York; four million people gave him a ticker-tape parade. The secretary of war made him a colonel. "Colonel Lindbergh," said the mayor, "New York City is yours—I give it to you."

He met the Rockefellers, the Guggenheims, the Morrows. He became rich. Rich people protected him. He lived in expensive mansions and estates. Reporters climbed fences and trees to take his picture. He married Anne Morrow, the daughter of the American ambassador to Mexico. He presented the *Spirit of St. Louis* to the Smithsonian. He didn't need trains; he flew everywhere. He flew from Los Angeles to New York in fourteen hours and forty-five minutes with his pregnant wife as navigator, who had to be carried from the plane when they landed. He flew to Japan and China by way of Canada and Alaska. He mapped out the first commercial airline routes for Transcontinental Air Transport (later TWA).

He flew survey trips for the Carnegie Institute over Arizona and New Mexico, and discovered ruins of an ancient pueblo. He filmed a lost Mayan site in Mexico from his plane. Airplanes, he said, gave humans the eyes of birds. And I thought, reading this, how perceptive—how true! What a powerful lift for the human spirit those first flimsy planes must have been. You could *see* things, at last. To see something, you rise up from the mess and look down. When you extricate yourself you can see it better, then you may define it, and so understand it.

It struck me this applied to people too. People, problems, muddles, mysteries. The solution to the maze is fly out of it. For someone like me, afraid of flying, this might not literally be possible, I realized. But we're talking about flights of the mind here, I thought—what the mind's eye can see, even hovering over a book, for example.

I glanced all around the library. I'd forgotten how good libraries made me feel.

He was smart. An inventor. He helped draw up plans for the *Spirit of St. Louis* himself. Later, in partnership with Dr. Alexis Carrel—Nobel Prize winner in medicine—he invented a perfusion pump designed to keep organs isolated from the body functioning, and tested it on the thyroid glands of cats and the spleens, ovaries, pituitaries and hearts of chickens. The technology set in motion by this pump led eventually to open-heart surgery, artificial hearts and my brain in this jar. So heroes confer boons upon us all.

He worked with Carrel at the Rockefeller Institute in New York, commuting from Princeton, New Jersey. They had visions of prolonging life indefinitely, though both concluded that the essence of life did not lie in the material. It was something else, a vital impulse. Science could isolate it, but science often killed it. Their goal was to isolate it yet keep it alive so its structure and function could be studied simultaneously, for in fact—they said— these were the same.

He also invented a flask through which one could observe and photograph living tissue cells in a circulating fluid. After midnight at the laboratory in New York, he spent hours alone gazing into this flask, watching leukocytes extend their pseudopods, then studying the resulting secretions.

He'd met Carrel in 1930, three years after the flight that made him a hero. In the same year, his wife gave birth to a son, and more than ever the reporters and photographers followed them relentlessly. To escape the perpetual publicity, they bought land in the isolated Sourland Mountains near Hopewell, New Jersey, and began construction of a house.

This was where it happened.

Their son had become America's favorite baby. For one thing, he was cuter than all other babies, and for another his name was Charles Lindbergh, Jr. He even had Lindy's dimple on his chin. He lived with his parents in Englewood Cliffs while the new house in Hopewell was being built.

They moved to Hopewell. The baby was kidnapped. On the ground outside the boy's second-story window were found a handmade ladder, a chisel and some footprints. Inside was a ransom note signed with two intersecting circles with three square holes

marked in a line across their diameters. Many words were mis-
spelled; deliberate or not? "Dear Sir! Have 50.000 $ redy 25 000
$ in 20 $ bills 1.5000 $ in 10 $ bills and 10000 $ in 5 $ bills. After
2–4 days we will inform you were to deliver the Mony. We warn
you for making anyding public or for notify the Police the chld
is in gute care."

In the driveway to the Norfolk, Virginia, Country Club a man
named Sam jumped onto the running board of the car of the ship
builder, John Hughes Curtis, and said he'd been selected as the
go-between by the kidnappers of the Lindbergh baby. All over
America, people were being chosen. A con man named Gaston
Means was chosen, and convinced Mrs. Evalyn Walsh McLean,
wife of the publisher of *The Washington Post,* to give him one
hundred thousand dollars to ransom the baby; she did it out of
patriotic duty. In the Cook County Jail in Chicago, Al Capone
offered a reward for the return of the child; he offered his services
to find the baby if they'd only let him out of jail. Colonels and
admirals and millionaires surrounded Lindbergh, sifting through
offers and phone calls and letters.

Dr. John F. Condon of the Bronx received a letter signed with
two intersecting circles and three square holes. "Dear Sir: If you
are willing to act as go-between in Lindbergh's cace please follow
stricly instruction." He met the baby's father and mother. "Will
you help me get back my baby?" Anne asked. When she cried,
he smiled and shook his big finger. "If one of those tears drops,
I shall go off the case immediately."

With Lindbergh in the car some one hundred yards away,
Condon handed over the ransom money in St. Raymond's Cemetery in the Bronx, and received a note in exchange. "the boy is
on Boad Nelly . . . you will find the Boad between Horseneck
Beach and gay Head near Elizabeth Island." But they couldn't
find the boat. Lindbergh flew up and down the New England
coast and all around Martha's Vineyard and the Elizabeth
Islands. No Boad Nelly.

A month later a child's body was found in a ditch half covered with leaves thirty yards off a road outside Hopewell. They thought it was him, but who could be certain? The body was badly decayed. Another month after that, Anne Morrow Lindbergh's maid, Violet Sharpe, committed suicide. Two years later, police arrested an immigrant German carpenter from the Bronx, Bruno Richard Hauptmann, and charged him with the kidnapping. They'd traced some ransom bills to him, and found more ransom money hidden in the walls of his garage.

He was charged with murdering the baby, tried, convicted and executed. This Hauptmann fascinated me too; to the end he said he was innocent. The ransom money had been given to him in a shoebox by a friend who went back to Germany and died, he said. No one bought the story then, but most of the books I read in the Poughkeepsie library pointed out that he was convicted on phony evidence. For example, after his arrest the police rented his house in the Bronx and went to live there to see what they could find. They nailed some holes in a section of the kidnap ladder and said these matched nailholes from the joists in the attic of Hauptmann's house, where a piece of wood had been removed. When the jury announced its verdict, Hauptmann said, "Little men, little pieces of wood, little scraps of paper."

Despite myself, this trial sucked me in. It wasn't enough to read about it in books, I had to see where it happened too; I had to put my fingers in the nail holes.

From behind me came an enormous sneeze; in the gray dust I noticed something collapse softly inside as the heavy door swung open. Someone had drained all the color from this room and replaced it with dust. I saw beetles on the floor. Lieutenant Miller, who couldn't stop sneezing, pointed out the place had been locked up for decades. It was down in the basement of the oldest barracks at New Jersey State Police Headquarters in Trenton, and no one ever came there anymore.

Nevertheless, the ladder was missing. Someone had used it for firewood. In cardboard boxes stacked on a row of steel cabinets against the far wall were trial records yellow at their edges: evidence, affidavits, testimony, clippings. These fell apart in my hands as I thumbed through them, though some had holes neatly incised.

What about fingerprints? Were there fingerprints of the Lindbergh baby?

Right here, said Lieutenant Miller, yanking open a drawer most of whose contents had been shredded into nests by mice. This is where they used to be. I rummaged around in the shredded paper, half expecting little teeth to clamp down on my thumb, and actually found in the back a manila envelope, nearly intact—only the gummed flap had been eaten—clearly labeled *Lindbergh Case Fingerprints*.

But it was empty.

No one ever comes here anymore? I was shaking my head to confirm this falsehood, to make me feel better. Lieutenant Miller shook his head too, because head shaking—or nodding, as I'd learned from Pork—was contagious.

In the Paradise Garage in Hopewell an old man with hairs in his ears and nose had once done a brisk business directing the curious to the Lindbergh estate. But hardly anyone asked anymore; I was the first this year. Were there Lindberghs still living there? No, after the kidnapping Mr. and Mrs. Lindbergh never lived there again. They gave the house to the State of New Jersey; it was now a reform school for boys.

Charles Lindbergh died in 1974.

Hopewell was filled with mouse-gray houses with clapboard shutters. Past the Masonic Temple I turned left on Amwell Road, but saw from the mailboxes that some called it Lindbergh Road. Beyond a narrow, crumbling railroad underpass were fields, woods, farmhouses and country estates, plus a few new ranches, a brand-new solar saltbox, one Lincoln Log home too. Barns leaned right out onto the road. I took another left down into a valley, past stone fences, storm fences, and a few cows in the fields, enough for gentleman farmers. Up a hill into woods to a driveway just before an old one-lane stone bridge. HIGHFIELDS, said the sign. KEEP OUT. I drove down this wooded driveway to a chain, parked the car and walked. Then I went back to the car and locked it; this was a reform school.

At a clearing in the woods a half mile up the road, the house came into view. Flat gray stones, shutters, steep pitched roofs, two wings and a midsection; basic twenties Period Revival on a large scale, with some vernacular touches in the sheds and outbuildings. A modest mansion. The drive swung around to a walled parking area, with a pair of vans sitting there, but no one was around. Not a sound came from the place. The house said nothing to me. I stood there at the edge of the clearing, staring up at it. Nothing.

I noted that the baby's nursery window faced south; this I identified from photographs. Below this window the ladder had been placed, but the top rung had failed to reach the window. A man could perhaps have crawled in that window, but climbing back out while holding onto a bundle wrapped in a blanket would be extremely difficult. I've done this, backed down onto ladders while cleaning out raingutters. You need both hands, and even then you're sucking air. I've never cared for heights regardless.

So some people think the child was dropped then, when the kidnapping happened. Charles and Anne Lindbergh in the house heard a noise, but didn't investigate. The kidnappers could have dropped the child, accidentally killing him, then buried him on their way out of Hopewell, but still decided to attempt to collect the ransom.

On the other hand, trial records indicated that a child from the orphanage up the road from where the body was found had also been missing; so the corpse could have been that child.

I've noticed that when you try to solve a problem, the evidence tends to break up into positive and negative ions. The governor of New Jersey called Hauptmann's wife—who insisted on his innocence—a woman who was either telling a truth that burned deeply in her heart, or staging a scene, like any great actress. There were lots of either/ors in this case. Either Hauptmann had kidnapped the child or he hadn't. Either that corpse was the Lindbergh baby or it wasn't. And if it wasn't?

In a case like this all the chaste facts scramble for cover, like ants you exposed by turning a rock. They add up to this or that outcome equally; but what they really want to do is mirror your brain, where facts tend to panic until they're a theory.

When the child's body was found it was so decayed that his doctor, called to the Swayze Morgue in Trenton, said, "If someone were to come in here and offer me ten million dollars, I simply wouldn't be able to identify those remains." A post-mortem examination showed that both second toes on the corpse overlapped the big toe; whereas the Lindbergh child's *little* toes both turned in and overlapped the next toe.

On the other hand, the left leg was missing from the corpse.

As for me, all my toes overlap. They appear to be fulfilling a prophecy. It happens to changelings stolen by gypsies as a protective reaction against losing their mothers.

The Lindbergh child had rickets too, because he was allergic to milk. I couldn't find out about birthmarks or lumps; no one mentioned them. Standing there watching that house, I waited for something to form a pattern, but my mind was too soft, too confused. Too many things were stirring it up. I thought of the dust in that room in Trenton and sneezed, though I hadn't sneezed when I was there. I shrugged and walked back to the car. The sun came out, trees looked raw. Their leaves hurt my eyes. Each one had its very own edge, perfect and inevitable, but who on earth could account for them all?

It occurred to me that the world doesn't operate randomly. If there's one thing I can't stand, it's the thought that *anything* could happen. If you went back and lived it again, I'm convinced, it would all occur exactly the same way. Flies know this—slugs, beetles, mice—but humans don't.

I began to feel I should keep everything I'd learned to myself. Some things you don't talk about. Excuse me, I'm the son of Charles Lindbergh, the famous aviator; somehow it didn't fit.

Of course, it couldn't be true. For one thing, I couldn't recognize any of the pictures of Anne Morrow Lindbergh. The woman whose memory Cleo Dannen had resurrected as my mother looked nothing like her.

Then I thought of the scar beneath my bottom lip. The Lindbergh baby had such a scar.

Little things like that were important, I knew. Driving out of Hopewell, I thought of little things and how important they could be. A matter of inches could throw off a survey. Also, water—water stays level, or it drops; the difference is hidden in details that serve other purposes too, like rocks on a hill, or trees and bushes, or the look of the soil. To see them you needed aerial photos—human minds need the eyes of birds—but then you had to interpret them also. Every last detail needed analysis to find out what it meant for you, or for your purposes.

So naturally little things were important. Lumps, scars, toes, also dimples. I had a dimple in the middle of my chin. The way you walk, how you use a spoon, your taste in clothes. Half the pictures I'd seen of Charles Lindbergh showed him with his left hand in his pocket. Now, not to put too great a face on it—one must be careful—I did this too. I often walked around with my left hand in my pocket.

On the other hand, I was short and Charles Lindbergh was tall. I wanted to see all sides of this question. The child was short too, but that's because he was a child. Actually, the corpse they found was thirty-three and one-third inches long, whereas Charles Lindbergh, Jr., measured by his doctor the week before the kidnapping, was only twenty-nine inches long.

Also, we were born the same year: 1930. At least, that's what it said on my driver's license.

Twenty-nine inches long, I thought. Only twenty-nine inches. How pathetic. Tears came to my eyes thinking of this poor twenty-nine-inch child stolen from his crib forever. In some heaven or hell, this act occurred over and over again: wrapped in a blanket, carried through darkness, divided from his mother. First your life was the same, then different. Everything pivoted on that difference, you seesawed up and down on it, but always landed in the same spot. This was because these things had been fixed. Once they happened, they were ordained. Thinking about them wouldn't change anything.

But don't get me wrong, thinking's important. I said this out loud—"Thinking's important"—and found as I drove that I was gesturing with my hand. And I wondered if Charles Lindbergh did this too, flying across the Atlantic; he probably talked to himself also, he must have. Often, talking with Pork, I would hesitate in saying certain things, or pause abruptly then fall silent. Was this an inherited trait as well? Getting tongue-tied like that? And why would I forget certain names—me, with my superb memory—or whistle certain songs, or say "davestating" instead of "devastating"? Approaching Manhattan, why did I take the Garden State Parkway instead of the Turnpike? Either way took you to the Holland Tunnel. Did the Garden State Parkway have some special significance I was yet unaware of?

A song came into my head—Benny Goodman's "Don't Be That Way"—and conjured up visions of men in uniforms, World War II canteens, silhouettes of bomber planes pasted on my ceiling. I wished I had a pencil and paper, as I wanted to make a note of that song. Maybe look up its date. With a little pocket-sized notebook and pencil to jot such things down I wouldn't forget them. And there were so many things to jot down! They raced through my mind now. I was often sloppy in my habits, my shirts were usually half untucked. I tied Windsor knots. Some days I had to shave twice, as my facial hair had always been heavy. When I made a sandwich, I always cut the bread crust off first. I ate bacon with my fingers. My handwriting sloped left. The smell of liver turned my stomach.

What was the truth about these things?

Walking down Liberty Street, I spotted myself in a plate-glass window. Someone I knew walked like that, slightly tipped to the side, in fact.

My lawyer wasn't much help. Talking to him, I felt as though

I'd just drunk about ten cups of coffee, and was so jumpy that when his phone rang I nearly leapt for it myself. I kept on noticing what he did with his hands or the way he paused before saying, "Charles." Didn't his secretary look at me funny? And my file was on his desk! He didn't have to search for it. Who told him I was coming?

Then I remembered I'd called him from Hopewell, and that calmed me down. I began to relax. I noticed my heart was still beating rapidly, and fingered my pulse, which seemed to help too. I could do this more or less undetected by him, as I'd pulled up my chair quite close to his desk, and my arms hung down below the top.

I'd always thought of James Faber, my lawyer, as a nice man with a big nose, older than me, a kind of father figure. He spoke with a deep, slow voice, his nose was large, with craterous nostrils rather tipped up and exposed in an obscene sort of way. His skin had a certain grayish tinge, and his chin was baggy, a chin approaching retirement. But he was very distinguished and never lost control. I was outwardly polite and felt myself nodding my head when he spoke, but inside regarded this man with disdain.

I asked him where my monthly check came from.

The estate dispersed funds through a trust company in Miami, he said. My eight hundred dollars a month came from there, via this office. He offered their phone number, not that it would help, since they weren't at liberty to disclose—he coughed—the name under which the estate was registered.

"Why not?"

"Terms of the estate."

"But why didn't you tell me?"

"You never asked, Charles." He said this shaking his head and folding his hands. Next question.

I asked him about my house in Windsor. Was the title with their papers here? All this happened when I was in college, this inheritance—I didn't look into it very carefully then.

"I'll check more thoroughly, Charles, and call you. But a cursory examination"—he was looking through folders—"reveals no record of that title. Nothing here mentions your house."

What about the name Lockwood? Was that in the file? George and Louise Lockwood?

"Offhand I don't see it. One thing I can do is put their names through the computer and see what it comes up with." Saying this, his eyes lit up. "We're in the process of computerizing our files. Shall I show you, Charles?"

I nodded and smiled, but when he stood up I tripped him. That is, I didn't remove my legs from his path when he walked around the desk, this distinguished man—just as an experiment. It unnerved me actually, the way his face was betraying something so close to his heart: his new computers. He was like a fisherman about to show you the little workshop where he ties his own flies. "Oh, I'm sorry, excuse me, how clumsy." *He* apologized, even though I'd tripped him, but as much as I enjoyed the feeling of disgust swelling up inside my chest like bread dough, disgust at his apologies, at this office with its mahogany paneling, at law firms that computerize, I also enjoyed being polite—not just the hypocrisy of it, the politeness too—and apologized myself, profusely, bowing and nodding my head at his apologies, while displaying at the same time all the enthusiasm I could muster for seeing these new computers.

And I *was* enthusiastic, that was the funny part. I felt it like a schoolboy, as we walked down a corridor past the receptionist's desk to a door James Faber opened. With awe, I glanced in at a long row of women busily typing away at computer terminals. No windows here; the floor was strewn with curls of paper. Their faces were slightly green, reflecting their display screens, and they all wore beatific smiles, or at least smiles of inner content, the kind you see on pregnant women.

"I'll put it through the computer," he said with his deep voice—in his own careful way he was beaming—"and call you at home. Lockwood, you say?"

George and Louise Lockwood. I wrote it down at the receptionist's desk, then shook his hand. I was smiling and nodding, backing away.

Outside, I ran all the way back to the car.

On the way home I bought a bottle of whiskey for medicinal purposes and a notebook for my pocket. I'd been away two days; this was Wednesday. I stopped by the office in Newburgh and told Pork I wouldn't be in the rest of that week either. I was taking my vacation. This was the end of September already, I'd worked all summer—not what I'd planned—and could afford to take a few weeks off now. We were scraping for things to do anyway, work was slow, which made Pork's assurances that they'd find a way to manage without me suspicious. I'd never thought Pork was capable of irony, but I didn't like those enthusiastic nods.

In Highland, the front door was unlocked and no one was home. Then I saw the kitchen all strewn with food. Packages of macaroni, cans of tomato sauce, pots and pans, cups, all scattered everywhere, on the counters and floor. The place was a mess. Also, it looked like my goblet was missing.

The other rooms were the same, especially the bedrooms. Every item in every closet and dresser had been taken out and thrown across these rooms. A window in one of the bathrooms was broken.

"Helga!" I phoned her office, but the line was busy. Then I called Maria, the cleaning lady. No answer. The police? Nothing valuable appeared to be missing except the goblet, but that I didn't care about. That wasn't what they were searching for anyway, as they must have found it early on, in the kitchen.

I sat there, not sure of what to do. I phoned James Faber's office, but he was out. He was supposed to call that afternoon anyway about George and Louise, though I doubted he'd find their names in his computer.

All at once I felt exhausted. I could no more put a can of tomato sauce away than climb a mountain. I knew these moods; to change a lightbulb would be impossible. You felt sad and weak, but the prospect of actually *doing* something weakened you further. It was like safety pins popping open in your heart, there was nothing you could do about it, everything felt futile. Part of this was the mess in the house, which profoundly depressed me. But what was going on? What were they looking for? And where, for example, was Helga? I roused myself and called her office again; she was in the city. I hung up the phone on the verge of tears. Helga, our home has been broken into! How come you're never around to protect it?

I lay on the couch and fell asleep immediately.

When the phone rang, dredging my sleep, I felt dragged by the shoulders from bottomless depths. I anticipated with pleasure and anger shouting as loud as I could at James Faber. It was all his fault—to hell with politeness!

"Hello!" I yelled.

"Dad?"

"Who's this?"

"Dad, Dad, my goodness stop shouting. I've been thinking about that lunch, Dad. I thought you might like to meet Mr. and Mrs. Fisch."

"Mr. and Mrs. Fisch?"

"The ones who adopted me."

My head was swimming, and somehow I thought this name, Mr. and Mrs. Fisch, was significant. I noted my left hand was in my pocket. *Fisch*—I should write that down. "Lunch, I can't have lunch. I'm busy this week." I realized all at once that this was Charles Lyndhurst. Junior.

"I called your office and they said you were on vacation."

"I'm busy with vacation. I'm painting my house."

"I thought it was natural wood."

"Painting the house in Windsor. I'm going to restore it."

"But you're in Highland."

"Making preparations. I'm about to leave."

He paused. "Let's make it next week, then."

"I'll be in Windsor next week."

"The week after next?"

I suddenly felt helpless, defeated. "That's fine," I said. "The week after next."

"What night's good for you?"

"Oh, any night. Any night's good."

"Friday?"

"Not Friday. Not during the week."

"Fine, let's make it Saturday, Dad. Or how about Sunday? We could have a nice Sunday dinner with Mr. and Mrs. Fisch," he said. "How does that sound? Sunday the thirteenth?"

"Wonderful. Son." Then I had an idea. "Son," I said—I was trying out the word—"remember you told me you found me, how? By hacking through computer files? Social Security?"

"Yes, yes, I did." Proud and eager and friendly.

"You can do this with any names?"

"Sure. I can try. It's a hobby too, Dad. I learned it doing Welfare files. I use their computer."

"Could you locate some people for me? I've been curious for years. They're probably dead."

"Still might be files. Depends on when they died. What's the name?"

"Lockwood. George Lockwood, Louise Lockwood. They once lived in Windsor."

"Lockwood. George. Lockwood. Louise. Once lived in Windsor." He was writing this down, I could tell. Good idea. "What's the zip code in Windsor?"

"13916."

"Sure thing, I'll give it a try. You'll be there tomorrow? Windsor?"

"Tomorrow, the next day. Why don't you call me here? I'll wait here before I leave, until you call me about it."

"Sure, I'll call there. I'll see what I can do. I'll call you first thing."

"First thing when?"

"When I find out something, Dad."

"Okay, son. Thanks."

10

"Dad?"

"Son?"

"Lockwood, George. Deceased. 196 28 7923. Last known address, Box 57, RD 2, McFall Road—"

"Wait a minute, let me get a pencil." Then I realized I had a notebook and pencil in my pocket, though I hadn't made use of them since I'd come home yesterday. I'd been sleeping a lot. "Okay," I said.

"That's Box 57, RD 2, McFall Road, Apalachin, New York."

"Apalachin? That's not too far from Windsor."

"I've got them both right here on the screen, Dad. Lockwood, Louise. 021 57 0803. Deceased, November 11, 1962. They don't have a date for George's death. Last known address, Louise, Box 57, RD 2, McFall Road, Apalachin, New York."

"Any children?"

"What?"

"Do they list any children, surviving relatives, anything?"

"No, that information doesn't appear."

"Thanks a lot, son. I appreciate it."

"No problem. See you the thirteenth. Twelve noon, Dad."

"The thirteenth. Twelve noon."

I noticed when I hung up that my legs were crossed in a peculiar way, more or less wrapped around each other; the toe of the upper leg was hooked behind the other's ankle. Since my notebook was open anyway, I decided to jot this down. While I was writing it, I realized I was scratching the side of my nose with my free hand, and noted that too.

I remembered I always buckled my pants before tucking in my shirt, despite the inconvenience, so I wrote this down. Sometimes I knotted my tie *after* I'd put on my coat. Apparently, I left loose ends to the last minute, then tidied them up quickly, unconsciously. I'd have to be careful to catch such traits, analyze them closely and make comparisons.

Already I felt better; the thought of being vigilant did it. On the other hand, it seemed that someone had pushed me out into a big river on a little boat without oars, and I didn't know where it was going.

In fact, I had no idea what the hell I was doing.

The house was still a mess, but Maria was coming today to clean it. I wrote her a note and a blank check, threw some clothes in a duffel bag—just in case—took my pipe this time, and jumped in the car.

Did Lindbergh smoke a pipe? I hadn't noticed this in any of the pictures. Did he drink? Was he faithful to his wife? How was his blood sugar? How did he die?

Faithful to his wife? A door cranked open in the back of my head; behind it were all sorts of possibilities, little gremlins. After all, I was an expert in illegitimate children. Maybe that was an inherited trait, the inclination to produce bastards. Even if you *were* clean-living, upright, and so forth.

The kidnapped baby could have been swapped for an illegitimate son, or vice versa, before or after the kidnapping. Maybe Lindbergh tricked the kidnappers—they took the wrong child. Scenarios and plots snapped through my mind, zigzagging fault lines like cracks in the plaster. All I had to do was knock on a surface (to see if it was hollow) and networks of lines appeared. If you were a bastard, it made sense, there was a reason for being raised by a succession of surrogate parents, while your real father hung around there in the wings.

I remembered Uncle Chuck had a dimple on his chin; a genuine, chrome-plated Kirk Douglas dimple. He was tall.

If I were Charles Lindbergh's son—just if—and if I were kid-napped, then found dead, but turned up alive a few years later, after everyone had adjusted to my death, that was good reason for my father, wasn't it, to keep me a secret? He wanted to spare his family.

I was driving over the Shawangunks on a shortcut from High-land to Route 17, and pulled over at a scenic overlook to write these thoughts down. Below me, the rolling valley lifted toward the Catskills up north. The waves of trees went from green to yellow to scarlet approaching the mountains. It was fall, the season of moribund leaves.

I felt happy; I was getting someplace.

Upstate, I drove past Windsor on Route 17, and all the way through Binghamton to the little town of Apalachin, ten miles or so west of Binghamton. A teenage girl in a gas station directed me to McFall Road, which came to an end in the hills above the town; Box 57 was near the dead end. This was another modest mansion, built like Lindbergh's of stone, but more recent, one story—maybe forties or fifties, when some California influence started washing back east.

A mansion like this, for George and Louise? It sat on a slight rise up behind carefully trimmed hedges. Planted discreetly next to the driveway was a For Sale sign: M. S. "MIKE" LYNCH, REAL-TOR. On today's market, this was a five- or six-hundred-thousand-dollar house. I wrote down the realtor's number and drove back to town.

A woman at the real estate office made arrangements for the caretaker to show me the place. This caretaker was a short, dumpy man—his wife wasn't home—and well into his sixties, with what I took to be a smug, doughy smile, though it may have been due to shyness, or maybe shy impatience, since he never looked di-rectly at me. He looked across a room, or out over the valley, smiled and spoke in a high pitch strangely like that of a brash young girl. He finished every sentence with an upward inflec-tion—as if to say, *I told you so*—and didn't introduce himself.

The caretaker's cottage, tucked in amongst some trees behind the house, was the size of tract homes in Highland. He made it clear to me that he and his wife came with the place if I bought it—rent-free. They'd been here for almost twenty-five years. Touring the house, I was admiring the slate floors—going overboard really, bending down to touch them, oohing and aahing —as well as the view from the French doors in the forty-foot family room, while trying to fathom how George and Louise could ever have afforded such a place. They weren't the types; subsistence farmers. Then it struck me that twenty-five years is a long time, and maybe this caretaker knew who they were.

"Yes, they were here before me. They were here for the raid."

What raid?

He lifted both eyebrows, looked out across the hills—we were standing on the front patio—and acted thoroughly amused that here I was touring this house and didn't know it was the site of the Famous Raid. So he filled me in.

On November 14, 1957, sixty-five of the top figures in the American and Cuban mafia gathered here for a meeting; the house was owned by Joseph M. Barbara, Sr. Vito Genovese came, as well as Carlo Gambino, Russell A. Buffalino, Joseph Profaci, and plenty of others. I thought this was heady company for George and Louise Lockwood, and failed to understand how they could have lived here if Joseph Barbara owned the house, when something the caretaker said—something about George and Louise watching from the trees, and later answering reporters' questions—made me realize they were the caretakers then.

And as he described this comic raid—it looked like a Keystone Cops movie, he said—I remembered reading about it back then in the papers, the famous Apalachin Gangland Convention, the first living proof that crime was not just crime, but a conspiracy. It was organized. They had meetings! When the caravan of state police arrived, the meeting broke up, the guests scattered, some ran into the woods—he gestured—but they didn't get far with their fancy shoes, their hats and coats snagging on trees, their diamond-studded belt buckles and gold wrist watches weighing them down. The caretaker chuckled. He was laughing at this picture, but also laughing at me, I could tell, for being so ignorant as not to have realized I'd been walking through History.

They threw them all in jail overnight, but couldn't find anything to charge them with—not even illegal parking—so had to let them go the next day. But by then it was international news.

But George and Louise? They worked here then? Driving back down McFall Road, I turned this over and over in my mind, until I felt the cargo there shifting. My head actually began to tilt, and I pulled over to suck on my pipe. As I was lighting it I saw the flame shaking a little at its base, then glanced up at the rearview mirror while smoke filled the car, and noticed a little Nissan pick-up truck creeping down the road behind me. It was the caretaker driving past, smiling. If he saw me, he didn't look over, but then again that was his way. He was like a gun sight one adjusts for by aiming ten feet left or right of the target.

Where was he going? To report on me? In my worked-up state, I actually thought this might be so. I felt I'd been climbing some rotten shale, and any minute it might begin to slide.

Things in my mind started growing. I once read of a ship whose cargo of beans got wet and sprouted, bursting the hold. Or a root cellar: all those pale tendrils searching for light, finding cracks and niches wherever they could. That's how my brain felt. I saw things I'd seen before, only now they were different. I was peeking through cracks in the barn in Windsor, but what I saw now were zombie versions of earlier memories, more decayed, more rubbery, unstable and sinister. They were half-dead bodies sprouting fungi-like growths, come to parasitic life with roots and sprouts and colorless flowers. They also looked like things you couldn't kill.

For example, it wasn't his *thumb* which Johnny stuck in a calf's mouth, in the barn, I now remembered.

Also, I saw him taking his luggage out of the Packard in the barn, and in the trunk was a pile of bloody sheets. I watched through cracks in a cow stall, frightened. If he was just now taking out his luggage, this had to be *before* hunting season, since he always arrived the weekend of opening Monday.

And later on, wasn't he burying something behind the barn? Or this could have been the time of the butchered cow. Except, it wasn't a cow this time, it was a horse. He'd killed a horse for sport and butchered it.

Nothing was right, I couldn't be sure.

We ate horsemeat. Louise cursed and swore. George was mean to animals. Our dogs had mange and were underfed and wormy. George and Louise never went to church. They beat me, I cried—I could see it so clearly! They beat me with a leather strap, an old bridle. Louise walked around like a man and she smoked. They made book with their new phone all that summer Johnny lived with us.

One of our dogs dragged his ass in the driveway, his worms were so bad. He went around in circles. The house smelled bad winters.

I turned on the radio to clear my head, then stepped out of the car and walked downhill, while behind me George Jones sang of growing old. I walked past a swamp, alive with frogs among the discarded tires. Little friendly gnats flew around my eyes.

Somewhere deep below memory something stirred its head and the bottom grew cloudy. I saw cliffs and banks I'd thought were solid dropping like pieces of cake in the water, while some profound dislocation underneath the water began boiling—I couldn't see much on the surface, but knew it was there, underneath.

Then I thought of entrails, all the entrails in the world.

Beyond the swamp was an apple orchard, but most of the trees were dead. Up ahead was a house with gingerbread trim and gray clapboard siding unpainted for a century. A dog loped out to the middle of the road looking down at the pavement, then lifted his head and barked with effort. He was an old dog. Like the caretaker, he wouldn't look at me, but I knew by the time I got there he'd be very annoyed, what with all that barking, so I turned and walked back to the car.

Down through Apalachin and back onto Route 17, then east through Binghamton, anticipating all the way—fighting it too—the urge to turn off at Windsor. Don't do it, Coop! Actually, I turned off long before Windsor, onto Route 11 outside of Binghamton, then up into the hills on Trim Street. The back way.

I turned on Ballyhock Road and drove past the house. It looked empty. No car in the driveway. I stopped on the road and looked back from maybe a half or quarter mile away. It sat in the late afternoon sun completely still like it *knew* it would be there after I died.

I thought of Bernice inside and all her knickknacks, but the knickknacks for some reason were in chaos. They were melting or boiling, or smashed all to pieces. Nothing was the same. Just inside the cellar entrance was a hole where Louise used to put the cat, to crawl around in the walls and catch mice. But one winter the house began to stink; the cat had gotten stuck in there somewhere. All winter long she rotted in the walls.

Of course, there was the septic smell too, but that came later. I pictured Bernice surrounded by smells. There were smells that clung to you, stewed you, in fact. When George peeked in the bathroom one time and saw me jerking off he made me sleep in the manure wagon behind the barn for punishment, and I smelled of that wagon for days—weeks!—afterward.

I remembered his face at the window like an apparition just above Louise's new washing machine; lifted eyebrows and round, startled mouth. "I got wet," he said when he barged in the door moments later and grabbed me by the neck—I'd quickly zipped up—and I never learned if this was a crude joke about my observed activity, or a reference to the washing machine, which was on at the time, and which drained directly outside through the window to the ground.

I shook my head and drove down to Route 79 and back onto 17. During the three-hour trip to Highland I tried my best to think of nothing. I felt drained, dried out. A sound went off in my brain like a gunshot, followed by its singing echo down miles of neural wires. I assumed this was cells blowing out. Memory fuses.

Two days later Bernice phoned me in Highland and sounded herself. Not normal; Bernice. She phoned to tell me Cleo Dannen had died. Funeral would be at the nursing home chapel, Our Lady of Mercy in the Bronx. Bernice said she intended to go, but then she didn't show up. For me, there was no hesitation. I'd grown up thinking Cleo Dannen was my mother, then that she'd died long ago, so I thought I'd better not miss a second chance to be at her funeral. Her son, or the man who'd said he was her son, glared at me through the whole Mass. Besides us, six nuns attended, and a handful of residents—all women—in housecoats.

Back at home I found a letter waiting whose address, printed out shakily in thin, bleak letters, made me think at first it was from Cleo. This was something I'd fantasized before; someone dies and a letter comes to *me,* their last words on earth. From the grave (it seemed) they would say something to the effect that I was the person most important in their life. They mailed it while alive, but I received it after they died, and in that arc or bridge was a message over and above what the words themselves said: *You are the chosen one.*

Of course, the words were important too. In the case of Cleo, I expected an explanation. Of everything. Language from the dead to clarify my origins and chase away shadows, then I could live at last free of ambiguities.

But it wasn't from Cleo. It was from my stepson, David; he was writing to announce that Valerie had given birth to a baby boy, Charles the Second. They named him after me!

A baby? They'd only known each other since April, and now it was October. Could David count, or did he realize this child wasn't his? Unless it was a preemie. Maybe Valerie had told him it wasn't his and he'd married her partly from charitable impulses. She was pregnant when she met him and her boyfriend had abandoned her, let's say. That David could be charitable wasn't out of the question. In his letter he announced a little moral revolution: he'd given up drinking and smoking, sold the trail bike, and bought an old Chevy. They were living in a trailer park, everyone lives in trailer parks in Florida. He signed the letter David Cooper, and Valerie added a note signed Valerie Cooper, so I was in it now. I was really a grandfather. At home, he'd always gone by his father's name, Spencer. David Spencer.

Then I realized that his young wife thought *I* was David's real father. And neither of them knew—or did they?—that I'd been her mother's lover. As for her mother's kinship with me, I prayed that Bernice hadn't told her daughter. There's plenty of things people don't tell each other, aren't there, Coop? And aren't they better left that way? Like a callus or healing wound, the skin grows over that ignorance, locking it in. You need another wound just to get to it.

When Helga came home she gushed over David's baby, which they'd phoned her about; she was genuinely happy. She wanted to go to Florida and help, but felt she might be in the way, so we phoned her brother Theon and sister Rika to scout the terrain. They needed some help, in Rika's opinion, Valerie did. Helga decided to fly to Orlando and stay with Theon for a week, while just more or less showing up at David's and Valerie's to see what she could do. She could visit her father as well while she was there.

From Orlando she phoned and marveled at Charles the Second, at his likeness to David, especially David's father. She liked Valerie too, and it seemed that Valerie hadn't mentioned that we—Valerie and I—had met. I still hadn't told Helga about Bernice, and frankly didn't want to. I felt the pressing need to keep them apart. So I wrote to Valerie and asked her not to reveal that I knew her mother, and while I was at it enclosed a check for a thousand dollars for her and David, my combined wedding and baby gift.

Things were slowing down. I began to feel numb. I remembered when, at the age of twenty-one, I'd first begun receiving my eight hundred dollars a month in the mail—actually, it was five hundred and something then. I just took it for granted. It was payment for someone who'd gone through the youth I'd gone through. At the age of twenty-one I didn't care who I was or where I'd come from, questions like that didn't interest me. I knew who my mother and father were—though my father was just a photograph on a dresser—and all I wanted to do was forget them. In my opinion, this was a solid foundation for a firm sense of identity.

Now I felt that I could be anyone. At the age of fifty-five I was free of everything, except uncertainty. I felt myself dragging this freedom around like a suitcase full of useless objects. Who was that beautiful woman, my mother, the one I'd envisioned beside Cleo Dannen's hospital bed? Carefully, I picked over the shards. Gangsters were connected with the Lindbergh kidnapping. This, to be sure, was uncertain, but did it have anything to do with George and Louise? Who was Johnny? Perhaps he was the kidnapper. At first this seemed ridiculous; nevertheless, like everything else, it had to be carefully analyzed. More closely scrutinized, it might yield up some meaning.

I flipped through my notebook, which I carried everywhere now, but found much of it indecipherable. Something about a bow tie. In shaky cursive—I must have been driving the car and writing simultaneously—was a mention of my fear of flying. I flew if I had to but needed three or four drinks, which helped, but also made me contemplate doing crazy things, like jumping up while strapped in my seat to apologize for my precipitate behavior.

How could I be related to Charles Lindbergh if I was afraid of flying?

I jotted this question down in the notebook, then remembered that Lindbergh was an engineer. An inventor! Since I'd invented things as well, this could very well be a connection, so I wrote it down, then closed the notebook, tapping it with my finger.

Over the next few days, when I wasn't rushing around, phoning James Faber or this person or that, or looking through books or jotting down notes or scrutinizing every scrap of behavior or detritus thrown up by memory or fantasy, I slept. I just sat there. I felt tired all the time. I watched a lot of TV.

When I dreamed, a disconcerting change took place: I couldn't control the dream, as I'd been able to in the past. For example, I dreamed that all my teeth fell out, but I failed at every attempt to put them back in.

Pork Vining came to dinner. Helga was back from Orlando, but staying in the city, so it was just Pork and me. I'd bought two bottles of sparkling wine, cheap stuff from California, but we didn't have any of those little cornucopia glasses. We started on the wine before dinner. At least drinking usually made me feel normal. Of course, it raised my blood sugar too, but what else was that but a means to enhance normalcy, like seeing everything upside down, or having X-ray vision and seeing people in their underwear? Nothing could be more banal. Drinking released demons you found out later were really grocers or stockbrokers.

All this occurred to me in a flash of stupor, and I began to grow passive. Maybe it was everything I'd been going through in the past few weeks, but the first bottle of wine, instead of picking me up, was thickening my mental exhaustion, so I left the other one corked and made some jasmine tea. We were eating Chinese tonight, in the kitchen, where Pork could watch me cook.

We ate as I cooked; ate a course, then I cooked another. Shredded beef Szechuan style, bamboo shoots and mushrooms, chicken with nuts. Eating, we discovered that we'd each at one time or another had fantasies of opening restaurants, and talked about converting Hudson Valley Consultants to, what? Hudson Valley Cuisine? The Hudson Compote. The Vineyard. The Coop.

I knew Pork liked food. He had the kind of body that absorbed it like a sponge. Everything he ate journeyed right out to his fingers and toes, and he tasted the food in more ways than most people. His nose was larger, his tongue had more surface, his appetite more volume. He had it both ways: food as fuel and food as pleasure, and didn't see any contradiction.

We talked. I was in a confiding mood, and decided I could tell Pork about my long lost illegitimate son showing up. I'd been wanting to tell someone, just to see if it was real. And Pork listened with sympathy and understanding, as I knew he would.

Yet, the telling didn't help. I still felt mentally exhausted. Instead of verifying things, confiding in Pork made me feel all the more cut off. I couldn't, for example, tell him that this son's mother was also my sister, or that the woman I thought was my mother wasn't—that would be too much. Could I tell him I sometimes wondered who the hell *I* was? I wanted to, but couldn't. Yet, the thought that I was holding back part of the story tainted the rest, so that instead of feeling relieved at getting it off my chest, I felt like I'd been lying.

Pork may have noticed this, I don't know. We grew silent; he looked thoughtful, even nervous. He had something on his mind, that was clear. He regarded me with, what? Understanding, pity, curiosity. Good old Pork. He wanted to say something. I noticed the way he handled his chopsticks, with the skill of a native Asian. They were extensions not just of his hand, but of his brain. He saw me looking, he looked too—holding them up for us both to see—then asked if I remembered what he'd broached that night Helga and I came to dinner at his place.

What was that, Pork?

About Vietnam.

I remembered, I perked up. When you find out a friend was a POW, you want to know the worst, of course. Talk about tainted! We all cast shadows, but here was a long one. At least, that's what I thought before hearing Pork's story. I had the usual suspicion about POWs: if they survived, they must have done something wrong. Subtly, I found myself adjusting my perception of Pork to account for the scars. If he'd been a good POW—

whatever *that* meant—he wouldn't be here now talking about it, would he?

Unless he'd paid an awful price.

He claimed he was the stubbornest POW they'd ever had, at least for the first few months. He knew all about the Geneva Convention—name, rank, serial number and date of birth—and knew the North Vietnamese didn't recognize it, because the Americans weren't soldiers but criminals. So he decided just to keep silent. Not to say anything. When questioned he stood at attention with his mouth closed, and they pried it open and mimed cutting out his tongue—they would serve it for a meal—but still he said nothing. And since he was keeping silent anyway—not opening his mouth—he threw away the little food they gave him, for the first few days at least, until he couldn't stand it anymore.

Pork told me this as I cooked, as we ate, and I listened with growing interest. For the first time in weeks, it seemed, I had something besides my own problems to think about. He was hit near Haiphong in an F-4 Phantom jet and sort of limped south along the coast almost a hundred miles before he went into a spin and ejected. He landed in some hills above a rice paddy, and managed to spend the night in the woods before they found him next day.

Both his arms were broken.

They force-marched him north. He refused to answer questions. He'd lost his dog tags, or someone had taken them, Pork wasn't sure. At a camp along the way, when he decided at last to eat, he couldn't lift anything to his mouth with those swollen, painful arms, so he had to eat kneeling with his face in the bowl. He couldn't lift his arms above his waist and could hardly bend them, but they hurt even more hanging by his side, so he improvised slings from his shirt, but his captors ripped them off. He refused to tell them his arms were broken, but they must have seen it from the swelling.

They stayed in one village for a week, and a man came to interrogate Pork. He stood at attention, stared straight ahead with his swollen arms sort of turned in and hanging in front of him, like an ape, and said nothing.

"So they put me in a pit about three feet high with a lid on it. I couldn't stand up, couldn't move around. One thing, sitting sort of curved like that I was able to rest my arms, so that helped. The bugs, the leeches, ants, spiders, things I couldn't see, they were crawling all over me, but I couldn't pick them off. I had to rub against the walls of the pit if I could, but my belly and chest I couldn't. My face.

"I was in there about a week. At first I tried to shit and piss in a little spot where I wasn't sitting, but after a while why bother? They didn't feed me but I still kept on having to go to the bathroom, so I just did it in my pants. When they let me out I felt like a zombie, a skunk, I was covered with my own excrement. Nobody came near me I stunk so much of earth and shit. Excuse me, Coop, great meal, I hope I'm not making you sick. You want me to stop, just say so."

"No, that's okay, Pork." We were sipping tea, on our second pot, before the last course. Pork held his cup in both hands, slurping politely. One thing he didn't do was nod. He didn't move his body very much at all. He spoke in a kind of earnest monotone, watching my reaction; uneasy, but controlled. I could sense he'd told this story before, but not very often. Only to certain people. And slowly it dawned on me that I'd have to spill out everything myself when he was finished, all the things that had happened to me in the last eight months. I couldn't very well hold back anything after this.

"So the week in that pit, I think what it did, it really popped something in the back of my head. I had to piss after that, I did it right in my pants. I ate like a pig, food all over. They had to teach me how to go to the bathroom again. How to take care of myself.

"It took us almost a month to get to Hanoi, because we kept making stops. I think they had to find out what to do with me. Not too many pilots were captured in that area. They put me in the Hanoi Hilton, Hoa Lo. They put me in the stocks because I wouldn't answer questions. Then they put me in solitary on bread and water. I used to run around and around the room as fast as I could, then fall asleep. By this time my arms were mostly healed, but they stuck out funny. I had to have them broken and reset at the VA hospital when I got back to the States. They operated and took out all these calcium deposits. I still can't bend either one of them all the way up." He demonstrated with a motion like a weightlifter doing a curl.

"So finally I decided to answer their questions, but what I did was give them phony information. I made up a name, Henry Nelson, I said I was from California, I was twenty-three years old. They said what village in California? Somehow they figured out I was lying, so they threw me in solitary, this time it was dark solitary. The place was completely boarded up. The problem was, here I had made up all this phony information and now I decided I better stick with it, so I tried to imagine in every detail the life in California of this Henry Nelson. His family history, his schooling, friends, financial class, tastes, opinions, abilities, everything. I figured they'd try to trip me up somehow, so I had to have an airtight story. Besides, it was a kind of mental exercise. It occupied the time.

"Problem was, in that dark cell—I couldn't even tell which was day and night—I felt like, like I don't know, Coop. Like I lost the outline to my personality, like I could *become* this Henry Nelson. It would be very easy. I began to get confused as to who was Henry and who was Pork. It scared me shitless, tell you the truth. The more I thought about it. I felt I had to stick with Henry, I had to be consistent, but I didn't want to lose Pork either, you know? So I had to make a kind of dividing line. Henry Nelson over here, Pork Vining over here. It was actually like I cut the cell in half, and saved the back part for Pork. That's where I went to be Pork. But if they took me out to question me, once I crossed over to the front of the cell and beyond that, outside, I was Henry, and I had all the facts of Henry's life. Back in the cell, I could cross back to Pork. I could withdraw sort of into myself, and curl up and be Pork in the privacy of myself.

"But it wasn't easy. I thought I was losing parts of myself, losing essential knowledge about me. I mean, the real me. When I was on the Pork side, I had to forget all about Henry, and vice versa on the Henry side. I got to be so good at keeping the two people separate, if I accidentally walked to the front of the cell, I'd just flip over to Henry. Like if I went to get my food and forgot about the dividing line, even if I wasn't prepared, *snap*, I was Henry. I ate as Henry and digested as Pork.

"But who was Pork? That was the real problem. I found I was *forgetting* things about myself. In that perpetual darkness, it was like your mind just opened up like a spigot and ran out. Henry felt real to me because all the details were fresh, but with Pork, I don't know—I felt like I could have just made him up. Like he was the phony one. It was hard for me to distinguish between my memory and my imagination. Memory was Pork, imagination was Henry, but it really wasn't that simple. For example, after a while, I had to remember all the things I'd made up about Henry, so that was memory too. As for Pork, I decided the important thing was to remember as many details about my life as I could. They had to be *facts*, not just feelings or vague pictures. I needed stubborn facts, hard information, to distinguish them from the things I'd made up. Not just my mother's face or the way I'd felt about her, but the color of her hair, the color of her eyes, her height, her weight. The exact time my father went to work in the morning. I started scratching some of this information on the wall in the back of my cell, but I coded it in case the guards found the scratches. I used letters for numbers and numbers for letters, and put it in a special order so I could feel it with my fingers in the darkness and go over some of the facts of my actual life in order not to lose them. It felt like, you know, the Jews? The wailing wall? Or Catholics with their rosary beads?

"My phone number. The exact number of stairs to the basement of our house—fourteen. All my friends' names and their phone numbers. The distance to downtown Boston from my house. I grew up in West Roxbury, Coop, did I mention that? Close to Boston. I counted the number of windows in our house—twenty-three; the number of doors—seventeen, including the garage door: thirteen interior doors, including linen closets, and four exterior; the number of clapboards from the basement to the roof—seventy-six on the gable end. When I was a kid I used to play a game bouncing a tennis ball on the side of the house onto each clapboard and catching it, going up a clapboard at a time; if I missed one I had to start over. So I knew the number of clapboards exactly.

"From there I went to facts about my bedroom, like the number of things in my closet, the number of toys I had, how many houses I could see from my window, things like that. So I was scratching all this stuff on the wall, getting it down, and something funny happened. I heard someone else scratching. I knew it wasn't a rat, this was human. Only problem was it came from the *front* of the cell. For a day or two, or whatever they were—I couldn't tell night from day in that darkness—I tried to ignore this, but I'm good at codes, Coop. I could see this had a pattern to it, the scratching I heard. It wasn't Morse code, it was something else simpler, like A was one scratch, B was two, and so forth, but after five scratches it went into combinations—you had to visualize a grid with lines of five letters each, so after E you had F, which was two scratches, pause, one scratch, G was two scratches, pause, two scratches, and so forth. I figured this out with one side of my head while with the other I was scratching the facts of my life on the wall. After a while, naturally I could understand what these scratches were saying. Very patient, one or two simple messages, like 'Hello. Who are you?' He scratched out his name. 'I am Captain Robert Messina.' There's lots of suspense in this kind of communication, Coop. I mean, you're sitting there waiting for the next letter, Jesus. You feel like screaming, *Out with it, man!*

"Finally, I had to answer this guy, or I thought I'd go nuts. The scratching was coming from the front of the cell, so I went up there to scratch back—I already had the code down—but naturally up there I wasn't Pork anymore, I was Henry Nelson. So we talked back and forth. Henry Nelson and Robert Messina. He told me about himself and I told him about myself, that is, about Henry Nelson. Actually, after a while I was burning to see this guy, or Henry Nelson was. I tried to picture his face, his build, the color of his hair, and so forth. I tried to imagine the facts of his life, to fill in the blanks of what he told me. Then finally they decided to let me out of solitary. I don't know how long I'd been in there. It could have been a month, it could have been five months. I had a little crisis here, because when I wasn't talking with Robert Messina I went back in the back of the cell to be Pork Vining. Now when they said they were going to let me out, I panicked. I didn't know if they planned to move me to a new cell or what. I couldn't leave Pork behind, my dividing line, but I had to stick with Henry too. No matter what they decided or discovered, I was Henry Nelson to my captors, my sanity depended on that. But I wanted to be able to be Pork to myself. And they said they would let me out the next day. The guard that brought my food said that.

"I decided the solution was to take the cell with me. I'd already thought about this before anyway, how inside that little place after a while I felt it actually made more sense to think of it as being inside me. You beat them, you outwitted your captors, by moving your prison cell into your mind. It wasn't very difficult at all to realize that this little physical space was actually contained within me, that is, inside the cave of my brain, inside what I could smell and taste and hear and feel. So it was just a small step to take it with me.

"So with this cell in my brain I could mentally move from Pork in the back of my mind to Henry in the front. This gave me a tremendous feeling of freedom and power. It was like I had a secret I could withhold, like when mad people have a secret they choose not to share with the rest of the world, which is that they're mad. They grew up mad, went to high school mad, to college mad, raised a family mad, but they guarded the secret so carefully no one could guess. That's what it felt like. I could inwardly laugh at my captors. *They didn't know!* I was like an imposter who's so good at what he does no one ever guesses. He fakes being a doctor or professor, he does it all his life, and no one ever guesses. A mad person tells himself he's capable at lunch of plunging a steak knife right into his best friend's heart—if only he knew—but he doesn't do it. But the inner joy, Coop, the satisfaction! You're playing a trick on them all!

"I forgot to mention, there was a bad period of transition in there. When they let me out of solitary my eyes were so used to the dark that at first I felt blinded. Like I had nails in my eyes. The worst thing was, I found out they'd let me out at *night.* They might have even done this out of compassion, the bastards, I don't know. When morning came I was *really* blinded; I couldn't see at all. Anyway, little by little I adjusted, I got my eyesight back. After one or two days I could see okay, and then I felt better. I felt pretty damn good actually, for somebody who went through the things that I did. The amazing thing was that I managed to get out of there with my sanity intact. I ascribe this to my decision to keep these two people separate, Pork and Henry. It was a matter of discretion. Discrete means separate; they didn't touch. This way I felt confident, in control. No one knew my secret. The North Vietnamese interrogated me, and I ticked off the facts of Henry Nelson's existence with ease. I even smiled at them. I felt pretty smug because in the back of my mind, the back of my cell, I had Pork Vining whole now; I had the facts of his life in place, they wouldn't fall out, and I could go there whenever I wanted. Only trouble was, in order to maintain consistency I had to tell the other POWs I was Henry Nelson too. It wasn't that I didn't trust them, just that most of the time if they let us talk there were guards around. So I had to tell them I was Henry, and I figured I could do that and then maybe later on, when it was safe, or maybe when the war was over, I could let them in on the secret, and they could have a good laugh with me about it too. I pictured us sitting around drinking beer someplace laughing uncontrollably about the trick I'd played. It was really hysterical!

"I met Robert Messina. Completely different from the way I pictured him, of course. This tall bony guy, very emaciated, sort of like Jimmy Stewart he looked like, but his face was more stark. We became pretty good friends. The North Vietnamese were going through a period of leniency at this time. They moved us to another prison, some of us. Son Tay, further from Hanoi, not as maximum security. Moved about five or six of us, including Bob Messina. They even—we could work in the fields out there, which to me was heaven after two years inside. Don't get me wrong, this was no country club. We still had the flying cockroaches in our cells, two inches long. Rats came up the drain holes. Spiders, mice, lizards, mosquitoes. Fucked-up weather all the time. Everyone had lice. They put men in the stocks. They didn't feed us very much, and everybody had lost thirty or forty pounds. The ones that survived stayed about there—thirty or forty pounds underweight—the ones that died kept on losing weight. It was common, if you grew too sick you died. Dysentery, edema, pneumonia. In the first six months at this camp, three men died.

"Anyway, Bob Messina decided to escape. I thought he was crazy, but he was stubborn. He thought now that we were out of Hanoi he had a reasonable chance of making it to the South, to South Vietnam, and finding the American lines. As far as I know, not one American ever succeeded in escaping from a POW camp in North Vietnam, but maybe I'm wrong. There was this tool shed where we worked in the fields, and Bob was in charge of the tools, so he started scratching a little pit in there a little at a time under some boards, and figured if he had about an hour he could dig a hole big enough to hide inside, then take off at night. I guess this part of it worked. Anyway, I never saw him again. Day before he did it I gave him my ring, sapphire ring, this one"—Pork held up his left hand—"and I told him my secret, even though he looked at me kind of funny, and I asked him if he made it to get this ring to somebody. That way they could get it to my family and they'd know I was alive.

"So he did it. When they discovered he was gone the guards made all sorts of noise, they locked us in our cells, didn't let us talk. This one guard that knew a little English said to me, 'Very stupid,' meaning Bob; he pointed at his own head, like a gun. Later on he was one of the guards that went out searching. Jesus, Coop, where'd you get that?"

"I made it." While Pork was talking I'd brought out the Bavarian cheesecake. Not exactly Chinese; but we'd already decided our restaurant would be eclectic. "In this story, Pork, is there anything else to turn someone's stomach? You're through with the gory touches, I take it?"

Pork stared at me, a little disgusted, but spoke calmly. "There is one thing, Coop, a little detail. You might want to wait." So we sat there with the cheesecake in the middle of the table while Pork finished his story. I cleared off the dishes, but left our glasses and the second bottle of wine for after dessert. Meanwhile, I was wondering if I could make as much sense of my own muddle as Pork made of his. I admired his control, his logic, his will. He was a little nervous, to be sure—his hands even shook—but none of this did he even bother to acknowledge.

"Anyway, a number of things happened after that. For one thing, I had to drop my disguise because one of my flight commanders was captured and brought to Son Tay, Major Winston Oaks, and of course he started calling me Pork, even though I winked and gritted my jaw and shook my head at him on the sly at first. He didn't get the hint. So, I had to tell the others. I think they were taken aback at first, but what the hell, Coop, in this situation—they knew it wasn't exactly the real world. Only thing about it real is you might wind up dead. You don't know what it's like. After a while the most important thing isn't hope or winning the war, or escaping, it's food. Stealing a little extra rice if you can. Learning what kind of beetles taste good.

"The guards caught on too. They figured out I wasn't Henry

Nelson. This had been 'seventy-two or 'seventy-three they would have thought I was someone important to lie like that, and they probably would have interrogated and tortured me to get at the truth. But it was 1975 and the war was almost over, so I don't think they really cared a lot. The one guard I told you about that knew English was the only one who cared. I could tell he knew something, he was curious about something, the way he watched me and smiled. He asked me things like, 'Where is Henry Nelson? What have you done with Captain Nelson?' It was weird, like he could read my mind, like he *knew* what was going on inside my head.

"Then one day I noticed his hand. I don't know how long it had been there. It could have been weeks, I don't know. My ring was on his thumb, the one I gave Bob Messina. I asked him what happened to Bob, and he smiled. 'What happened to Captain Nelson?' he asked. I told him I wanted my ring back, and he said it wasn't my ring, it was Captain Nelson's. If you see Captain Nelson, he said—and the bastard grinned—tell him I have his ring.

"Coop, I can't tell you, it was awful. I can't tell you how depressing this was. It was bad enough having to give up my secret, but to have it thrown in my face like this was worse than breaking my arms or being in that pit, which just happens to your body. Worse than the stocks. This guard—we called him Ho—I felt he could see through my mind, like he knew everything I'd been going through for the past three years, he knew exactly the strategies I'd devised, the lies I'd told, the mental exercises, whatever, everything I'd done just to preserve a little bit of sanity in that hell hole. I felt like after that effort, after all that effort, I didn't have any secrets left, and this man, this little Vietnamese man could just drive me crazy just by looking at me. Christ. He was around all the time. I noticed he held his hand up a lot, or stood with his hand on that side out toward me, the one with the ring. He made sure I saw it every day, nine hundred times a day.

"Actually, nothing much happened after that, until we were

released. We all knew it was coming, but while the other POWs, their spirits were rising, mine were at their lowest ebb. Early on—I was in captivity for four years, Coop—early on I learned how to cope, I was healthy in mind and body, as healthy as I could be, while all around me was despair. It's because there were two of me, you might say. But now it was the opposite; I felt defeated, crushed. I even started losing weight—while the rest of the men, it was like—"

All at once the phone rang and I jumped. Then we both just sat there, in a spell. At last Pork picked it up—it was right behind him, on the wall. "It's Helga, Coop."

"What's she want?" I stood up to take the phone.

"Oh Coop."

"Helga, what's wrong?"

"Coop, forgive me."

"What's happening, Helga? Where are you?"

"Coop, Coop."

"Honey, what's the matter?"

"Coop," she said. Then she must have hung up because the line went dead. I replaced the phone.

"That was Helga," I told Pork, shrugging uncomfortably. We sat there and looked at each other, but I avoided his eyes. I stared at the nose. Something all over the world was wrong, I could tell—some rising infection or disease. Even Helga had caught it, though by now I began to wonder whether she'd even called, whether I hadn't dreamed it. Staring at Pork, I questioned him mentally—was that phone call real, or what? But what I said out loud was, "Cheesecake?"

"No thanks." He turned away. I pulled out my pipe, filled it and lit up.

"So what happened?" I finally asked. Pork's big hands were resting on the table, and I glanced at the sapphire ring. "You got the ring back, right?" Pork looked down at it too.

"Affirmative, I got the ring back. The war ended and he gave it back to me. In a little envelope. 'For Captain Henry Nelson,' he said, pressing it into my hand." Suddenly Pork stood up. "You can guess what was in the envelope, Coop."

"The ring."

"That and something else." Pork was dragging himself around the room, looking for his coat, eyes darting everywhere.

"Pork, don't leave."

He stopped and regarded me, his big face hanging in the air. "What was in the envelope, Coop? You're good at guessing. You can figure things out."

I thought I knew, but didn't want to say. "A message?"

"No."

"Dog tags?"

"His finger. Bob Messina's finger. We can safely assume it was his," said Pork.

I noticed all the smoke in the kitchen, from my pipe. Pork's coat was in his hand, he was walking toward the door. "Stick around, Pork. There's another bottle. Let's talk more. I want to tell you something. Something I need your opinion on, Pork."

He shot one mournful look at me, full of speechless appeal, then pulled on his coat without a word, opened the door, and left.

PART III

11

Ms. Helga Cooper
Room 211, Union Hotel
826 Tenth Avenue
N.Y.C.

Dear Ms. Cooper,

As per our agreement of 8/12/85, NYC Welfare Agency, Inc., agrees to lease the Union Hotel for a period of not less than two years commencing 9/1/85. The yearly fee shall be $240,000, payment in quarterly sums, to wit, $60,000 on 9/1/85, $60,000 on 12/1/85, $60,000 on 3/1/86, and $60,-000 on 6/1/86, seriatim through 6/1/87. Enclosed find our contract. As we discussed, lessee agrees to transfer management of the property to NYC Welfare Agency, Inc., upon commencement of leasing period.

It was a lovely dinner, for which we all thank you warmly. Shall we see you again before you leave for Florida? Do keep us posted on the Schaeffer property.

As ever,
Charles Lyndhurst, Jr.

I regarded this letter with a species of horror and morbid curiosity I hadn't experienced since coming upon a geek at a carnival on my ninth birthday. Helga and Charles Lyndhurst, Jr.? They had a business relationship, it appeared. Did he know she was my wife? Did they talk about me?

I was in Helga's room at the Union Hotel in the city, but where was Helga? She hadn't been home to Highland in more than a week. She wasn't in Florida; I'd phoned them all there. This room, whose existence I'd been completely unaware of, had been revealed to me by Helga's cousin Woody—he even gave me the key—but I'd been here two days, and no Helga.

Signs of Helga, yes. Correspondence, such as the letter from Charles Lyndhurst, Jr., which I'd just read for the two hundredth time. I was tired of reading it. No contract inside; that was undoubtedly filed away in one of Helga's caches, a deposit box, an office somewhere. She had fifty lives, all of them missing. I tore the letter into little shreds and let them drift to the floor.

This room was a haven in a neighborhood and building I would never have imagined Helga venturing near. She'd apparently constructed for herself a way of walling all that out: fresh paint, a decent bed, and various useful items of furniture such as a bookcase, easy chairs, a writing table, even pictures on the wall, old oils and watercolors. Did the other rooms here look the same, or was this Helga's alone, her private hideaway? On the whole, the place was not promising. Its hallways made you want to crawl through them, and the one elevator smelled of events that occur after death.

But this room was cozy. Clothes in the closet. Some pots and pans in the kitchenette, which made a little cubbyhole in a corner. Funny things as well. Brass fittings and couplings, a ship's compass, lots of paperweights (but little paper), some model ships—one ship in a bottle—flea market stuff. It could be that Helga bought these things in the city and sold them in Highland or Newburgh on consignment, but there was junk here also. In one corner on the floor sat an old watering can with some hoses sticking out. Some jars with rubber tubes and stoppers and spools of thread; a kind of spindle with kite string on it, attached to something that resembled a meat rack. All these objects looked poised. They watched me carefully, waiting for Helga. I'd decided just that morning that the things around me were mainly the outer limit of my attention, but they appeared to resist this notion.

The room had the atmosphere of a secondhand store.

Actually, everything was arranged very neatly. Most of the things were laid out on the floor against the far wall, although some sat on dressers and bookcases, even chairs. This was a tidy little efficiency apartment, tucked away in a Welfare hotel. It was green. One double bed. I assumed this was where she always stayed when she came to the city, so she couldn't be in the city now—could she? Woody didn't know; he shared my concern. Since the phone call the night Pork came to dinner I hadn't heard a peep from Helga. Twice in this room the phone had rung and I'd answered it, but the other end had hung up.

And what did her phone call that night *mean?* It frightened me to think of, but I also felt annoyed. When I remembered her voice, analyzed it carefully, she appeared to be apologizing for something, but what? For disappearing like this? She was begging forgiveness in advance. Maybe she ran off with a ski instructor, or an airplane pilot.

In this room of Helga's I'd found no food at all in the cupboards, and one cup of yogurt in the tiny refrigerator. Helga undoubtedly preferred eating out.

I poured myself some bourbon, sat on the edge of the bed, and imagined feelings of frustration and anger. I was trying them out. The room had one window looking out onto Tenth Avenue— which I preferred not to see—and another frosted window in the bathroom which opened to an air shaft.

I did a flow chart in my mind. Helga was missing, yes or no? A, yes, she was missing. B, she wasn't *missing* (in the wide sense), she'd been kidnapped. Yes or no? Yes, halt. No, back to A, she was missing, on to C, she ran away. One, she ran away with all sorts of illicit money from fishy real estate deals. Two, she found out Charles Lyndhurst was my son, and ran away in disgust. Three, Bernice had contacted her. Three-A, she learned that David's baby wasn't his. Four, mobsters—they'd scared her away. They were trying to get to me because I was Lindbergh's son.

But why would they care whose son I was? None of the above, I hissed out loud. Back to A, she was missing, on to D, she was dead, halt.

Good work, Coop. You really figured it out.

I stood up and kicked a chair across the room, but immediately regretted my rashness. In order to preserve my self-control and deal with these problems rationally, I'd decided that no one should know I was in that room. I checked the towels I'd already stuffed beneath the door. I'd seen some seedy characters in this hotel, but of course they were all on Welfare. My preference would have been not to walk down the hallways, but to use the fire escape, or lower myself by sheets down the air shaft, which must have possessed an exit at the bottom. They did, didn't they, air shafts? At least *buildings* should be fair!

It could very well have been that someone had followed me here. The little pockmarks in the sidewalk and the singing hisses everywhere—like gamma rays or frozen wires—could have been muffled gunshots. I wadded up some Kleenex from a box on Helga's writing table and stuffed it in the keyhole of the door. The window was another problem. Once, on my knees, I'd peeked out. Across the street were some ambiguous-looking warehouses with corrugated overhead doors, and a Korean or Chinese grocery on the corner. Buses behind a chain-link fence. The wind blew hard, and trash filled the air. There weren't too many people, but I knew what was out there—the city—and wanted no part of it.

Now I found some blankets on a shelf in the closet, and pulled one down, only to release a shower of moth flakes and moth balls and to set off little squealing voices in my ears. In that shallow closet—Helga's clothes were all at diagonals as though in a chorus line—I shook out the blanket, half opened, and carried it to the window, careful to approach from the side, against the wall.

A little green box hung on the far wall, out of which one could pull a cord and attach it to a hook across the room. A clothesline. I'd found clothespins in a small boat-shaped basket in the kitchen, and with these fastened the blanket to the curtain rod over the window. Of course, the window already had curtains, but they were flimsy, and the shade was missing.

Then, cursing under my breath, I swept the letter I'd torn up into an old dustpan with a long wire handle. This was a dustpan from the thirties or forties with a green sheet-metal pocket, much like the one Louise had used in Windsor. When I dumped it in the trash, I felt like I'd won a round in a boxing match, though I knew instinctively that the problem with this battle was the harder you fought the more you strengthened the opposition. It was like trying not to sleep—the effort made you more tired.

Then I poured myself more bourbon. Ten High.

It was almost six, and I hadn't eaten all day. But I wasn't very hungry. I hadn't slept much for the last two days either. The room made noises at night, actually—whispers, they sounded like; the distant rustling of dried leaves and twigs—and these effectively prevented me from sleeping while I lay there on Helga's double bed, eyes wide open.

I walked around the room and thought of Helga. Walked very slowly and varied the pattern, in order to demonstrate that I wasn't pacing. If I wasn't pacing, then things weren't too bad. Helga was missing, but she was bound to show up.

There was Bernice in Windsor, Valerie and David in Orlando, also Charles Lyndhurst, Jr., just uptown from here. Pork Vining in Newburgh. Cleo Dannen buried in the Bronx. To all these, my life was connected. If I tried to solve the problem of my origins, or the mystery of Helga's disappearance, the thinking spread out on a network of connections, fibers of kinship and road maps of various important focal points. The Lindbergh estate in Hopewell, for example. The house in Apalachin. So Pork was right—

your brain spread out beyond your skull. Mentally, you could travel for miles. Everything had an answer—it was all mapped out, there were hundreds of connections. All it called for was the right interpretation.

It occurred to me that Helga didn't usually laugh, but when she did she couldn't stop. It was like thinking—the circuits either opened or closed, no in between. This is how a computer operates, in fact; every pathway in the process confronts either an open or closed switch.

And Helga was very much like that. Never in between. Also, she was in control all the time. Even when she laughed uncontrollably, she was in control. It was a laugh free and open, it pooled in her throat, and once she started she couldn't stop, that is, unless she wanted to. Something in it verged on the uncontrollable, it was the closest she ever came to desperation, but there was also something artificial about it, as in much of the laughter we hear. She could *make* herself laugh, though once she did it caught and more or less took over, and then she couldn't stop. It was like when I got angry, in fact.

What *was* Helga hiding, anyway? She had too much equanimity not to be hiding something. She could have been in disguise; someone disguised as Helga.

I sat on the edge of the bed. We didn't make love much anymore—two or three times a month—but when we did she clung to me for dear life, and I felt like a man on a parachute with someone else to save. It didn't feel right; I was shorter than her. She made love like she laughed, with artificial passion that bred its own reality. Very carefully, she lost control, and she always smiled. She liked to kiss.

The way she talked of suicide at Pork's—you'd think she just disappeared into the contemplation of herself.

When all this is over, I thought, when I've got it all figured out, I could take a *real* vacation, say to the Grand Canyon. There I was, fifty-five years old and I'd never been to the Grand Canyon. What kind of American was I?

As I stood up and walked toward the bathroom to pee, I began crying. I couldn't stop it, even while I peed. I'd struck a huge blank space in my thoughts, a chasm, and felt my insides sinking. If Helga was dead, where was she now? *No place,* I said, and immediately responded with a guttural *No!* My heartbeat was taking off, and I shook my head, crying, I actually started to laugh through my tears.

When you're dead you're dead, a voice said. It was mine. Well then, I thought. At least you're not around to regret being dead.

I was washing my hands, and pictured my head smashing against the porcelain sink and the metal fixtures in that little cramped bathroom. I could do that to myself—lower my head and ram it against all those hard surfaces, damage myself horribly—or someone else could do it for me, by way of punishment. You're done for, Coop. I shook my head. Actually, I was beginning to feel a little better. In the mirror I saw I was basically tired—pale as well—and that seemed to account for everything. It was that tired feeling you get when your body takes revenge on you for making it fatigued and coerces you to stay awake. Your heartbeat doubles when you start nodding off.

I dialed Charles Lyndhurst, Jr.

"Hello."

"Hello, son? Charles?"

"Who's this? Dad?" I could hear his voice lift. "Dad, I've been trying to call you all day!"

"Was it anything special, son?" Hint, hint. The real question in my mind was whether he knew that the Helga of his hotel-leasing was my wife. If he didn't, how could I even ask him if he knew where she was? "I haven't been home all day," I said.

"Was it anything special, ha ha, very good, Pop. Anything special is dinner tomorrow. You didn't forget? With Mr. and Mrs. Fisch."

Of course I'd forgotten. I'd blocked it out entirely. "Noon, was it, son? How could I forget? I'm in the city now, in fact. I came down to the city for the weekend, son, to be here tomorrow." I concluded from this conversation that today was Saturday. "Noon you said, wasn't it?"

"Noon, yes noon. You're in the city now?"

"At my hotel." And I held my breath, waiting for him to inquire what hotel that might be. I could risk it, I decided—the Union Hotel, son—but he didn't ask.

"Wonderful, Dad! I knew you'd remember. You have my address?"

"Two Sixty-four West Ninety-first Street."

"Just up from Broadway. I'm in the office, downstairs. Just when you go in the door."

"Fine, son, see you tomorrow."

"Tomorrow," he echoed.

I hung up, lay back on my bed, and lit my pipe. I filled the room with smoke, contemplating with extreme apprehension the task of wading through the city tomorrow to get up to Ninety-first Street. Maybe Sunday morning wouldn't be so bad. *Wouldn't be so bad.* The words floated up in the smoke. I was falling asleep, I knew, and placed the pipe in its ashtray on the bedside table, thus demonstrating what a careful man I was.

I woke up hearing whispers and soft scuffling movements. The room was so dark I couldn't see my hands. Then a wave of fear shot up and licked my heart, carrying me bolt upright in bed: the lights were out, but I hadn't turned them out.

A plate crashed to the floor in the kitchenette. *Who's there?* I said.

Just us, said a whisper.

I thought of roaches and mice, their little scurrying feet. Actually, the strange thing about this place was that I hadn't seen a single cockroach since arriving here. I ascribed this to the lack of food.

A piece of metal clinked. I had the feeling of things falling into place, resuming their postures, as, when you wake up in the morning, the dresser repositions itself beside the window, the piano takes its place across the room, and so forth. Carefully—so as not to step on anything unpleasant—I climbed out of bed and switched on the light. It seemed to catch everything prepared. The brass couplings, ships, bottles, water can, hoses. They stared at me with a quality of feigned innocence. They appeared to be accusing me of not sufficiently appreciating how tedious their existence was. Theirs was a life of utility and service. Actually, I felt envious. They were waiting for their owner to return, tolerating for now this intruder, me. I noticed pieces of broken plate on the floor of the kitchenette, and it occurred to me that this was some sort of protest, as when Buddhist monks immolated themselves during the Vietnam war.

There was an old tea strainer in with all the things against the far wall, insolently lying at a diagonal between a jar filled with rubber stoppers and the watering can. From somewhere, it seemed—from far away, yet still in this room—came hoarse laughter, a low hissing sound. Then I realized this was the radiator: it knocked and hissed beneath the window I'd blanketed, and I thought I could *see* the heat it gave off.

Forgive me, I told the room, and switched off the light. Then I lay there on the bed completely still, not daring to move, while the hissing sound, like a blank tape turned up, filled the room.

I felt small the next morning walking up Tenth Avenue, as though all this mental and emotional strain—the lack of sleep too—had shrunk me a bit. Traffic was light, and once I'd made my way east toward Columbus Avenue, the people turned inside out with all their accusations showing, the public mumblers and the walking explanations had thinned out, and all I had to wade against were a few conventional paranoid types, some even well dressed. One or two couples actually looked like they were coming from church, because they were beaming idiotic charity to everyone they passed.

I had the strange sensation of approaching a man on the sidewalk who in the distance appeared small, but neglected to grow larger as I drew closer. I thought he must be a dwarf, until at the last moment, in the nick of time—just before we passed—he assumed normal proportions.

But this sensation kept on recurring. Suddenly I felt benign. I knew what was happening—they weren't seeing me. I was seeing them, but from their point of view I hardly existed, I was nearly transparent, and so they could simply maintain their scale, which was all of a piece, because it hadn't been sliced up yet by the various other people like me seizing our viewpoints within it. In a way, it was like the streets were still asleep. People walked carefully. They were at that stage of being small in God's eye, on the one morning of the week—Sunday—when God was still allowed to see everywhere. That's why most people were hiding. Only Broadway was in any manner of speaking crowded, so I avoided it, coming up on Ninety-first Street from Columbus, then turning west.

I was early, eleven thirty, so I more or less walked past my son's building from across the street a few times, regarding it with foreboding. It was one of those buildings that resemble a huge cash register, only very long—it occupied almost the whole block. Work was proceeding on much of the ground floor behind a long wooden fence and walkway extending the length of the street. I knew at a glance this was another Welfare building; the people near it walked in slow motion. The whole place had a kind of glaze around it, as though it existed in a different dimension. For some crazy reason I thought of a massive nursery school.

Interesting weather, I thought, and looked up at the sky. Actually, I couldn't really tell what the weather was doing. It was hard for me to figure out whether it was even warm or cold.

All at once I wondered what was happening to me. It was a moment of clarity such as I'd never experienced before and never have since—God's eye shining on everything for an instant—and I stood there absolutely still on the sidewalk. I knew I looked unkempt. I hadn't been to work in more than three weeks—my "vacation" stretching on indefinitely—and I knew they were doing just fine back there at Hudson Valley Consultants without me. Also, I felt old. I was feeling older than I ever had before. At the age of fifty-five, I felt like an old man; the world was passing me by. I could go back to Highland right now and resume a normal life, even without Helga. Women had left me before, I was used to it. I could work for ten more years at my profession (too late to change it now) and retire with dignity, or I could cross the street and become embroiled in something I'd fail to understand, call a strange man son and shake him by the hand.

I repeated this little ditty to myself a few times: *couldn't understand, shake him by the hand.*

I noticed a pawnshop a few doors up, on the corner of Broadway, open even on Sunday morning. In the window were ghetto blasters of all sizes, switchblades, conga drums, tape recorders, all with bright red price tags. A small gray cassette tape recorder caught my eye; this was exactly what I needed. I walked in and bought it on the spot, from a pale sleepy-eyed man with garlic on his breath.

This thing was small enough to carry unnoticed in my coat pocket, and had an earplug and a little mike the size of an earplug for recording. I tried it out on the sidewalk: *couldn't understand, shake him by the hand.*

I pressed Rewind and Play, and heard my voice emerge from the complicated innards of the thing: *couldn't understand, shake him by the hand.* It wobbled a bit, but that might have been the original, not the copy. Armed with this machine, I crossed West Ninety-first Street to confront Charles Lyndhurst, Jr.

A wooden ramp led between plywood fences to the lobby of the place. In front of the door a sign said: COMING SOON, BROADWAY GALLERIA, FOURTEEN SHOPS. In the lobby, a few old people sat on couches under relief murals of futuristic strong men and orbiting planets. A door across the hall displayed my son's name on a brass plate. I knocked; immediately, it flew open.

"Dad!"

His arms were open; we embraced. I hadn't remembered him being this tall. Nor did I care for the smell of his cologne. Somewhere behind him, a figure disappeared through a door. All I saw was his back, then the door closed softly, and I shuddered. Who was it?

Charles Lyndhurst, Jr., held me at arm's length by the elbows. He'd dressed for this occasion in a double-breasted suit—I inferred they were coming back—and an open-collared brown silky shirt, with the top two buttons undone, exposing a lot of curly hair on his chest. It was positively pubic. He smiled broadly, but his tall face looked spongier than ever. It was something about his skin, as though he attacked it every morning with a pumice stone in order to soften it up. Also, his face possessed a sickly, pale, brownish color, and his black peaked hair was thin and long. With a loose-lipped smile he regarded me, but I found it difficult to look in his eyes. They were brown too; I thought of dead mossy earth under trees.

"So good of you to come," he said.

I nodded and pulled out my pipe. "Mind if I smoke?"

"We're going right up," he said sharply. "Abner doesn't like smokers, I'm afraid."

"Abner?"

"Mr. Fisch."

I looked around the office. A row of antique oak file cabinets lined one wall. There were three desks here, and I concluded from this that Charles had several secretaries or assistants. Two of the desks had computer terminals, and programs in boxes lay stacked on a table against the far wall.

Someone had taped the Round Tuit poster on a wall, the same as in our office at Hudson Valley. Above one desk was a Care Bear calendar.

At the largest desk of all, in the back, Charles Lyndhurst opened the top drawer and took out a key. "We'll just let ourselves in," he said. "We'll surprise them."

"They're waiting for us, are they?" I wasn't sure what I meant by this. Also, standing there, I didn't know what to do with my arms.

"It's at their apartment."

"Remodeling yours?"

"Anna wanted to cook something German."

"Anna," I said. It felt like this little conversation was in code. Why did I say "Remodeling yours?" There must have been a reason. I began to feel vigilant, and watched Charles Lyndhurst cross the room in front of me, trying to read his expression and his manner. The smile on his face appeared somewhat smug, but I wasn't sure why. I decided to watch his hands; they often tell more. He wore fingerless gloves and had long pointed nails.

"This way," he said. With his bony fingers closed over that key he held the door for me.

We walked down a long hallway boarded up along its length. Wallboard dust everywhere, metal studs in stacks on the floor. At the first corridor we passed, he nodded. "I live down there." We took the next hallway to an elevator.

"They should paint lines on the floor," I said. "Like hospitals."

"This is a new concept for Welfare," said Charles. "Shops. We thought we'd try to gentrify the place. Multiple economic levels too. Forty percent Welfare. Theoretically, you don't know if your neighbor's on Welfare."

But the elevator smelled faintly of urine regardless. It was freshly painted yellow over scratched graffiti.

At the door of Apartment 619, my son cocked his key, smiling broadly. "Are you ready for this?" he asked.

"Roger, contact."

He unlocked the door and ushered me in.

Three people looked up from a greenish living room, and all at once I felt underwater. Two of them I didn't know, but the third, who stood up with a look of alarm—though she managed an abashed, querulous grin too—was Bernice. "Charlie!" she said.

"Bernice!"

"Carol." She shot an angry glance at our son.

He was struggling with a smile, rubbing his hands together. "Surprise."

The other two stood up. They looked somber; angry even. I

don't know it if was the state I was in, but I felt frightened and suspicious. These people already *knew* each other, and I felt I'd intruded. They were planning something, or talking about me.

"Dad," said Charles. "Meet Mr. and Mrs. Fisch. Abner and Anna."

Abner Fisch, a large barrel-chested man of around sixty or seventy, with a white brush mustache, held out his hand. He had round, popping eyes—the kind that scare children—and his bloated face was as smooth as a balloon, thus making him look younger than he probably was. Slightly fat faces tend not to wrinkle. He scowled, squeezing my hand.

"Charlie, I didn't know you'd be coming," said Bernice.

"I didn't either," I said. "I mean you." Despite myself, my heart went soft this close to Bernice. Her husky voice felt like a physical thing, something you could touch.

"I thought I'd surprise you both," said our son.

"Pleased to meet you, sir," said Mr. Fisch. But he didn't look like he was. I wondered if he addressed everyone in this military fashion, or just didn't know what to call me. His gestures and words were curt; he discarded my hand as though he'd had enough of it. "Your coat."

I panicked, because the tape recorder was already running. "I'll just keep it on," I said. "My blood sugar. I get chills easily." It was a light ski jacket actually, with big pockets.

"Well, young man," said Anna Fisch, "speak to the manager . . ." Saying this, she appeared to experience an attack of shyness, as everyone was looking at her. Her husband was positively scowling.

"Out with it, Anna!" We were all still standing there. She muttered something about turning up the heat, and nodded her head toward Charles Lyndhurst. I understood this as a mild joke; the manager was *here*, with us. Meanwhile I was reaching for her hand, but she didn't notice. "*Anna*," said Abner. Confused, Anna looked around, mumbled "Oh," took my hand. In stature she was considerably shorter than her husband, and very trim;

from the back, I imagined, one could mistake her for a woman of twenty, especially as her hair was all brown, though I assumed she'd colored it.

But her face was ravaged; it was a map of haphazard wrinkles without pattern. She hadn't just aged, she'd exploded, and here in front of us was the walking debris.

It occurred to me that this was the source of Mr. Fisch's apparent disgust with his wife; from the front she showed her age.

"Have a seat, sir," he said.

"Call me Charlie."

"Charlie it is, sir."

I sat on the couch between Charles Lyndhurst, Jr., and Anna. Abner lowered himself—with some difficulty, I noticed—into a recliner across the room, and Bernice sat on the edge of a rocker. Then she stood up and swaggered across the room, grinning—I couldn't help loving that swagger!—and pecked me on the cheek, a gesture she'd evidently resolved to accomplish at whatever cost. She was blushing and grinning defiantly, both, one eye up and one eye down. Her hand was in mine; I squeezed it. She walked back to her seat, queen of the room, and sat swiveling her head in triumph, having slipped right in past all my suspicious unease as only a sister could. I noticed how short she was, like me, and felt a pang of regret at that thought—*like me.*

"Well, here we all are," said Charles Lyndhurst, Jr.

Everyone sat there in silence. Bernice grinned, Abner scowled, Anna looked confused, and Charles Lyndhurst, Jr., held his breath in expectation. He appeared to be about to spill into a cataract of solicitation.

As for me, I felt a little better. It was partly Bernice. We had a secret bond, a shameful one, yes, but something to cling to when you felt uncomfortable. It was also partly the tape recorder, which I knew was getting this all down.

On the other hand I couldn't entirely shake the feeling that they'd been talking intimately when I walked in, Bernice and the Fisches. Not just intimately in the sense of friendship or kinship;

they'd been arguing something too, and this seemed to imply an acquaintance previous to this gathering, of long standing in fact. I settled back in my chair, determined to observe the others and let them make the first move. I was resolved not to be caught unawares, not to take the offensive, but to defend myself vigorously if they should take it. It felt good to be careful—like sitting on a wall above the fray.

On the glass coffee table in front of us were peanuts in one dish and pale yellow and green mints in another. Through the coffee table, one could see the dark, inky American oriental the Fisches had walked upon half their lives. On the wall above Abner hung a mirror with leaves of gold wrapping the corners. Beside it were silhouettes of mandolins and G clefs.

The walls and upholstery were green. Everywhere you sat—on the couches and chairs—were sheets of clear plastic. The backs of chairs too. Across the room, just inside the archway—beyond which I noted a dining room table set in white linen and tarnished silver—was a Steinway grand, with a music stand beside it.

"Mrs. Fisch gives lessons," said Abner, who I observed was watching me carefully.

The only windows were in that dining room, muffled in heavy beige drapes. To my right was the door, to my left the dining room. I remarked all this with care, and tried to picture a floor plan from overhead. A hallway behind the piano evidently led to the bedrooms and kitchen. I could smell something sweet, with onions. Something baking.

Actually, I was hot in my coat, but tried not to show it.

"I wanted you to meet my real parents," Charles Lyndhurst, Jr., was saying to the Fisches.

"He's been searching *so* long," said Anna beside me, turning but not looking up. Curvature of the spine.

"I don't know but what it might be," said Bernice, "disappointing. Ha ha."

Charles Lyndhurst threw his head back and laughed uproariously, then jumped up rubbing his gloved hands. "Disappointing," he said. "Very good, Mom. Disappointing, wonderful." He

was shaking his head, and looked over at Anna, as if to say, See
what a card my real mother is? "Can you imagine how it feels,"
he asked, "to have all *four* of my parents here with me?" He sat
down. "So to speak."

"I'm serious," said Bernice. "We're no prizes, Charlie and me.
Oh, maybe *Charlie* . . ." She looked over at me, scratching her
thigh. "I was pleased to find out that Charlie's successful." She
looked proud. She was my sister.

Did the Fisches know we weren't married? It appeared so.
Bernice must have told them. "Chuckie tells me that you are"—
Abner's face appeared to pinch itself—"a water engineer."

Chuckie? "That's right," I said, but then I clammed up. I
wasn't sure yet how far to go into anything, and wanted to play
it safe.

"With your own firm in Newburgh?" Abner wanted me to
impress him, I could tell—to establish my credentials.

"A small firm," I said.

"Hardly small," said—Chuckie. "Dad's being modest," he explained. "Hudson Valley Consultants completed two point six
million dollars worth of business last year. This year they may
double that."

I couldn't help asking how he knew this.

"You told me," he said, looking genuinely startled. So I
thought it must be so.

For the first time Abner appeared to be nearly smiling.
"Good," he said. I had the feeling this had all been rehearsed. We
were performing rituals to propitiate the godhead.

"And this water business," said Anna. "What exactly is it that
you do?"

I explained as succinctly as I could what sort of projects our firm
took on, but couldn't help warming to the subject a bit. It occurred to me that all the water in New York City was invisible,
except for the rivers, of course. New York was already entirely
engineered, whereas I worked out on the edge of the unrecon-
structed. The cutting edge, I said.

"Insightful comment," said Bernice.

I was an important part of that human impulse to domesticate all the land and water which would otherwise simply lie around unused, Mr. and Mrs. Fisch. In New York City that might be hard to imagine.

"But pretty soon," said Carol, "the whole world will be like New York City. As far as being engineered goes."

"Then, my friend, you'll be out of work," said Abner.

"In that case, I'll go on Welfare," I said, looking over at Charles Lyndhurst, Jr.—Chuckie—and everyone laughed, even Abner.

I felt in control. I knew what I was doing.

"But this remains a serious question," said Abner. "As the American economy transforms itself into a service economy. When all the houses are built, all the goods manufactured," he said, "we shall all be either the administrators of Welfare, and other such services, medical services, or"—he held up his hands like the Pope—"the recipients of them."

"Exactly," I said. "One or the other."

Sitting on the edge of his chair, Chuckie looked proudly from Abner to me.

"I don't know about that," said Bernice. "You both sound a little crazy about this to me. In the far distant future, maybe, I don't know. If the engineers don't blow us all up."

"How can a water engineer blow us up?" Anna Fisch appeared genuinely puzzled.

"Anna," said Abner, scowling. When he addressed her his voice rose two or three decibels. "Carol was speaking figuratively."

"The exact meaning of what I said," said Bernice, squirming in her chair—she was smiling, but the shadows of other emotions passed across her face—anger, impatience—"is that all the crazy engineers in this world, including water ones, are going to engineer us out of existence, in my opinion. They'll have everything so perfectly planned and mapped out, so far as whatever goes— your water, your wars, your illnesses, whatever it is that needs to be engineered, and I noticed that when engineers get together that means everything. So what's left? Artificial hearts, artificial brains. It's not funny anymore."

"No one said it was, my dear."

I couldn't tell from this whether Abner was agreeing or disagreeing with Bernice. He raised himself a little in his chair. I guessed what this meant; he was repressing something, though it might have been his bowels.

"But don't you think that science has worked miracles in this century?" asked Anna.

"Oh Christ." Abner shook his head, disgusted.

"Abner, *leave me alone,*" snapped his wife.

"Miracles?" said Bernice. "Such as indoor plumbing?"

That was the nineteenth century, Bernice.

"Bombs, atomic power, Three Mile Island. The Glen Canyon Dam. Smog, toxic wastes, cancer in everything. *Hamburg* has cancer. Miracles, all right."

"Depends on how you cook it," said my son Chuckie. He looked a little worried. Maybe puzzled. But I sensed this was a normal conversation. That is, it was following paths laid out in advance by the ghosts of these people—their personalities. Your personality always scouts the terrain.

"Bernice," I said, "did you drive a car here? Take a train? A cab? Did you ride the elevator or climb six flights of stairs? Wash your hands after you went to the bathroom? You can criticize engineers," I said, glancing around the room, "but don't take them for granted."

"I wasn't taking them for granted, as far as that goes. Whoever engineered my car was diabolical."

We talked like this for a while, like a family, in little intimate outbursts and recriminations. For some reason Abner treated Bernice with kid gloves, though toward his wife he was openly contemptuous. This was as it was destined to be, I sensed. Meanwhile, most of Bernice's remarks were belligerent. Her spite was laced with smiles, but I couldn't help wondering where it came from. It occurred to me that it was entirely possible that they already knew each other well, Bernice and the Fisches. Chuckie had discovered Bernice a year or so ago; she'd probably been here to dinner quite often.

I felt in my pocket to assure myself that the tape recorder was still going. My son, who'd been sitting on the edge of the couch listening to our talk with a kind of gluttonous anxiety, stood up and excused himself—to go to the bathroom, I assumed. He'd been sitting on my right, Anna on my left. I noticed a pocket watch lying there on the couch in his place beside me; it looked antique. Casually, I let my hand drop across it. No one observed me. I slipped it into my pocket. Then, when he came back, I stood up too. "My turn," I said.

Pissing in the bathroom, I felt very hungry. I hadn't eaten much at all in the past few days, and hunger felt like the revenge of normalcy. I smiled at myself in the mirror and winked, rubbing my hands, licking my lips. I raised my eyebrows and leered at the mirror. In my pocket, I checked the recorder and saw that the tape was two-thirds used up, so I took this opportunity to turn it over.

Dinner was sauerbraten with potato pancakes, fresh rolls and butter. For some reason it felt like a picnic. Then Anna brought in some baked pigs' feet, and it didn't stop there. Smoked herring, borscht and tossed salad after that. The borscht was a deep rich purple—I pictured it staining my insides—and very sweet, the best dish in the meal. Abner kept the wine flowing—white German wines, all—and his wife did all the serving, as Bernice didn't even offer to help.

Then again, neither did I.

I was starved. I ate like a starving man, spilling food on the table, much to the embarrassment (I was sure) of my son. When I finished it looked like a dog had been sitting at my place. "Wonderful dinner," I said, and they all looked at me. Bernice grinned. I suppressed a belch.

I asked Bernice where she was staying, but she seemed puzzled by the question. How's Windsor? I asked her.

"Windsor?" she replied.

Of course, it was my fate to be surrounded by people with their heads screwed on wrong. For a dizzying instant, I thought these were all twins or lookalikes of the people I thought I was with. "Windsor, *Windsor*," said Chuckie, with the habitual distress of a son addressing his absentminded mother. "C'mon, Mom."

"Oh. Windsor."

But all this put me on the alert once more. Something else was going on, I felt sure. Looking around the dining room table, I saw once again that all eyes were on me. Abner Fisch's especially; one eye had widened and appeared to be engorging itself on the sight of my face. He bored in, actually leaning forward across the table.

I decided to relax; what harm could looking do? Let him have a good look, tomorrow I'll be somewhere else—the Grand Canyon. I felt very strongly that these people couldn't touch me.

"Speaking of Windsor," said Chuckie, addressing me, "did you locate your friends there? The Lockwoods?"

The question took me by surprise. The Lockwoods. Should these people know about them? "They're dead," I said.

"Yes, I know, I remember. I told you they were deceased, Dad. Later on I found out where they were buried by cross-checking IRS files."

"Where?" Across the table, Bernice's sprung eyes (I could swear one actually wobbled a little) appeared querulous and puzzled, watching me and our son.

"Mount Emerald Cemetery, Binghamton."

"Oh," I said. I decided we should drop this subject. Anna was serving a chocolate torte.

"Friends of yours?" asked Chuckie with a smile.

"Landlords," I lied. "I owed them money."

"One never owes the dead, sir," said Abner.

"Of course, exactly. One never owes the dead."

"They can hardly collect, can they?" He was looking right at me, smiling.

"Of course not. How could they?" I sipped some wine. In fact, I gulped it down. What was this all supposed to signify? The atmosphere of secret meanings, winks and mutual suspicions made it hard for me to breathe. Even Anna seemed caught up in it. Glancing over at me on the sly, she whispered something to her husband, with an anxious, conspiratorial air. He scowled in reply.

"Dessert, Mr. . . . ?" He reached a slice of torte in my direction.

"Cooper," I said.

Chuckie's face stiffened. "Lyndhurst," he said softly.

"Mr. Cooper," said Abner Fisch. "You and Carol. That is, Mrs. Englehard—"

"Lyndhurst," Bernice muttered.

"You are my son's parents, are you not? That is, his natural parents. My adopted son. You have satisfied yourself as to the— the authenticity of his claim?"

We hadn't, but what could I say?

"Not exactly," said Bernice.

"Of course we have," I said with a smile.

"Yes, I thought so." With the briefest flicker of a glance at Bernice, Abner continued addressing me. I decided the best way through this was to be agreeable. "You strike me as a careful man," he said. "Vigilant."

"Vigilant, yes, absolutely."

"A man with an eye to the future, sir."

"Yes, the future."

"Who takes care of himself."

"Takes care of himself."

"And his family. His offspring."

I saw where all this was leading, but didn't flinch. "By all means," I said. Across the table, Bernice winked and squirmed. She saw it too.

"Accordingly," he said, "have you discussed . . . ? Have you thought of making provisions for . . . ?" He looked over at Chuckie.

"*Dad,*" said Charles Lyndhurst, Jr. "I mean, Abner . . . " His face was red from anger, shame, or both, and he squirmed in his chair like a boneless man. "Dad," he said again, meaning me this time. He'd swiveled his head up toward me—*up,* because he was nearly doubled over at his place—and the watery eyes, the baboon grimace, contained, I could see, a genuine plea. "Dad, I didn't bring you here to discuss such things. I had no idea—"

"Nevertheless," bellowed Abner Fisch, "such things must be discussed, mustn't they?" He appeared to be asking me. I shrugged. I let my eyes go blank. My face betrayed nothing. "One never owes the dead. But the living. To the living one has an obligation." He looked around the table. "And one had best fulfill it before one dies oneself."

All this talk of dying was making me uncomfortable, so I smiled and attacked my chocolate torte.

"Please, Abner." Chuckie was all doubled up and twisting his red face. I could see he wanted to clasp his hands together.

"Abner and I have settled fifteen—"

"Anna has no idea of the amount. Keep your mouth shut, Anna. Don't interrupt." He addressed his wife but looked at me. "In our estate, we had set aside twenty-five thousand dollars for Chuckie, after our decease. In Ginny Maes and treasury bills, Mr.—Charlie. This was before, of course, Chuckie had located his natural parents. With our blessing, to be sure. Whether this discovery mitigates our obligation to this—lad we brought up with—love and affection—"

"The cost of raising a child these days," shot in Anna.

"I leave that for you to decide, sir." Abner Fisch folded his hands on his chest.

All eyes were on me. I could see Bernice was beginning to enjoy this. She smiled, she grinned, she scratched her head. "Yes, of course," I said. "Absolutely," I nodded.

"Abner—"

"Hold your tongue, Chuckie. Excuse me. Yes, of course, *what,* may I ask?"

"Your responsibility has been mitigated," I said.

"Oh, I can't *stand* this," said Chuckie, and stood up at his place. It struck me all at once that he was putting on an act; they'd planned this carefully, and he was playing his role to the hilt. Overplaying it, in fact.

"Sit down, Chuckie. I thought, Mr.—sir—if you could match such an amount—"

"Oh, I'm sure he could do it," said Bernice. "He's rich, right, Charlie?" She waved at me from across the table.

"Sure," I said.

"What?"

"I can match that amount. Twenty-five thousand? I can double it."

Abner looked like someone who'd charged a door only to find it swing open in front of him. The momentum carried him through, he couldn't stop. "For if you could assume this obligation—of love—we could then make plans to settle our estate—on *our* natural child."

"What?" Chuckie sat bolt upright in his chair. I thought I smelled smoke. Bernice was giggling.

"You have a natural child?" I asked.

Anna took this opportunity to begin clearing the table. "Abner!" she shouted from the kitchen.

"Chuckie didn't know," said Abner. "Yes, we do, sir. We hope to make for her the sort of generous settlement—to shoulder our responsibility—"

"I was thinking you should have invited her here too," said Bernice.

"Abner, smoke!" Anna shouted from the kitchen. It was true; the smell had grown stronger. With difficulty, Mr. Fisch lurched up and lumbered toward the kitchen, with the rest of us in tow. Here, the smoke was visible. Abner pulled the oven open, but nothing was in it—no fire there.

"Down here," said Chuckie from the hallway. From a closed room at the end of the hall, smoke curled out of the crack around the door. "Everyone out," said my son. "Out through the living room," he shouted.

"Don't open that door!" Abner Fisch boomed with alarm.

"And let the place burn?" Charles Lyndhurst, Jr., was ushering his adoptive father out of the hallway into the living room. By this time the thick smoke was burning our eyes; Anna coughed as Bernice led her out. I felt the door, but it wasn't hot. Chuckie came back with the key in his fist.

"I can help, I know about fires," I said. "I'm a water engineer."

He unlocked the door and a wall of smoke collapsed on top of us. We couldn't see fire; Chuckie flicked on the light switch. We coughed. In the middle of this room was a large white plastic bucket with smoke pouring out of it. As it turned out, the room had its own door to the outside hallway, and Chuckie swung it open while I carried the bucket outside, averting my face—it smelled like roofing tar. In the hallway, Abner, Anna and Carol huddled down by the elevator. There was smoke in the hallway, and some of the other residents had come out in housecoats and curlers, with expressions of alarm. A bell began clanging. I could see roofing shingles smoldering in the bucket. On the floor of the hallway was a can of charcoal lighter.

I went back into the room to see if anything else was burning. The smoke was still thick, but what I saw there froze me on the spot, regardless of smoke. This windowless room was filled with photographs, model planes, trophies, books, medals, busts, pennants and so forth, and the planes were all copies of the *Spirit of St. Louis*, the photographs and busts all of Charles Lindbergh. Framed newspaper headlines about Lindbergh's famous flight, about the Lindbergh child's kidnapping. LINDBERGH DOES IT! TO PARIS IN 33½ HOURS.

I felt my heart beating in my neck, making the veins there thick as cords.

"Dad, everything okay in there?" In the hallway my son was dousing the bucket with a fire extinguisher.

"Charlie? Mr. Cooper, sir!" I heard the voice of Abner Fisch. He was lumbering down the hallway toward the door. Looking around, I noticed the key still in the lock of the inner door. I pulled it out, slipped it in my pocket, and flicked off the light. At the doorway I ran into Abner Fisch; he felt like an immovable object. He seized my arm, his eyes bulged grotesquely. "Are you all right?" he asked, jerking me out of that room with one pull.

"I'm fine," I said. "My eyes sting."

He slammed the door tight behind us.

12

We were standing across the street, where I'd stood by myself several hours before, watching the last of the fire engines depart, and waiting for a cab to take Mr. and Mrs. Fisch to their hotel. They didn't want to leave their apartment, but Chuckie had insisted, at least until tomorrow, when his maintenance crew could check for smoke damage. They couldn't sleep there tonight with that smell, he said.

Oh yes they could, said Abner. I've slept with smells worse than that before. And this gross man looked over at his wife.

But Chuckie pulled rank as the building's manager, and the Fisches now each had a suitcase in their hands. In *his* hand, Chuckie still held the bucket of roofing shingles, for the fire chief to come by and pick up and inspect. Bernice had already left for her hotel or wherever she was staying. At the end, she'd become furtive and suspicious, and seemed to want no part of the rest of us. And who could blame her? I felt the same way too; I couldn't wait to get out of there. Mr. and Mrs. Fisch were smoldering on the sidewalk, and Chuckie was pacing back and forth, shaking his head. Who would do such a thing? he asked. And why?

As far as that went, I had my own theory, but I wasn't sharing it. In the crowd on the street when the fire engines came I'd spotted a familiar face, though at first I couldn't place it. He was tall and burly, his features were creased, and he swiveled his head, acting sneaky and secretive. I caught him looking over at me, and almost suspected that he *wanted* me to see him. Then I began to think I'd spotted him quite a bit recently, though until now

I hadn't consciously registered it. At any rate, I couldn't place him until the crowd had dissolved and him with it, when it suddenly came to me—Cleo Dannen's son. I didn't even know his name. But it was the same man who'd pulled me out of her hiccuping presence at the hospital, who'd called himself her son, and who'd threatened to kill me if I didn't stay away from her.

He'd been following me, I felt certain of it now. But why? And why was that room full of Lindbergh memorabilia? In the *Fisches'* apartment, no less.

At last a cab pulled up, and I shook hands with Mr. and Mrs. Fisch. Though we instinctively avoided eye contact, we said vague things about meeting again and resuming our discussion. Then they climbed in making the leaden and disgruntled noises of old people.

I knew all about it; I was old too.

Charles Lyndhurst, Jr., and I embraced on the sidewalk, a manly embrace. He promised to be in touch, my son, and I actually felt a twinge of affection. Somehow I knew now that he hadn't planned that discussion about money with the Fisches; he was as much of its victim as I was.

He wanted to know how long I'd be in the city, and I told him just until tomorrow. Call me up, he said. I will, I said, inwardly vowing *Never*. A twinge of affection was wholly enough, and I walked off feeling liberated, abandoned—bursting with shrugs and sighs of relief.

It suddenly occurred to me that I'd never even asked him about Helga. But then again, how could I? The explanations I'd be forced to make felt like flypaper. They would stick to me, he would shake his head and grin.

It was five or six o'clock I guessed, dark already. On Broadway I found a bar playing Latin music, ordered a beer, and sat at a table way in the back. The place was nearly empty—just a few dark-skinned men at the bar.

I took out my cassette player, rewound the tape, plugged in the earphone and drank deeply of my beer. The music was loud, but my little earplug blocked most of it out. I pressed Play, nearly rubbing my hands in anticipation.

The knocking sound, I guessed, was footsteps. Echoing voices, but I couldn't make them out. Everything sounded muffled and distant, except for a cough—mine, I assumed—and some fuzzy rubbing and squeaking sounds which may have had something to do with my coat.

I realized I should have pinned the microphone up behind my collar, or fastened it to my sleeve. A clank, a hum—this was the elevator. More muffled steps, and voices sounding garbled and chewed. I pictured people wearing muzzles filled with cotton. "Charlie!" said a voice in the distance. My own voice came back loud but distorted, a kind of blunt object broken at its edges. When I spoke the distortion was enormous, but when others spoke it sounded like words you'd hear through walls. Most of this was incomprehensible except in waves, as when a radio station fades in and out. "Your own firm in Newburgh," squawk, crash rub. With the earphone in one ear, the other ear blocked by my finger, Latin music in the distance. "Up near 9W . . ." "The Roosevelt House . . ." Much of what I heard sounded like someone prying nails out of boards inside my skull. There was a great deal of hissing; people spoke in hisses and ripples. I couldn't recognize half of what was said, my memory of it was nothing like this. At first I thought that even by means of fragments I'd be able to reconstruct the content of our conversation, and thus examine its minute implications, but the fragments I now heard were broken from larger pieces I couldn't even remember. Someone was talking about automobile fatalities. Also, people *spoke* in fragments, in bursts. Voices crossed each other. I began to think I'd hot-wired another conversation, or this was something already on the tape—I hadn't really recorded anything—when finally in a comprehensible (if distorted) voice I heard myself blurt out—much too loudly in my judgment—"In that case I'll go on Welfare." And everyone laughed! The laughter sounded like coughs, hisses, rustling leaves, scraping chairs, but nonetheless it was evidently the laughter of a polite, alert group of people in a room somewhere.

But much of what I heard was disconcertingly banal. Actually, I began to get bored after a while, and advanced the tape a few times. Still, everywhere it was the same. Talk of Reagan and the farmers, Germany after the war. A long, broken, incomprehensible story of a neighbor downstairs and her daughter's problems with renting a house in Arizona. I must have blocked this out at the time, because I hardly remembered it. Anna told it, in her wavering singsong, whose inflections all descended. She'd been sitting on my left; otherwise I wouldn't have picked up a word. Periodically, Abner interrupted with a booming interjection or denial, though on the tape it sounded like someone shouting far away from across a canyon.

I couldn't find any secret meanings.

Advancing the tape, it seemed that more and more the hiss was dominant, the sort of noise you might get by recording a leaking pipe from inside. Intimate and dead and flat.

All at once I thought I heard something familiar. It sounded like a name I knew well: Hauptmann. Was this Abner speaking? Or Chuckie. The voice was male. Hauptmann! I could have sworn it was that. Of course, I hadn't heard it when I was there or I surely would have remembered, since I knew the name well. Bruno Hauptmann was the man accused of kidnapping the Lindbergh child. The rest of what was said came out terribly distorted, but I thought I heard "Windsor"—I did remember talking about Windsor—and perhaps even "Apalachin," though of this I wasn't certain.

Hauptmann and Apalachin? I pressed Rewind and played it again, but now the tape was dead—a blank. Then I realized I'd touched Record, not Play; by now whatever I'd heard had been erased.

But what had I heard? I gulped my beer and felt for my pulse. Slowly, with care, I pulled out my pipe and filled the bowl.

Of course, I hadn't heard a thing. I'd heard noise. Behind the noise, on the other hand, was plenty. Important things were said in that apartment, and my only problem was that I hadn't been sufficiently alert. Something was going on, I felt certain. Why was it that I couldn't even recognize half the things that were said—of those I could understand, that is?

I lit my pipe, ordered another beer and listened to more. I found that I had to fight the sense that it was banal or ordinary. I refused to be bored. If a fragment by Abner sounded stupid or plain, if the intonations were flat and inexpressive, the silences hardly pregnant—just blank—I refused to accept this at face value. I listened through the tape to the bitter end, to the exclamations of "fire" and "smoke," the suddenly scraping chairs, rustling squawks, footsteps, crashing sounds, clinking dishes, and felt that one or two patterns had very clearly suggested themselves. It had all built up to that suspicious fire. And then, of course, the Lindbergh room! With another listen I'd no doubt catch more. There was probably some way you could engineer the tape to eliminate the hiss so that more of what was said could be heard. I could hire someone to transcribe it, too, though I might lose important intonations and hints that way.

I stood up feeling excited, flushed. The Latin music had been replaced by disco, or maybe it was Latin disco. A few women sat at the bar, and one looked inquiringly in my direction. I knew at that moment I must have appeared proud and confident, bursting with, what? *Faith*, no doubt. I slipped the recorder in my pocket and walked out, winking at the whores.

Out on the street I was shocked to learn it was nine o'clock already. Someone touched my arm, but this failed to startle me. "Not tonight," I said, smiling regardless; inwardly, I blessed her. Then I walked down Broadway to Ninety-first Street, and down Ninety-first to my son's building.

Lights were on in most of the windows. Crossing the street, I walked up the ramp. With Chuckie's key I unlocked the front door and experienced the feeling that all doors were open to me that night, since, as I'd surmised, this was a master key. I walked through the lobby, nodded at two old gentlemen there, and turned left down the same dimly lit corridor we'd walked through earlier that day.

It looked different, though. It felt like a warehouse. On my left, behind the construction equipment—piles of metal studs, tubs of wallboard compound, stacks of drywall—stood what appeared to be a corrugated metal wall, or a series of overhead doors. This hallway was so dimly lit I wasn't sure. It could have been that aqua fiberglass they use for carports, nailed up over hasty studwalls. Up ahead someone walking knocked into something, startling a can, which rolled across the hallway with an echo, and this frankly scared me. I walked past the corridor where my son had said he lived and took the next hallway to the right.

Down here should have been the elevator, but I couldn't find it. This building was actually larger than I'd thought, for the hallway I was in seemed to go on forever. It jogged left, straightened out, and kept on going. Stale smells of fish and chicken in the air. Behind doors were sounds of television sets, coughs, shouts, dishes, cries of babies, loud music, vacuum cleaners.

Real life went on behind those doors.

But no one came out. I spotted a sign saying STAIRWAY and decided to take it. The door heaved open much too slowly, I felt half asleep pushing it. I was tired; I needed rest. The metal stairs rang with a terrible echo as I climbed, and this stairwell was lit in the most perfunctory manner, just occasional bare lightbulbs hanging from frayed cords.

Below me, other footsteps were climbing. Of course, there was nothing particularly sinister about this. Since these were stairs, people naturally used them. On the other hand the smells here were bad, and some of the graffiti suggested what people used them *for*. I even thought I saw bloodstains, though that was no doubt my morbid imagination fed by fuzzy blood sugar and lack of sleep.

On one landing, a teenage boy lay in a sleeping bag, sound asleep. He didn't wake up when I tiptoed past. The footsteps below me became louder, so to compensate I walked as softly as

I could. I stopped for a minute to let my heart slow down, and pictured myself tumbling down these steps having suffered a heart attack—dead at fifty-five.

That made me feel better, and I climbed on. When I thought I'd reached the sixth floor—or did I want the fifth?—I pushed a door open, shocked to find it led not to a corridor but another set of stairs, wooden this time. They were narrower and steep. They struck me as the sort of steps you might see in old theaters, leading up to a balcony or attic high behind the stage. I began the climb to a door far above me lit by a bulb in a green metal shade. My legs were heavy and I felt annoyed; this wasn't bringing me any closer to my goal. And it was *steep*; I climbed in half steps, like a toddler. At last I was there, and as I pushed at the door, the one below me swung open as well, but I didn't wait around to see who it was.

Here was a huge empty ballroom or attic with great lumps of things stored everywhere. Some of it was furniture, but sheets thrown across everything made it difficult to tell. Ceiling-high windows showed the city outside, and I realized these were the only source of light, even at night.

In that murky darkness I saw parts of statues, reclining figures, ambiguous sculptures, arms, legs and heads. They were draped with sheets which only partially covered them. Much of it was art nouveauish; sleek granite forms, pockmarked and dark, and some panel reliefs also—evidently taken from demolished buildings— like the one in the hallway downstairs.

I wandered around in this cavernous room, making my way toward its far end. In the darkness I spotted a small red light and made that my goal. Somewhere behind me the door swung open and footsteps emerged. I decided not to panic. The red light was what I thought it would be—a freight elevator—but when I pushed the button the noise felt enormous in that big hollow place. The motor hummed, cables squealed and rumbled, and something resembling a huge wooden crate labored up toward me from below, making clanks.

Glass broke. Someone threw something. As I stepped on the

freight elevator and pulled the down lever, they all ran out with their Uzis and shotguns, razing the place, all the mobsters of my dreams.

Actually, nothing of the sort occurred. What happened was that my brain went off like a pinwheel, sending out sparks and tracers. I'd repressed my fright enough till it snapped, and that, combined with my worked-up state, the darkness, my fuzzed-over senses and dizzy fatigue, made the place explode just as I descended. I think that's the way my mind often worked—imagine the worst in order to spare it the necessity of occurring. It was a form of absolution; I forgave reality its sins in advance.

I felt like I'd opened a pressure valve, and sensed relief descending that elevator, but the only trouble with such moments was, increasingly lately, I couldn't always remember afterward whether they actually had occurred or not. For example, the footsteps. Were those imagined too? This is where the tape recorder came in. I realized I should have turned it on long ago.

At a floor or two below I stopped and emerged in a sort of utility room, a small place with metal shelves, a sink, mops. I pushed the door open and came out into a corridor. Once again there were doorways with sounds behind them, the noise of other people's lives. The numbers on the doors all began with six.

Around a corner I found Apartment 619 with a blank door nearby. This I unlocked quickly and slipped past. The room was dark and smelled strongly of smoke. As I remembered, the light switch was across the room beside the other door, and I stumbled blindly in that direction, groping the walls until I found the door, and next to it the switch.

Light filled the place. I felt so grateful to see that no one had taken this room away, or filled it with bear traps, or vandalized the things inside it, that I dropped to my knees with my forehead to the floor and nearly fell asleep. I collapsed on my side and sprawled there, exhausted. Actually, I must have slept, or half slept, though my eyes were wide open. They stared at a small brown depression in the wooden floor.

When I recovered my wits I began inspecting this room. It was just as I'd remembered it. Wooden replicas of the *Spirit of St. Louis* hung from the ceiling, bronze statues of the plane stood on shelves, headlines and photographs hung on the walls, and busts of Lindbergh were everywhere. I'd seen a deli in Brooklyn like this except it was a Kennedy shrine. The yellow walls here had no windows. The framed headlines about Lindbergh hanging on the walls were fascinating; they chronicled the famous trip to Paris and its aftermath. LINDBERGH SPEEDS ACROSS NORTH ATLANTIC; SIGHTED PASSING ST. JOHN'S, N.F. AT 7:15 PM. Intrepid St. Louis Aviator's Trackless Route Across Atlantic. DE NEW-YORK AU BOURGET EN AVION. LINDBERGH LANDS IN PARIS. GREAT OVATION GREETS AIR HERO. "Am I Here," He Asks, as City Goes Wild with Frenzy of Joy. GIGANTIC CROWD RUSHES ON FIELD AND PULLS HAGGARD FLYER FROM HIS AIRPLANE. The Irish Coast Was a Beautiful Sight to Him. COULD HAVE GONE 500 MILES FARTHER. Ate Only One and a Half of His Five Sandwiches. LINDBERGH LANDS AT CAPITAL TODAY. MOTHER SHARES HONORS. 37,000 Telegrams Arrive for Lindbergh. MILLIONS ROAR WELCOME TO LINDBERGH IN CITY'S GREATEST TRIUMPHAL PAGEANT. Called "Lucky" But Says Luck Isn't All.

All this carried me back to my childhood, when I'd first realized that people and events had actually existed prior to my birth. What a startling discovery! It shrouded the previous decades in mystery and wonder. I remembered people talking about Lindbergh, speaking his name with a certain reverence. And despite myself, I began to cry. I couldn't help it. His picture was everywhere here, and he looked so young and slack-jowled, so confident and vulnerable too, though in the photographs of the various parades honoring him you could also detect a kind of numb awe, even anger—pinch me, I'm dreaming, I don't like to dream—that I felt involuntarily a sense of kinship with the man. I felt that numb awe as well—it was a form of reverence, and just as irritating. You wake up and discover that you *are* the chosen one.

I began thumbing through books. Half in the bookcase took

Lindbergh as their subject, the other half were by him. "It was
an odyssey like that of the heroes of antiquity, and altered irrevo-
cably the way people looked at the map." Actually, I'd seen many
of these books before, in the Poughkeepsie Public Library, so I
tried to confine myself to anything that looked unusual or suspicious. In a brownish folder was a thirty-page pamphlet from the
Missouri Historical Society listing decorations, awards, trophies
and gifts presented to Lindbergh in connection with his flight.
After the several thousand items listed came a selection of offers
declined, including a home in Flushing Meadows, various motion
picture contracts (one for five million dollars), a live monkey and
a gift of 150,000 francs from Mme. de la Meurthe in France,
returned with thanks and the request that it be used for families
of men who'd lost their lives in plane crashes.

Another folder caught my eye. This contained clippings about
the Lindbergh baby kidnapping, probably too painful or shameful
an episode to frame on the wall in the judgment of whatever priest
had erected this shrine. I found nothing here I didn't already
know. However, at the back, under all the clippings, was a typewritten manuscript with a strange title. "History of the Monkey-
Faced Girl," it said. I thumbed through these slightly yellowed
pages, at the end of which was a letter written in longhand and
signed and dated by Abner Fisch in October of 1944. Even if it
had nothing to do with Lindbergh, this looked enticing, so I
folded it up and put it in my pocket.

One entire shelf consisted of duplicate copies of Lindbergh's
book about the flight to Paris, *The Spirit of St. Louis*. Only one
had a jacket, and I pulled this down. On the front page was this
inscription: *To Abner and Anna—the two A's—with gratitude
and affection, Charles A. Lindbergh, July 24, 1953.*

I looked around the room with this book in my hands and felt
a kind of chill of awe, or maybe it was fear. The Fisches knew
Lindbergh; he'd signed this himself! With gratitude and affection, Charles A. Lindbergh.

Of course, it could have been a forgery. I felt at that moment more mentally alert than I'd been in days, and didn't want to discount any possibilities. Even if my own secrets weren't hidden in this room someplace, I knew I was close to them—trembling on the verge, in fact—and didn't want to blow it now.

Everything had to be scrutinized carefully.

I thumbed through the book, which wasn't just about the flight to Paris; it was a kind of autobiography too. Lindbergh occupied the time crossing the Atlantic by remembering his past. He recalled his youth barnstorming the Midwest, doing crazy tricks, tailspins, loop-the-loops. He walked on the wings and did the hanging by the teeth trick, but confessed a harness was attached to his back. He'd dropped out of college to learn how to fly, flew the airmail planes between Chicago and St. Louis, crashed a few times—bailed out twice.

His friends called him Slim. Slim, weren't you scared? In the months before he left for Paris, four other pilots died trying to make the same flight. Two had died the year before. The preparations for takeoff he compared to a funeral procession. Of course (I told myself), we must keep in mind this book was written twenty-five years after the fact. There may be some embellishment here. By the time he wrote this book he'd become famous, married a beautiful heiress, had a son and the son had been kidnapped and murdered. By the way, Slim, are you sure that was your son they found? Did you check it out carefully?

No comment. Over.

Across the ocean at night, Charles Lindbergh flew around great mountain ranges of towering thunderheads, through canyons of clouds with a few stars overhead and a thin strip of moon-glazed water below. He thought he might die; the engine could fail. "Logic's not enough to calm my senses." Amen, Slim.

I was interested in how he stayed awake on this trip, since I myself had experienced such little sleep in the past few days that I sometimes wondered whether I'd ever sleep again. He sat in that little pipsqueak of a plane in the same cramped position for thirty-three and a half hours; no sleep the night before either. He couldn't let himself sleep because he had to keep his hand on the stick; in a matter of seconds the plane could veer off course. I couldn't help feeling the similarity here. I had to keep awake and alert too, so as not to miss a clue. Against the necessity of sleep we both opposed the necessity of exercising vigilance. In my case, my body obliged by glowing with a kind of low-level inner radiation (this had something to do with my blood sugar too) whose buzz became a substitute for sleep, or at least prevented it in large doses. Who could sleep while buzzing and glowing?

In Lindbergh's case, sleep came in fitful little bursts.

> Over and over again, I fall asleep with my eyes open, knowing I'm falling asleep, unable to prevent it; having all the sensations of falling asleep, as one does in bed at night; and then, seconds or minutes later, having all the sensations of waking up. When I fall asleep this way, my eyes are cut off from my ordinary mind as though they were shut, but they become directly connected to this new, extraordinary mind which grows increasingly competent to deal with their impressions . . .

This new, extraordinary mind. I knew what he meant; in extreme situations, it just takes over. Slim, we're on the same wavelength! We're both walking zombies. When you have a goal, a mission to fulfill, the body doesn't matter anymore; shoot it full of holes and it keeps on going.

He heard voices. "There's no longer weight to my body, no longer hardness to the stick. The feeling of flesh is gone." He found himself staring at the instrument panel, but without turning his head—through the back of his skull—he could *see* all the phantoms gathered there behind him. "Is this death? Am I now more man or spirit?"

These phantoms were members of his family, especially his father. In flying alone, he had them for company. His father had taught him to be independent. In the plane he remembered his father saying: "One boy's a boy. Two boys are half a boy. Three boys are no boy at all." So Slim was a loner too. He was twenty-five years old in that plane. For an eerie moment I felt he was *my* son.

Slim, you loved your father?

Loved him? He taught me everything I knew. He called me "boss," believe it or not. How many do you want, boss, he'd ask, hunting turtles. He taught me how to handle turtles, how to swim and hunt. I walked behind him with a loaded gun at the age of seven. Age didn't make any difference to him. He let me use an axe when I had strength enough to swing it. I drove his Ford car when I was twelve.

That's a father for you, Slim.

There's only one for each of us, Coop.

And *his* father, Slim? We're dealing with fathers and sons here now.

When I was a lad, a buzzsaw cut off my grandfather's arm, and everyone expected him to die. When he recovered, he asked to see the arm. They brought it to him in a small, rough coffin, and he told it good-bye. "You have been a good friend to me for fifty years," he said. "But you can't be with me anymore. Good-bye."

That's bravery for you, Slim! (I couldn't help it, I found myself crying.) Bravery like that—it runs in families.

Darn right it does. All my sons are brave.

All of them, Slim? Are you keeping tabs?

Where I am, up here, I can see everything.

Past and future too?

I can see all your secrets. I know when you're awake. I know if you've been bad or good.

Dad, have I been good? I found myself shouting this out, and strangely enough someone answered. From behind a door or wall a voice said, "Charlie?" and instinctively I ducked, expecting the room to come crashing down around me. Footsteps came from the Fisches' apartment. I slammed the book closed, replacing it on the shelf, and looked around wildly, swiveling my head for a place to hide. "Charlie?" The door swung open and Bernice stepped in.

"Charlie, what are you doing here, Charlie?"

"I could ask you the same question, Bernice. What the hell are you doing in the Fisches' apartment?" She swaggered across the room, half grinning, half startled. She was taken aback, I could tell. Standing there in front of me, she sort of listed to the side. I thought maybe I'd woken her up, but she was fully dressed.

"I'm staying here, Charlie. They invited me to stay."

"But they're gone. They're in a hotel."

"That's right, but they asked me to keep an eye on the place. I think they thought someone wanted to break in, Charlie."

"Why would anyone," I asked, "want to do that?"

"I can't imagine," she shrugged. Then she cocked her head, staring into my face. "God, Charlie, you don't look too good. You should try sitting down. You could try raising your feet up a little. You look kind of pale."

I sat in an easy chair, and Bernice with her feet pushed a magazine stand in front of me, for my legs. I was gulping air like a fish out of water, but tried not to show it. "So Bernice, Carol, you're close to the Fisches? You've been here before?"

"A number of times. I'm their adopted son's mother, as you know, Charlie, being his father. I don't know, they act like they like me."

"Does *he* know you're here? Our, you know. Charles Lynd-hurst?"

"I doubt it. He wanted everyone out."

"I wonder why?" I mumbled. "You knew about this room?"

"They showed me it, Charlie."

"How come they didn't show me?"

Bernice shrugged.

"And what exactly," I asked carefully, "does it *mean?* Do you know what the significance of this place is, Bernice?" I tried not to sound too conspiratorial. In fact, I labored to keep my voice as neutral as possible, in order not to appear to be suggesting anything. Bernice glanced around the room, looked the books up and down, but I could tell this was all perfunctory on her part.

"I don't know, Charlie. How should I know? I guess they like

Charles Lindbergh, wouldn't you say? I noticed they were beaming when they showed me the place, and I thought at the time, they must worship this man."

"Oh come on, Bernice. It's more than that. Did they *know* Charles Lindbergh?"

"Abner says he met him once. At a banquet someplace."

Then I thought of something else. "What did Abner *do*, Bernice? Before he retired?"

"Charlie, all these questions. What did Abner do? I'm not sure, something to do with fish I think. I think he wholesaled fish. I don't know, I forgot. Chuckie told me. Maybe it was produce. Import, or something."

"Bernice, were you following me tonight?"

"Oh Charlie! Following you? Why would I be following you?"

"Why would you be guarding this place?"

"Guarding, it's not exactly guarding. I don't have a gun or anything."

Somehow, when she said this it frightened me. I looked at her carefully, watching her hands, which I noted were nervously fidgeting up and down her waist, drumming and scratching. "Could it be," I asked, "that they don't want me to discover something?"

"My goodness, what could that be?"

"Come off it, Bernice."

"*Carol.*"

"You know very well what I'm talking about." I couldn't bring myself to say it, and wanted her to instead. "You were with Cleo Dannen when she told me that day. She told me you were my *sister.* I assume this means we had the same *father.*"

"Oh *that*," said Bernice with an ill-concealed grin. "It could also mean we had the same *mother*, as far as that goes."

"The same mother?"

She nodded. Her nervous gestures struck me as a macabre dance, and I thought of neon signs—that grin flashing on and off—while she fluttered and twitched in place before me. It was obvious to me that all this was a thin veneer of dissimulation, a kind of nervous cheerfulness pasted over guilty knowledge.

The same mother?

All at once she squealed, the door burst open, and Charles Lyndhurst, Jr., stepped in, looking like a banshee dressed in clothes.

"Well, you two! I thought I heard voices. Mom and Dad, you're both here together!" Bernice sat down in a chair next to mine. This room had a little single bed also, up against the wall, with some cushions on the back to make it serve as a couch.

"Yes, we are. That's right."

"Dad, is that your key in the door?" Charles Lyndhurst, Jr., had entered by way of the door to the outside corridor, the same way I'd let myself in.

"Yes, son, actually—I think it's yours. I found it."

"I *thought* I recognized that key!" My son's body looked so tense I began to feel sorry for him. I could see it moving slowly, the spine inside unfolding impatiently, then curling up again. His fingers in their fingerless mittens were perfectly straight and splayed out like spokes. His face had gone rigid, with the largely voluntary expression of someone who smells something bad and wants everyone to know it.

Around his neck was wrapped a scarf. "Well, shall we go?" he offered.

Bernice and I looked at each other.

"I don't mean to be—boorish, Dad. And you too, Mom. But I *do* think that Abner and Anna would be extremely upset if they knew you were here. This *is* their home, after all."

"And what if they knew you were here, Chuckie?" Bernice flashed her nicest grin. "As for me, they invited me to stay the night. Charlie's my guest, your father," she said.

"They could hardly have *invited* you, Mom. When did they *invite* you?"

"After the fire."

"But they *knew*"—his eyes had widened and mouth curled

down; I expected him next to bare his teeth—"they *knew* this place was supposed to stay empty."

"Why?" I asked.

"I told them," he said.

"I mean why was it supposed to stay empty?"

"Fire regulations."

"Suspicious fire, if you ask me," I said.

"Exactly. The arson squad arrives tomorrow morning, Dad. Until then, this room was to remain untouched." Standing there in the middle of the floor, he squeezed each word out like someone decorating cakes, bent over and frowning with extreme concentration and distaste.

"Well, *you're* here," said Bernice.

"I'm the *manager*," he said. "Mom."

"We're all here," I said, "in this room."

"Yes, we are. But it's time for us to leave."

"Why?" I asked.

"There was a *fire* in here."

"But why *this* room?" I felt my voice rising. "Just what is it about this room, anyway? Why is it here? Who started that fire? It was obviously started. And what *is* all this stuff, can you tell me that, son? I mean, I know what it *is*, but what does it *mean?* Maybe you could enlighten me on this matter." I stood up, and saw my son actually take a step backward, so it seemed this was working. He'd never seen me angry, I realized. Bernice stood too. "Charles Lindbergh," I shouted, "who was Charles Lindbergh? I *know* who Charles Lindbergh was, but what exactly, what's the *relationship* here?"

"He was my father."

We all turned our heads toward this voice, which came from the door to the corridor. And there stood Cleo Dannen's son, who glared at us with bitter exultation. It was painful to see. This tall and burly man with a crease across the middle of his features was holding out his hands in supplication. I sat in my chair; Charles Lyndhurst, Jr., slinked to the couch. "He was my father, I'm

convinced of it now." He stepped into the room and closed the
door. "Hello, you," he nodded to me. "Bernice," he nodded.
"Charles."

"You know each other?" I asked my son.

"We've met," said Charles Lyndhurst, Jr.

I fought back an impulse to cross myself.

As Cleo Dannen's son spoke—I still didn't know his name—I
felt I knew every word, grimace, and gesture the man was going
to make or say. It was creepy, and I couldn't help squirming, but
the more he spoke the more it also struck me as perfectly ludi-
crous. He was Charles Lindbergh's son? After a while I could
barely suppress the laughter I felt building up inside me, about
to boil over.

He confessed he'd been listening outside, at the door, and by
way of explanation began talking about his mother, whom he'd
discovered (only after her death) had worked as a governess before
he was born.

A governess? I thought. Oh yes, a governess, and I lowered my
head when a giggle rose up. I felt Bernice's hand touch my arm.

You poor, deluded man! I thought. You don't know half of it.

Then, he said, he found all this Lindbergh memorabilia among
her personal effects, after her death. Much like what we see here,
he gestured. Books, clippings, photographs, letters. He found
them in a trunk his mother kept in her room. Actually, what he
discovered was probably only a fraction of her collection. Since
the Fisches were friends of his mother, who knows, this may have
been hers. She may have given all this to them when she went
into the nursing home, he said.

Friends of his mother? But this was hilarious! By now he was
pacing back and forth, alternately snapping his fingers and gesturing wildly, and I tried not to watch him, realizing that if I did the
laughter wouldn't stop. I coughed to suppress it.

The upshot, he said, was that through certain evidence he'd
assembled, he determined that the man she'd told him was his
father was not his real father. *Not his real father!* He put two and

two together and did some research into the kidnapping of the Lindbergh baby. Did we know, he asked, that the corpse they discovered was never positively identified as that of Charles Lindbergh, Jr.? Furthermore, photos of the child showed a scar on his chin, very much like this one—he pointed to his chin. And the toes on my right foot are turned in, he said, like the Lindbergh baby's. Further investigation uncovered suspicious documents— he'd even written to the surviving members of the Lindbergh family, but received no reply. Of course, at first he resisted the notion. He'd been at this for months—deciphered innumerable hints—had given up his job as well—compared baby photos— went through the files of the kidnapping case—put two and two together—fingerprints, birthmarks, inherited traits—the dimple on his chin—

But I'd had enough. I realized that no one was listening to poor Cleo's son anyway, they were all watching *me*, they couldn't pretend to ignore it anymore. Doubled over, laughing uncontrollably, I rose to my feet in that ridiculous company and staggered toward the door. I couldn't stop laughing. Cleo's son stepped aside—he'd stopped talking, what was the use of it?—and it seemed he even hastened to open the door for me. I felt like someone at a very funny play who finally has to leave, for his health. Laughter like that felt like pumping my weak heart up with air until it was ready to burst. These misled people were all actors in a farce, I felt—just a pack of cards—but my reaction had effectively silenced them. On the other hand, I didn't want to suffer a heart attack right there in their midst. They'd probably think I was faking it. So I left, still laughing, with the assembled company watching me all the way.

And when I reached the hallway the door slammed shut behind me.

13

I stood at the door to Helga's room at the Union Hotel with feelings of anxiety, having recovered from the worst bout of pure hysterics I'd ever experienced in my life.

What bothered me was the thought of those objects in there. I made a lot of noise with the key, rattled the door knob, even kicked the door a few times, to give them fair warning. When I finally stepped in and flicked on the light, they seemed innocent enough, but I saw dust in the air. Nothing was quite the same, of course. The watering can with the hoses now stood over by the closet, and the tea strainer lay next to the bed at a suggestive angle. There appeared to be a certain order, a species of regimentation, but obviously different from the one I'd left behind that morning, or the morning of the previous day, that is. It was two A.M. now.

I threw myself on the bed, exhausted, knowing I wouldn't be able to sleep. Something sharp and hard pressed my side, and I reached underneath with vexation, thinking it was one of those maverick objects. But it turned out to be the tape recorder in my pocket. The tape recorder! I sat bolt upright, slamming the heel of my palm to my forehead, mumbling over and over, *the tape recorder.* If only I'd had the presence of mind to turn it on back there.

Something else was in the pocket. This was the typewritten manuscript I'd found. I pulled it out and unfolded it on the bed. Looking closer I saw it was a carbon copy, smeared here and there, but legible all the way through. Since I couldn't sleep—my heart wouldn't let me—I lay there and read it, sinking deeper into the words with each page, with each name I recognized, each coded message.

History of the Monkey-Faced Girl

Because of my birth, my mother lost her happiness. But now I may hold my chin up high. If she could see me now, my mother would be enraptured. What hidden beauty, what joy, lie underneath the surface of things! She almost lost her life when I was born. Then, when she looked at me, she turned away and said she would not have me. This I was told later by a moon-faced somebody who did not love me very much, I think. My mother asked, how could she be my mother? My *real* mother had to be a monkey!

The moon-faced somebody was my foster sister, who tormented me with stories of my birth, so she could watch me lose my temper. The temper I was famous for as a child. I threw myself to the ground and tore out my hair and screamed as loud as I could. Heartrending cries and bloodcurdling screams. My "sister" told me that my face was covered with black hair when I was born and that I also had a full set of teeth and *bit* my mother as I came out, almost killing her! Kinder people have said that these stories are not true. That the hair did not appear on my face until I was three. Except for this hair, and my early menstruation, they said that I was normal. But I have no way of knowing who is right, an aroma of mystery envelops my birth. Because I have never met my parents. Do they know what has happened to me now? As I have before stated, my mother would be enraptured if she could see me today. For I am now beautiful, who once was ugly. Due to the miracles of science. Am human who once was thought of as an animal. Am normal who once was displayed as a freak. If my mother could see me!

And if I could see her? Would I embrace her? No, I would not. I would smile and walk away and stare at my mirror instead, and think to myself thoughts of love and cruelty, which to me are one and the same thing.

I am fourteen years old. My doctor, who performed the operation, and my secret benefactor, through messages sent to me, have urged me to pour out the story of my childhood. And so consign it to oblivion. By writing it down I may put it behind me. Cleopatra, my guardian, says that I may one day forget all the pain. But can I forget being exhibited? My earliest memories are of being stared at, maybe this is why I have always thought I was special! At first I thought people admired me! Later, I noticed that children were frightened. I noticed that pregnant women turned away. I learned that this was because they thought the sight of my face would cause their children to be born with hairy faces too.

Now people are like a black-and-white tile floor. We are the black squares, and the white squares are the people who are normal. We see the white squares as the top pieces, and they look down on us. But now I see them in the true light. I can be a white square too! Even if I stay black inside.

On display, I sat before a loom. To keep me occupied, because I was always very restless growing up. I was wild and wooly and full of fleas, and so, I didn't sleep very much. I wandered about everyplace. My hands got into everything. Into other children's hair. Into women's purses and men's pockets. Into books of matches and cigarettes. I was acting like the monkey they expected me to be. I learned to make my tantrums wild. My eyes widened and I gritted my teeth with just the right amount of snapping, growling and screeching. I ran around and scratched at everything, including myself. I noticed at the sideshow before they taught me the loom they encouraged my tantrums, but the laughter of the people watching me made me attack a pretty little girl one day. With golden curls and a sneering sort of smile. I noticed that I loved and hated her at the same time. Yes, at that moment I pictured myself smothering this girl with kisses, and strangling her at the same time, or maybe tearing her apart. I was very strong. I pictured myself murdering that little girl and carrying her body through the trees, weeping sadly as I did so. Sadly and unconsolably.

Well, they pulled me off her at once, all that she got were some scratches, a bite, and a memory to give her nightmares for the rest of her life, I sincerely hope. I was left panting in the debris of the aftermath. This was at the sideshow, a world of dreams, a roaring bustle. A whirlpool of gaiety and laughter, but a pit of black despair for some people too. The unlucky ones.

Who was this little girl with the golden curls, to me? She was normal life. The world outside of carnivals and sideshows. School, parents, friends, and playgrounds. Pampered illnesses, good-night kisses, soft bedclothes, and closets full of frilly clothing. This was why I hated her, even though I *did* have frilly clothing myself, they dressed me in it because it looked funny.

After that, I was kept on a leash. I was unable to restrain my real self anymore. I snarled at the audience! If a mouse had run by I would have jumped it and swallowed it whole! I remember thinking at the time I could eat mice or garter snakes easily if the "geeks" at our sideshow could. Even though I knew I would be scolded by Cleopatra. When she came to visit on the weekends, or evenings, she scolded me for my misbehavior. It was Cleopatra who had taken on the burden of educating me. Teaching me to sew, write, love music, play piano, draw, paint, recite and read.

It was Cleopatra who brought me cakes and fruits. Who wiped my hairy face when she saw me. Who kissed me with affection and examined my clothes for tears or rips and the bottoms of my shoes for holes or tacks.

And it was Cleopatra who thought of seating me at the loom. Why did she do this? Firstly, it occupied me. In the second place, it earned me extra spending money, I could buy the fine and frilly things my heart so longed for. And last, it proved to the audience as well to myself that even monkeys can be useful and domestic. And what fun it was to weave, as it turned out! Such an experience, that lifted me for a time out of my monkey antics and made me forget my whole life, was a consolation, to me. I made the loom hum with excitement. I could weave at blinding speed with my nimble fingers. Adults marveled at this!

As I weaved, the barker told the story of my birth. Not the true story, but a tissue of lies. And I sat there at the loom while smiling smugly to myself at the thought-provoking possibility that people could believe such "bunk." Imagine yourself at a carnival sideshow. Or Coney Island or Ocean City. Or the New York World's Fair in 1939, where I was given my first big chance when they discovered that Frances Murphy, the Gorilla Lady in the Strange as it Seems Show, was a man! They needed a quick replacement, and it was me: Bernice, the Monkey-Faced Girl. The audience, having gawked at the Alligator Boy (my friend), next finds its attention directed to my booth. As they watch me weave, they hear the "strange but true" tale of my Brazilian father, the captain of a merchant ship. Who accepted payment on one of his voyages of a live gorilla in a cage, for the goods that he sold, and brought it home as a pet to the beautiful suburbs of Buenos Aires, in South America. At first my mother was madder than a wet hen about this. The gorilla shook his cage when he saw her, and growled and bared his yellow teeth. Alas, this was not anger, but love. One day when my father was gone and the cage was accidentally left unlocked, the ape escaped and threw himself at my mother's feet. He brought her food. Brought her gifts of pretty rocks from outside. He became her servant, when my father was gone on a voyage. In the cage he pined away for love. But outside the cage he danced and clapped his hands. Once, to her surprise, he lifted her skirt, to look beneath it, but she slapped his hand, and he slunk off, the wild old ape, hanging his head. Deeply ashamed.

To make it up to her, he brought her flowers. Flowers of every description. Flowers he picked himself in the lush tropical forest near my parents' house. And my female parent accepted these flowers, to give him comfort, as he had suffered enough, according to this preposterous story. But I noticed the rubes listened with their eyes wide open. Touched by these flowers, my mother taught the simian to dance. She took him on walks. Held his paw. This dalliance then turned to shameless play. My mother grew more bold and wanton, but at the last minute her scruples interposed, much to this ape's deeply felt frustration. Later my father returned from his voyage, the desperate ape was back in his cage, the cage being again left unlocked. Well, that evening my father lay with my mother and the horrible creature crept into their bedroom and sprang forth on my father's back in a fit of jealous rage! Beating him and biting him so badly that he fainted away, later dying from his wounds!

This terrible beast then rolled the limp man aside and finished the act which my father had begun! And I was the result of that unfortunate union!

So went the story. As I have mentioned previously, the gullible rubes were enchanted. They leered at me with pity. But I learned to pay them no mind. Though sometimes I could scarcely frustrate my desire to rip off my clothes and dance in their faces! To bite one of their hands reaching out, since I noticed how much they savored this story. Or just to leap across their heads and climb up a tree and be off. Swinging through the branches.

But most of the time I sat there quietly at the loom and pondered wistfully on the ways of Fate that had made me grow up with a hairy face. I ignored their prying fingers and eyes. It was a job. We all learned to ignore the rubes. The Living Skeleton fell asleep, often. The Alligator Boy read a book. Our lives were normal and dull. We never held a banquet of freaks to welcome a newcomer with food thrown around and dancing on the table. Everyone running around half distracted hither and thither. Chants of "One of us, one of us, ooga booga, one of us." There was a movie in which sideshow freaks did these things, it made me terribly ashamed to see it. At the same time, I could not but think to myself, that our lives were nothing like the movies. They were quite ordinary. So rare and yet so common. To my disgust. We never *did* anything, ever! We shunned public places. My adopted family sat at home in our trailer listening to the radio. Reading or knitting. Before bed we prayed together, then all went to sleep at the same exact hour. In the morning time, the men of the family walked around in their underwear with hair all uncombed. Faces unshaven. Mrs. Dannen scratched Mr. Dannen's back. That was their name. She was the cashier at the sideshow, he was the barker. Jo-Jo, a young acrobat, lived with us, as did Andrew the Alligator boy. My "sister" Jo-Jo was the one who told me the other stories of my birth. The ones that made me fly into a rage, that my mother didn't want me. Cleopatra lived with us too when I was very young, before she went into the world beyond. The world of normal people. After that, she visited us on weekends.

Cleopatra was Mr. Dannen's sister. Now Cleopatra had worked at the carnival also, before my time. She was known as Cleopatra, the Rubber-Legged Girl. She could walk on her hands as well as her feet. She did perfect upstarts, in other words leaping to her feet from a position of lying down on her back. She walked the rolling globe at the entrance to the sideshow, but her great claim to fame was to weave in and out of the rungs of a ladder like a veritable serpent. None of these things could she do anymore, when I was young, as the result of premature arthritis. In the later years, she needed a cane, and, after that, a wheelchair.

If we were in town, she would see me on weekends, sometimes taking me to a museum. It chased the gloom away. She in her wheelchair, I in my veil. I had to be careful in public, as I have always had a tendency to be incontinent, due to improper toilet training. It was necessary, I found, to restrain myself from spitting or laughing immoderately in public. The painter I liked the most in the museums was Rembrandt van Rijn. I stared despairingly at his self-portrait, there was even a simian quality which it had. Unknown founts of strength tapped by despair. He had known tragedy, and I felt the same about myself, the disappointment of my wasted life, the non-performance of my aspirations. We knew each other well. Rembrandt van Rijn and me.

Cleopatra had known tragedy too, it was also written on her face. A face which had prematurely aged. Though it still possessed some of its previous impish beauty. When she was young, before I was born, her impish beauty had attracted a man. A habitué of the Dannen carnival as it traveled through New York and New Jersey, on its circuit. Jo-Jo told me the story of this man and Cleopatra.

Now Cleopatra was married at the time, but her husband neglected her. He worked in New York City, living there with their son when the carnival was "on the road." The man she had attracted, in contrast to her husband, was tall and handsome, with curly hair. The kind of man who wore flight jackets and silk scarves. In the fashion of those times.

He courted her. She fell in love with him. But something went wrong. Enter Olga Kuyper, the Flying Angel. A tall Dutch girl who had lately joined the carnival. She turned the head of Cleo's lover, in time she stole him away from her.

Cleopatra was short and energetic. Boyishly pretty. Olga, on the contrary, was a tall statuesque female with a Roman nose. High were her cheekbones and her hair was reddish brown. I have seen pictures of her and have been struck by her full round mouth, which gave her a most unusual attractiveness.

Some contests are intensely interesting, others are dull and insipid. In every contest there must be a winner and a loser. We love the contest when we have got the full worth of it, but no one cares to lose. In the contest for a man's love, some women do nothing and win, while others jump around all over the place, which is really not the way at all. Olga won. Or, as was more likely the case, Cleopatra lost. Well, Cleopatra plotted her revenge. I have heard many stories. She threw acid in Olga's face. Severed the ropes of her trapeze. Loosened the stays on her safety net. Burned her beautiful hair. Cut a tendon in her leg. Or simply jumped on her back in a moment of rage (as I would have done), reaching around to scratch out her eyes with her long sharp nails.

But none of this was the way it really happened. Instead, she slugged her rival in the face with her fist closed around a roll of dimes. An old carnival trick. Breaking her nose and knocking out two teeth in one blow.

Oh! How I have often pictured myself in Cleopatra's shoes! Feeling that pretty face split beneath my knuckles! Hearing the crack of skin and bone! Watching the blood start! Smelling her fear—for it has a smell, to sensitive noses, such as my own. A thrill of excitement tingles through my whole being when I think of that moment!

What vivid pictures it calls to mind! To think was to act, and Cleopatra acted, despite the protests of a world of downtrodden beasts called men. I noticed this has always been a lesson to me. But how truly fickle and two-sided everything in life is, for Cleopatra, upon delivering this blow, immediately regretted it. A few days later, she begged the forgiveness of Olga and her lover. People scoffed at her, calling her a fool, but she sought to make amends by placing herself at the service of her rival. Always hanging around the two of them. Running errands, buying them gifts. Holding Olga's jacket during her performances. She bought a fur coat for Olga. Around this time Cleo's husband divorced her, as news of her immoral life at the carnival had reached him. She thought this was proper punishment for her sinful behavior, and it made her redouble her self-punishment efforts. The climax was, when Olga became pregnant. She had to leave the sideshow. Eventually, she gave birth to a child out of wedlock, and Cleopatra volunteered to take it off the hands of Olga and her lover. She placed it in a home. And so, in this way, Cleopatra made herself their faithful servant for a time.

What happened to Olga Kuyper after she left the carnival, I do not know. She went to parts unknown. Some say she married, but not the man whose heart she stole from Cleopatra. As for Cleopatra, I don't want to sound too "pick-upy," but I owe so much to her! She turned her attention to me, as I have before stated, and educated me, raising me up from the slough of despair and despondency I lived in. And now I shall leave the sideshow! Having lost my chief means of attraction. And Cleopatra shall be my guardian, and we shall live in luxury, thanks to my secret benefactor, whoever he may be, wink wink. I can add two plus two. My secret benefactor has long used Cleo to carry out his charity, has he not? And perhaps Cleopatra has pointed out to him (to you) worthy objects of that charity? She refuses to reveal his (your) identity, but I can draw my own conclusions. I picture a man, tall of course. With a dimple on his chin. He wears flight jackets and silk scarves, he has earned the lifelong devotion of someone whose love he once spurned. So now you know why I have told this story, your excellent self. Have I "hit the mark"?

And so, my life shall change. Will I be happy? Will I have my revenge on the rubes and smug gawkers? I once lived in direst poverty, who now shall live in luxury. All because of a chance hormonal imbalance! Those who are normal, cannot know how this feels. Already I have learned to imitate a young lady's manners. I drink my tea ever so daintily. I know enough not to jump around too much. I am, in truth, a *good* little monkey! For I have learned that behaving well consists of aping good behavior.

Surely my doctor knows this. He was there, he removed the bandages. He held the mirror before my face. I thought at the time, now I begin a new life! Leaving the old one behind forever. There, it is gone. When I saw my face, so clean and pure, all aglow with new skin, I screeched in triumph. It must have surprised my doctor, but there you are. Having been so humble and quiet during all those painful operations. Such a good patient. Such a good monkey! But when I saw my new beauty, it was too wonderful to be true. Well, I screamed with savage joy! Ready to sink my teeth into the world!

October 3, 1944

Dear Mr. Lyndhurst,

You will please excuse the contents of this memoir as the excited outpourings of an angry but brilliant young girl. Our daughter didn't know whom she was writing it for, and I think she sometimes hardly knew what she was saying. As Cleo pointed out to me, there is much here to give us pause. But I hope you will see as I do a great deal to warm our hearts as well. If that day ever comes on which Anna and I may make ourselves known to our daughter, I will have this memoir bound in leather and presented to her on a pillow of gold, as proof of our undying affection. When we gave her up to those who thought they knew where she belonged (as ever, I exclude Cleo from this charge), it tore our hearts out. We never went to see her on display; it would have been our ruin. And people who say that we sold her for gain lie through their teeth. I have enemies, sir; enough said on that score. (I am sure you've experienced this envy yourself.)

Now we must give her up a second time, without having yet won her back. Yes, we give her into good hands. And I have seen the photographs; marvelous, simply marvelous. You will forgive me, however, if I shed one more tear, a tear of gratitude and regret. (I can hardly stop Anna from crying, to be frank.) Please keep me informed as to the state of her soul and the growth of her mind.

This copy of her memoir is yours; I retain the original. Cleo will still see us periodically, but I will be anxious to hear from you also, as one who has had much experience in life, has won some acclaim, and now has taken it upon himself to give of himself to others. Please treat our little girl well; she is about to become a woman. You can see for yourself how sensitive she is. Give her good companions and books, the best schools, the best culture and taste. Please do not neglect to send us pictures. You know where I can be found. Once again I assure you that we will not interfere or make ourselves known until such time as you find it appropriate. But think of us, sir! Do not neglect us!

I acknowledge the receipt of your kind check, deposited into our account at Chase Manhattan.

Sincerely,
Abner Fisch

14

From the relative comfort of my jar today, I find it difficult to place in sensible order all I discovered, or thought I discovered, after reading this story—all the extraordinary conclusions I came to that night. I was far less calm then than now, since I knew myself to be on the verge of revelations, and therefore felt in that room like a cinder popping around inside a stove, a spark of pure vision bouncing off the walls.

One must keep in mind my lack of sleep, my heightened suspicions, my sense of displacement in that room, as well as the current of fear and confusion running beneath it all due to Helga's unexplained disappearance. I heard voices. I think I did. But I glimpsed the truth too. Parts of my mind blew their circuits, leaping gaps in their search for facts. Knowing what I know now, I see how generally ragged historical facts are around the edges, a phenomenon of material decay, I've since concluded. It's what happens to old documents, letters, charts and charters, images, clothes, concepts and names. They veil themselves in rags and ashes.

At first, I just lay there stunned and thought of obviously crazy explanations. This was all a hoax, or a monkey had typed it, as when people said, given enough time (trillions of years, for example), monkeys pecking away at random could type the complete works of Shakespeare.

Then I remembered having seen an acrobat named Jo-Jo at a carnival in Windsor when I was a child. I think it was Jo-Jo. Was this the same carnival, the Dannen carnival? Maybe I saw Bernice there too.

Bernice, the beautiful love of my youth! If this story was true, she grew up hairy, then had an operation. And Cleo was her guardian. But why was she *my* guardian also? *I* wasn't some sort of freak too, was I?

All at once I sat up, feeling my body flush, my heart lurch forward. *Olga gave birth to a child out of wedlock.* This sentence looped through my mind nonstop, along with the other one. *Cleopatra placed it in a home.*

I felt myself swaying forward and back, arms wrapped around my chest, while I tried to figure this one out. Suppose that child was me. Just suppose. Its father was Olga's lover, who was also Bernice's secret benefactor. He payed for Bernice's operation, he took her into his home, or provided a home for Cleo and her. So he was Uncle Chuck, number one. And number two, Uncle Chuck was the Mr. Lyndhurst to whom Abner's letter was addressed, since the home had to be East Seventy-eighth Street, where Bernice went to live at the age of fourteen. A few months later I arrived there too, the son of Olga Kuyper and this Mr. Lyndhurst. Lyndhurst? The name Chuckie and Social Security had thrust upon me, Bernice's name, though I recognized it now as a congenial pseudonym. They used it to protect him. Who else could Abner be alluding to in his letter when he said the man had won "some acclaim"?

Abner! I leaped out of bed, I may even have shouted, or grunted, I don't know, scattering around objects and junk. According to his letter, Abner and Anna were Bernice's parents. Therefore, she couldn't be my sister. She didn't know this herself, not yet. They'd found her again, Abner and Anna, by means of our mutual son—so to speak—and they were undoubtedly ready now, forty years later, to acknowledge her as theirs. Now that I'd taken Chuckie off their hands.

But that made Chuckie their grandson. My God. Of course, *they* didn't know this. Did they?

My head swam in circles, and I couldn't for a while organize all that was crashing around me. I did feel underwater, I felt smothered by everything, but at the same time, beneath it all, beneath the questions and swirling answers, lay this wonderful consolation: Bernice and I were not incestuous lovers. I thought that I must have known this all along. Weren't there instincts triggered by hormones or pheromones which prevented you from mating with your own sister? I'd heard this someplace. . . .

I walked back and forth, flung myself on the bed, and read Bernice's story again. The lover Olga Kuyper had stolen from Cleo had to be this man named Lyndhurst. Was he my father? Was Olga Kuyper my mother? I marshaled all the evidence, tried to organize it into piles, but like pyramids of marbles they collapsed repeatedly, they skittered all over, I had to keep chasing them. Lyndhurst. Yes. I know his real name, of course. Don't I? I laughed out loud. Then, as I lay there on the bed, something actually scurried past a corner of my eye, just beyond the bedclothes, on the floor across the room. I thought of roaches or mice again, but stare as I might at that spot—trying to catch whatever it was, or to draw it out, as the sun draws out moisture—nothing moved.

Move? said the objects scattered on the floor (with their hands to their chests)—how could *we* move?

Then I thought, *Bernice!* and rose straight out of the bed a few inches. I thought of phoning her at the Fisches' apartment, if she was still there, but picturing the mad scene I'd left in that room—Bernice, Chuckie, and Cleo Dannen's son—I again felt confused, felt the careful piles collapsing.

Cleo Dannen's son. Here was another factor in the equation. He was probably the son from her marriage to the drunken stockbroker, the man who divorced her when Mr. Lyndhurst showed up. He thought he was *Lindbergh's* son, but of course that was crazy. Megalomania.

As for Abner and Anna, they'd inherited all those Lindbergh mementos from Cleo. They were Cleo's old friends, because of Bernice. Maybe that's how Cleo met them; when Bernice turned out to be a monkey-faced infant, her parents searched for a carnival and found the Dannens'. Did Cleo—or her brother—pay for Bernice? Did they *purchase* Bernice from the Fisches? Later came along our secret benefactor, this man named Lyndhurst, the man Cleo had vowed to serve—Uncle Chuck—and when she brought Abner and Anna's daughter to his attention, he offered to rehabilitate her, with Cleo's help and the wonders of science. Then, still later, when Bernice wanted someone to adopt *our* child—hers and mine—she naturally turned to Cleo, who naturally went to Abner and Anna, her friends. They could return the favor, couldn't they?

I felt proud of myself. I was keeping things straight, they were falling into place. I was getting someplace, I could tell, and waving that typewritten manuscript at the ceiling—carbon, actually—kissing it once too, I remembered my cousin, Bernice—the girl they called my cousin—when I first went to live on East Seventy-eighth Street. Even then (it occurred to me now) there was something wonderfully *new* about her face, there may have been little faint blue lines on it too. A kind of cheesy texture. The blue lines I remembered as veins—they showed when she was angry or aroused—but of course they could have been stitches too. Seams where her new face had been pieced together.

But Cleo Dannen's son and my son? I didn't like the fact that they had met. It sounded suspicious. And what about the mysterious Mr. Lyndhurst? Was he really Charles Lindbergh? Here, I still felt somewhat uncertain, and was forced, in the absence of absolute proof, to rely upon conviction. With that as a base I could search for clues, sort through them carefully, and analyze them rationally. What I actually had to do was process information. I'd accessed plenty. Now I had to process it.

I tried to remember Uncle Chuck. Did he wear silk scarves? Then again, did Charles Lindbergh even wear them? Silk scarves were just a bit much for the Charles Lindbergh *I* knew. Then I thought of something Uncle Chuck had said, or something Cleo said once; maybe she addressed him as Colonel. Yes, that was it. Or Slim. Or maybe Lucky.

Then I thought of Olga Kuyper, the angel. The Flying Angel.

But something was missing. I knew there was something I wanted to remember, it loomed up ahead like a buttress in thought. I could *feel* its shadow. It was like having a word or name on the tip of your tongue, like the time I tried to remember the name of a certain mayor of New York, but all I could think of was the Spanish Civil War. I concluded this meant that he must have been mayor when that war was going on, but somehow I sensed there was more to it than that. It took a few days to make the connection (not that I was thinking about it unceasingly), which went something like, Civil War, Civil Guard, Guardia Civil, La Guardia. Henry La Guardia. Or was it Thomas?

I could do something like that with Bernice's story, I thought— let the names jog my memory—but the damn whispers around me were getting louder. They diverted my concentration. Whispers, rustling, the distant sound of dry leaves. A handkerchief thrown amid that little community of objects on the floor had assumed a sinister aspect. It had a face, it looked like a boy. The strange thing was, though, the more I looked at it the less I could tell what on earth it was, whether a handkerchief or a face or anything at all. It didn't look like a thing I could recognize.

I noticed a jar of pills there too. This I hadn't seen before.

I thought of Jo-Jo. That was a name to conjure with. Maybe that was the thing, the shadow or whatever, which was activating my memory glands. Jo-Jo, Jody, Jujube. Jo-Jo made you think of a dog, a trained dog who jumps on horses' backs.

I was getting nowhere. The name drew a blank.

It occurred to me that there are no guileless memories, just as, for example, there is no guileless love.

I thought I heard laughter. My brain felt overcrowded, as when you stuff your mouth and try to speak—I couldn't think, couldn't articulate. After the rush of mental and emotional ecstasy when I'd first read Carol's story—after the discovery that she wasn't my sister—things were going stale. The threads had run out. Carol? Bernice. Maybe that was it, Carol, Clairol. She'd changed her name to put Bernice the Monkey-Faced Girl behind her, of course. On the other hand, she was still Bernice when I knew her on East Seventy-eighth Street. So the change came after that.

The Spirit of St. Louis. Louis, Louise. Didn't I know someone named Louise?

More whispered laughter, laughter of creatures lacking in vocal cords. I looked at the time: two A.M. So my watch had stopped. I realized I must have been falling asleep. I was thinking, I could *be* that handkerchief, I could *be* that spindle, that watering can. The fog I was in let things be put together in new ways, it was generous but not fastidious. It didn't care about the truth, for example. It was exciting, though. The possibilities were endless. Griffins, minotaurs, Lindbergh's sons.

I thought I could be a shoe.

You wouldn't like it, said a voice.

Something crashed to the floor, and a blast of cold air went through my soul. I woke up having just in my sleep experienced a kind of membrane opening, a tissue of memory unsticking, but already whatever it was had slipped away. A name, or a word.

The lights were out, but I hadn't turned them out. I could swear I hadn't. Rattle and scurry of things on the floor when I jumped out of bed to turn the lights on. Over by the objects, on the floor beside the dresser, were pieces of glass and wood. This was a bottle which had been sitting on the dresser, containing within it a ship made of toothpicks. Now it was all smashed on the floor.

A name or word. I thought perhaps I could choose what it was. As when I'd once had the power to control my dreams, I could decide what it was. Going one step further, I could also decide whether I was Charles Lindbergh's son or not. Over here, all the evidence said I was, and over here all the evidence said I wasn't. All right, Coop. What do you choose?

But this was frivolous, and I erased the question with a few sweeps of my paw. "Shall we try again?" I asked myself out loud. "Have another go at it? Lyndhurst. Olga Kuyper."

I sat up. It was like electrodes in my brain. That name Kuyper had triggered something, but I couldn't put my finger on it. Then all at once I didn't know who I was. I thought of those people who show up at bus stations without any memory of where they've been or who they are. Just flotsam in the fog . . .

Olga, Helga. We had a certain connection here. I tugged a little more, pulled a little further. This was the sort of thing, if you pulled too hard you'd lose it, it was tricky. Also, it was a big, heavy thing. Baggy and loose, it came from another planet entirely. It wasn't anything like I'd expected, it came dragging seaweed and kelp and debris, and smelling bad as well. But it came. I pulled it in, then I had it: Kuyper was Helga's mother's name. Helga's mother, who'd died long ago. Out of my memory of some document or application—it may have been our marriage license—the name shaped itself, the soft letters hardened: *Mother's Maiden Name:* Kuyper.

Didn't Helga have an uncle named Kuyper, still alive? In Miami or someplace? I was certain of this. Pretty sure. I thought so.

This wasn't exactly what I'd hoped for, not the discovery I was supposed to make, so maybe it was true. It had nothing to do with Lindbergh, for example. Or did it? Our secret benefactor was Olga's lover. Steady now, Coop. Let's keep this mess straight. I felt like crying because all my threads were snarling. Of course, the names could just be pure coincidence. Two people named Kuyper, completely unrelated. But Olga and Helga? Think of *those* names.

There were other things too. Helga's father's name was Max, Max Clausen. Had he married once or twice? I couldn't remember. And Helga and Chuckie had a business relationship; he was Abner and Anna's grandson! But these were peripheral matters, or so I thought, and my job was to keep my eye on the brass ring itself. It helped, remembering Helga's mother's name, but it also demonstrated clearly (I thought) that something was still missing, some link.

This may have been why everything now appeared covered with fuzz when it should have been clear and hard-edged. And the noise, that hissing sound, or whispers, or laughter. Olga, Helga.

I jumped when the phone rang, it sounded so terrifying. This was the loudest phone I'd ever heard in my life. I answered it, but the party on the other end was keeping mum. "Who is this?" I shouted. Then I thought of something practical, at least. "Could you tell me what time it is?" The line went dead.

But now I had to adjust back down to the audio level of this strange little room, and it felt like sinking back into static. Low-level radiation.

He'll consent to anything that will bring us harm, said a voice. I realized that the speaker was the jar of pills.

He doesn't trust you?

Not anymore.

I lay there still on the bed, while reaching down carefully in my pocket to switch on the tape recorder. Slowly, with caution—only moving a fraction of an inch at a time—I pulled out the thin plastic cord with the microphone at its end, dangling it over the edge of the bed.

Besides, said another voice, if you complain you'll be thrown on the junk heap, if that's your attitude.

At this a collective shudder rose up, I could feel it in that room. I opened my pocket and glanced at the tape recorder, getting all this down. Across the room, the spindle with its meat rack lingered in the background, keeping its own counsel. Then I saw it: a cockroach. It scampered across the floor from the spindle toward the closet. I had to move now, I knew it—to shake off that drowsy feeling, the lassitude I felt. Watching that cockroach scuttle into the closet, I told myself: Now I will jump to my feet. But I couldn't.

At last one leg moved. Slowly, I felt myself climb off the bed. Moving very slowly, I held completely still for a minute or two, feeling the motion echo. Like moving underwater. Meanwhile, a button was counseling patience and praising the virtues of simplicity. Brass is brass, it was saying. Another roach ran into the closet.

On my feet, near the closet, I felt wobbly but a little more in control. I sensed the presence of someone or something in there. The closet door was actually a curtain, open a crack, and I could see a few roaches ascending the side wall, venturing out upon the wooden dowel and down a coathanger to something in the back. Whatever it was was obscured by the clothes on hangers, unclear in the single overhead light from the room behind me.

Powerful currents came from that closet. I turned and saw all the objects gathered behind me, the watering can, shoes, pills, bottles, tea strainer, spindle, buttons, all crowded around the closet door like a congregation. I even thought I heard drumming, but of course it turned out to be the heart in my chest, throbbing away.

Turning back, I tore open the curtain. From the rear of the closet a roach flew down, landing on my leg. Behind Helga's clothes was a leather carrying bag, too large for a purse—something she took on flights—and from it came more roaches, they flew down around me with a dry hiss or rattling sound, and I tried not to panic, brushing at my legs. Meanwhile, I stared at this carrying bag, whose top was open. In it was a small package or box. One corner had been torn open, and it appeared that the roaches came out of that. Was this a lunch Helga had neglected to dispose of? I looked closer and gradually realized that I'd recognized this box right away, perhaps not admitting it to myself, although why Helga would have taken my mother's ashes, would have brought them to this place, I couldn't understand.

I reached for it, brushing roaches off, while backing out of the closet and kicking at the junk and trash behind me. I tripped over something, fell, jumped up, felt a substance draining from the hole in the box. Saw the little pile of ashes on the floor. *My mother's ashes!* I pinched the hole closed. I held the box so the hole was on top. I shook it a little; it felt half empty. Some roaches might still be inside, but they'd have to stay.

And it *was* my mother's ashes all right, the package I'd been mailed thirty-five years ago. It had an outer wrapping I'd never removed with the return address of a mortuary in Miami, Florida. I hadn't looked at this box in decades, largely due to shame. Taking it with me on moves from Yale to Albany to Nyack to Highland, I'd stored it away as quickly as possible, perpetually deferring her last wishes to sprinkle the ashes on the East River.

The wrapping had been half torn off by someone, then hastily replaced. Beneath it, a label on the box said *Olga Cooper*. But in parentheses after Cooper, it said *Kuyper. Olga Cooper (née Kuyper).*

I held the box in my hands. My mother was an angel. The woman Cleopatra had punched in the face, the same face I recalled so vividly at the hospital—that beautiful face!—she was my mother. And she was that man's lover, our secret benefactor—we know who, don't we? I was their son. And when she died, a lawyer or someone—executor of the will—mailed the ashes to me at Yale, and now here they were.

I processed this information with outward calm, all the while sinking down a whirlpool. For the last link was there, had been there all along, staring me right in the face, though I'd closed my eyes. Why had Helga taken these ashes? Because Olga Kuyper was *her* mother too . . .

One of us, I said to myself. It made a nice chant. *Olga Helga, one of us.*

I turned to run, but felt something dragging: the mike from my cassette recorder, still hanging from my pocket. As I stuffed it hastily back, hopping on each foot in succession to pull on my shoes, lashing out and kicking at the objects by my feet—as I looked all around me in fear, I noticed through cracks of light around the blanket pinned over the window that it was dawn.

I cradled the box carefully, brushed a roach off my arm, and ran from that room singing to myself—I couldn't help it—*One of us, one of us, Olga Helga, one of us . . .*

From the Queensboro Bridge the ashes spiraled down in a thin white line to the cold water below. A few roaches dropped too. I tore the label off the box and stuffed it in my pocket, then let the box fall. It felt at that moment as though all my existence, all of my past and future too, had been sucked into my mind and blown out again. I was empty, cleared. Things looked perfectly ordinary and dull. The metal railing was a metal railing, and the water below was gray and cold. It held no associations.

Behind me the traffic honked and beeped, thick as soup, and the concrete pavement bearing it up looked raw in the light. I found myself blinking. On Fifty-ninth Street I caught a cab. "Where's a good place for breakfast?" I asked.

"The Belmore."

"Where's that?"

"Park Avenue South."

So he drove me to the Belmore Cafeteria, though it took forever in the morning rush hour. I couldn't go back to the Union Hotel, I'd already decided that. I had my wallet, my cassette recorder. After breakfast I planned to leave the city for good.

"Helga's my sister," I told the cabbie.

He grunted.

"Kuyper's her mother's name," I explained.

Sitting back, I thought of Helga's phone call the night Pork Vining had come to dinner. She'd discovered the ashes before me, those ashes I'd been trying to find, and had spirited them out of the house when she opened the wrapper and recognized the name. Dear, sweet Helga. I wanted to scream, but sat there very calmly.

"I've lost and gained a sister in a day."

"Good for you," he said. He was leaning to the side—to roll down the window and spit outside, I assumed—but then I noticed the screen sliding shut between front and back, blocking off communication.

The Belmore Cafeteria was filled with cabbies drinking coffee. I sat to an order of eggs and sausage feeling utterly exhausted, barely able to eat. Sitting there, I noticed the egg whites had been nibbled all around the edges until only the yolks were left. Had I done that?

And here I must reveal a little secret. Shake of the head, and a guilty shrug. Helga was my wife, of course. I courted her in Nyack in 1970 and we married the year after. But I'd known her long before that; had met her on East Seventy-eighth Street, in fact. Helga was the girl I've referred to as Karin, Bernice's friend, the one I used to rouse Bernice's jealousy back then—the one who was with me in the library that time when Bernice walked in— that was Helga. I gave her name as Karin to protect the innocent.

Later, in Nyack, I found her again. I'd traced her there, after years of searching in vain for Bernice. If I couldn't have one, I was determined to have the other. I joined the cast of *The Crucible* precisely in order to court her, twenty-five years after she'd touched me so intimately that evening in the library. Of course, she didn't recognize or recall me. So my conquest was especially gratifying, having been accomplished twice. On the stage I stormed around as John Proctor, just as years before I'd been her Count of Monte Cristo. Maybe she recognized me, I don't know. I doubt it though. If she did, she never let on, and hasn't since. But I knew it was her, because I'd researched it. On East Seventy-eighth Street, she'd lived just a block away from Bernice and me. Unable to learn anything about Bernice or my family, I inquired of porters and neighbors of Helga and hers. Eventually I learned her married name and the fact that she was now living in Nyack. In Nyack, I hung around her house after rehearsals. I invited myself in when her husband was gone and her five-year-old David in bed. I met her at shopping centers. I joined the Unitarian Church, to be close to her. And through carefully devised small talk, I coaxed her to talk about her youth in New York City, thus confirming my discovery. I even contemplated directing this talk toward the topic of Bernice—maybe Helga knew where she was, I thought—but realized that wouldn't be possible without giving myself away.

Besides, Helga was just fine. She'd grown less frail, far more beautiful, than the Helga—or Karin—I'd victimized twenty-five years before. I'd never forgotten her devotion to me, her steadfast love even during my affair with Bernice.

Dear, sweet Helga was actually my very first love. Then she was my wife. And now she was my sister.

I remembered that on East Seventy-eighth Street her mother had often visited mine, or the woman I thought was mine, Cleo Dannen, for reasons now obvious to me. She wanted to see Cleo, her former rival, her friend, but there was someone else she wanted to see also, wasn't there? Didn't she usually bring me a gift? A bar of soap, a book, an ocarina? Of course she did. She must have.

Undoubtedly, she was respectable by then, having given up the carnival and her lover. She'd married Helga's father, Max; Helga, at least, was legitimate. And Max was still alive in Orlando, still hanging on. I could talk to him, perhaps, to confirm this. Discreetly.

But Helga, could I talk with her? Even if I could find her now? Eating breakfast at the Belmore, I shook my head, drained. Better let it go. She'd seen the name on the ashes, she'd discovered the horrible truth. How could I even face her again?

PART IV

15

"Well, Charlie, we all more or less wanted to . . . disabuse you of the notion that you were Charles Lindbergh's son."

"You mean that was all *planned?* In that room?"

"More or less. We improvised a lot of it too. Patrick was good, don't you think?"

"Patrick?"

"Cleo Dannen's son."

"What about the fire?"

"We planned that too."

"*Why?*"

"Well, we had to get you into that room somehow."

"I mean why disabuse me? Why did you want to do it?"

"In the first place, it looked like something you were getting pretty crazy about. I mean, Charlie, you weren't acting normal, I noticed."

"And in the second place?"

"The second place is Charles Lindbergh already has enough sons. He doesn't need any more."

"He doesn't need you to protect him either. He's dead."

"But his family is very much alive."

"You can say that again."

"Charlie, don't start."

"Am I his son or not? That's all I want to know. You haven't told me anything to prove I'm not."

"You haven't told me anything to prove you are."

"Bernice, you started this, remember? You accosted me in a

playground in Newburgh and told me you were my sister."

"I didn't, Cleo did."

"I didn't want to listen. I wasn't interested at all. If I didn't believe you then, why should I believe you now?"

"I'm not your sister."

"I know. But you told me you were."

"I thought I was, but I'm not."

"When you thought you were, Bernice, at that point in time— who did you think was our father? Uncle Chuck?"

"I suspected."

"And who the hell did you think Uncle Chuck was? That's the question, is it not?"

"I suppose that's one of the questions."

"Was he Charles Lindbergh?"

"Charlie, it didn't work, did it? What we did. You still have this crazy idea."

"I just want to settle it once and for all."

"Did he look like Charles Lindbergh? You saw as much of the man as I did."

"That's just it. In a way he did. I don't know, Bernice, it was such a long time ago. He wore flight jackets. He had a dimple on his chin."

"Charlie, lots of people have dimples on their chins. *You* have one."

"Exactly. Also, he was tall."

"Well, I don't know. From *your* perspective . . ."

"He only showed up weekends."

"What's that supposed to prove?"

"He led two lives, Bernice. It could have been. He kept us under wraps in that apartment, watched over by our guardian, Cleo."

"And why would Charles Lindbergh do that?"

"Because, I don't know. Maybe we were his children. Or some of us. He took an interest in us. He was playing philanthropist."

"Well, if you say so, Charlie. You must know what you're talking about. But it still sounds to me like delusions of grandeur."

"Bernice, I wouldn't even *have* such delusions if you hadn't given them to me."

"I told you, it was Cleo."

"You and Cleo together."

"I just went along. I wanted to see you again."

"You wanted a free house."

"Did *you* pay for it, Charlie? I noticed you were getting checks every month in the mail, you told me. That's more than I got. Some philanthropy. When they booted us out they kept you on the dole, but not me. I should be getting something, don't you think? The least you can do is not begrudge me this house."

"What happened after the baby, Bernice?"

"After I had Chuckie?"

"On East Seventy-eighth Street. They sent me to boarding school. Where did you go?"

"First of all, Cleo took the baby off my hands. I didn't know it at the time, but what she did was she gave it to Abner and Anna. Then Cleo and I moved out. To Long Island. I had to take care of her, because of her legs."

"No more Uncle Chuck?"

"No more Uncle Chuck, no more cousins, but I heard later that Raymond died. Of an aneurism. I already told you I went to college, I got married, what else? To answer quickly, fast, I don't think I could. The main thing was, I remember thinking at the time, the world just turned stale for me. I mean, West Babylon, which is where we went, was not exactly the Upper East Side. We lived in a house like a bird cage, somewhat. I lost interest in books, I gave up ballet, the piano, those things. I started gaining weight, too, which I've lost most of it since then. But for a little while there I was—I was what you might call fat."

"And you never saw Uncle Chuck again?"

"Never."

"What about Cleo?"

"I don't know, she might have. Her legs got better. She might have seen him again."

"Why did she say I was Charles Lindbergh's son?"

"Here we go again. To get your attention."

"That's what *she* said."

"Then maybe it's true."

"It's weak, Bernice. That's no way to get someone's attention. And why Charles Lindbergh? Why not John Dillinger, or FDR, or Sacco or Vanzetti, or someone else famous?"

"Well, first of all maybe she was interested in Charles Lindbergh. Maybe she was in love with him, Charlie."

"In love? Then she knew him?"

"In the context of reading about him. She read about him in the papers just like everyone else. Also, she saw him once, this she told me, the time he landed his plane out on Long Island near the town she used to work in. Before you and me were born."

"Naturally."

"His plane circled a field near a carnival and everyone went out to see it, she said. When they heard Lindy was overhead, the whole town ran outside. Well, it was seven-thirty A.M., Charlie, so Mr. Lindbergh must have had a lovely view of the latest fashions in pajamas, ha ha. He landed and stayed in the town overnight, in the mayor's house, and then Cleo saw him come out the next morning. They were all lined up on the street outside, half the town, waiting to see him come out."

"Then what happened?"

"Then he took off."

"And that's all?"

"Well, maybe that's enough for someone like Cleo, I don't know. She thought she saw him everywhere after that. She collected all this stuff. Clippings and books. She went to the kidnapping trial, when that happened. Cleo was never that—balanced, Charlie. You should remember that. I don't know but what it might have been an obsession, you could say."

"And the things in that room at the Fisches' apartment. Those were Cleo's?"

"Most of it. Some of it was theirs. They shared a common interest. Abner met Lindbergh one time, as I told you. They all belonged to the Lindbergh Club of the Bronx, Cleo and the Fisches."

"Come on."

"It's true."

"Are you making this up or what, Bernice?"

"Do chickens have teeth? Can pigs fly? Why would I—why would I *want* to make it up?"

"To hide something from me. I know you're hiding something."

"Why would I hide something, number one, and number two, I've got nothing to hide. Who cares, as far as that goes? It's all water under the bridge. What difference does it make? I mean, remembering those things. That's what I was talking about, Charlie, it could drive a person crazy."

"Yes, it could. You're exactly right. If a person doesn't—take precautions."

"And what's that supposed to mean? Wipe that grin off your face, please, you grin at the most inappropriate times. Charlie, you're so tense, look at you! You're tight as a drum, relax a little, please. Roll over—"

I pressed Stop and glanced up at James Faber with a look of profound significance. I was here on Liberty Street to present my lawyer with evidence that certain people had entrapped me into sneaking into Abner's apartment, had even staged a fire, these fanatics, in order to make me think I was not Charles Lindbergh's son. Their ultimate ruse was to flood the market with claims to be a Lindbergh—here, I had in mind Cleo Dannen's son—thus making such claims common. Cheap, even.

And why would they do this? Go to such lengths?

James Faber cleared his throat. "More?" I asked, holding my finger cocked over the cassette player.

"No, that's quite enough, Charles."

"Just one more, James, wait. It gets worse, we started shouting." Reaching down into the paper bag at my feet, I fumbled for another tape with shaking hands. I might have dropped a few too. Each cassette was clearly labeled—*Whose House, Sideshow, Cleo, Charles Lindbergh*—according to the dominant topic in the conversation. I was looking for the one titled *East Seventy-eighth Street*. I'd already explained to James how I'd made these tapes, by hiding the tape recorder under our bed, where Bernice and I did most of our talking. In bed was where I tried to draw her out. Of course, this meant recording certain private activities also, at least initially, but these I'd done my best to erase. Then I'd had the tapes transcribed; the typewritten manuscripts lay in a stack on James Faber's desk. That way he could read them at his leisure without being subject to embarrassing sounds, and I could keep my tapes.

I'd gone to Windsor to live with Bernice after leaving the Belmore Cafeteria in New York City. It was now April, just about spring, a year since Bernice and Cleo had accosted me on that playground in Newburgh, and five months since I'd sprinkled Olga Kuyper's ashes on the East River, then fled the city and driven to Windsor.

"It's right here someplace, just a second, here it is." Rummaging through that bag of clattering cassettes, half bent over, reading each label, I felt my lawyer's cold flat eyes upon me. I wanted him to hear Bernice's laughable account of East Seventy-eighth Street and our mysterious benefactor, the man named Charles Lyndhurst.

Of course, it could be true. I couldn't entirely discount the possibility. But even though the origins Bernice had invented for me were less prosaic than most (she no doubt thought they would please me) they were hardly sufficient for a man who'd discovered that his wife was his sister and his son's mother wasn't.

Besides, I knew what Bernice was after—my money. Living with her in Windsor confirmed this. I shouldn't have gone there, of course, I should have left her alone to drive herself crazy. But where could I go after fleeing the Union Hotel? I couldn't face Helga again, wherever she was. If I'd gone back to Highland, Helga might have shown up. And since I'd discovered Bernice wasn't my sister, I thought we could be friends. Lovers, even. But I should have known this wouldn't work.

"Here it is James, just this part, just a little." I snapped in the tape and held the Forward button for exactly fourteen seconds.

"—which is fine for someone like you, with your looks. I don't care if you were a lizard, I loved you."

"You forced yourself on me. You raped me, Charlie."

"You, you witch. How can you say that? It was you, you made the first advances."

"Sure. I crept into *your* room."

"You invited me in. You told me what time."

"And when Raymond caught you—"

"Cleo. It was Cleo."

"No, Charlie, it was Raymond. He grabbed you by the neck."

"How could he grab me by the neck on the bottom. You were on top!"

"Stop shouting Ch—"

I pressed the Forward button again. *Here it is James, just this part, here it is.*

"Cleo told me later."

"Told you that you were my sister, or that she wanted *him* to think that you were?"

"I don't know, Charlie, it's so fuzzy long ago. I think what she did was, she wanted him to take me in too. So she just told him I was your sister from the same mother but a different lover, before he met her. Then when he heard this, he wanted us brought up like brother and sister, but he didn't want us to know about it, so they called us cousins."

"You were there first."

"By just a few months, as a matter of fact. You were his son, you were living here in Windsor with some people he hired. So when he started the orphanage he figured you could live there too, and he could be close to you. The way he figured it, he could see you now and then."

"Orphanage, what orphanage?"

"Well, that's what it was, if you really want to know about it, Charlie. You could call it an orphanage. That's really what it was."

"You could call it a madhouse. You could call it anything."

"Try orphanage. You could call it an orphanage for the rich."

"Orphans can't be rich."

"I don't mean just orphans, I mean illegitimate children. Bastards, the word is."

"Rich bastards?"

"Well, their parents were rich. I mean, their fathers. It was a bastard place. A school for bastards. An orphanage for rich bastards, you could say."

"Bernice, you have to be dead to put your children in an orphanage. It doesn't make sense. What kind of rich people put their kids in an *orphanage*?"

"Actually, you put your finger on it, Charlie. What kind of rich people? That's a good question. Takes a certain kind. I would say rich people like your gamblers or whatever. It could be those kind of rich people. They die fairly easily, I've noticed. They could die anytime. So I guess they wanted to be ahead of the game."

"You mean racketeers? Crooks?"

"You could say that, Charlie. Successful men in their line."

"All that wealth, you're telling me—"

"Wealth is wealth, what's the difference?"

"And you and me—"

"Cousin Raymond, the kids, Charlotte, Dana, Patrick—"

"We were children of *gangsters?* Bernice, I can tell, you're making this up."

"I'm sure you'd prefer being son of a hero."

"Absolutely not. I would not prefer it. I'd prefer having nothing but ordinary parents. I didn't ask for this, Bernice. God knows. You're telling me stories, and I don't have to believe them. You expect me to believe such a story? I prefer my own."

"Which is what?"

"That Uncle Chuck was Charles Lindbergh. I was his illegitimate son . . ."

"Uncle Chuck was Charles Lyndhurst. He was just some sort of gangster, Charlie."

". . . and because Charles Lindbergh was a famous man, he had to more or less hide me away."

"Suppose there was a man named Charles Lyndhurst, Charlie, just suppose. Maybe he used to work for the city, for the Department of Public Services or something. Let's say he was Tammany Hall too. He got caught with his hand in the till, where he worked. Skimming money from these different orphanages which the city was paying them room and board for, but some of the money he kept for himself. People get caught doing things like that, Charlie. Maybe that's what happened. Let's say he got caught, they had a large scandal, he went into hiding, underground you could say, but then, since he knew something in the orphanage line of business, he set up a real fancy orphanage of his own, for special clients, you know the type of people. How does that sound?"

"Doubtful."

"I like it, Charlie. I like my story. It's a true story."

"Where did you get it?"

"From Cleo, where else?"

"Okay, Bernice. Now here's mine. A little monkey told me this one. Suppose Charles Lindbergh met Cleo at a carnival. He met my mother there too, she was an acrobat. The Flying Angel. Let's say he fell in love with this Flying Angel, he got her pregnant, she gave birth to me. Then Cleo offered to take me off their hands. She sent me to this house to live with George and Louise. Maybe I got swapped for his kidnapped baby too, I don't know, I haven't figured that part out yet. In that case I'm not the illegitimate son, I'm the other one. I'm Charles Lindbergh, Jr. Anyway, later on, after Cleo got better, I went to live with her in the city, you were there too, and *he* came around now and then, just to see us. My father. Charles Lindbergh. How does that sound?"

"Suspicious."

"Also, he gave me this house."

"No, no. It was Cleo's."

"So she gave it to me."

"But she should have given it to *me*, Charlie. She told me so herself. It was just because you were—you."

"There, see, I caught you! I was *who?*"

"You were the man, you went to Yale, you got an inheritance, you got me pregnant too. You had it easy, men have it easy, the only consequences they have to deal with are the spoils. You got the booty, Charlie. You got the gold mine, I got the shaft."

"Bernice, you move in here, you take over my life. You're not even *related* to me."

"We had the same guardian."

"That's not a blood relation. And where the hell did you get keys to my house?"

"From Cleo, where else? She had some old ones. You know those old thumblatch keys, you can't find those anymore. I went—"

Pressing Stop and glancing up at James Faber once more with a look—I could feel myself compose it—of smug but humble triumph, I thought of the things I hadn't told Bernice in Windsor, things that would surely have made her change *her* story. For example, I hadn't told her about Abner's letter. Did she know that Abner and Anna were her parents? She thought she knew everything, but she didn't even know her own mother and father! Looking at James, I tried not to smirk or laugh. "It's all in the transcripts," I said.

"This must have cost you a pretty penny, Charles." He patted the stack of transcribed conversations, neither smiling nor frowning—a very cautious man. His skin had a certain white or gray tinge, and amid the folds of his face his lips were so fine they seemed to have been cut with a razor.

"Look through it carefully," I said. "Check it for accuracy. I want your—considered opinion, James. Why are they doing this? What, exactly, are these people trying to hide?"

"I'll take a look, Charles. Offhand, I would say they have nothing to hide."

"Ha ha, very good." I felt myself flush. "You see the lengths to which they'll go. The sort of trash they'll conjure up."

He looked at me for a long, painful moment—behind his mask, I could see him debating what to say—then finally swiveled to the side in his chair. "And your family, Charles? How are they doing?"

"My *family?*" I couldn't help it, I jumped up, looking all around the room. "My *family*, which one? I've got dozens, hundreds!"

"Sit down, Charles, I meant nothing by the comment. I was thinking of Helga and the boy, is it Michael?"

"David." I sat down. "I haven't seen Helga in five months, to be exact. This is not—this thing isn't child's play, James. I've begun to suspect that they—that they kidnapped Helga."

"I see."

Actually, I wasn't sure about this. In fact, I'd just thought of it now. They could have done that; I wouldn't put it past them. Kidnap Helga, kill her, who knows? One thing I could do was talk to her father, Max. If he was still coherent, not yet too senile, he could answer some questions, I imagined.

Besides, I missed Helga, even if I didn't dare face her again.
It surprised me to realize how much stability she'd given my life.
I'd learned this—gradually, to be sure—while living with Bernice
in Windsor for the winter.

Living with Bernice! Where else could I go? At the Union
Hotel I'd learned that Bernice wasn't my sister and that Helga
was, so Highland was out; I couldn't go back there. Even returning to Hudson Valley Consultants—just the thought of it—
turned my stomach, so I merely phoned in some rather hasty
excuses to the office, intending to make my early retirement
official later on, at which time I could vote myself a pension.

Then I drove to Windsor directly from the city, in fulfillment
of a lifelong ambition to live with my first and only love. Windsor
was my true home, I thought, and when I arrived it did seem as
though my entire center of gravity had shifted there.

But it didn't work out. Living with Bernice became a night-
mare. I think she was going crazy, for one thing. I had it on tape,
some of it, and James Faber could judge for himself. We could
have her declared incompetent as a first step toward putting her
away, then I could have my house back.

A severe winter didn't help. We seldom left the house during
the day, and part of the problem must have been that we simply
got on each other's nerves. Meanwhile, I began recording our
conversations in bed, unbeknownst to her. Bed was where we
talked. I asked her about Charles Lindbergh, about Cleo, about
East Seventy-eighth Street. I asked her about her life before East
Seventy-eighth Street, but she grew silent and tense, pretending
that this period of time was so painful she couldn't bring herself
to recall it now. When I brought up the manuscript I'd found—
the "Monkey-Faced Girl"—she became nervous and acted like I
was crazy and denied she'd ever written such a thing.

It's nothing to be ashamed of, I told her. Some people are not
like the rest of us.

You can say that again, she replied.

Of course, it could have been a fake. She could have planted
the manuscript in that room, where she knew I'd find it. However,

I was certain it was genuine, though I couldn't prove it, as I'd left it behind when I fled the Union Hotel. But various clues and hints in Windsor confirmed its authenticity. For example, more than once I thought I detected hair on her face. It made me wonder whether she didn't secretly shave. I even thought I could see those faint blue lines where her face had been pieced together years ago.

Then one night as we made love she bit me. Not a playful nip, or a helpless, open-mouthed clamp of the lips, but a ferocious, painful animal bite which broke the skin on the fleshy part of my chest, near the armpit, drawing blood. Even when I screamed she didn't let go.

It withered me instantly; I suspect that's what she wanted. The bruise festered and turned many colors, forcing me to go to the doctor. After that, we made love less often. And how typical of her to blame *me* for this bite. I'd been hurting her, she said, bruising her with my hands. It was like the time I woke up in the middle of the night to find Bernice shaking me violently at the foot of the bed. She had dragged me out of bed to shake me, then to excuse herself claimed that I'd been beating the furniture.

After living with Bernice a month or so, I began to feel damp all the time. My clothes felt damp. In fact, we both began experiencing deteriorating health. Bernice's eczema flared up, causing her to scratch herself day and night. She nearly scratched herself raw. She became incontinent, wetting herself at least once a day, and she often made involuntary, jerky movements while smacking her lips audibly. These movements she ascribed to the Thorazine she was taking.

And why would Bernice be taking Thorazine?

As for me, it felt as though my body was at last becoming a stranger. I found it difficult to breathe, my chest became constricted. I experienced frequent headaches, or not exactly headaches—more like a pressure on top of my head. I had to go to the bathroom often, as old people do. When I turned my head I could feel something rubbing at the base of my skull, like cloth against cloth.

Sometimes I fell asleep only to wake up frightened, but of what

I wasn't sure. I easily became tired. It required a great effort just to stand up if I'd been sitting a long time. All the time now my heart was growing smaller. I pictured it shrinking. Morning, noon and night, I experienced that familiar forward lunge and sudden gulp when my heart seemed to pucker or quicken in my chest.

In the mirror I saw that I'd aged. At last my hair was turning gray. My face had wrinkled. Some of this was neglect. Since we spent that winter mostly indoors, I didn't bother to shave very often. My hair grew long, but it was stringy and unkempt, as I seldom washed it. Also, my clothes seemed looser, my shoes larger. Blisters and sores appeared on my feet. I felt my entire existence contracting. Bernice didn't help, by mocking my appearance. She pointed out several times a day that I looked old, that I walked stooped, that my fingernails were dirty or my breath smelled bad. She seemed to enjoy thus tormenting me for something I couldn't help, for the betrayal of nature which all of us experience in growing old. But two could play that game. I mocked her for her jerky movements, her wobbling eyeballs, her scratching, and especially for wetting herself. Old man, she called me. Witch, I called her.

Then she changed her tactics. To get at me, she mocked my father, Charles Lindbergh, since in her view I mentioned him too much. Charles Lindbergh, she said, who was Charles Lindbergh? You think he's your father? He was a fascist, that's what he was. A Nazi, Charlie, he sympathized with the Nazis.

I couldn't refrain from asking Bernice how she had obtained this information.

I've read about him, she said.

Then if you've read about him, you know that those accusations were false.

He flew to Germany to meet Göring, she said.

An intelligence mission, Bernice. That was in 1936. He was there to gauge the strength of the German Luftwaffe.

Which he thought was too strong for anybody at all, Charlie, so he made speeches to keep America out of the war.

So did lots of people. That doesn't make them Nazis.

Then what about this? Did you know about this? When he gave the *Spirit of St. Louis* to the Smithsonian, you know what they found on your hero's plane? They found a swastika scratched on the propeller shaft.

At first this seemed too absurd to even answer. But it did disturb me. It disturbed me profoundly. So I drove to the public library in Binghamton one day, trying to locate a reference to this swastika on the propeller shaft, and found out that a worker who assembled the plane had put it there—for good luck, he said.

Likely story, said Bernice.

But why was she out to destroy my conception of Charles Lindbergh? She obviously knew too much about him not to be up to some insidious tricks. Of course, she wouldn't concede the most important thing she knew—as if I didn't know it too. As far as I could see, it was all part of a campaign to hush me up, to keep my convictions under wraps. Maybe she was after Lindbergh's inheritance, for example, and if Cleo's son got there first with a prior claim they would split it between them.

On the other hand, Bernice had already admitted that Cleo's son was pretending that night, at Abner's apartment.

Could it be, however, that she was pretending now? By appearing to be engaged in a campaign to disabuse me of the notion that I was Charles Lindbergh's son—who knows?—she could be trying to make me believe it all the more. If she made me think I was Lindbergh's son, she could then claim my house and my monthly check. Since I wasn't Charles Cooper anymore, she could weasel into Charles Cooper's legacy.

Still, I'd already concluded that Charles Cooper's legacy came from Charles Lindbergh. It was Lindbergh who left me the house and the money.

Of course, I could let her have those things, the house and the money. Though I was reluctant to give them up without a fight, the most important thing to me was still the truth. Why, for example, was all that Lindbergh memorabilia in Abner's apartment? And why had Bernice read so much about Lindbergh? With one eye upon stripping Charles Lindbergh's career of its glamour, as though to protect me from the contamination of being his offspring, and the other upon that absurd story of Charles Lyndhurst and the orphanage for children of racketeers, no wonder she seemed crazy half the time.

Then again, maybe she was shrewd. It could be she was actually protecting the Lindbergh family from me, but she disguised it very cleverly as defamation of his character in order to scare me off.

She needn't have worried. I had no intention of pressing my claims upon the surviving members of the Lindbergh clan, or in any way causing them undue embarrassment. Though I knew I was Lindbergh's son, I wouldn't harass them—they'd suffered enough already, hadn't they? I knew how it felt, to be hounded and harassed. I would leave them alone, since—unlike Bernice —it wasn't money I was after anyway. It was the name—the vindication of a life.

Our son came to visit on Christmas, Charles Lyndhurst, Jr. Chuckie. We cleaned the house, cleaned ourselves, but all Christmas Day couldn't control our irritation at having been forced to put such a good face on things. No one liked their presents. Chuckie smiled at us with bitter irony, rubbing the backs of his fingers to warm them. I gave him a fine leather wallet; Bernice gave him some cologne. And he gave us a rotisserie grill, with a motor to turn the meat on its spit.

Bernice and I gave each other books and underwear. She gave me a book about famous bridges, and I gave her one about Princess Diana. It was pathetic; we all sat there with undisguised contempt for these gifts, which we'd purchased in a spirit of resentment in the first place. Chuckie left early, to drive back to New York.

In January the winter got worse, but February was better. Then, as the ground thawed in March, the leach field from the septic tank backed up into the cellar and the smell of leachate began to rise into the house. Leachate is distilled waste and decay, grayish black in color. The smell makes you think of nothing less than dead flesh and corruption, the poison of mortality. We bought fans for the cellar windows, but it didn't work. With quick-drying cement I filled in the places where the leachate entered the cellar, but this was a laid-up stone wall, entirely porous. For each spot I patched it found a detour, and resumed its stinking flow.

Down there in the cellar the smell was especially sharp and penetrating—it went to your head and stomach, both—in contrast to the dull, spreading odor upstairs, which infrequently enabled you to forget it; until you remembered, with a rush of depression. In the cellar was no forgetting, so after these futile efforts to block out the leachate I avoided going down there, it frightened me too much. Lying in bed, smelling that smell, I pictured the cellar floor covered with messy coils of entrails.

We stopped taking baths. Dishwater we threw outside instead of draining down the sink. We flushed the toilet only once a day. Any use of water activated the leach field, which then entered the cellar. This economy purchased some relief, but then it rained, washing all the leachate still waiting in the soil down into the cellar.

We lit incense, but incense only sweetened the smell, making it all the more corrupt and sickly. It was like coating a bitter pill with sugar, thus making you taste it instead of just swallowing. Pipe smoke was better—the tobacco smell was knottier, more muscular, and there were times it actually managed to crowd out the septic smell—so I smoked incessantly, smoked until my tongue and the roof of my mouth grew hot and raw.

At Agway, I purchased some powdered enzymes designed to scour out leach fields, and flushed them down the drains. They did nothing but help the smell spread outside. I phoned for a truck to come and pump out the septic tank, and for a week this afforded some relief. But once it filled up again, once the leach fields started leaching again, the smell returned, as though the earth itself had become incontinent.

We slept in the barn a few nights. Actually, this horror drew us back together for a while, and we clung to each other in desperation. We knew nothing would work, we were cursed. Oh Bernice! Our bodies had cursed us, our waste had cursed us, our issue, our progeny, our past, our deceptions.

I left when she began to grow violent, in self-defense she had the nerve to claim. The details of this unnerve me now, but suffice it to say it had mostly to do with biting and scratching, so as to draw blood. I was tempted in retaliation to tell her about my wife, Helga, about her actual identity. Not about her being my sister, that would be too much. But I could tell Bernice that my wife was the friend of her youth, the girl with whom she had once tormented me, and with whom I subsequently tormented her, thus tricking her into loving me.

But I didn't. I wanted to keep Helga, even the thought of Helga, out of this morass. I still had a great deal of affection for Helga—though what *kind* of affection was another question now—and concluded from this that I was doomed to love what I couldn't have, and to have what love had poisoned and corrupted.

From Windsor, I drove to Binghamton and hired a Manpower girl to transcribe my tapes; it took about a week. I slept in my car, at a roadside rest stop outside of town.

Then I drove to New York to present the transcriptions to my lawyer, James Faber. I thought he might give them the right interpretation; perhaps he could see things I couldn't see. I sat there and waited while he thumbed through these documents, turning pages with care, but much too quickly. He licked a finger now and then. I could tell he wasn't reading. "Right there," I jumped up and jabbed a page with my finger. "That was the time she bit me."

"I see." He stood up. "Well, Charles, this is—fascinating. I'll look them over carefully and see what I can do. What exactly is it," he added with a certain confidential air—patronizing, actually—"that you want me to do?"

"They're hiding something from me," I said.

"And what might that be?"

"The story of my life, you could say. The identity of my father. I don't know, it could be they want my property as well. They want some way to make claims on my property."

"Your property? And this Bernice, or Carol—"

"Lyndhurst," I said. "Actually, it's Englehard."

"She once told you that she was your sister?"

"Yes, but she isn't."

"Therefore, she has no legal claim on your property."

"She's living in my house, James. I can't get her out. Did you ever find that title to my house?"

"No. We don't have it here." He'd come around from behind his desk. I stood up too, though I didn't want to.

"You ran George and Louise Lockwood through your computers?"

"Yes, we did. Nothing."

"Strange," I said. I was rooted to the spot, standing there in front of his desk, suddenly conscious of my decrepit appearance. I needed a shave, my fingers were dirty. Having lost my pipe tool, I'd resorted in recent months to my fingers and thumb.

"Incidentally, Charles." He'd taken my elbow, I had no choice but to move, so I picked up my cassette player and bag of tapes. "Where should we be sending your checks now? I noticed you haven't deposited the last four. We've been mailing them to Highland. Shall we send them to Windsor?"

I panicked, I froze, I felt ready to weep. I knew my face must have contained a rather desperate plea. With that bag in my arms, I searched his smiling mouth, his clever gaze—he was watching me. We were standing at the door; his secretary looked up. All at once I shrugged and grinned, defeated. I nodded my head, waved the back of one hand. Walking out, I said, "Sure. I get it. Send them to Windsor. Make them out, while you're at it, to Carol Englehard, on my behalf. She needs it more than me."

And I swaggered down the hallway, feeling their glittering eyes upon me.

16

From James Faber's office I drove to La Guardia Airport, intending to fly to Orlando and speak with Helga's father. What my lawyer didn't know was that I had learned that Helga was my sister. Whereas, James Faber, what had *he* done? No doubt married his childhood sweetheart and raised a string of complacent, successful children. That was his claim to fame, the middle-class prig. If he only knew!

It bothered me that he was in on it too, but what could I do? Let them have the house, the money, everything—I had Charles Lindbergh. Not that this was easy, having a famous man for your father. There were many burdens associated with being son to a hero. Invidious comparisons, standards impossibly high. Think of the sons or siblings of U.S. presidents. John-John Kennedy, Donald Nixon, Billy Carter, Ronald Reagan, Jr. We were all askew versions of the powerful, all dragged into the icy gaze of the public, who naturally then applied warped expectations to us, either too many or not enough.

Dad, your advice?

Shoulder your burden, son.

At La Guardia I parked in long-term parking and purchased a ticket to Orlando. When flight time came, however, I couldn't bring myself to board the plane. I'd always been somewhat afraid of flying, but now I was actually terrified. Was it the flying or the lack of exertion? You filed in, sat down, did nothing—soft human beings all in rows—while as the plane climbed, that huge mass of hardness down below successively swallowed people, cars, buildings, and roads.

I found a bar and drank on the earth while the plane took off without me. Next to the bar was a little open café selling sandwiches, and there I ate dinner, at a table beside a window looking out at the planes taking off and landing. I could try again tomorrow.

Later, in one of the lounges at La Guardia where a wing of the airport bulged, I sat and read a *Times* someone had left there. I noticed other people who also looked like they had no place to go. They were hanging around, like me, cultivating their immobility. Or maybe they had no choice. Some of them looked like bums. A group of German students with suitcases and backpacks alternately sat around bored, or jumped up and snapped each other's photos, but after a few hours they left.

As evening fell, more bums showed up. Old men and young, black and white, some with beards and long hair, gap-toothed, slow, wearing worn overcoats and shoes held together with scraps of twine. It was no retired pilots association. They nodded at me, as though I were one of them. I buried myself in the *Times* and read a story about a dead body found in a suitcase at the Oakland airport. A Korean woman had stowed away, but then the suitcase went unclaimed and she couldn't get out. They discovered it by smell.

I fell asleep. In the middle of the night a sound woke me up. On the wide ledges beneath the windows, some bums were sleeping, right on the heating vents, but others had stood on these ledges and were jumping from them onto the floor. These were old men; some had long beards. I couldn't imagine what this was all about until I saw one holding out his arms. He closed his eyes, the cords in his neck went taut, he jumped, and landed with surprising ease. Others didn't even bother to climb onto the ledges; on the floor they squatted, extending their arms. They strained their limbs like men lifting weights, as though by a sheer act of will they could get off the ground. And a few actually did.

One floated up two or three feet; another managed to fly to one of those window ledges. But I could see that the effort cost them. They landed and lay there exhausted, sprawled out. Such an inhuman effort, to fly.

The next morning I tried again. I purchased another ticket to Orlando—the old one was no good—but once more I simply couldn't get on the plane. I was terrified. "Sir, we're boarding," said a flight attendant. I stood up and ran away from her, out of the lounge and up the concourse. Ran as fast as my little shuffling steps would allow. People turned to watch. I was more or less huddled into myself, fists balled together. They wouldn't look at me so strangely, I thought, if they knew I had a kind heart. They didn't know I was a gentle, generous person.

I drove back to Highland, defeated. I hadn't been there in—how long?—five or six months, though I'd called several times to see if Helga had returned, with the intention of hanging up should she answer the phone. But she didn't. Where was she, Helga?

At home, I sat at the kitchen table and scribbled a codicil to my will in which I left fifty thousand dollars to my natural son, Charles Lyndhurst, Jr., and my house in Windsor to Bernice. I posted it to James Faber, adding a note confirming the disposition of my monthly checks. Sign them over to Bernice, I said.

Then I walked to my bedroom and slept, having amputated those people from my life with one painless operation. I slept like the dead.

Something strange woke me up. It sounded like the cry of a cat, a distant howl or meow, muffled at first, then louder. Or the faraway whine of a car turning over but not catching. At first. Then it broke out into thin, piercing cries, and as crazy as it seemed I thought it was a baby. In my house.

I walked down the hallway and stood at the door to my study a moment, listening with wonder to these cries and sobs, also a few exclamations of sorts, in which the letter *e* was dominant. I tried the knob; pushed the door open. Someone had transformed my study into a nursery, with changing tables, pink dressers, stuffed toys, and mobiles of tinkling fish. It was warm. All my things had been removed, and against the far wall, where my desk once stood, was a white crib with little blue lambs frisking about on the headboard. A crib toy was stretched across the top, toward which a shrunken, pink hand—the size of a jumbo shrimp—reached in frustration. It balled in a fist, a howl rose up.

I tiptoed closer. When it saw me, this baby stopped all its noise in suspended amazement at the apparition of my face. It lay there on its back in a blue sleeping suit—blue for boys, I remembered—with convict stripes on the arms and legs, lay there in its pink face watching me, and even had the sense of drama to say, "Oooohhhhh." And to reach up, clasping and unclasping its hand.

This sound was like someone practicing amazement before a mirror. Several clouds then passed across his face, expressions helplessly trying themselves out. He appeared to be uncertain as to what they signified. One of them—a brand of sorrow or resent-ment—startled him so much he grew scared, and his face col-lapsed inward, though only for a moment—then it swelled out again like a sail, and he was smiling. I didn't flatter myself that he was smiling because he was happy to see me; on the contrary, he was happy because he'd remembered how to smile. And this doubled the smile, a sound bubbled up, something like "beesh," and I thought he even laughed. Because he was laughing, my face amused him.

I lifted him out by his armpits, realizing I'd never lifted a baby before, never even held one. He smelled sour and sweet at the same time. His head bobbed in a funny way, mouth round and puckered—I thought of a fish out of water—until it found a niche between my neck and shoulder and more or less frantically settled in there, turning this way and that but resting in between.

I'd never seen or felt flesh that smooth and milky before. With my big dirty crooked finger I touched his pink cheek, and immediately he sniffed, his mouth opened blindly, rooting around like a leech.

In that room was a rocking chair, and I sat in it, humming to this baby. It seemed like the right thing to do, when you find a strange baby in your house. I rocked back and forth, feeling the outline of his body, all those miniature details, traced against mine. He pressed up against me like a large adult hand. He squirmed a lot, but it never occurred to me, and therefore not to him, that he would cry. Some funny climbing motions erupted once or twice, arms and legs moving up and down. His head continued to swivel too, each time with a kind of determined, resolute settling of its weight afterward. I think he liked my smell, but maybe he had to decide which smelled better, the shoulder or the neck. I felt capsules of his breath on my neck—little explosions of condensed warmth—and soon he was sleeping.

I didn't dare stop rocking. Besides, it was easy; he weighed hardly more than a bag of groceries.

So there I sat rocking a baby in my study.

After a while—it may have been fifteen minutes, or as much as an hour—someone unlocked the front door and walked in half-singing half-shouting, "Hello?" I could tell it wasn't Helga. Whoever it was came straight down the hallway and pushed open the door to my study, emitting a little muffled shriek. "Who are you?" she asked.

"Good question," I said.

I recognized her at once—Bernice's daughter, Valerie—but it took her longer to place me, though when she did the sigh of relief filled the room. "Mr. *Cooper*," she exclaimed. "You look so— different. I didn't *recognize* you at first. I thought—some *stranger* was stealing my baby. I didn't *realize* it was his—*grandfather,* Mr. Cooper. Imagine my surprise! Where did *you* come from?"

"The airport," I said.

"So you found little Charlie."

"He found me, you could say."

"Ha ha, I hope he wasn't too much trouble." She was walking

forward reaching for the baby, but I didn't want to give him up that easily.

"He's sleeping," I said.

"No he isn't. His eyes are wide open." I pulled in my chin to look down, and she was right. He hadn't moved at all, but his big eyes were open, watching his mother. All at once his entire body balled up, his rear end pushed out, he uttered a cry, and the arms and legs of him started clawing across my middle. So happy was he to see his mother that he became angry, he shook his little head like a fist. She took him from me, opened her coat, lifted her sweatshirt—she was braless—and held him to a breast. I noticed it was leaking. "Where's David?" she asked, without looking up.

"I have no idea."

"He's not here?"

"I don't think so."

"*Shit,* excuse me, Mr. Cooper, he was supposed to be here. He's not supposed to leave Charlie alone. When I'm working. He knows that. Do you know what time it is?"

I looked at my watch. "Three o'clock."

"Shit. Darn it."

I could hear little Charlie sucking with greed. I saw him too, but tried not to stare. Stretched across Valerie's bare middle, tucked up beneath the folds of her sweatshirt, he clung to her breast and drank. Her other breast hung down against his hip.

A watery sound like a drain letting go came from his body. "Oops," said his mother.

I realized she was standing there in the middle of that room— one hand still held her purse by the strap—and jumped up to offer her the rocking chair. She took it without a word.

I didn't know what to say. "You're working?" I asked. I shouldn't have, but I scratched my face, where a beard was on its way. I hadn't shaved in weeks, had neglected my hygiene some-what as well, so little flakes came down when I scratched.

I had to remind myself that this was Bernice's daughter, feeling pangs of anxiety and dread as I did so.

"At Mr. Vining's," she said.

"Mr. Vining's? In Newburgh?"

"No, the new office," she said. "In Kingston. It's a long way to drive, living here, but what the hell, heck—it's a good job, I'm typing, answering the phone, but he lets me do some drafting too. Just a little, it's a start."

"This is Pork Vining you are talking about, of course."

"Vining and Cooper, Land and Water Consultants."

I thought it considerate of Pork to include me like that, though he hadn't exactly asked. Vining and Cooper. "What happened to Florida?"

"David lost his job."

The other chair in that room was one of my Windsor chairs, left over from my study, so I shuffled over and sat down in it, to rest. I couldn't keep everything straight. First of all, was Hudson Valley Consultants still open in Newburgh? It was November when I'd phoned them last, six months ago.

And Valerie and David living here. "Does he have a job now?"

"No, he's still looking."

"Oh." I wanted to light my pipe, but thought the baby wouldn't like it.

"It's a funny world," said Valerie, apropos of nothing. She pulled little Charlie off her nipple—it sounded like pulling a cork from a bottle—and held him to her shoulder, patting his back. His mouth hung open but his eyes were closed, and it occurred to me that he'd fallen asleep sucking. What bliss. "Could you hand me one of those diapers?" She pointed to the plastic changing table beside me, whose stacked tiers reminded me of a parking garage. "Make it two."

I gave her two disposable diapers. One she placed beneath his head, on her shoulder, while continuing to burp him. At last—it was much too loud for his size—came a sudden release of air and a stream of white liquid from that toothless mouth.

Then, very quickly and efficiently, laying the child across her lap, she unzipped him and changed his diaper, folding up something soft and wet inside the old one. "Hand me the wipes," she said. I watched this operation with amazement. This was how it was done, how you handled those little bodies with their tiny entrances and exits. As a water engineer, I felt drawn to it immediately. Before she taped on the new diaper, I saw that his genitals were just as detailed in miniature as his little hands and fingers and fingernails. Everything was there, but reduced in scale. Was this true of *everything?* His thoughts, his words, his prearranged destiny? For me, the laws of chance had broken down, but for this child they started up all over again. They had another chance.

Valerie handed me the old diaper—folded up carefully, with soiled wipes inside—and nodded to a pail with a lid by the door. For the first time in months I felt useful.

Then she offered the child her other breast, which was dripping like an open spigot. He'd woken up groggy during the change, but came to life in proximity to that nipple, bobbed his head frantically, missed it once, searched around, clamped down and finally settled in, as though finding his purpose in life at last.

When Charlie finished, she pulled down her sweatshirt and I relaxed a little. Once more he slept as she burped him on her shoulder. "Let me do that," I said.

"Sure." She handed me the baby, and a pad for my shoulder. "Not too hard." I tapped his back.

"What happens if he doesn't burp?"

"He will."

And he did, after a minute or two. A full, adult burp of satisfaction. It seemed to propel him deeper into sleep.

"You can put him down now, Mr. Cooper."

"Call me Charlie."

"That would be confusing, wouldn't it? Charlie here, Charlie there? Excuse me, I'm sorry, support his neck!"

"What?"

"When you lay a baby down you have to keep your hand on the back of his neck. He's all limp there, like, I don't know. A rag doll. Even when he's awake." She'd taken him from me to demonstrate, placing him in the crib with one hand cradling the back of his neck.

I felt alarmed. "Is something wrong with him?"

"It's *all* babies."

"Oh."

We stood there watching him sleep, arms flung back, satisfied stomach bulging up with milk. His eyeballs moved beneath their delicate lids. Was he David's? I couldn't tell. He didn't look like David, he looked like a baby, a wholly different species.

"I could call you Grandpa." She looked at me, smiling. "I never had one myself."

"You do now," I said, though I was actually thinking of Abner Fisch. She appeared to appreciate the remark and touched my arm.

"Mr. Cooper, I mean Gramps, where *were* you? No one could find you."

"I was in Windsor," I said.

"The phone was disconnected."

"I know." We'd neglected to pay the bill. "And Helga," I said. "David's mother? Has she been here?"

"No, she hasn't," Valerie said. "I don't think so. We've only been living here two or three weeks. I don't think she's been here."

Valerie didn't seem terribly concerned. From a pay phone in downtown Windsor last month I'd called Highland several times, to see if Helga had returned. From wherever she was.

She looked at me. "Of course, I see her every day." I felt as though someone had kicked me in the chest. I found the Windsor chair again and sat down. Valerie's sweatshirt, wet with milk stains, said DURAN DURAN.

"You see her every day?"

"At the office. Vining and Cooper, remember?"

I reeled this in slowly. It was *that* Cooper. Pork and Helga had joined forces. Land and Water Consultants. Thunder Mountain Lake!

Pork and Helga? I felt for my pulse. I pulled out my pipe and filled it. "Mr. Cooper, Gramps?" Valerie nodded to the crib.

"Oh. Sorry." But I had to smoke. "Let's go out of here," I said, standing up.

We settled in the living room, or I did, while Valerie washed some dishes in the kitchen. Every now and then she popped her head in the door to comment on something, mostly about David. The day David threw out all his heavy-metal records. Framed in the kitchen doorway she looked remarkably thin for someone nursing a baby. I tried to see her mother's face in hers, but couldn't. A scar rested on her upper lip. Had that been there before?

And all the while, puffing away like mad on my pipe, I thought of Pork and Helga, the thoughts of a man who'd lost all foresight. It used to be that I could *see* the future like a road up ahead unwinding at my feet. But Pork and Helga?

The baby woke up. David came home. Valerie placed little Charlie on a blanket on the living room floor, where he rocked back and forth on his belly and played idly with some empty baby-food jars. It seemed that he could roll over onto his back, but couldn't get back to his stomach, so I was obliged to perform this service for him. Very gently, supporting his neck. I'd put the pipe out already and tried to wave most of the smoke from the room.

When he walked in David said, "Dad!" and we embraced. "You need a shave," he said. He looked at me funny—puzzled, I think—while trying his best not to show it, I could tell.

"I'm growing a beard," I said.

"Oh, great," he said. But I couldn't determine whether this was sarcastic or sincere. It occurred to me that I'd never known such things about David, the tone he was using; he probably didn't himself. Though he'd thrown away all his heavy-metal records, he looked no different. He still wore his earring. His hair was still long, especially in front, where it fell across his eyes, and he often had to brush it away. David.

He and Valerie had a tiff of sorts in the kitchen, mostly having to do with leaving the baby alone in the house. They restrained themselves because of me, I could tell. David had had an appointment, he said, to see about getting his old job back at KFC. How did it go? I'll know tomorrow.

"Gramps, you got some mail," sang Valerie. "Some of it's been here since we moved in."

"*Gramps?*" said David.

"He's Charlie's *grandfather*," Valerie pointed out.

"Oh," said David, watching me anxiously.

The mail was bills, flyers, checks. A lot of Hudson Valley Consultant business had been forwarded here, including an eviction notice for the office. Overdue rent. And a notice to appear in court concerning the suit of Roderick Donohue against Hudson Valley Consultants, Incorporated, for three million dollars. Roderick Donohue was the paraplegic teenager who'd gotten that way by driving his car into a ditch I'd designed. The court date was in February.

I concluded from this that Hudson Valley Consultants existed no longer.

A letter from the Social Security Administration asked me to return to their Kingston office, and reminded me of the penalties for falsification of identity. This struck me as funny, and I laughed out loud. Baby Charlie looked up, as did David, engaged in play with the child on the floor, doing things to raise his laughter. Taking away baby jars, putting them back. "Beesh?" said the baby.

Before dinner I called Pork's number in Newburgh, but got a recording. No longer in service.

Dinner was clam spaghetti—pretty good. But all I could think of was Helga, my sister. Helga and Pork. Helga, my wife. David's high cheekbones, I noticed, bore a remarkable resemblance to hers. He was growing into her appearance, and my heart went out to him. But thank God he wasn't mine!

Meanwhile, Valerie had launched into a complicated story— assisted now and then by her husband—which I only half followed, concerning the mobile home they'd rented outside of

Orlando. It seems that they didn't notice it at first, but after they moved in they saw hoses running from their trailer into the woods behind it. Also, several thick extension cords, plugged into an outlet in the utility room and leading out through a dryer vent.

A dryer? I said.

They did not *have* a dryer, the cords led out of the hole where a dryer *vent* used to be. One day David followed these cords and hoses, and found they led to a shack in the woods where a bearded man cultivated marijuana plants. In pots, I thought I heard Valerie say, and wondered, why in pots? In the middle of the woods?

He didn't have a *bathroom,* Valerie said. He was shitting in the woods.

And we were paying his electric and water, said David.

When they complained to the landlord about paying this man's bills, the landlord complained that he didn't know they were going to have a *baby* in the house; or mobile home. He hadn't counted on that. It seemed that the landlord was on this guy's side.

So Mr. Krueger, said Valerie, recommended a lawyer to them, which turned out not to be helpful at all. I was feeding the baby as Valerie talked, mashed up spaghetti on a little baby spoon.

Mr. Krueger? I asked.

Mom's uncle, said David.

I thought he lived in Miami, I said. I thought his name was Kuyper.

He moved to Orlando. No, it isn't Kuyper, said David. I've never heard of that name. It's Krueger. Albert Krueger.

And I realized I'd always known it was Krueger, though the memory came as a bit of a shock. I turned this over in my mind, missing the denouement of Valerie's story.

Krueger. Albert Krueger. Helga's mother's brother. Of course, this could have been another uncle. I fed baby Charlie some more spaghetti, outwardly calm. But Helga had never mentioned other uncles. How old was he now? He must have been old. Something was wrong.

I had to admit, when I examined things closely, and went back in my mind to that horrible night at the Union Hotel, the night I read Bernice's story and found my mother's ashes, the night everything came crashing down around me—I had to admit that in thinking I recognized Kuyper as the name of Helga's mother, I could have been misremembering Krueger. It was dawning on me that this could have happened, given my worked-up state that night. In the foggy parts of memory, Kuyper has a shape not unlike Krueger. The parts of memory with the torn pages.

I felt my mind sagging.

It could very well be that there was no connection at all between my mother—Olga Kuyper—and Helga. Sitting there at dinner, I began to shake my head. What were the odds? Given the population, say, of the Hudson Valley and New York City, the chances that Helga was also my sister, or half-sister—that we had the same mother—were pretty low.

On the other hand, I reminded myself that the laws of chance had broken down. Then again, my evidence for this was the fact that Helga had turned out to be my sister.

Helga's mother had visited Cleo Dannen often, on East Seventy-eighth Street. But that of itself didn't mean that she was Olga Kuyper. She died in the years between East Seventy-eighth Street and Nyack, so my fuzzy memory of her was confined to that earlier period. And she wasn't that beautiful, come to think of it. Hardly an angel. But people change, don't they? Think of Cleo. Or Bernice!

I'd never believed that much in chance anyway. If Helga was my sister, it was fate, not chance. Chance was just destiny wearing a mask to make it look more alarming. These things were usually plotted out in advance, probably quite dispassionately. For example, what about the ashes? What about Helga's phone call the night Pork came to dinner? *Oh Coop, I'm so sorry.* Why had she left me? It *had* to be Kuyper. That is, her mother's maiden name. Helga had left me for shame at having discovered that she'd married her brother.

I fed Charlie some more mashed spaghetti. She's my sister, I muttered under my breath. I think she is, I said. I felt things unraveling. Then I looked up and noticed Valerie and David, having finished their story, watching me carefully. "Duran Duran?" I said, reading Valerie's sweatshirt.

"It's a rock group," she said, though I noticed she flushed a bit.

"I asked you not to wear that," said her husband.

"He likes Amy Grant," Valerie said, clearing the table. "He likes inflicting his values on people." She looked over at him. "David, help." Slowly, David stood, glared at his wife, and carried his plate to the sink, where he scraped it into the garbage disposal. Over the roar of the disposal, Valerie shouted to me, "He tried to make me throw out all my Duran Duran records. But I wouldn't."

"Who's Amy Grant?" I asked. But no one heard me.

The next morning, while David slept, and after Valerie left for work at nine—but before she arrived—I obtained the number of Vining and Cooper in Kingston from Information, and called them up.

Helga answered the phone. "Vining and Cooper." Her voice, her inflection—with that slight hint of German—went straight to my heart. "Who is this, please?" she said.

"Helga?"

"Yes, this is Helga. Who is speaking?"

"Your husband."

"Coop? Oh, Coop. Coop, this is you?"

I checked myself. "Yes."

"Are you home, then?"

"Yes, I am."

"Then you know?"

This gave me some pause. I realized I didn't know anything. "I don't know anything," I said.

"Coop, where have you been?" She said *haff*, more or less.

"Tell me what I should know and I'll tell you where I've been."

She paused. I thought she took a deep breath. "On your behalf, we have filed under Chapter Seven, for Hudson Valley Consultants. The corporation has been placed in receivership. Coop, we tried to find you but couldn't. The nail in the coffin was that lawsuit, you know? The boy in the wheelchair?"

"The boy in the wheelchair?"

"And Pork and I have formed a new company."

"Pork and *you?*"

"Surely, he told you?"

"That you formed a new company? No. I heard it from David's wife yesterday."

"Yes, David's wife. I hope this is agreeable to you. I told David they could live there, and then—when she needed work, Valerie, his wife? She turned out to be quite good, it seems. Pork insists that she go back to school. She would make a good architect. We may put her through school."

"*We?* Pork and you?"

"He did not *tell* you? Oh, Coop, he was—Pork was supposed to tell you that night. The night he came to dinner. He insisted that he tell you himself."

"Like a man."

"But he did not? What did you think when I phoned? I phoned to apologize."

"Helga, I didn't know what to think. We talked about a lot of things, Pork and me. He talked a lot. But not about you."

"The poor man," said Helga. "He must have lost his nerve."

"I feel sorry for him, I do. Is he there?"

"No, he isn't. He's out in the field."

"And you plan to marry?"

"Not immediately. First, I will file for divorce."

"I see." I was sitting at the kitchen table, watching the apple trees outside think about blossoming. "Thanks for warning me."

"Oh Coop, don't be bitter."

"Someday we'll have to have a long talk. You, me and Pork."

"I don't think he could bear it, Coop. He admires you so much. He felt so badly. I assumed—I assumed you'd run off when you heard. When Pork broke the news."

"The news he never broke."

"*Me*, he didn't tell. *I* thought you knew. He didn't tell *me* he had lost his nerve."

I looked all around the kitchen, looked out the window, looked at my shoes. But I didn't see anything. Pork and Helga. "Helga, I want to ask you two questions. Two questions, that's all."

"Certainly."

I paused and said it slowly. "Why did you take my mother's ashes?"

"Your mother's ashes? I found them in a box and took them with me to New York to sprinkle on the river. As you told me you had never done, for thirty years. I felt so badly that you had not done this. And when I found them in the closet, the closet in the spare room, I thought to perform—this service for you."

"This last service."

"Yes."

"So you did it?"

"Not yet." Helga hesitated. "My new work keeps me away from the city more than I wish."

"But you *will* do it, won't you?"

"Of course. On your behalf."

"Fine. Don't bother. I've already done it. And Helga dear, one more question. What was your mother's maiden name?"

"Please explain to me what you mean, that you've already done it."

"Helga, your mother's maiden name. A simple question."

"I can't imagine, Coop—why should this concern you?"

"It concerns me. What was it?"

"Her maiden name was Krueger. Margaret Krueger. Now, if you please—"

I hung up the phone, washing my hands of Helga. When it rang, I ignored it. Margaret Krueger. The name felt like something whose name I didn't know. A coin with its face worn off, a dumb thing in my hand. It was, I realized, an entirely meaningless name.

Five minutes later the phone rang again and I let it ring, though this time it woke up the baby, who first started making fussing noises, then began bawling. I heard David stumble from his room down the hallway into the nursery, mumbling reassuring sounds.

I'd made a mistake. As far as I was concerned, if Helga wasn't my sister she was nobody. I felt her draining from my heart, like a fluid. Evidently, I'd inflated her importance. On the phone, her voice sounded surprisingly tinny and small. She wasn't my sister, and pretty soon she wouldn't be my wife. Given her behavior, she didn't deserve either. *Neither one,* I said, smacking my fist in my palm. *Let Pork have her!*

Of course, she could have been lying. About her mother's maiden name. I jumped up and ran down the hallway, toward the spare bedroom. Valerie and David were using his old room, so the spare bedroom was still mostly storage.

We kept important papers in an antique oak filing cabinet, and this I began to ransack. Old check stubs, paper bags full of former tax returns and records, insurance policies, contracts, car registration and so forth. I pulled out one of Helga's insurance policies, but it told me nothing. I was looking for a birth certificate or marriage license or something of that nature, and digging through the drawers of this file cabinet I literally began to claw at the papers, pulling them out, hurling them halfway across the room.

In the back of the third drawer down was a folder with Helga's old passport. With it was an application for a new passport, never mailed in. I pulled this out, holding it up. Under *Father's Name* it said Maximilian Clausen. Under *Mother's Maiden Name,* Margaret Krueger. I dropped it to the floor. And as it fell I simply stared at it falling, while the name for what it was dropped out of my mind, at about the same speed.

Oops, I thought.

I realized that I must have known this all along. Weren't there instincts triggered by hormones or pheromones which prevented you from mating with your sister? I'd read this once . . .

In my own bedroom I found my jacket with the label from my mother's box of ashes still in the pocket. It still said *Olga Cooper (née Kuyper)*. I let it drop too, then looked around and noticed what a mess this room was in. I hadn't made my bed, which resembled a collapsed parachute. Debris everywhere. Three ashtrays overflowing, because Maria, the cleaning lady, didn't do ashtrays (they made her sick), and these had been here since last October.

Good work, Coop. You blew it.

At least I found out who my mother was.

You could have done that thirty years ago. Just once—just one time—if you'd carefully looked at the box of her ashes. If you'd obeyed her wishes when it came in the mail. If you'd removed the damn *wrapper*, even.

Well, look at it this way. I could have thrown it in the trash.

Oh yes, how wonderful. Dutiful son. I realized I was crying.

"Dad?"

David stood at the door to my bedroom, with the baby in his arms. "Are you okay, Dad?"

"I'm okay. Sure."

He was dressed to go out, wearing his coat. "I was wondering, could you watch Charlie, Dad? I have to—I'm supposed to—"

"Sure, I'll watch him."

"Valerie says he gets a bottle at noon. Try to hold him off if he wants it before then. You could entertain him."

"Entertain him?"

"He might take a nap, or something. Put him in front of the TV. Bottle's in the refrigerator, you warm it up in hot water on the stove."

"Hot water?"

"Just put the whole bottle in a pan of hot water until the milk warms up. Don't get it too hot. It's Valerie's milk. She pumps out her breasts. Thanks a lot, Dad."

"No problem, son."

David handed me the baby.

17

And now, more than ever, I became convinced that I was Charles Lindbergh's son. It was all I had left, the last shred of self-respect to cling to. Everything else had been stripped away—Helga, Bernice, my childhood, my work. But you can't strip away genes. Biology. This remains firm, it has realness. Hardness.

I played my tapes often, when Valerie and David were gone at work. David was back at KFC, and I took care of baby Charlie days. I played the tapes for him as well as for me; it was my way of telling him my story. The *East Seventy-eighth Street* tape, the *Cleo* tape. Often I played the part about Charles Lindbergh landing at a field near a carnival in the town where Cleo worked. That was the key right there, I suspected, where it all began. I preferred this to the foolish story of the orphanage for racketeers run by Charles Lyndhurst. Playing these tapes, I asked baby Charlie which one he chose.

"Beesh," he replied.

Sometimes I played the tape of our dinner at Abner and Anna's, just for old time's sake, but the technical quality of that one was poor. Usually, if I wanted to review things in my mind, or just relieve the tedium, during those portions of the day when I wasn't feeding baby Charlie, or changing his diaper, or taking him for a walk, I played the Bernice tapes. These were the best. Also, I liked her husky voice. At times I just listened to her voice, not to what she said. The note she struck, not the words themselves.

In this way I began to think increasingly of Bernice, to whom, in a way, I'd been unfair. I tried calling her in Windsor, but the phone was still disconnected. I phoned some places in Binghamton to get prices on installing a new septic tank. That was one thing I could do. I could do that for her. A sand filtration system, which was what that hardpan soil needed, would cost around five or six thousand dollars, but after what we'd been through it was worth it. We could put it out by the barn, in the back—well away from the house.

Also, I wondered whether Bernice had yet seen Valerie's baby. When I'd mentioned it in Windsor, she hadn't expressed exorbitant interest. She didn't (as Helga had done) hop on the first plane for Orlando.

Well, that was how it happened, by my playing the tapes and thinking of taking baby Charlie to Windsor for a visit.

The question was, should I secure David and Valerie's permission to take the baby away for a few days? It seemed I was the one chiefly in charge of him, regardless. I even got up with him nights, since his parents argued about whether or not to go into his room if he cried in the night. He'll *expect* it, said Valerie, if you walk him at night.

But I didn't mind walking him at night, since I was usually awake when he started crying anyway.

Actually, I thought I understood him better than they did. Not that they didn't love him—especially Valerie—but being gone all day they couldn't see him at his best. I knew when he was bored, when he wanted to eat or watch TV. They fretted over why he cried, and tried to distract him, but I sensed this was misguided. The fact was that he *wanted* to cry. It fulfilled a need. And when he wanted to stop, he stopped.

The way I figured it, when he cried he needed someone to listen, so I went into his room to walk him.

I knew when he wanted to go outside, and wheeled him down our hill in his stroller, past the apple trees whirling with blossoms in April and May. We took long, complicated walks all April, May and June, and he seldom fell asleep. We saw birds, flowers, new grass, buds, then leaves on the trees. It was spring. Everything we saw I pointed out for Charlie to apply his word to, "beesh."

In the house, flies and moths came around occasionally, because it was their time of year, and these I tried to make Charlie notice, but he wasn't interested. I was beginning to see things through his eyes, and thought I'd like to notice them too; if he noticed them, then I could notice them. But he didn't, so I couldn't.

He played with all sorts of things. Little round things, pretty colored things, square things with pages, things made of wood. He liked a small cylindrical object with a silver top and red thumb latch. I forgot the name—I used it to light my pipe. I gave him my used ones to play with.

In the room we cooked food in, he played beneath—the place where we ate. He was beginning to pull himself up to his feet, for which he used the things we sat on. Chairs.

I wondered about his future. Would they find a cure for cancer? For AIDS? Would Star Wars protect him or invite destruction upon his head? Valerie had joined an antinuke group—for her baby's future, she said—and this became the chief topic of discussion at the dinner table, the madness of overkill and of weapons in space. I tried to picture a future in which we all lived in a garden watched over by benign machines, but somehow it didn't work. Computers humming while human beings played.

I couldn't believe it.

Charlie got confused for a while, and when he learned his first words began calling me *Da*. He liked to pull my thing, I can't recall the name—the hair on my face. My *beard*. It was white.

Or he pulled himself to his feet at the couch and managed to turn around and lean back with his arms spread out—the posture of crucifixion—belly pushed out, half lolling there, watching me, who was in fact watching him. He was *bored*. He wanted me to make him laugh. Sometimes his face became tired with the waiting.

His favorite toys were my tools. Tools for banging things,

screwing things, squeezing things, loosening things. He carried them around and lost them, but then again I was doing that too. I was losing everything. I lost the thing I smoked with and had to buy another. I lost the names of my tools and the thing I smoked with too—simple names, really. I couldn't remember them.

He learned to imitate me. When I fed him solid food, he sometimes took it out of his mouth and offered it to me, shaking his head. "Tttssit!" he said, whatever that meant.

He placed two small things in a plastic container, shook it around and dumped them out. They were round, shiny things. He picked one up and put it in again. The container was one of those things you carry water in.

I went to the store with Charlie, who pointed to the things we should buy. When we left, someone gave me a large bag with those things in it.

We did a lot of the same things. Got up, ate, dressed, looked at things. I gave up thinking of him as a baby, or a midget, and just began thinking of him as another human being, only smaller, with a human being's normal interest in things. Often I just sat with my hands on my knees and watched him, or looked out the window.

Some things happened. He identified a small object on the rug. It was a tiny thing, a piece of lint perhaps, or a fingernail paring, which he picked up very carefully, and sitting—he could sit up now, he could crawl—placed in my hand, telling me what it was. It was beesh. Beesh he would see across the room and crawl toward frantically, shouting out *"Beesh,"* and pick it up with his little thumb and finger, then place it in my hand, as a gift. Then he would want it back. This time, however, I lost it—it fell through my fingers perhaps, or blew off, or maybe it was never there—so I had to throw up my hands in grief or innocence, unable to restore beesh to its proper owner, while the latter wailed.

Most of the time, however, he was happy.

I made arrangements by phone to have the new septic tank installed in Windsor. Valerie left for work at nine, David at ten. At ten thirty one morning, I threw some bottles, formula, and disposable diapers in a little carrying case, strapped Charlie into the thing he sat in—it was like a tall throne—and began the drive to Windsor. I had every intention of returning eventually, of course, but decided it was best not to alarm David and Valerie in advance by telling them where I was going. They'd become too protective, regardless. They didn't want me walking him at night, since now he woke every single night, and even after I walked him he didn't care to sleep anymore, so Valerie had to feed him.

The solution to this was to take him off their hands. Not for good, just a little while. We drove down Chapel Hill Road to Route 44, and west on 44 toward the Shawangunks. This was my shortcut to Route 17, the road to Windsor. A marvelous June day without clouds.

Out of Highland the road dips down into a town called Modena, and that's where Charlie spotted it, right on the road. "Beesh," he shouted, extending his arm, and I saw it there too, a round shiny beesh just like the one I'd lost.

It was on the opposite side, in the lane for the—carts, or whatever, that drive the other way. I stopped, pulled all the way off the road and onto someone's—what? Grassy area in front of their building. I told Charlie I'd be right back—I was wrong—and ran up the road to get that thing.

And there it was. Like I said, it was shiny. Not too small, not too large. I could see what it was very clearly, and bent to pick it up in the road, this thing, this beesh, when something hard struck me, all the hardness of the world, hardness itself. Then I heard the screeching tires. It was like waking up.

I lay on the ground looking at the sky. Scuffling sounds. Crickets and birds. Beneath me, the ground had that realness. That hardness. Of the people looking down at me, one held Charlie, so I thought I'd better smile, but couldn't. When I opened my mouth to speak nothing came out. In a sudden panic I took my pulse, expecting a drumroll. However, it was calm. In fact, I couldn't find it. Nothing. Not a thing.

And I realized that this was what I'd been searching for all that time, all those years of pulse taking—for this nothing to calm me. I needed that reassurance of quietude. As a consequence, even the entrails didn't bother me. I'd managed to spot them down by my belly, squeezing out. (I should mention that my shirt was untucked.) Entrails were the secret inside things, the softness. They were everywhere, they made hardness beautiful, and I closed my eyes upon this thought—perfectly happy—they made hardness beautiful—and sank at that moment down into my brain. Down networks of neural cables, down miles of cells and crazy wires singing. Down tunnels and complicated folds of tissue.

And I'm still there, still in the coils. For a while I felt my cortex wrinkling and hardening like a prune, from the outside in. Neuritic plaque forming, shrinking my little fist of thought. But nothing's ever over, not quite. I'm still searching out wrinkles of truth in the folds, clues and hints to confirm my conviction. The brain's a huge maze, and all this takes time. Read the label on my jar; you'll see I've been here a good year already.

And why? Why would they keep me alive like this? Because I'm Charles Lindbergh's son, of course. That's my significance. I can't see too well, but hearing I'm good at, and several times a day, through storms of little footsteps and screams, I hear someone read my label out loud. Through the sound of a pump hammering wetly in the background. Sound waves transmitted by the Pyrex walls pass through the liquid medium—a mixture of ox blood serum and Tyrode's solution—and strike my cerebral cortex, which absorbs them like a sponge.

Look at this! they say. Something, something, something. Apparatus designed by Charles Lindbergh. The Lindbergh-Carrel Perfusion Pump. Designed by Charles Lindbergh and Doctor Alexis Carrel at the Rockefeller Institute in 1935.

Then someone always says, I didn't know he *invented* things. I thought he flew *planes.*

But whose brain is it? someone else says. And that's when I laugh. Silently, of course. Folded in the folds, I laugh and laugh . . .

Chuckie, what's this?

Intestines. What else?

No, this is *it*. See? A brain.

Oh, you're right. Is it him?

What's left of him.

How cruel. It's unnatural. Mom, please, let's go. Is he still *alive* in there? It's not fair, it's not human. Who did this? What right did they have?

Your guess is as good as mine.

It says, Equipment property of the Lindbergh estate. Designed by Charles Lindbergh. Lindbergh, why Lindbergh?

I'm sure I can't imagine.

Mom, what's the story? Is this why you brought me here? He really is Lindbergh's son, is that it?

Oh, Chuckie, don't be silly. Your father suffered delusions of grandeur. Wouldn't I know who he really is? Charlie? Can you hear me? Are you Lindbergh's son?

Mom. Not so loud.

Besides, I noticed when it says who the equipment is property of, that's the *equipment*, not what's inside. The contents inside belong to you and me by rights.

You mean, because we're his legal heirs.

That's right.

And you think he—what's inside is still *alive?*

Ask him, why don't you?

How creepy, how terrible. What can he do in there? He can't *do* anything.

That's what you think. If the word got out, he could do plenty.

Like what? He's helpless.

Oh, plenty. Just plenty. Legally, in other words.

You mean, because if he's still alive—

He can still own property. It's a way to take it with you.

But, Mom. Mom. What would probate court say?

Good question, Chuckie. I'm glad you thought of it. Let's say if—just if—he was still alive in there, in other words, legally, as far as that goes, someone could get a court order, for example. If he was one of those people in a coma, let's say, I know your father, I know what he'd want. I'd want it too. The poor man suffered so much. He'd want us to pull his plug, is what he'd want.

Not so loud, Mom.

He'd want us to put him out of his misery. If you were him, Chuckie, what would you want?

Some way to die.

Someone could just pull his plug right now.

Oh, Mom. How could we?

You could just try it.

No, you.

What would happen?

I don't know.

Let's find out.